D0180634

TOM DEWITT

For my son Bryan and the inspiration he provides, and for my daughter Ashleigh whose love is unconditional.

"Power tends to corrupt, and absolute power corrupts absolutely. Great men are almost always bad men."

John Emerich Edward Dalberg Acton and Others

CONTENTS

Prologue	1
Chapter 1	14
Chapter 2	20
Chapter 3	31
Chapter 4	40
Chapter 5	47
Chapter 6	54
Chapter 7	73
Chapter 8	79
Chapter 9	93
Chapter 10	107
Chapter 11	114
Chapter 12	126
Chapter 13	131
Chapter 14	134
Chapter 15	160
Chapter 16	165
Chapter 17	171
Chapter 18	175
Chapter 19	180
Chapter 20	183

Chapter 21	190
Chapter 22	195
Chapter 23	204
Chapter 24	219
Chapter 25	224
Chapter 26	233
Chapter 27	242
Chapter 28	250
Chapter 29	269
Chapter 30	279
Chapter 31	289
Chapter 32	301
Chapter 33	319
Chapter 34	322
Chapter 35	331
Chapter 36	338
Chapter 37	344
Chapter 38	352
Chapter 39	360
Chapter 40	365
Chapter 41	372
Chapter 42	387
Chapter 43	393
Chapter 44	398
Chapter 45	410
Chapter 46	420
Chapter 47	429
Epilogue	435

PROLOGUE

The Mirror Reflects the Face of Evil

T he morning was dreary, the sky heavy with impending snow. Large clouds hung in the air blocking the sun's light, casting gray shadows on the landscape and enveloping all into the darkness of winter. It was 8:46 a.m. on this dreariest of days that Connie Parker dropped off her daughter Dana, and best friend Brenda, like she had every day since the beginning of the school year.

"Thanks, Mrs. Parker," Brenda said, sliding out of the back seat.

"Dana, good luck on your chemistry test today."

"Got it, Mom. I'm gonna nail this one."

Connie had no doubts about the results. Unlike her son, who excelled athletically, Dana was an exceptional student.

"See you tonight, Dana, bundle up on the way home, they're calling for snow this afternoon."

"Ok, mom."

Both girls ran from the vehicle and into the side door of the school.

Connie wanted to spend as much time with Dana during her formative years as possible, so she decided to drive her to school each day. Part of the deal included Brenda, which was no problem at all as she lived next door. The extra time allowed her to tune into the conversations between her daughter and friend; and, when the opportunity presented itself, to be part of the discussion. Boys were a popular topic, and this short ride in the morning kept her parenting skills sharp until she drove through the traffic circle and dropped them both at the side entrance of Kelly Wash High School, home of the Trojans.

Ms. Wilcox, the volunteer traffic controller, kept law and order among the parents driving their children. A blow on her whistle and a wave with her hand provided clear instructions to wrong-way drivers and those that violated the flow of the established traffic pattern. For some reason, Connie never received more than a wave and a smile from Ms. Wilcox as she drove through the small circle. Connie would wave back and provide a warm smile that could melt the coldest of hearts. That is just the way Connie was.

Connie pulled the 2016 Ford Edge out of the "drop zone" as it was called and decided to head to the mall for a little bit of shopping. Christmas was coming, and she wanted to get a jump on the season. Connie would spend an hour at the local coffee shop located outside the mall, catching up on her email over a white chocolate peppermint with no cream, and be perfectly positioned at a mall entrance by 10:00 a.m. when the shops all opened. She turned on her satellite radio and sang along with the Christmas songs as she drove. The music always transported her back to her childhood and great family memories, adding to her holiday spirit. This time of year made her nostalgic and grateful for her life, and this morning was no exception as her mind drifted to earlier times.

Connie Parker was told that she was one of the most beautiful women in Casper, Wyoming. She did not think that was true anymore. It was 1994 when the panel of judges declared her runner up, Miss Wyoming. *That was so long ago*, she thought and laughed out loud at the idea of a magic mirror that she would frequently ask as she aged, "Who was the fairest of them all?"

She married her high school sweetheart two years later, and the newlyweds immediately started living the American

2

Dream. Recalling her wedding day brought joy into her heart as she drove and the hope that one day, her children would experience the same. Douglas was their oldest child and a junior, and while Dana was a freshman, she was developing into a beautiful woman very quickly. Connie felt very comfortable with her decision to stay engaged with her during the mornings.

She turned off Wyoming Blvd and was abruptly pulled back to reality as her car hit a deep pothole driving into the empty parking lot near Macy's. The jolt rattled her arms as she clenched intuitively on the steering wheel while pressing the brake.

Startled and shaken, she pulled into a parking spot and stepped out into the cold to check the left front tire for damage. As she knelt to inspect the tire, a pick-up truck with flashing lights pulled up next to her. The driver's side door opened and a middle-aged man in coveralls jumped out.

"Looks like you might have banged her bad. I saw you hit the pothole," he said.

Still looking at the tire, Connie started to stand and turn to thank her helper.

"I know. You would think they would fix that so close to the turnoff," she remarked.

And then Connie felt it. Something was wrong. A hand grabbed her shoulder, then moved to lock her into a bear hug. His massive arm crushed her breasts, and a cloth placed over her nose and mouth hindered her breathing. She tried to scream, but the rag muffled the sound. His hold was firm. Then blackness filled her vision.

After a while, Connie awoke. It took her eyes a moment to adjust to the dim light of her surroundings, and then panic hit her. Her wrists were shackled to a chain that linked through a supporting ring anchored to the cinder block. When she pulled on the chain, they made a deafening sound, the iron links sliding through their metal guide rings in the darkness. She was standing with her back against a wall staring into darkness. Her legs were pulled apart and held by sets of chains that prevented her from walking without pulling her arms backward. Each leg appeared affixed to a guide ring attached to a post on each side of her.

She screamed, "Help me!" only once before her plea died in the darkness around her. It was quiet, only the dim gray objects her eyes could faintly see and an earthy smell that filled her nostrils indicated she was awake. *Where am I? How did I get here?* She tried to recall. Then she remembered and with that memory, her mind raced, and heart beat wildly as panic joined her fear. She was afraid of passing out when she heard boots on the wooden floor scraping above her, and realized her captor was human and not the darkness she felt consuming her from inside. Gathering her strength against this man was her defense. In defiance, she screamed, "Let me the hell out of here!" The scraping noise ceased, and she heard the stride of the person above stop and change direction.

A door opened, and an overhead light came on above the stairs to illuminate the way down to her. The intruding brightness created shadows in the room allowing Connie to see her surroundings with a greater degree of clarity. Connie heard her captor descend the wooden stairs, each step of a boot on creaking treads, creating a scraping noise followed by a hollow sound that echoed around her. In her new view created from the open door and light, she surveyed her surroundings and saw the chains that held her. To her right, she observed a table close to her containing a lighter resting on the table's top. On each side of her, there were two full-length mirrors, each attached to the wall, which hung at a slight inward tilt. On her left, she observed what appeared to be an automobile mechanics chest containing five drawers. She was able to make out the silver handles on each, which contrasted with the dreariness and damp smell of the basement. There were no windows, but in the light cast down the stairs, she noticed several torches attached to the walls.

The man from the pick-up truck, dressed in a long flowing robe stepped off the last stair and was now standing in the room with her. He had a strong muscular build and silver hair, which he pulled into a ponytail and held in place with a thin golden hairband, seen only by its sparkle as it caught the light as he moved. His robe was dark red and buttoned closed. Attached was a decorative gold pin on the upper right shoulder that appeared to be in the shape of a circle with an arrow piercing the center. Around his neck hung a golden hilted knife attached to a chain connected to the scabbard about halfway down his body.

"Good morning, or should I say good afternoon. We just passed noon," he said with a slight southern drawl.

The man walked across the room toward her.

"Who are you?" she shouted. "What do you want with me?"

Responding with an English accent he said, "I want to spend the afternoon with you. I've never had the companionship of such a beautiful woman before."

"Please," she said, "Let me go. My husband and I have money. We will give you want ever you want."

"I know," he said as a matter of fact. "I know who you are. I'm not looking for money or any other possessions."

Connie pulled her chains in the act of desperation, making a loud, clattering sound. They were not coming off. As if in response, the man lifted the lighter from the table next to her, flicked it once to ensure it lit and walked to the first torch. He lifted his hand slowly and touched the flame to the torch. Gradually, the kerosene-soaked cloth caught fire, with the smell of the burning fuel filling her nose.

"Do you know Latin?" he asked her without his false English accent.

"No!" she shot back quickly, struggling with her chains.

"Then, I will have to translate for you as we walk through our little ritual, here in my church," he said.

Spreading his arms and turning in a circle, he signaled that all items in the room would play a part in what was to come.

"*Primum enim*," he said with perfect diction. "The first to you," he said and blew her a kiss with his left hand as he moved to the second torch.

He flicked the lighter again and raised it to the second torch. "*Secundum ad me*," he said as he lit the second torch. "The second to me."

A third torch was on the opposite wall from Connie, and in the flickering light, she could see a painted symbol on the cinder block that looked like the biblical story of Adam and Eve in the Garden of Eden. A serpent hovered close to Eve's shoulder, its eyes painted with specks of silver glimmering in the torchlight, dangling down from a tree branch and watching. Adam stood next to Eve, preparing to bite the fruit she provided. Eve's hand remained stretched out toward him in the act of giving. "'*Ad tertium Deorum ignotum*' – the third to Gods unknown. Do you know God?" he asked.

She remained silent.

"Most people don't," he said, stating his belief. "But they should."

The fourth torch was on the wall to her right, and she turned to observe his next pronouncement. This wall, too, was covered by a mural painting of what looked like an Egyptian god with a dog head. The god stood next to a measuring scale with two small pans connected by chains to a bar above them, balanced by a center post. On one side in the measuring pan hung a human heart and the other side a feather. Next to the scale sat a beast with its mouth open.

"'*In quarta ad deos oblivione delebitur*' – 'the fourth to the forgotten Gods.' Do you read history? This picture has an interesting story."

He pointed to the mural. She remained silent.

"We shall see how your heart is measured. Lighter than a feather, no doubt," he said smiling. The man walked over to her and pointed with his eyes to the remaining torch above her right hand. He stepped up onto a small stool and leaned above her as he performed his last click of the lighter and touched it to the cloth. She could smell perfume on his robe. Clearly, he had bathed and prepared himself for this moment. The last torch caught fire, bouncing its reflection off the mirrors on the wall and illuminating the darkness. "'*Quinque omnis reveletur*,' 'let all be revealed.'"

He seemed pleased with himself for completing his tasks. Connie could feel panic again as she sensed the man's ritual unfolding in front of her and the part she would play.

"You don't need to do this," she pleaded, "Please…"

"But I do."

He walked to the light switch and turned off the overhead light. The basement glowed and flickered from the torchlight. Small whiffs of smoke rose to the ceiling and sparks from the torches dropped onto the cement floor.

The man walked to the mechanics' tool chest, pulled a drawer open and took out a cotter pin. Walking over to the wall, he inserted the pin into a small hole in the chain anchor above her head.

"Now try," he said, running a finger along her cheek. Connie shouted and pulled away, but the chains caught firmly in place, causing the shackles to bite into her wrist. Only her sobs and pleading filled the room. The chains, for now, were silenced.

"Now, we are ready," he said as he opened the second drawer. Connie saw an ax and screamed.

"Oh please," he said, trying to calm her down. "It's too early to use that. Why are you screaming already? And by the way, the screams are only for you. We are miles from town. My closest neighbor is two miles that way," he said, pointing over his shoulder while looking in the drawer he just opened.

"Where is that thing? Oh well, maybe later."

He casually closed the drawer, then looked directly into her eyes.

Oh my God – this man is insane! What did I do to him?

"Why, why are you doing this?" Connie sobbed. "Please

let me go. I have two children; they need me."

"So do I," he replied. "*Need* you that is."

He walked around to her face, leaned close and looked into her eyes, then whispered, "This will only hurt a minute."

"No!"

He slowly pulled the knife out of the scabbard. The chains locked her hands above her head as she squirmed in hopes of freeing herself. Once again, he mounted the step stool, reached the top, and placed the blade at the bottom of her sleeve, making a quick cut to the material. He pointed the blade down to cut away the sleeve of her shirt, the ripping sound from the knife slicing the material mixing with his heavy breathing. He carefully worked his way from her wrist to her shoulder. As he began to finish, he cut too quickly, and the knife entered the skin, drawing blood. She cried out and pulled away, but the chains held in her position.

"Oops, that wasn't intentional."

He repeated this for the other arm; and when he reached the shoulder, he cut away the fabric on both sides while being extra careful.

Then leaning in said, "This is the fun part." He placed the blade inside the top of her blouse and quickly cut away the buttons on her shirt, exposing her bra. He peeled the shirt off of her and then slid the knife under one bra strap on her shoulder, and then the second cutting each in a quick motion watching each loop fall around her arms. He moved the blade to the front center, and in one swift upward cut, the bra fell off.

"My God, these are beautiful," he said.

He reached over and placed his hands on her breast. "So round and soft." She recoiled in disgust.

"Don't touch me, you bastard!" she hissed.

She swung at the man, but the chain grabbed her wrists and prevented her from being able to bring all her hatred into a strike against him.

"Let's see what the rest of you looks like," he said as he dropped to one knee and put the blade down to her ankle.

A drop of blood dropped from where he accidentally cut her and hit him on the cheek.

"Did you see that?" he asked her, wiping the drop from his face. "You are already starting to share yourself with me."

Connie shouted and pulled on the chains.

"If I get loose, I'll kill you."

"But you won't," he said quite calmly.

He put the knife blade under Connie's pants and started to cut up the leg to her hips, pulling away the cloth as he did. He moved to the other leg, firmly locked into position by the chain, and cut away the pants on the other leg, slicing up to her hips. He unzipped her pants as she thrashed and twisted.

"Careful," he said with a tone of warning. "I am going to put the knife in your pants to cut away the rest of the fabric and don't want to hurt you again. Please try and calm down."

Connie broke down into tears, unable to muster any more strength to resist the man and his knife. He slowly slid the blade through the zipper opening and jerked downward, cutting in three violent slices which pulled on Connie's arms as the chains held fast. The pants, now cut and ripped, were torn away, exposing her thong underwear. He stepped back to survey his picture of Venus in chains.

"What do you want?" she sobbed.

He looked at her face a moment and then locked his eyes with hers.

"Do you remember me?"

"No," a faint whisper was all Connie could utter.

"Are you sure?" he chided. "Think about it. 9th grade, Mr. Perry's English Literature class. I remember it like it was yesterday. We'd just finished two weeks of American writers. You know, Hawthorne to Hemingway. It was time to look at English poets and of course, my favorite, William Shakespeare! Mr. Perry announced we were going to read Romeo and Juliet aloud. I could barely contain my excitement. I don't think you noticed me in the back of the room, I looked a little different then. A little heavier, but I digress. I noticed you, though. I always noticed you. It was no surprise that Mr. Perry picked you to read Juliet's part. Then he asked the class, 'who wanted to read Romeo'?"

The robed man reached out and touched her breast again, looking into her eyes and smiling as he did so. Connie thrashed with as much force as she could muster.

"Get AWAY!"

He slowly moved his hand from her chest and leaned closely into her face and spoke, "I raised my hand and almost came out of my seat as I waved it in the air that morning. I wanted to read the part so much! And Mr. Perry did not pick me. He picked that jock in the third row who could not even spell Romeo."

He paused and shifted back into his English accent.

"But alas, disappointment is my middle name."

He returned to his normal voice again and stepped away.

"But not because I didn't try that day. I was always content to sit in the back and away from everyone. I never raised my hand in class. But I did that day. I wanted to read that part. I loved you..."

He paused, as though reliving the moment in his mind.

"Reading that part," slowly citing his words with perfect diction and locking his eyes with Connie's, "was the closest I was ever going to get to telling you, my Juliet."

He struck a pose in front of her, reminiscent of many actors performing Shakespeare. Staring upward toward an imaginary balcony, he stood with feet apart and one hand pointing skyward.

"But soft, what light through yonder window breaks? It is the east, and Juliet is the sun."

Connie tried hard to focus, find a weakness, something she could say or do that might set her free. She could not remember the moment in class, let alone reading Romeo and Juliet aloud. Connie could see that he put the knife on the table along with her destroyed clothing. Then, sudden pain as she felt a slap on her face. With cheeks stinging, her ears started to ring from the blow intended to keep her focused on his conversation. Connie pulled on the chains again, somehow believing in the surreal world spinning around her that if she pulled them hard enough, they would break, but they were still firm. She began to sob again.

"I don't remember! I can't remember," she stammered.

"Yes, and that is why we are here."

He shifted to his normal voice once more and each time he changed persona added to the fear Connie experienced, knowing that the man in front of her was unreachable with reason.

"We are at my church. The Church of Truth. There are five torches on the walls, each representing the path you will take to reveal what is in your heart."

Once again, he pointed to each torch. Then, he held up his five fingers in front of her, counting each finger with his other hand.

"What do you mean? I don't understand."

"I have professed my love for you. You, in turn, have five opportunities to profess your love for me. Each sacrament of our 'Service of the Torch' will bring us *closer together*," he said, a thin crooked smile forming on his lips. "Then after the fifth sacrament, your true feelings will be revealed." Connie now understood the shrouded purpose behind the service he described and felt her presence with evil.

He quickly stood up and leaned in to kiss her, saying, "All for you, my dear Connie. For your salvation. You turned away from me years ago."

As his lips opened to kiss her, Connie spit in defiance, her spittle covering his lips and cheek. He recoiled suddenly, surprised by her response. Yet, he quickly regained his composure.

"Why thank you, my dear. I am going to need this."

He reached up and promptly removed the pin from the chain anchor that held her in place, releasing the slack. In

TOM DEWITT

one effortless move, he spun Connie around and positioned her back to him. She faced the wall, the chains slipping through their loops, clattering loudly in the confined downstairs room, each rattle heralding the coming despair. Now, she could see the reason for the tilted mirrors. As she looked into them, they focused on the activity directly behind her. She could see the crooked smile form again on her captor's lips, knowing she would see all of him, with her. He placed his leg between hers and spread them apart. Once positioned correctly, her captor replaced the pin into the chain anchor.

He placed his hand on his cheek, collecting her spit as he leaned in to kiss the hair on the back of her head. She saw it all in the mirror. Unable to move her arms and legs more than a couple of links, Connie reared back with her head and smacked her assailant in the nose, creating a crunching noise. She watched him stumble backward, howling in pain and surprise. His nose was bleeding a steady stream that flowed into his mouth. Composing himself, he laughed while wiping away the wave of blood flowing onto his lip with his tongue, savoring the salty iron flavor.

"All sacrifice requires blood, my dear Juliet. So let's begin," he said and unbuttoned his robe. Connie screamed.

Later, after his service was completed, he looked upon his Juliet and wondered if she looked like what Shakespeare would have imagined. There were some slight differences between the stories that he keenly noted. Shakespeare had his Juliet commit suicide by burying Romeo's dagger into her heart. His Juliet died differently. He smiled as he recalled the sacraments he performed to find the truth; and sadly realized that unlike the star crossed lovers of Shakespeare, his Juliet never returned his love. The Service of Torches revealed his answer. There could be no doubt about the result. Therefore, without her love, he was justified to sacrifice her. His Juliet didn't remember him even though he had loved her to the depths of his soul. He would make special note of these differences when he captured the activities of the service in his journal later that evening. Shakespeare, he concluded, was not the only author that could write a tragic ending.

◆ ◆ ◆

It was 8:46 a.m. when Connie Parker dropped her daughter and best friend at school that morning without incident. It was a peaceful drive home. She had considered going to the mall to do some shopping but had elected to head home instead because of the announced snow. She pulled her SUV onto her street, singing Christmas carols until she reached her house and reflected on the season and joy she felt in her life. When she entered the kitchen, she poured herself a mug of coffee and sat at the table. She looked through the small stack of catalogs and flyers, each with holiday sales, wondering what gifts she would surprise her family with for Christmas. She loved her life.

CHAPTER 1

I t was raining like hell. Big drops bounced off the car with a rhythm that only a summertime thundershower in DC could produce. Officer Jefferson Grant of the Washington, DC Metropolitan Police Department sat on Benning Road in his parked car and listened to the raindrops make music on his roof. He had seen nothing that would make his impromptu stakeout worth his time. The only thing Grant had observed was the car clock tick off the second hour of what was turning into an uneventful night. Yet, one of his most reliable sources swore that "Strange things was happenin' that night'" outside of the funeral home. When he pried for more information, his informant walked away saying, "You'll see. I ain't saying nothing more - less you got real money to spend for me to talk." She was his best informant, but sometimes she could be a real pain.

Grant worked the DC streets his whole adult life and was six years from retirement. One of the older police officers on the force, he was more interested in solving cases and putting away criminals than politicking for rank and prestige. Grant turned down numerous promotions to sergeant to stay on the streets. His sergeant thought he was crazy but respected his commitment and experience. Because of these traits, his boss provided extra time for Grant to work with street sources and investigate problems despite not being a detective. Grant liked the role he played. He was still fit, or so he thought despite what his wife told him. He maintained a low profile, collected information, and provided reports to his chain of command. He felt like he connected with the people he had sworn to serve and found protecting them the most rewarding part of his job. They were simple people trying to survive in a world that erupted without warning into shootings from drug deals or gang hits. Over the years, his sources provided information that led to several criminals being put away. To most on the streets, he was a hero for his police work. To others, they knew not to get sideways with Officer Grant.

So here he was, doing it old school, sitting in civilian clothes in the family mini-van waiting for something to happen. No high-tech surveillance, no warrant to search, and not getting paid overtime. Just sitting on a side street at half-past ten, looking through the rain and black night waiting for something to happen. As he played through the endless cycle of checking the smartphone for email, looking at the funeral home, and scanning the street, something happened. Grant looked in his rearview mirror and saw a big truck lumbering up the road. The truck slowed when it arrived at the funeral home. The vehicle made a right into the driveway and drove around the back, disappearing behind the building.

He needed to move to see what was happening. Making sure there was not a second vehicle trailing the first, Grant opened the door was instantly soaked. He sprinted across the street and headed to an area on the left side of the funeral home. Behind him was an open field with a row of boxwood shrubs that could offer cover next to a large gray transformer attached to other utility equipment. Not the best for providing concealment, but he could get low enough and still see the parking lot.

He watched as the truck pulled forward, then backward. As the truck driver jockeyed to get into position, the backup lights alternated with brake lights, creating an eerie light show until the driver turned off the engine. Grant saw two men open both doors of a delivery entrance into the back of the home. They bent down with something in their hands and wedged the doors open, so far as Grant could tell through the downpour. Three more people came out of the home, pulling up collars on their rain gear as they stepped outside into the torrent. As if on cue, lightning flashed, lighting up the players at the door. The men inside the door were in suits; but that was not uncommon for a funeral home, he surmised. *Everyone else wore rain gear, so no help there*, his cop mind reported. The responding thunder echoed in the distance.

The driver sprung from the front door and yelled, "Get the forklift!" then moved around to open the back of the truck. Grant was startled as a side door to the funeral home opened about 100 feet from him, and the inside light shot into the night. A young woman jumped onto a forklift sheltered from the monsoon by a driveway roof and started the engine. He completely missed seeing the vehicle when he dashed across the street. She drove past the boxwoods a mere 20 feet away, close enough for Grant to see her blonde hair tucked under a rain cap, and headed for the truck. From Grant's vantage point, he could see straight into the back of the delivery vehicle and make out large gray objects inside the cargo area.

"Ok, everyone knows the drill; let's get this done!" shouted one of the guys over the rain, falling even harder now. The rain made it difficult to make out details of the activity, but he could not risk moving any closer. There was nothing but the parking lot blacktop between him and the action.

The forklift pointed its lifting arms into the back of the truck to start unloading. The truck driver hopped into the cargo area and used a pen flashlight to guide the forklift into the darkness. Grant could not see much more as the vehicle pulled up to the truck and began to load its cargo. The forklift backed up, completed extracting the shipment, and stopped. The operator slowly turned the vehicle and moved the cargo to the loading dock. When she did, Grant recognized immediately that they were unloading a shipment of caskets. The forklift pulled up to the platform, and two men gave lowering directions with their hands, easing the coffin onto a dolly. One man connected a cable assembly to the side of the casket's frame, paused as if to get affirmation that the cable connected, and disappeared into the funeral home with his partner and the coffin. The woman turned and maneuvered to the back of the truck. The rain continued to pour.

"What the hell?" Grant mumbled.

"Who needs to connect a cable to a casket?" he said out loud.

Grant never witnessed casket deliveries before, but he was pretty sure that they did not require a battery or power to be transported.

Why is the casket not in its shipping container? Did I see that?

His mind started to fill with questions making a mental checklist as he did so. *Just observe and make no assumptions*, he told himself. *You can figure out what's happening later.*

The forklift unloaded a second and a third casket. Each time, the men on the loading dock connected a cable to the coffin, validated the cable insertion, and departed. After the third time, Grant had their routine. He loved being a cop and was amazed at how his brain captured the information around him. Grant made a mental note.

Two people near the truck at all times, the driver helps the forklift operator, two men in suits, who were different each time, would load the casket on a wheeled dolly, connect a cable and take the coffin inside.

He noticed there was one person who looked to be supervising the operation and never moved; just stood and watched as the raindrops bounced off his rain gear.

The forklift returned to the back of the truck for the fourth run. As it backed away from the truck's cargo hold, the driver rushed the procedure, and the forklift did not come to a full stop before making the turn to the delivery door. Grant watched in disbelief as the casket began to slide on the slippery forks of the vehicle. The two men by the side of the truck sprinted to steady the coffin.

"Stop, Stop!" the supervising man yelled, waving his arms. The two men grabbed the casket and tried to steady it, but the weight of the box and slick soled shoes on the wet pavement made its drop inevitable. Responding to the Supervisor, she hit the brakes, causing the sideways momentum and lack of friction on the wet arms of the forklift to work against the two men. The casket came down with a crash, bursting open to reveal a man's body that rolled out into the night. Grant had difficulty seeing and squinted hard to focus his vision. He could see what he thought were several plastic tube connections on the man's body, and it appeared that small LED lights were flashing inside the casket and around the man.

The man supervising quickly moved to the side of the open casket. Everyone froze. In one continuous motion, he pulled out what looked like a Sig P226 pistol, pointed it at the man on the ground, and fired three shots at point-blank range. The body recoiled on impact, and pieces of the man's skull flew back into the open casket, mixing with the rainwater collecting in the silk-lined box.

Grant stared in disbelief and rubbed the rain out of his eyes for additional clarity. The man looked at the forklift driver, holstered his pistol, and calmly said, "Clean this up, now!"

"Yes, Sir, I am really sorry about this," she started.

The supervisor cut her off.

"DO your job, no more screw-ups. Figure out a way to prevent this from happening again. Do we understand each other?"

"Yes, Sir!"

The man in charge turned and walked away. The two standing men helped the forklift operator get the body back in the casket, and this time there was no doubt, Grant saw the LED lights and plastic tubing. They closed the lid, and the two inside helpers came out to assist. The four men lifted the casket and slid it onto the loading dock. All four jumped up onto the dock and counting down from five aloud, lifted the coffin onto the dolly as they hit number one. The men and the coffin disappeared inside. Two men closed the delivery doors, and the woman drove the forklift inside a shed located in the corner of the parking lot near Grant. She parked it, jumped off, and locked the door behind her. She sprinted past the officer, oblivious to his observation, and entered the funeral home via the side door she exited from earlier. The driver of the cargo truck started its engine and drove out of the parking lot. In under three minutes, there was no evidence that anything happened, leaving Grant alone in the pouring rain to wonder why anyone would shoot a dead man.

CHAPTER 2

The prosecuting attorney Franklin Hayes rose as the honorable Justin A. Markstrum entered the courtroom in Austin, Texas, at precisely 8:15 p.m. Hayes found it odd that there was no bailiff to tell the six people in the room to "All rise." The defense attorney Breckinridge stood up instinctively, and the defendant next to him slowly rose and bent at the waist, poking out his rear end behind him. He appeared to do so more to stretch his legs than show disrespect for the official that entered the court. His attorney looked at him with disdain and said so only his client could hear, "Stand up." The defendant was an imposing man, and when he stood fully erect, his six-foot two height complimented a back-woodsman trim of 245 pounds made hard by years of manual labor. In a different life, he could have been an excellent line-backer for a football team, but that was not the path he chose.

Judge Markstrum took his seat, turned on his laptop, and looked at the court recorder. The court recorder moved her mic closer to the judge and placed her fingers on the re-cording keyboard and nodded that she was ready to start. Judge Markstrum called the court to order, saying, "We are now on the record."

Both attorneys seated themselves. The defendant, dressed in his bright orange jumpsuit and handcuffed hands front, sat down with an audible flop. Hayes watched Judge Markstrum do some last-second positioning of items on the desk. Hayes could see parts of the judge's laptop screen, and assumed it showed Markstrum's prepared comments and information from the trial of "John Brooks versus the State of Texas." Markstrum looked up, scanned the defendant rolling a pencil through his fingers, and calmly said, "Mr. Brooks – do you know why you are here?"

His attorney responded for him, "He does your honor and-" the judge cut him off.

"Thank you, Mr. Breckinridge," he said in his pronounced Texas accent, "but I would like to hear the defendant respond."

Breckinridge looked at Brooks again, and this time audibly said, "Stand up." Brooks stood, faced the judge, and said, "Yeah, I know. Time to pay."

Markstrum continued.

"The people of Texas have found you guilty of 5 counts of 1st-degree murder and recommended the death penalty. We are here tonight to pronounce your sentence. Is there anything you want to say before I do so?"

"Yes, Sir. I do," Brooks responded, trying to mimic the judge's accent.

"Go ahead," the judge ordered, slightly irritated at the insult to the court.

"Well," Brooks started, "I know you are probably gonna give me death row but don't care much if you do. My wife and kids deserved to die. They left me no choice. The wife was doin' every redneck she could get a holt of in town. And the kids- they was making up lies to protect their mom. They was all in it together, and I knew I would git even with 'em."

Brooks stopped and lowered his voice. He began speaking much slower and looked like he had a moment of reflection, then proceeded with his statement.

"I planned it for a while. At first, I thought I would use a pistol, then the idea of my huntin' knife sounded good, but in the end, it was me and my shotgun."

Brooks changed the rhythm, volume, and cadence of his voice, speaking faster as he delivered the end of his personal admission.

"I waited for them all to be asleep, then God directed my finger to the trigger. Now that's justice!"

Hayes watched Markstrum's face turn red and could only guess at how many murderers the Judge dealt with in his career. *Kudos to the judge for keeping it together when dealing a man like Brooks. I wonder how he does it.* Hayes did not have to wait long to see. Markstrum stared at Brooks, and Hayes saw the Judge's lips move while counting to three, composing himself before making his next comments.

"Mr. Brooks, do you feel any remorse or regret for your action?" Markstrum asked.

Brooks looked down at the desk, contemplating the question. Then he looked up as though asking for more divine direction mumbling something under his breath. His gaze turned to his lawyer's eyes, he smiled, then looked back at the judge.

"Nope."

It was just that simple.

"Mr. Brooks," Markstrum began, southern accent cutting the quiet of the Texas courtroom. "If there were anything that I could say that would give me hope that one day you might redeem yourself and ask God for forgiveness, I would spend my time saying it. However, I fear my words would be lost to you and, therefore, will not waste the court's time. There is no compassion or reasonableness found in a man like you. Hearing the evidence presented at trial, the recommendation of the jury, and your comments tonight, I believe I can only express remorse for the loss of your family."

He paused for effect.

"I can now rest, knowing that the evil you have brought to your community will soon be gone."

The judge continued.

"Mr. Brooks, on behalf of the people of Texas and the

authority and trust placed in me by the United States Department of Justice, I hereby remand you to LIFE in the Special Operational Unfenced Prison, sentence to begin immediately."

He pounded his gavel to drive home his decision. He looked at the two motionless figures in the corner and directed.

"Gentlemen, the prisoner is yours. Do your duty."

Hayes saw one of the men draw his pistol to cover the second agent that moved to where Brooks stood. The agent moved around behind Brooks and with a slight push, said, "Let's go," directing him to the door. His partner slowly backed out of the courtroom; pistol leveled at Brooks and holding the door open. At the exit, the second man placed his gun into the small of Brook's back and said, "Keep moving." All three exited the courtroom, and the double doors closed. The judge then declared, "The state's case of Texas vs. John Brooks is now closed" and pounded the gavel once more.

Markstrum rose as did the two attorneys, and Hayes watched the court reporter begin disconnecting the microphone and packaging her keypad and power source. The judge walked around his bench and toward the two of them.

"This case was a hard one gentleman. Breckinridge, Hayes, thank you for your professionalism and your conduct during the trial."

He shook each of their hands in turn.

The court recorder, having completed her packing, said, "Goodnight, Your Honor, gentleman. Mr. Breckinridge, I will be in touch shortly with tonight's transcript."

Breckinridge smiled and acknowledged the court reporter with a thumbs up as she exited the courtroom.

Markstrum looked at both lawyers and said, "Y'all have a good evening. I'm looking forward to seeing you both in court again soon. Breckie – it's time. Bring him in."

The judge turned and walked through the door he entered earlier and disappeared into his chambers. Both men returned to their tables to collect their pencils and note pads and, once placed in their briefcases, turned to leave. Breckinridge sent a text message to his driver to have the car out front in 15 minutes. He looked up from his phone. There was nothing but silence as both men looked at each other. Then Hayes broke the stillness of the courtroom.

"What the hell?"

"Come on, Franklin, let's take a walk," Breckinridge said.

The two men opened the court's short bar doors and walked down the carpeted path leading out of the courtroom. Once in the hall, both stopped and stood to look out of the window. Breckinridge started the conversation.

"Okay, I know you have questions. Ask them, and I will answer them the best that I can."

Hayes spoke calmly.

"First of all, where was everyone? No bailiff, no local police or state troopers? And were those guys feds that took your client out?"

"Short answer is 'yes,' they were feds. This was a closed session, and even though we are in Texas, the feds had oversight of the final sentence."

"Wait. That's just not done."

"What's your next question?"

Hayes stopped for a moment and realized that not all the answers he wanted would come tonight. He asked the next one hoping for a better response.

"What is the Special Operations Unfenced Prison?" he whispered, leaning into Breckinridge. "Is that why the Feds were here?"

A court clerk hustled by, probably burning the late-night oil for some judge, and their conversation stopped.

"Let's start walking to the door. It's pretty quiet here tonight, but I think we can walk and talk. Don't you?" Breckinridge asked, trying to send the clear message: *let's go home.* Both men started walking.

Hayes persisted.

"What is the Special Operations Unfenced Prison?"

"I don't know. I can only surmise it's a new prison system the feds control directly, some high supermax security place for guys like Brooks. This is my third case where my client was sent there to do their time."

"Which brings me to my next question," Hayes pressed, "Why did the judge give him life when the jury recommended the death penalty? The judge obviously concurred with the jury's recommendation."

"Look, Texas has gotten a bad rap for being one of the last states that uses the death penalty. There is A LOT of pressure coming from the state legislature AND the governor to get rid of it. The smart guys are all saying it's going to cost someone an election. Times are changing, and even the people of Texas don't want the death penalty anymore."

"So all of a sudden, Texas is going to listen to the federal government. What kind of BS is that?"

As the men walked down the hall, it was apparent that they were alone in the building except for the maintenance teams scurrying to bring the building back to pristine shape for the next day of justice. As they got closer to the main exit, their shoes echoed off each of the walls and ceiling every time their leather soles hit the freshly buffed marble tiled floor.

It was Breckinridge's turn to lower his voice and lean closer.

"Texas is not listening or bowing down to the federal government. You can't take away a century of state's rights. Hell, every President and Governor we've had would haunt us for eternity if we did that."

Hayes also lowered his voice.

"What then?"

Breckinridge paused, checked the surroundings with his eyes to verify they were alone. He looked at Hayes and calmly stated, "We made a deal."

Hayes was incredulous.

"What! What kind of deal?"

The men reached the security guards standing near

their metal detectors, guarding the exit to the building.

"Goodnight, Mr. Breckinridge, Mr. Hayes," Officer Johnson said.

"Goodnight, Mike," both said in unison as they opened the main door and exited into the street.

"What kind of deal?" Hayes asked again, pressing for more information once outside.

"I don't know the details. I just know that tonight the judge said to 'bring you in,' so that's what I am doing right now. I am bringing you in."

Hayes stopped for a moment to focus on what Breckinridge just said.

"What do you mean, 'bring me in'?"

"Look, Franklin, this is what I know, swear to God, ok? The judge liked the way you handled the prosecution. You were aggressive, creative, and had your facts lined up perfectly. Not hard with a case like this when a guy decides to kill his family, and there is a forensics trail a mile long to back it up. But you did a great job keeping that forensics trail clean and ensuring our system did not screw this up. You know as well as I do, lots of guys get off because of goofs with evidence, but not you. You made this case a slam dunk."

"Ok, enough sunshine. What kind of deal did we make with the feds?" Hayes asked impatiently.

Breckinridge paused.

"Let's just say you, and I are going to get a lot of these high visibility cases. These cases are the big ones that result in the death penalty. The DA is going to make you the prosecutor for each of them."

"What?"

"Listen to me. The DA is in the program. The DA will provide you your top cover."

"Top cover?"

"Yes, the protection your supervisor gives you to continue your job uninterrupted. Jesus, don't you know anything about politics?"

"Screw you, Breckinridge!"

"Sorry, I deserved that," he apologized.

Hayes nodded and accepted the gesture. Breckinridge continued.

"Now listen to me. For tonight's services, you are going to receive a special bonus. It will be personal to you and paid to your checking account on record for your regular pay. You do not have to put it in an offshore account, and it's all legal. You will pay taxes on the money you receive to both the fed and Texas. You will receive a W-2 from the federal government for your services and placed in a special federal pay band. Each case you prosecute will have a unique case code tied to this program. This is all above board."

"Are you serious, Breckinridge?"

"Quite. You heard the judge tell me it's time. Well, your hard work and record has made you the judge's pick for the job."

"So, what is my job?"

"Your job is to make sure the prosecution's case is locked down solid. That everything you prosecute moves as smoothly as this one."

"Well, that's my job anyway, to fight your defense."

Breckinridge paused for a moment.

"Yes," he said, drawing out the word. "This is where it gets a little gray. Once we know guilt, *not prove but know guilt*, my job as a defender is to let you win, regardless of the merits of the case. As a matter of fact, my job is to help you win."

"Are you saying I will always win? Where the hell is justice?" Hayes asked, completely puzzled by the conversation.

"Listen to me before you get all self-righteous. The death penalty is on its way out in Texas, but it's not going to happen soon. We entered this deal with the feds because they have a prototype prison system that they need to put into play. I was told in confidence that it is going to shake up the system and make society much safer. They need inmates to test the prototype, and they only want the ones that we would send to meet their maker."

Hayes was stunned, but what Breckinridge was saying was starting to make sense. His mind was processing the information as fast as it was coming in. Breckinridge continued.

"There are key people in the Courts that have agreed to be a part of the special pay band. Our judge tonight and the DA are some of those people. My firm is part of this deal, and while it's a little trickier to pay for the defense, the feds have worked it out for cases like this. My firm is a temporary extension of the government, like being deputized for the case. That way, I can serve as a public defender. Everyone has to get something to make this work."

Hayes thought a moment. He signed up to practice law, not get involved in some federal deal.

"What happens if this gets out or fails?"

"Well, then there are a lot of folks that are going down with this one. The Governor herself agreed that we will produce as many inmates for the new federal prison as possible, but only those where we know there is guilt and the sentence would be the death penalty. To do this, we need prosecutors who can do their job and defense lawyers that let them, as well as *assist* them."

"Are you talking about throwing out client-attorney privilege and everything else protecting the defendant? Are you saying you'll share info with me, and together, we make sure we have evidence to make it stick? Do I hear that, right?"

Hayes could feel the anger start to rise as this deal, and the extent of government involvement with the feds was explained to him. Breckinridge saw the expression of disapproval on Hayes' face.

"Look, you have defended people before that you know are guilty. Now, under this agreement, we will make sure that the guilty are truly guilty. Isn't that what we signed up to do? Hell, isn't that the real justice, killers not getting off on BS technical claims or undue influence of public opinion where people don't know the facts but have powerful friends or slick lawyers who twist the law and smile nicely for the jurors?"

Hayes agreed, Breckinridge's points were solid. He was starting to see some value in this program.

"And tonight, the way the sentence was levied?" Hayes asked, beginning to cool down.

"Closing up the loose ends, Franklin. These trials are very public. The press is involved in most of them, and it hits the local media almost every day. Sometimes the case goes national. Everyone has an opinion, juries are influenced regardless of sequestration, and it turns into a flat out circus."

"The people do need their circus, Breckie."

Hayes smiled as he comprehended what was being said by his new friend and felt secure enough to use his nickname. Breckinridge stopped for a moment and looked at Hayes, surprised by his switch to a casual demeanor, and then continued.

"That's right, Franklin. So, when the judge has a closed session like this evening, no one publicly sees the feds, there is no press, and we announce later that during sentencing, the judge reduced the sentence to life instead of the death penalty. The state is now a hero. This is why. The people that support the death penalty know that the jury recommended it, and take comfort knowing Texas can still sentence a man to death. They blame those 'damned liberal judges' for converting it to a life sentence. The people that don't support the death penalty, which is the majority of the voter base, applaud the decision. So you see, the state gets all the credit for showing compassion with the majority. This means votes. The feds get what they want, more inmates, and we pick up a little extra in the paycheck, all legally. Everyone wins."

"So how much extra? What did we make tonight?"

Breckinridge paused, then smiled.

"$100,000 for legal services rendered. It will be that for each case where the defendant goes to the fed's new prison. And by the way, I hear the DA is expanding personnel support to make sure you have the staff you need to get this done. The

Judge already told the DA we would have this conversation. Your new staffing does not include my team. My folks will also be part of supporting your effort."

Hayes was dumbfounded. The headlights from Breckinridge's car indicated to both men the conversation was coming to an end. As the car pulled up to the curb, Breckinridge opened the car door, turned, and looked at Hayes.

"Welcome to the team. Goodnight, Franklin – call me in the morning and let's set up lunch. It looks like we are going to be working together quite a lot."

Breckinridge shook his hand before he got in the car and drove off. Hayes looked around and realized his car was in the main parking garage. As he started his quarter-mile walk, he looked up at the Texas night sky filled with stars and thought, *They sure are big and bright*. He smiled as he knew next year he would have his car pick him up out front. Man, his wife was going to love the pay raise.

CHAPTER 3

John Brooks was taken at gunpoint by two federal agents out of the courtroom, down a flight of stairs, and exited the side door where an armored government black SUV was waiting to pick them up. The car's driver had the engine running and was communicating via his small headset with the two agents bringing Brooks out of the courtroom.

Agent Munoz was the first of the two agents to emerge from the doorway and continued to cover Brooks and Agent McCarron as the two approached the SUV. McCarron positioned Brooks in front of the back door where Munoz had a clear shot, opened it, and shuffled Brooks around the door. Brooks felt his head pushed down, keeping it low and being guided into the back seat. The driver turned and pointed his pistol at Brooks' head and remained silent as McCarron moved around the vehicle, opened the opposite door, leaned the middle seat forward, and took his position in the rear jump seat behind Brooks. Munoz moved around to the side door and took his place next to the prisoner.

"Ok," Munoz said. "Let's go."

None of the agents fastened their seat belts to allow a quicker response if something happened during transit. Brooks looked at Munoz.

"Well, how about putting mine on at least?" referencing the seatbelt.

The two agents in the back laughed at his comment.

"Kiss my ass," Munoz said.

Brooks starting watching the street signs and landmarks as the driver pulled the SUV out on West 14th street, turned right on Lavaca, made the light on 15th street, and headed west.

"Hey, where y'all taking me? You guys is feds, so I think we're not going to the normal lock-up."

Munoz looked at McCarron in the jump seat and nodded. McCarron opened a small pouch with a hypodermic needle and small vial of clear blue liquid. Brooks could see him insert the needle into the small jar, pull the serum into the hypodermic, and clear the air from the syringe, shooting a short spurt into the air hitting the ceiling of the vehicle.

"Ok, Brooks – we are going to give you something to sleep. We have a long trip in front of us, and we don't want to be watching your ass the whole way." Munoz announced. "Do I need to hold you down, or can the Agent just give it to you?"

"I'm fine-"

Before Brooks finished, McCarron pushed the needle through the jumpsuit into Brook's top right shoulder. Brooks jumped slightly when he felt the needle pinprick and said, "You boys coulda given me a second or two to git ready."

McCarron pulled the needle out and put both the vial and the hypodermic back into its small pouch. Brooks watched as the street signs passed and started to feel lightheaded. *I gotta hold on*, he said to himself as the SUV turned off of Lamar, made a left onto Windsor Road, and headed for the MoPac Expressway and his new home.

The car had passed the turn for Harris Blvd., when Brooks started counting down. When he reached ten, he smiled. They were approaching Jarratt Ave., and he saw the lights from another vehicle coming up the street, knowing what would happen when he hit the number one. Out of nowhere, another SUV, moving at 40 miles per hour, timed its collision to T-bone the black SUV on the car's back right panel.

"Watch out!" Munoz yelled to the driver, "Car right!"

The two vehicles collided, causing the black SUV to spin as the laws of physics attempted to get the two crashing cars to look straight at each other. Brooks felt himself thrown against his door and banged his head against the glass, the impact force passing mostly straight through his body. He crunched into the door, pressed against it by the initial impact, unable to move his body as though pinned to the door by an invisible hand. As the vehicles settled, Brooks fell over to his right side, dazed and close to losing consciousness. Munoz lifted off his seat as the SUV spun underneath him. The propulsive force of the collision pushed him into the back of the driver's seat, which guided his body headfirst into Brooks' door, knocking him out. Munoz crumpled on top of Brooks and remained pinned between Brooks and the driver's seat. Brooks saw McCarron thrown into the backside of the SUV and, while bouncing airborne, watched McCarron's face impact the rear of the jump seat as the SUV spun and responded to the force of the collision. Both cars came to a rest in under 10 seconds. The combined vehicles created a barrier of twisted metal and broken glass across the road.

As Brook's vision slowly returned, he observed all traffic on the street had stopped, and saw people leaving their vehicles to assist. In the spirit in which faith in humanity is restored, he saw motorists grab their flares and light them as an advanced warning to arriving motorists to slow down. Others began directing traffic as the number of cars approaching the scene slowed, then stopped, stacking up behind each other. Several motorists grabbed their first aid kits and blankets and started to run towards the accident.

The driver of the government SUV was more fortunate than the passengers. Seat belted in, he was thrown around, but the seat belt and inflating side airbag held him firm. He unfastened his seat belt and pushed the driver side door open, pulling the deflated airbag with it. Still shaken from the collision, Brooks watched as the driver got out, he looked disoriented and was having difficulty standing. The driver saw a man coming straight at him from the driver's side of the other vehicle.

"Didn't you see your STOP sign?" the agent yelled.

"I saw it," the man answered.

Brooks lifted his head and watched through the windshield as the driver of his vehicle reach for his pistol inside his jacket. The other man facing the agent coolly raised his gun and fired two shots. Brooks saw the first round catch the driver square in the throat, and the second one appeared to graze his head. The driver brought his hand to his bloody neck and began to gasp for air making a gurgling sound as he did so; falling to the street choking his last breaths. The bystanders heading to the accident stopped immediately. Several laid on the ground, looking to get as low as they could while hugging the concrete road. Those not falling to the ground ran back to their vehicles and looked for cover.

The shooter hurried by the fallen driver and opened the side door of the government SUV. He pulled Brooks out of his seat, trying to steady him on his feet. Munoz's unconscious body fell on to the pavement.

"Johnny," the man slapped him quickly on both cheeks. "Johnny, you ok, cuz?"

Brooks nodded his head slowly.

"Frank, is that you?"

"Yeah, are you Ok?"

"A little groggy, the feds give me something to sleep. The other guy has the keys to my cuffs," he said through his drug-induced haze.

"Hey, dipshit, you got Johnny? Is he ok?" another man yelled from the other side of the government vehicle.

"Yeah, he's fine, Buddy! – Margie here yet?"

Brooks heard the sound of another car approaching from Jarratt Ave., and locking its tires to answer the question. The Ford Taurus sedan skidded to a stop on the road. Their escape car had arrived.

"She just pulled up – hurry up, will ya!"

"Ok – I got Johnny and a fed here – you take care of the guy in the back and get his keys. Johnny is all handcuffed up."

Frank turned his attention to Brooks.

"Can you walk, cuz?"

"Yeah – give me your pistol Frank," Brooks said, lifting his two cuffed hands to his cousin.

He handed his pistol to Brooks. Brooks stood up, shaking like a newborn calf, firmly gripped the pistol in both hands, and fired two shots into Munoz's chest.

"You kiss MY ass, fed!"

Frank grabbed him around the waist.

"Here, lean on me, cuz. We gotta go!"

Buddy fired two shots on the other side of the SUV. McCarron's fate was the same as Munoz. Frank and Brooks struggled around the front of the government SUV and crouched down behind it. Brooks heard one of the motorist yell, "The guy in Orange is shooting people. We gotta stop them!"

Buddy yelled, "Looks like we got folks reaching for their hardware. This could get excitin'!"

Both crashed cars starting receiving fire, bullets zinging from left and right from the small arms fired by the stopped motorists. This caused the bulletproof glass to starburst and the other rounds to make "thump, thump" sounds as the bullets made contact with the reinforced siding of the black SUV. The other SUV did not absorb the rounds as well as glass shattered, and bullets entered the front quarter panel, ricocheting off the engine block.

"Holy shit – they're shootin' at us!" Frank exclaimed as several more pistol shots hit the SUV. "Git over here, Buddy, and help me out!"

"You gotta love Texas," Buddy shouted over the last round of pistol fire.

The gunfire escalated, and it became apparent that they were caught in a crossfire from both sides of the stopped cars, though the heaviest was coming from the direction of the parkway.

"Git their heads down, Buddy, so that we can move!" Frank yelled from between the cars.

Buddy stood briefly, and he felt the zip of bullets passing close and heard more of the "thump, thump" into the side of the vehicle and watched as more stars appeared in the glass. He emptied the clip of his .45 shooting back at the new citizen deputies over the hood of the black SUV, causing a lull in the firing they needed. Using the cover of the crashed SUV's, both men grabbed Brook's rock-solid frame and pulled him to the Ford that concealed itself behind the crashed vehicles. They moved out of the way just as a round fired from a rifle flattened the passenger front tire of their SUV and blew off the hub cap loosed in the collision creating a hellish noise as it hit and bounced on the pavement. A second bullet shattered the front windshield.

"Jesus!" The women driver yelled from the escape car, "Hurry up! I ain't getting shot by another redneck!"

Frank opened the back door of the Ford and Brooks felt himself pushed into the back seat headfirst.

"Buddy, did you get the keys?"

"Got'em!" came the response.

Frank slid over the trunk and opened the other side, grabbed the jumpsuit and pulled Brooks through the backseat by the shoulders. Buddy jumped in on the floor behind the front seats and pulled the back door closed. Frank jumped in the front door that Margie opened and said, "Let's go!"

In the distance, they could begin to hear the sirens of the Austin Police Department responding to frantic calls about a shoot-out at Windsor and Jarratt. Margie slammed the car in reverse and hit the curb backing up, which threw Frank and Buddy around like paper in a wind storm. She turned the Ford sedan in a flurry of smoke and screeching tires as she headed the car back down Jarratt Ave., howling a rebel yell into the night as their right rear light was shot out, throwing pieces of colored plastic onto the street. Frank recovered from his bounce and shut his door on the fly, grinning as if he just won the Jackpot at Vegas. Margie, seeing no followers, dropped her speed to the limit and cruised along as if nothing happened.

"Is he gonna be okay?" Margie asked.

"He'll be fine – he's a bit groggy," Buddy responded, pulling himself up on to the seat and using trial and error with the keys to unlock the foot shackles and handcuffs. "But he can still talk a little bit."

It did not seem to Brooks that they had driven far when Margie made a right that caused him to roll in the back seat and bounce slightly as the car pulled into what he believed was a driveway. He could hear the garage door already opening as Margie drove into the noise of the unit's chain rattling loudly as it pulled the door open. The two cousins got out and walked into the garage. Margie pulled into the garage and turned off the ignition. Brooks could hear the garage door close and knew they were free. The Austin police zoomed by, sirens wailing as they chased a phantom car into the night. When the garage door shut entirely, Frank and Buddy opened the back door of the vehicle and pulled Brooks out.

"Where are we?" Brooks asked.

"We're at a friend of mines," Buddy replied. "We are going to lay low here a couple of weeks until the heat cools – then make our next move."

"Arizona? We decided Arizona, right?" Margie asked.

"Y'all got a plan?" Brooks asked.

"Yep," Buddy replied. "Johnny, our plan is we'll take both cars, stay on the back roads and off the interstate. We'll head south first into Mexico by Big Bend and then loop up back into the USA, cross on foot if we need to. Thanks to the newspapers and the internet covering the trial, we got plenty of new friends that will help us along the way."

"Thanks, cuz. Didn't need you to tell me the plan. I just wanted to know if you had one," Brooks said.

"Johnny, you ok?" Margie asked. "You're not hit, are

you?"

"No, still hazy, got a knot on my head and getting really tired - but thanks, y'all."

Brooks looked at Buddy, looking a little hurt by his comment about the plan.

"It's a good plan," Brooks added.

Buddy smiled, turned and looked at Frank.

"Ain't no way Johnny will spend a day more in prison for what he did."

"I ain't ever going to prison," Brooks said loud enough for everyone to hear.

The temporary excitement of the escape was over, and Brooks started to feel himself slip into darkness. He felt his arms lift, and two sets of hands support him and knew he was being carried by his two cousins as he walked into the house. Brooks kicked the threshold to the door with his foot, providing him a returning moment to clarity. He felt grateful for his family that had saved him. *Not my cheatin' woman and lying kids*, was his final thought as the blackness finally claimed him.

◆ ◆ ◆

The phone rang, and Agent Willis answered, "175."

"How did it go?"

The voice on the other end was their Supervisor. Willis looked around at his two fellow agents, McCarron and Munoz, in the room and glared. They understood his facial expression. In reaction to knowing it was their boss, both discarded their reading material, sat up straight and paid attention to Willis' side of the conversation as though the man on the other end of the phone had walked into the room.

"The Brooks transfer was successful, no biological rejection and initial reports indicate normal brain activity. Visualization is 97%, and he's already made several contributions to the local community to include a shootout as part of his escape. We'll continue to monitor for any abnormalities in the life support functions. All indicators are that he is fine, and we now have number 100 tucked away in the SOUP."

"Any problems with the transfer?"

"The new injection worked instantaneously. Mental activity data indicates the immediate transfer of cognitive functions and a successfully replaced consciousness. We were able to sustain number 100 at Jumpstart until full bio integration occurred with the Jacket and the Box."

"Any new information about how long we can sustain Jumpstart with the new drug before Jacket integration?"

"Not yet, the lab is still working the data we provided on 100, but if he is like the previous 47 inmates, all indicators show an average pre-Jacket VLS of 3 hrs."

There was a pause on the other end of the phone and then, "Great job. Pass my congratulations along to your team. Get me the updated lab results. I am going to need them soon."

"Yes, Sir."

Click.

CHAPTER 4

O fficer Grant walked in the Washington afternoon heat along the path past the Vietnam Women's Memorial on the way to his meeting. Tourists and locals alike filled the National Mall for daily runs, pickup games of Ultimate Frisbee, and touring the Nation's monuments. Grant looked like one of them, wearing a pair of cargo shorts and his embroidered hat with the Washington Capitals logo. The Caps, as they were called, were the DC professional hockey team that had inspired its fans by bringing home the National Hockey League championship a couple of years earlier. In addition to the hat, he picked his favorite light blue t-shirt listing the locations of the 76 Spirit Tour by Earth, Wind, and Fire; or "EWF" as he often referred to them.

Grant recently acquired his new shirt off Amazon to replace his original, long worn out from endless washings and wearing. As he walked along the path to the Lincoln Memorial, he reflected fondly on that December night, riding with his older brother and sister up to the Baltimore Civic Center for an evening of horns and soul. The Emotions on tour with EWF were terrific, but you just could not beat the sound of the EWF brass, and outstanding vocals blending together. He had to work hard to complete his chores and do personal favors for his siblings in the weeks leading up to the concert. In the end, he earned the ticket and a spot in the car backseat to create one of the best memories of his early teen years. *Good memor-*

ies, he thought.

Grant was meeting with one of his best informants this afternoon. He needed to know the details of her experiences with the funeral home and how she knew something was going to happen there. He also had many questions of his own and wanted some answers.

To schedule this meeting, Grant had walked casually to the food stand at the path intersection on the southwest side of the pond with Constitution gardens last week. After getting his hotdog and diet coke, Grant strolled behind the kiosk and sat on a park bench next to a green park tourist sign with a map of the national mall in bright colors. Once he finished his meal, he moved to the trashcans flanking the benches, discarded his lunch, and returned to the sign. Leaning over to read it, he palmed a magnetic box with a coin inside to the back underside. In this instance, it was a penny letting his source know they would meet at the Lincoln Memorial on the steps. Grant and his informant used a simple system of coins and the national monuments for meeting places; the nickel, Jefferson Memorial, and the Quarter, the Washington Monument. While Grant hated cloak and dagger precautions, this source was worth protecting at all costs. Grant would know the signal was received when he would receive a text message from the phone he gave her for just this purpose. The text consisted of a smiley face emoticon. Twenty-four hours later, from the "sent" time on the message, they would meet at the designated memorial. Today, his meeting was set for 12:23. When the meeting was over, Grant would buy an "item" on e-Bay owned by his source to pay for the information.

As he approached the Lincoln memorial, he saw her on the steps midway between the bottom where the reflecting pool started and the top of the monument. Almost the same age as Grant, she was dressed in her patched blue jeans and a yellow, loose-fitting top to stay cool in the summer heat. She was wearing a large hat, made from straw with a wide brim to keep the sun out of her eyes, and to hide her facial features if someone were to try and recognize her. Her head was down, indicating she checked out her surroundings and did not see anything to prevent them from the meeting. It all looked good. Grant walked up to her, trying his best to sing "Shining Star," a major EWF hit and crowd-pleaser.

"I don't know why you do that. You can't sing that shit," she said, looking up into Grant's face and flashing a smile.

Grant smiled back. Of all his sources, she had the best personality, and over the years, they developed as close a friendship as this business would allow. While never mentioning her name or revealing her identity, Grant had taken to calling her Maggie after his favorite aunt. The name must have agreed with her because she never corrected him or gave him grief about its use.

"You try, Maggie," he retorted. "It's not as easy as you think to hit those notes."

He sat down on the concrete step next to her.

"This is gonna cost you," she started.

"All down to business, I see."

"Hell yeah, it's hot today. Don't need to be hangin' round here with you."

"How much?" Grant said, leaning forward to stretch his back.

"One thousand or I'm walking."

"I'll give you $800 if the information is good."

"You cops is always trying to git the upper hand!" she said so only he could hear.

Then she paused, knowing that this was the most he ever offered to pay her for information. She looked at him, and he gave her the "don't mess with me" look formed by closing his eyes halfway and tightening his lips. It seemed extra menacing under his Caps hat. Like Maggie, Grant also had a good deal of street time. He knew how much the information was worth, and he knew how much he could afford.

"Ok – $800. It must be important to you. Did you check out the place like I told you?"

His silence gave her the answer she wanted.

"Maggie, let me ask the questions."

She nodded her head and said, "Okay, your dime."

Grant proceeded. "How did you find out about the deliveries?" he asked, trying to keep his body language as casual as possible.

"I got sources, too. 'Bout six months ago, one of them had their couzin pass. You heard 'bout the shootin' in South East by the brothers selling dope out of a barbershop?"

Grant nodded.

"That was him – stupid fool trying to buy weed from one of them, and the deal goes sideways."

Grant remembered the incident when news came into the station. The owners of the barbershop were arrested in early 2018 and eventually convicted for drug sales. DC police believed that some of the drugs made it on the street and were being sold by guys that worked at the shop before the owner's arrest. One of the deals had gone wrong, and a young man was shot and killed.

Maggie continued.

"Well, my guy wants to see his couzin one last time but knows that the bad guys know who he is and will be waiting at the funeral home. So rather than go to the home for the homecomin' service, he waits till nighttime when he can sneak into the parlor where his cousin is layin' to say goodbye. But is he surprised when he gets there! There's some big truck in the back and guys in suits is offloading caskets like cordwood. Not just normal folks. These got guns!"

Grant listened intently, relating what she was saying with his personal experience.

"How did he know they had guns?"

"Cause one of the guys sees him walking toward them. My guy was figuring the back door in is the best way into the parlor and all, and bumps into all this mess. Then one of the suits, a brother at that, comes over and tells him he should hang out someplace else and puts his hands on his hips, pulling back his suit jacket so my guy can see he is carrying."

This information was reinforcing what Grant had seen. Maggie's story seemed pretty solid.

"Now ain't that some craziness. So he comes to see me and wants to know if I know what's goin' on. And I say to him, 'I ain't no rocket scientist' and tell him to stay clear given his rep on the street."

"Okay, so what was your next move?"

"Well, I figured before I told you about this, I need to see for myself. So I go a week later and nothin'. Then a couple of nights later, when I'm back this side of DC staying with my boy, I try again. Still nothin'. I'm startin' to think my man be trippin'. So, I hang out on the corner for one last night, and I see it. A big truck is coming my way, and he turns into the home and parks around back. I walk across the street and go to the back, and the same thing happens to me. Brother with a gun tells me to go away, nothing to see and shit. So I leave, and that's when I told you to go check it out."

"Did you see anything else?"

"Yes. Like my guy, I see the big truck was parked around back, and they had a forklift being drivin' by some lady, and she was pulling caskets out of the truck and driving them to a loading dock for the home. There were guys in suits, and they were hustling everywhere. Those guys were SERIOUS, know what I mean? Not PLAYIN'. So when the brother tells me to leave, I did it. You don't pay me to git my ass shot."

Grant nodded in agreement.

"Yes, I don't pay you to get your ass shot," he said grinning. "If you did, then we couldn't do any more monument meetings on concrete steps like this."

"Look, smart man. Something is happenin' there. This is not a one-time thing. Can you tell me why that many white folks are bringin' caskets to a funeral home in South East at night and why them people are carrying guns and wearing suits?"

"No, Maggie, I can't; but I am going to find out. Anything

else?"

She stopped to recall any remaining details.

"They did have cameras all over, but that's not nothing today. Everybody got those."

"Do you think they caught you on camera?"

"Don't know how I wasn't. They was everywhere."

"Have you noticed anyone following you? Anything that might be different since you visited the home?"

"No. Nothing yet, but as I says, I move around a lot and stay at lots of folk's places that I am helpin' with their problems."

He stood up, stretching his legs and did a windmill with his waist to loosen his back. He hated getting old. Six more years, he reminded himself, and it was pension time.

"What's you doing spinning like a top? You gettin' old?"

"Cut the teasing, Maggie. Down to business. As you said, I'm paying for this."

He smiled to let her know he was open to the harassment, and that he *was* starting to feel old.

"Did your source see anything else?"

"No, he acted like he was all cool, but I think it scared him."

"Why do you think that?"

"Cause I ain't seen him in a couple of weeks. That ain't like him."

"How about you? You worried?"

"Not 'bout me. But he was a good man. You should look into where he went too. Don't know what you will find. Somethin' ain't right!"

Grant did not want to mention he visited the home. He could understand Maggie's concern for her source. Grant looked at her and said, "Put surround sound speakers on e-bay with a 54 inch TV."

Still sitting, she nodded that she understood. Grant paused and then said, "Maggie, you take care and watch yourself."

She smiled at him.

"You watch your own shit. I got mine altogether."

Grant smiled back at Maggie and walked down the stairs. When he reached the reflecting pool, he turned to look up at the Lincoln Memorial. She was walking off in the opposite direction. He agreed, the info was all adding up that something was happening at the funeral home. Now he needed to do some digging. He turned and headed back to his car.

CHAPTER 5

Aaron McAllister, Chief of Staff to the President of the United States, sat in his office outside of the Oval Office. *How the hell am I going to do this?* He hung up the phone less than three minutes ago and already saw a firestorm coming. He was read on to the VLS Program, but what the man on the telephone proposed was political and not operational. He struggled with the favor he was just asked. Granted, he owed his friend for many favors over the years that he'd never called in. Now that day had come.

He pulled up the President's schedule and saw he had a five-minute window before the meeting with the Vice President to discuss NASA's next steps. Elon Musk was surpassing NASA's progress with his own Big Falcon Rocket (BFR) as it was known publicly. Privately, McAllister was told that Musk drew it on a whiteboard and said he wanted a Big Fucking Rocket to get to Mars. Maybe because of the rocket's name, his team moved out quickly and appeared to be passing milestones faster than NASA's planning and oversight could keep up. Having a private company get to Mars or start asteroid mining was something this administration was not going to deal with today; but they had a responsibility to lay down the economic framework and policy implications for the future. Musk renamed the rocket to "Starship," but McAllister was all in on the unofficial definition of BFR. He loved American ingenuity, whatever it was called.

Smiling, McAllister wondered how The Supervisor knew he could grab five minutes with POTUS before the meeting. It did not matter. He picked up his NASA briefing book and walked into the Oval Office. POTUS was hunched over his desk, finishing the same brief. Pushing away from the Resolute Desk, he stood up. "Should be an interesting meeting with the VP and his team."

"I think it's going to be a little more interesting than you think, Mr. President."

The President picked up immediately that his Chief of Staff had something on his mind. The President buzzed his secretary outside the Oval Office.

"Betty, hold the VP and his team until I call again."

"Yes, Mr. President," came the reply, and POTUS ended the intercom call.

"What do you have?"

"Sir, you are read in on the operational activities of VLS – Virtual Life Solution. In the last two years, significant progress was made on the prototype, and we believe it is time to apply oversight and get Congress officially involved in continued funding."

"Yes – Artificial Intelligence Research," the president said. "Ok, Aaron, so what makes this so interesting?"

"I've talked with the Program Executive, and we agree: we think a special joint committee of Congress is necessary to provide governance."

"Ok, so I ask again: why is this something we need to discuss?"

"Mr. President, we are also recommending the VP be part of the Committee, but not chair it. Additionally, senior members of both House and Senate Judiciary Committees that comprise this special group are meeting next Monday to begin the program briefings, and the VP needs to be there if he is going to fill a role in this effort."

The President nodded. He understood the problem.

"Well, he's not going to like that. The VP had some personal time scheduled in Arizona. Additionally, he was going to meet with some of our people on the ground to start up our efforts in the Southwestern states while he was out there."

McAllister said nothing knowing the importance of fundraising for the campaign and waited for the President's next comments.

"How important is this, Aaron?"

"Pretty important, Mr. President. I've known the Program Executive for about eight years. A straight shooter and responsible for some of the major technological breakthroughs in Defense with AI technology. He would not ask this if he thought he had another way."

POTUS nodded. "Betty, is the VP here yet?" he said, pushing the phone's intercom button.

"Yes, sir. Everyone is here."

"Send in the VP and ask the rest to wait about five minutes."

The door to the Oval Office opened, and Vice President of the United States Harold Morrison the Third or "Trip" as his friends called him, walked in.

"Good morning Mr. President," he said as he moved across the carpet emblazoned with the US Seal to greet the President.

"Morning Trip," the President said as he moved from behind the desk and shook his VP's hand and then pointed to the sofa.

McAllister remembered when the party asked the President to consider Morrison for his VP. During Morrison's interview with the President, McAllister could tell that the VP candidate was liked immediately. True to his background, Morrison was a tough rust belt politician and influential voice for Republicans in Illinois. His platform and reputation would bring in the votes for every state from Pennsylvania to Iowa; and if lucky, New York as well. What the President had liked best about Morrison is you got what you saw, and you got it straight. Six months later, on Election Day, Morrison worked his political magic and delivered his states and New York as hoped. Now, after two and a half years in office, the respect turned to trust. The VP was an integral part of the team. The President gave his Vice President more responsibility and oversight for areas typically not offered to the position by previous presidents. He tasked jobs to Morrison as a sign of respect and to solidify the trust between the two men. The President knew that Morrison welcomed the added work-load. The extra tasks helped his VP build relationships with Congress while lengthening Morrison's resume; preparing him for when he would run for the top position. Morrison would be the logical heir apparent for the party, and if things continued as they were, The President would personally provide Morrison's endorsement to the party. Stable leadership from two consecutive presidents; the country had not seen that in a while. America was long overdue for a White House with a vision for the future and Chief Executives willing to take action to turn that vision into reality.

"Good to see you, Mr. Vice President," McAllister said.

"Morning Chief, always glad to see you as well," he commented as he took his usual seat on the sofa.

POTUS looked at the Chief as the sign to start.

"Mr. Vice President, you are aware of the VLS program, correct?" McAllister began.

"I've not been briefed in a while, but I know we have gotten some great technology for Defense, Justice, and Homeland from the program. Artificial Intelligence stuff, I believe."

Pretty good for not being briefed recently, McAllister thought. He shared the President's respect and trust for the man.

The Chief of Staff continued with a, "Yes Sir," and handed the VP a one-page summary marked "Top Secret."

"The program has reached a point where it needs oversight. A special joint Committee is forming in Congress."

The VP quickly scanned the paper and recalled the program briefing he'd received. He knew immediately where this conversation was heading. Very seldom do committees involve him in his role as President of the Senate, though there are times when it happens. It looks like there was more to this program than Research and Development if they were building a joint committee. Morrison nodded his head as a signal for the Chief to continue.

"The Program Executive feels your involvement on the Committee will be necessary to represent the White House as well as Congress. This program could change the way we operate our prisons in this country, and if successful, this means we will have great news for the voters this fall with our domestic agenda and justice reform. We anticipate this program will need the involvement of the Attorney General at some point; a central oversight Committee to prioritize technology sharing across the Departments; and of course, to ensure funding from Congress. This is why, Sir, you are a logical choice to sit on the Committee."

The VP smiled and thought, *easy enough to read the tea leaves on this one.* He looked at the Chief with puzzlement.

"Am I leading it?"

"No, Sir, we think it best that your schedule remain flexible enough to continue support for the efforts you are working."

"Trip, I need you available to work the campaign. I don't want you bogged down in leading this," the President added.

Ok – this makes sense, and the President wasn't pushing yet, so what's the ask? He did not have to wait long to hear it.

"The Committee is meeting this Monday, Mr. Vice President."

There it is! His mind exclaimed without changing the calm exterior he was showing the President and the Chief of Staff.

Speaking coolly while handing the Chief back the summary, he stated, "I'm in Arizona next week. I've scheduled a full week of fundraising to kick things off for the campaign.

Some of these meetings took months to work the schedules. I can't just tell these donors I am canceling because of a committee meeting."

The President looked at his Chief and then his Vice. It was apparent to both men that the President was weighing each side before making his decision. There was measurable tension in the room, and everyone could feel it. Seconds ticked away in silence. McAllister was relieved when the President asked, "How soon can we get the Committee meeting on Monday, Aaron?"

"We can start at 10:00 a.m. It will run for approximately two hours," McAllister said with confidence.

The Supervisor told McAllister he might run into problems with the VP and that he would ensure the Committee was ready to start at 10:00. The President made his decision.

"Trip, I want you on the Hill at 10:00 for this. You can get to Phoenix with the time difference around 4:00 p.m. That still gives you Monday night for work and hitting your schedule. You can brief the Chief or me on the flight out on any details of the Committee meeting. Then I want you and Rebecca to take a couple of extra days for yourself. I don't want you back in DC before Tuesday of the following week. That's an order."

With a faint smile toward his Vice after a pause, the President added, "I'll reschedule our breakfast strategy meeting for Tuesday rather than Monday morning."

McAllister noticed a change in Morrison's expression. The two men really did respect each other, and the Vice President appeared to be taken aback by the President's generosity to change his schedule for him. Morrison knew this was going to mess up his personal agenda, but he could be flexible if POTUS were asking him to do this. Instead of planning a getaway with Rebecca this weekend, he could make it up on the backside and that would keep him out of the doghouse on the home front. Morrison promised his wife this trip and was determined to keep that part of his life alive. He loved his wife and knew what the next 12 years could mean for their marriage if they were fortunate to remain in the White House. The rest of the meetings could be adjusted. He looked at the President with sincere gratitude.

"Yes, Mr. President, I'll be there on Monday at 10:00."

The President looked relieved. "Ok, Aaron, let's get the guys in here from NASA so I can hear how they are going to keep an eye on Musk."

As the Chief of Staff walked over to open the door to the waiting scientist and managers outside, the Vice President thought, *this Monday meeting better be worth it, or I'm going to have someone's ass.*

CHAPTER 6

The Supervisor and his team stood up as the members of the Special Joint Judiciary Committee walked into the hearing room at precisely 10:00 am. Outside the chamber, standing guard were members of the Supervisor's team. He was not taking chances with the Capitol Police or even the Secret Service detail to protect this session. What he and his team were going to discuss was not for public disclosure and would quickly become one of the nation's closest secrets if he had his way. The meeting room was a small board room cleared for sensitive discussions in the Russell Senate Building and would serve his purpose of building a team with the new committee perfectly.

The Supervisor had gotten the attention of the right people to make this happen. The Vice President was reluctant to alter his schedule, but POTUS told him to be here. His friend McAllister filled him in afterward on their meeting. The VP said, "Yes, Sir," but the Supervisor knew he had not made friends with his request. The last place the Supervisor wanted to be was on the VP's blacklist, but the VP was critical to the project moving forward.

The Supervisor had reached his milestone to put 100 inmates in VLS successfully. Now it was time for this Committee to make his program official. This status would give the Supervisor the authority to run the program under the direction of the Committee and free him up to focus on op-

EVIL WALKS AMONG US

erations. In return, each of the Committee members would ensure funding was available to expand and maintain the program, and keep opposition to their efforts within Congress to a minimum. Vice President Harold Morrison walked over to the Supervisor and shook his hand. The two men stared eye to eye like two prizefighters getting ready to throw the first punch.

"This better be good, you jumped pretty high to pull me here," the Vice President said, squeezing the handshake a little more than usual.

"I promise you, Mr. Vice President, this will not be a waste of your time."

The handshake ended. Morrison smiled and walked around the table to take his seat. The Supervisor took his. The meeting members sat at a long rectangular table, politicians on one side, and the Supervisor and his team on the other. It looked more like a negotiation than an oversight Committee, but the Supervisor wanted the setting to be more intimate. He was going to address something new to this group and needed "buy-in" as partners working together; not the typical testimony where witnesses provided information while talking up to Committee members asking their questions from their elevated chairs.

As the Vice President sat down, he calmly stated, "The first session of the Special Joint Judiciary Committee is called to order. Because of the secrecy associated with this program, all records of this session will be taken and maintained by you," he said, staring at the Supervisor, "and that this program is at the highest classification with special code name clearance. As I understand it, you've asked us to refer to you as the Supervisor."

The Supervisor nodded and affirmed.

"That's correct, Mr. Vice President. Following standard procedures, each member of this Committee will be allowed access to review code name information and proceedings of this meeting for 48 hours after the meeting's conclusion. My team will be available in the 'basement' of both the House and Senate, at your convenience, while you review and sign the record of our discussions. As to my title, my name is not as important as the role I perform. For programs like this, personal names put the executives at risk. I appreciate your indulgence."

Each nodded their approval. The Vice President sat in the middle of the group. On his right was the Senate President Pro Tem and Judiciary Chairman Carter Hurst, Republican from Texas and on his right, Senate Ranking Committee Member Amanda Sheldon, Democrat from Georgia. On Morrison's left was the House Judiciary Chairman Elizabeth Katz, Republican from Virginia and on her left, House Committee Ranking Member Thomas Sweet, and Democrat from New York. All lined up in order of precedence.

"Let's begin," Morrison said and nodded to the Supervisor, "Your show."

The Supervisor stood, made eye contact with his audience, and began.

"I do not need to give any of you a history lesson about our criminal justice system and the rising costs of incarceration. Much of this information you received as a read-ahead before this meeting. I think we can all agree that there are significant social, political, and fiscal issues associated with our system. This year's appropriations will total $184 Billion to handle the process from arrest to prison for each inmate found guilty in our courtrooms."

The Supervisor looked side to side, then continued.

"I would like to remind each of you that the citizens and voters of the United States feel less secure today than ever before."

The Supervisor paused once again. *Good, there was no interruption.* He made his point, and there was no dispute with his comments. It was always tough to get consensus in a bipartisan Committee on the most basic facts. The Supervisor continued.

"Crime, terrorism, and mass shootings all contribute to society's feelings; and frankly, each time a major event occurs, the people look to the government to fix it. This morning, I am here to report, there is a solution."

The Supervisor stopped to survey the group of law-makers in front of him. The Republicans were looking forward with interest; Congressman Sweet crossed his arms and sat back in his chair. He was already withdrawing.

"What we will discuss may sound like a bit of science fiction to you, but I can assure you it's real and working today."

He looked at a member of his team who, on cue, pulled up the presentation on his computer and activated a TV mounted the wall. A display of slides began, the first read "Virtual Life Solution."

"Our program is called the 'Virtual Life Solution,' or 'VLS,'" the Supervisor began.

Morrison looked straight forward and sighed.

"Damned Acronyms, do we have to condense everything to three letters?"

The Committee chuckled, each one understanding the Vice President's frustration with the Washington DC language defined by three and four-letter catchphrases designed to form a working word or sexy-sounding letters to help people's memory and provide a standard reference to descriptions that could be quite complex if each word was spoken. The Supervisor knew Morrison had a reputation for hating all this secrecy with names like "the Supervisor," but was told by Mc-Allister, that beneath his outer toughness, the Vice President understood the necessity in code name projects and the need to not reveal the identity of the man behind the curtain who took all the risks.

The Supervisor continued, ignoring the comment.

"Next Slide."

The projector showed a brief event history and several line graphs representing dollar amounts since the start of the program.

"VLS was started fifteen years ago as Artificial Intelligence began to mature as a science. Dr. Janice O'Neal, with us this morning and the only member of our team not to operate under a descriptive code name, pioneered the development of the basic systems and constructs for the Department of Defense. Nine years ago, she moved to our team to work on building an artificial reality component to our solution. Since then, she has successfully developed the underlying technology framework for VLS."

"Why no code name for Dr. O'Neil?" the Vice President asked.

"Dr. O'Neil supports multiple AI programs throughout the government, Mr. Vice President. As such, there is no way for the public to link her to VLS and our efforts," the Supervisor explained.

The Supervisor paused to allow each member of the Committee to associate Dr. O'Neil with the program's technology successes and establish the ground rules for her involvement.

"To date, development costs are just under $500 million or $56 million per year," the Supervisor continued.

"Congratulations, Dr. O'Neal," Amanda Sheldon said. "I don't understand it yet, but building something this important for under $500 Million is an accomplishment."

Dr. O'Neal responded with a smile that worked to convince many lawmakers around the beltway that she was a dedicated professional with a brilliant mind, and was savvy with political matters; the Supervisor had come to rely upon her immensely.

"Thank you, Senator. I have a great team assisting me."

Sheldon nodded to O'Neil, grateful for the acknowledgment of her compliment. Congressman Sweet leaned forward and commented, "I would also like to pass along my congratulations to Dr. O'Neil. She and I are both alumni of Carnegie Mellon. I have followed your research and read your papers, Dr. O'Neil, on the applications of Artificial Intelligence to resolve various problems within society and am fascinated by your ideas and their implementation. If this is one of those ideas, then I am looking forward to your portion of the presentation."

Sweet sat back in his chair again and crossed his arms, an unmistakable signal to all present that he would engage only with Dr. O'Neil. The Supervisor allowed exchanges like these with Dr. O'Neil and was encouraged by the comments. *Collaboration between his team and this Committee was critical to being successful, even if it required only one conversation at a time.* Getting back to business, the Supervisor continued.

"I want to point out that there is a one-time construction cost that I will address later in my presentation of approximately $120 million. Overall, our obligations are under $1 billion for all program costs to date, including labor, since the history of the program."

Senator Hurst broke the silence, and with a slight smile.

"Well, Mr. Supervisor, just what did the American people get for your efficient management of our tax dollars?"

"We built this nation a maximum-security prison system that will house 1,500 inmates and requires only 3 guards to secure," the Supervisor answered.

There was silence as each member processed the implications of his statement.

"Oh come on, Mr. Supervisor," Amanda Sheldon said, breaking the silence. "What kind of nonsense is this?"

"I assure you, Senator Sheldon. It's real."

"You built a prison to hold 1,500 of our worst criminals and terrorists. Well, where is it? I've seen nothing about this."

She appeared flustered and shuffled through the read-ahead papers in front of her for supporting information.

The Supervisor paused, then calmly stated, "It's here in DC, located 70 feet under a funeral home located in South East."

It was Congressman Sweet's turn. He uncrossed his arms and slowly leaned forward.

"So let me get this straight. Are you telling us that we have a maximum-security facility that will house the nation's most dangerous criminals in the center of Washington, DC - underneath a funeral home?"

"Yes, Congressman. That's what I am telling you."

Sweet sat back in his seat and murmured, "That's impressive."

The room had gotten quiet. The Vice President smiled.

"Proceed, Mr. Supervisor. You have our attention."

"Next slide," he directed, and the program information displayed.

"VLS is an active program in its final prototype phase that currently houses 100 of our nation's worst criminals and terrorists."

"Wait – stop!" Congresswomen Katz interrupted. "This facility is operational?"

"Yes, Congresswomen, it is," The Supervisor replied and then looked to Hurst.

The room exploded with questions directed at the Supervisor and each other. Senator Hurst stepped in.

"Mr. Vice President, ladies, and gentleman, please," he pleaded. "Please hold your questions. Let us allow the Supervisor and Dr. O'Neal to provide their information before we begin to overwhelm them with questions. We have time, and I assure you: we will get all our questions answered before leaving today."

As the room calmed, Morrison ignored Hurst's request to hold all questions.

"If we have 100 inmates currently incarcerated, where did they come from?" he asked.

Okay! I have the VP engaged, and he wants to ask questions, the Supervisor thought. *This was a good start.* He would have to make sure Morrison was comfortable before leaving and knew the VP had travel plans after the meeting. The Supervisor resigned himself to future interruptions and answered the Vice President's inquiry.

"Many came from our existing high-security prisons and were routine transfers, some came from Areas of Operations in Iraq and Afghanistan, and some came from our facility at Guantanamo Bay. The last ten came from convictions in our court system. Each of our inmates is sentenced to death or Life imprisonment."

Anticipating the next question, the Supervisor turned to Hurst and nodded.

"Senator Hurst, would you add additional information to my explanation?"

All eyes turned to Hurst, who calmly said, "Next slide."

Senator Hurst stood and began to talk directly to the information.

"The state of Texas was chosen to be the first state to test a new program two years ago. I've had program clearance for the last two years to participate in the Texas portion but not at this level. Like you, I am hearing much of this for the first time today and thought VLS was an AI research effort. My part was to work with the State Judicial System and the Governor to ensure that criminals charged with murder would not walk off because of technicalities in our judicial system. We picked the best and the brightest. Judges were selected to hear the cases, and prosecutors and defenders were chosen to prove guilt and close all the loopholes. Judges administered the cases justly, but there was no slip-ups with evidence or slick lawyer defenders. Convicted criminals, the worst of the worse, were tried, convicted, and sent into the Special Operational Unfenced Prison or as we call it in Texas – the SOUP."

Morrison moaned and then asked sarcastically of Hurst, "Another acronym for us, Senator?"

Hurst ignored the moan and continued.

"Publicly, they received the death penalty or life, and that's the way the news reported it. But after the Judge's final sentencing, done in a closed session away from the press, they're shipped to DC."

Hurst looked at the Supervisor, and with a slight pointing hand gesture, turned the presentation back over and sat down.

"Next slide."

The next slide appeared with a single word "PROCESS" as the title.

"With your indulgence, I would like to walk you through how we incarcerated our first 100 inmates and their experiences in VLS," the Supervisor began. "The first 100 inmates each experienced the same procedure to be placed in the SOUP. Incidentally, we call it that in Virginia as well, Senator."

"Only logical," the Vice President commented.

The Supervisor continued.

"We used various techniques to achieve this and tested newly developed procedures to enhance operations. My team is continuously working to improve our methods."

The operator highlighted the first hidden topic on the slide, and it appeared for all to see. It simply read "INITIATION."

The Supervisor continued.

"Each inmate receives an injection of a standard Benzodiazepine sedative to induce unconsciousness. Contained within the sedative is a chemical compound that we have developed that places the brain into an enhanced dream state. The compound taps into the brain's memory center, where it can draw upon the inmate's previous experiences while also inducing a release of various amounts of adrenaline, dopamine, serotonin, oxytocin, and endorphin – all creating a euphoric state with the adrenal energy to sustain it."

"Can you control their dreams?" Katz asked.

"Not successfully, Congresswoman. At this point, we are opening the inmate's mind to a positive state of illusion. What they think about after the injection is unique to each inmate. What we do know is their mind is ready to accept new memories that continue their current dream, or at least the positive emotions and illusions generated by the sedative. We give them one new memory. That memory tells each inmate that what they are experiencing is real. We call this Jumpstarting. This is how we transition the inmate's existing reality and replace it with their new reality in the SOUP."

"How long does this drug last?" Sweet asked.

"Our most current drug will sustain them in this positive state for three hours and gives us time to exert control on the inmate during their transport with minimal risk to the transporting agents."

The Supervisor nodded for the next step in the presentation to be shown. The screen highlighted "PREPARATION." He continued.

"We take our Inmates to special facilities that are within the three-hour travel time after being injected."

"What happens if it takes longer than three hours to reach the facility?" Morrison added.

"In unique cases, agents will withhold the sedative for some time to put them in the time window, but this is not the preferred method. We expect as the sedative is improved, the sedation time will increase, thereby affording more travel time before the body recovers from the effects. Increasing the sedation time will decrease the amount of 'forward preparation' required before transport to DC. This reduces facility and workforce costs."

Senator Hurst asked the next question.

"What happens in 'forward preparation'?"

"Scientists from the team equip each inmate with their Jacket and Box, Senator; which I will show you now. Next slide."

The image revealed a metallic collection of overlapping belts, which reminded the Senator of a wire mesh suit that extended from the head to the feet. At the head appeared to be a ring with a variety of fiber strands standing in mid-air. At various intervals starting at the neck, each belt strand had its sensor array wrapped along the belt as well as a canvas cloth overtop to protect the sensor. Along the length of the suit, there were also larger connector plugs terminated at each end, as well as a variety of plastic tubes with various size connectors. One master wiring assembly protruded from the side wrapped nicely with two other larger plastic tubes.

"This ladies and gentleman is the 'Jacket.' We credit this technological breakthrough to NASA's research on Space Suits, new health care life support as well as magneto/fiber bonding. The Jacket will be fixed to the inmate's body and fit nearly as snug as a glove when complete. The first step is to dress the body in our special protective suit. This will facilitate the Jacket connections to the environment, as well as protect the body."

Automation began on the TV that showed an individual in their suit and how the jacket would fit attached to a human being.

"The Jacket is the mechanism that allows the inmate to experience the five senses. At the crown of the Jacket is the biodata housing, which connects the inmate with VLS reality. We call this portion of the Jacket, 'The Crown.' The other items are power cords and various tubing that support biological functions such as feeding and waste removal."

Sheldon asked the next question.

"How do you care for the inmates? In other words, feeding, cleaning, and maintaining their health?"

"In addition to the sedative, we have also created our own protein solution that prevents muscular atrophy, bone decay, and other problems that occur when the body remains stationary for long periods. This drug, combined with lowering the body temperature slightly and the suit keeps the outer skin intact. We estimate that our inmates can survive 40 or so years without a significant impact on the body. This protein solution passes through a standard mixture of 'liquid food' that is designed to provide all the basic nutritional needs. There are no solids ingested by the body."

The Supervisor could see the look of disbelief on Sheldon's face.

"Senator Sheldon, there is nothing that we have done here for inmate sustainment that is not already being done to some degree today. Our inmates receive better physiological and bio system care than hospital patients kept alive on life support machines, and through the other functions of the Jacket, live a complete life that is indistinguishable from you and me. We estimate that most inmates will live longer in VLS than in our world, which we call Real Space, because they will die of natural causes and not violence or drug addiction. This particular technology was developed by us and operational-ized by NASA as part of their experiments in prolonged space travel."

The Supervisor paused to let the Committee digest the information. He was moving into a very technical realm and clearly wanted to ensure the Committee members under-stood most of the information he was providing. Congress-man Sweet, an engineer by education, was fascinated with the design and continued to look at the chart.

"Can you zoom in on the Crown?" he asked.

The picture was enlarged to show the detail of the con-nections. Sweet continued to study the diagram while asking the next questions.

"How long does it take to prepare the inmate, and how are they connected to the SOUP?"

"Preparation time takes approximately 30 minutes to suit the inmate and configure the Jacket. Another 10 minutes to connect to the Box. Then about a minute to make the final Crown connection, and our inmate is in the SOUP. The major-ity of the next 24 hours are spent running diagnostic routines and fine-tuning the parameters of the Jacket. After about 48 hours, the probability of becoming a fulltime resident of the SOUP is 99.997%. As to the details of the connection Con-gressman, we have a slide dedicated to that detail coming up shortly. If you indulge us until then, we will answer all your questions."

The Congressman nodded his approval. Again, the

Supervisor anticipated the next question and offered additional information.

"Most inmates we have were interned within the last two years. This only occurred after the VLS environment was thoroughly tested and found functional. We've only lost one inmate, and that was not because of the technology."

Each lawmaker provided approving nods, many still marveling at how this technology worked and not wanting to ask about the exception mentioned.

The Vice Present also stared at the diagram on the screen.

"Ok, what's the Box?"

The Supervisor directed his assistant.

"Skip ahead two," and one slide quickly flashed and vanished, and the second slide appeared on the TV.

"Am I seeing this right?" The Vice Present said. "Is that a casket?"

"Yes, Mr. Vice President, it is. But it's been modified," the Supervisor responded, walking over to the TV. "Our team agreed that the standard casket was the most economical and configurable Box on the market. Inside we have added a power pack here."

Placing a finger on the TV, he touched the location on the casket diagram.

"We have bio tube connectors here and here, internal diagnostic processors here, and connections for the jacket to provide sensor input here and here."

"What are those hooks on the inside of the casket?" Hurst asked.

"Those connect the Jacket to the Box and stabilize the sensors when they are in proximity to the inmate. We do not need to have the sensors touch the skin. The jacket provides all readings for each of the organs, nervous system, etc. if they are within five centimeters of the body. Our suit does not obstruct the reading, but we do want to keep the sensors close."

"And that cluster at the top of the Box?" Morrison asked.

"Congressman Sweet, here is the answer to your last question. That, Mr. Vice President, is the connection junction between the VLS and the Jacket crown. There are over 5,000 individual Nanosensors and connections that run from the Crown of the Jacket. These connect to the top of the Box by way of a unique optical signature on each strand. This signature facilitates each of these connections without human intervention. Dr. O'Neil, do you have anything to add?"

Dr. O'Neal nodded.

"Thank you, sir. The Jacket and Box are 'forward deployed' to where the inmate will require preparation. The Jacket Crown, which controls each of the sensors, connects to the Box at the top into what we call the junction."

The Supervisor pointed to the location on the diagram.

"Each Box is equipped with segments of its own VLS code and processor in the junction, which can keep the inmate out of the SOUP for an additional 12 hours. This transport configuration allows the inmate to interact with their new reality while being shipped to the facility."

"How do you ship the inmate?" Congressman Sweet asked.

The Supervisor provided the answer.

"We place the Box on public transportation as a deceased person's remains, and the agents escort the inmate to DC and the funeral home."

"So how are all the inmates kept in the SOUP?"

It was Sheldon this time with the question.

"Let's run the video," the Supervisor said.

The video flickered on the screen and then showed a long cavernous opening underground.

"I commented earlier that there were construction costs. This is how we accomplished our construction in the earlier phases. Our video shows that we took advantage of metro subway upgrades recently and worked to do additional tunnel construction in the direction of our facility. To most observers, we were working at the Metro. We closed the access tunnel when the underground construction was complete to deny any access from outside the facility."

The video now showed the crew working the construction and finishing the facility interior, and then a completed job with corridors and offices. As the footage entered its last 90 seconds, it showed the storage areas for the inmates.

"It may be hard to make out in this portion of the video, but each Box fits into a container with a sealed door. The container connects to the Box and houses the diagnostic and technical connections to monitor the inmate."

The image on the screen changed to provide a closer look at the operation.

"Ah, that's a better look."

The video showed a Box being lifted and slid into a rectangular container by a forklift looking vehicle. The coffin was inserted, and the outside door closed and locked automatically. As it did so, a plug connected the Box with the container and illuminated diagrams of information on the door. Each layout displayed critical Biosystems and monitoring indicators. In the top center of the container, a button turned green.

"The green button indicates that all connections to the Box are correct. This will be the limit of what a non-technical person will need to know that is providing care. Any other color and a VLS member is alerted automatically."

The video shot of the storage facility pulled back to show approximately 1,500 containers in a square room, each with their doors closed, several of which had green indicators. It looked like a massive mausoleum, each Box perfectly aligned horizontally and vertically, reaching to a height of 20 feet off the polished floor.

"Mr. Vice President, Ladies, and Gentlemen, what are your questions at this point?"

The group deferred first to the Vice President, who began the conversation.

"I get the connection between the casket and the funeral home now. It's a very ingenious way to operate without causing suspicion with the local population; but I am not sure that you answered Senator Sheldon's question. Let me ask it another way - tell me again about the staffing levels. I mean, can the inmates escape?"

To this, Sheldon nodded to affirm the question was correct.

"For the first time in the history of this nation, Mr. Vice President, our guards are trained to keep the public out, not to keep the inmates in. In theory, this operation could run with no guards."

The Supervisor paused.

"There is no escape. As we've shown, each Jacket creates a physical containment system within the Box. The Box when closed locks in three places to secure the link between the Jacket Crown and the VLS junction. Lastly, the Box is locked into the container to facilitate the diagnostic connection between the coffin Box and the inmate status monitor."

The Committee members were following the presentation and were engaged. This was a good sign of collaboration and the future of his program, the Supervisor thought.

"Think about it, Mr. Vice President, ladies, and gentleman. This is a high-security prison with no escape. No more prison riots, no more organized crime operating out of prisons, no more huge taxpayer expenses, and land that can be reclaimed by the local authorities for other purposes. The list goes on. In essence, when inmates are in the SOUP, they are done with humanity and DO spend the rest of their life in prison. There is no parole or recidivism with this group of criminals."

There was more nodding from all at the table. Hurst followed with the next question.

"So when the inmate dies of natural causes, what happens?"

"Dr. O'Neal – will you take this one?" the Supervisor requested, and then sat down.

Dr. O'Neal remained seated and explained, "The system

will alert my VLS team that the inmate is within the last two minutes of their life."

"Two minutes – can you do that?" Sweet asked, showing more interest as an engineer fascinated with the program and less as a Congressman.

Dr. O'Neal responded.

"Yes sir, we can."

"Amazing!" Sweet exclaimed, shaking his head slowly as though that would cement the facts for him. Dr. O'Neal continued.

"Once we are alerted that the individual is within the last two minutes of their life, a routine will automatically open the door behind the containment unit. When this starts, the Box will decouple from the container, and the crown will disengage from the junction severing the connection with the SOUP. The inmate enters into what we call 'Conversion Time.'"

"Conversion Time – what do you mean?" Katz asked.

Dr. O'Neal cleared her throat.

"An interesting event occurs that we are still studying, but it appears the inmate's brain holds the last memory image in VLS reality after the Jacket crown disconnects from the junction. For a short moment, the inmate continues to see the VLS reality around them. Then, there is a 'pixilation' of the current VLS image, almost as though they were watching a picture taken with their phone slowly transition from the full image to the tiny dots that make the picture. We call this 30-seconds the 'Conversion Time' or 'CT.'"

All eyes looked to the Vice President.

"Ok – explain CT. If we can anticipate the last two minutes before death – why not let them die before disconnecting?" the Vice President asked.

Dr. O'Neal looked at the Supervisor for direction on the response. Sensing her reluctance, he picked up the conversation.

"CT is the final moments when the inmate realizes, just

before they die, that they are in an artificial system. Their mind's reality shifts back to Real Space and returns them to their last real memory. In these 30 seconds or so, we would hope that they would ask forgiveness for what they have done. Hence, conversion time."

"That's sick," Sheldon said with disgust. "I agree with the Vice President, why not just let them die without CT?"

The Supervisor's tone changed from briefer to VLS Executive. He stood and looked directly into the eyes of the Committee.

"Because Senator Sheldon, the people we house in VLS are sick, perverted, and some of the world's most evil people. We send them to our maximum-security facilities to atone for their debt to society. But one major problem is our criminals do not reform as we would hope. As the Senator knows from her state, recidivism is very high among the criminal population. Established facts show that your state releases 20,000 prisoners back into the community every year, and two out of three of those released are rearrested within three years. Nearly one in three are re-convicted within this time frame, resulting in re-incarceration. They very seldom feel remorse for the innocent lives they have destroyed; and, if granted parole, kill or harm more people. I believe CT is our only remaining hope that inmates will ask forgiveness in their final moments of life for what they have done to others. After all, isn't regret and reform the real purpose behind incarceration?"

The room felt awkward. From the look on his face, the Supervisor regretted getting preachy with the Senator; but the stakes were high for his program as well as the nation's citizens. He pulled his suit jacket front down and slightly brushed away imaginary lint. In doing so, he regained his composure. Sheldon looked down at the table, also embarrassed by her outburst as well as her state's statistics. The Supervisor thought, *Come on Senator, we have to implement this solution together. Work with me here.* Senator Sheldon said nothing. *I will hear from her office later and will need to be prepared to give her an apology. Keep your cool!*

The Supervisor continued in his calm briefing voice, "As Dr. O'Neal was explaining, a fireproof door at the rear of the containment unit opens. Behind each unit, we have built the unit's cremation chamber. When we have confirmation that the inmate is deceased, the Box moves into the chamber, and the door closes, protecting the container unit. Then the body and all contents are burned. The unit is now ready to receive another inmate."

"Very efficient," Sweet remarked and leaned his chair backward again as if to relax for a Sunday football game. "Efficient, indeed."

"Let's take a break, shall we?" the Vice President announced.

CHAPTER 7

T he Supervisor stood in the back of the briefing room and contemplated the mood of the committee. He needed to keep this program viable, not only for the nation and its citizens but for him as well. The Supervisor wondered if the committee had made the connection between him and Carter Hurst. It was a friendship that went back to an earlier time when he was known as Matthew Boyd, a name that no longer provided relevance in his life and was discarded when VLS, his life's real purpose, presented itself. What the committee could not know was that the Senator's family and his were connected by the event that provided the reason for the program that he was fighting so hard to keep alive.

Memories from his past pushed themselves into current events and provided him with a reminder for today's purpose. Twenty-two years ago was the worst night for the two families. They enjoyed dinner together and laughed well into the night on the back patio of the Hurst home. The kids played inside, the perfect ages and interests to bond them together into lifelong friends. It was about 1 a.m. when the evening broke up, and each wished each other a good night, numerous times. Wine flowed, and while the men stuck to sipping their whiskey, their wives killed a bottle or two of the most elegant Pinot Gris. They made plans for the next get-together, and the family piled into the car for the ride home. Hurst's wife Ashley and his wife Elizabeth were still talking and laughing, holding hands through the passenger side window as the car pulled out of the driveway, vowing to drink less wine at the next dinner. Carter stood in the driveway, pushing the vehicle out magically with his hands while imitating the motions made by the evening weather personalities.

On the way home, a presumed drunk driver passed close to their car and swerved in front, causing Matthew to hit the brakes and turn the wheel quickly to avoid a collision. His car hit the curb hard, jarring all the passengers and the force bounced the vehicle back into its lane. The car in front of them continued on its way as though nothing had happened. Matthew stopped the car and did a quick visual inspection. No broken pieces, rims were intact, and nothing was dripping. A quick accounting showed that the family was ok, and the car seemed to have survived. Their trip home continued, and they laughed loudly in the quiet night as they told jokes heard in school and discussed family secrets. When they got home, Matthew raised the garage door, but he did not pull the car in.

"I'm going to make sure the car is ok. I'll be in soon."

"Fine, but I have to pee," she said, whispering so only he could hear. "Hurry, I'll be waiting for you upstairs."

She made a smile that left no room for what she had in mind. Elizabeth began giggling and bolted out of the door into the garage, followed by her two boys that had urgent business of their own. He reached into the glove compartment, found his flashlight, and took it out. He turned it on and started looking at the right front tire that hit the curb. As he bent to one knee to inspect it, he heard it- a single shot from within the house. As he looked up, he listened to a second shot and saw the muzzle flash lite the darkened home then eerily return to darkness. He heard Elizabeth's scream. He remained frozen on one knee, the situation too surreal to register that something was very wrong. As he began to sense the reality of what was occurring, his adrenaline launched him into action. He took off into the garage, grabbing a crowbar off his worktable and sprinted into the house. He heard the third shot and then a fourth. Both muzzle flashes cast brief silhouettes on the stairway wall of a shooter, and then a woman going to the floor. Blinded by rage and the understanding of what was occurring, he charged up the stairs facing the strobe light effect from each additional muzzle flash, unaware of the rounds that penetrated the drywall and blew holes in the railing, sending pieces of wood down to the lower floor. He felt a sting in his left shoulder but was focused only on the shooter.

And then he had him. He swung the crowbar with all his might straight at the man's head, sure that he would kill him. But as his arm came forward, he tripped on Elizabeth's sprawled body; causing his aim to miss its mark and hit the man in his lower arm instead. This sent the pistol flying down the hallway and causing screams and curses to come from the shooter.

As Matthew struggled to regain his balance and prevent himself from falling back down the stairs, he grasped for the handrail and dropped the crowbar. The shooter reached for the crowbar, but Matthew kicked it over the side of the stairs, crashing onto the hardwood floor below. Regaining his balance, he tackled the shooter. In a split second, he was on him; pounding his fist into every part of the man's face that he could hit. He felt a blow to his head and reeled backward. Struggling to keep consciousness as his ears rang, blood dripped into his left eye. Matthew lunged back on the man and was able to get both hands wrapped around his neck, and in a primordial rage, he squeezed. With all his might, he hoped to break whatever he could of the man's trachea. He felt another blow to his head and one up into his chin, yet he continued to squeeze the life out of the individual whose body twisted and contorted under him. He wanted to kill the bastard that brought this new pain into his life. And then it ended. No more resistance from the shooter, no more blows being thrown into his body as he released his hands from around the man's neck. He crawled over to Elizabeth and knew she was dead. Grief replaced rage, and his own body shook uncontrollably.

"Matthew! Are you alright?"

It was his neighbor awoken by the shots.

"Up here," he whispered and then louder, "Up here!"

He heard his neighbor charge up the stairs causing his flashlight beam to dance on the wall with each stride.

"Holy Shit!"

"Phone in our bedroom, Carl. Call the police."

Carl bolted into the bedroom, and he could hear bits and pieces of the conversation as he lay there in the dark, "wife shot, shooter unconscious and husband in need of emergency care."

Carl rushed back to the hallway and knelt to check his wounds. Matthew brushed him off.

"Find my boys."

Seconds turned to minutes and minutes into eternity before the sound of sirens and shouts broke the silence. The lights in the house were turned on, and he was blinded abruptly by the sudden brightness of the hallway lamp. The sounds of heavy shoes and orders from the police and paramedics all merged into one great noise. As he felt arms lift him and cause a shooting pain in his shoulder, the maddening sounds faded while they carried him down the stairs. He was placed onto a gurney and rolled to the ambulance. Two paramedics lifted him into the vehicle, the legs collapsing under the stretcher as he slid towards the back. The paramedics climbed in and introduced themselves and offered assurances for his immediate care. He felt one tear away the fabric of his shirt on the left shoulder while the other started an IV and tried to explain where he was and where they were going. As the ambulance raced towards St. David's Medical Center, he knew his family was gone. He began to weep.

He awoke the next morning, light streaming through the window of his room signaling the beginning of a new day. He did not know where he was, and his only companion was a memory of him killing a man in his house, too surreal to believe, but somehow he knew it was true. He was unsure how long he laid in his bed, staring at the roof of his room and replaying his hate-filled charge up the stairs with his desire to exact revenge on the man shooting at him before he fell into a dreamless sleep. He awoke again and heard a woman talking with Carter.

"He's had a traumatic event. Even when he is fully awake, he may still exhibit symptoms of shock. It may take him days to understand everything that has happened and months, if not longer to process it. He will need you now more than ever."

The woman was right. Later that day, his worse fears were confirmed. His family was gone. Both boys and Elizabeth died at the scene. Carter broke the news but provided little detail. Ashley stayed with Carter, holding his hand as both struggled to find the right words. Afterward, Ashley excused herself as the tears appeared and streaked her face. Carter wiped his away.

The days swirled in a kaleidoscope of events that had no meaning for Matthew as he dealt with his never-ending dream, repeating over and over, the image of the evening burning into his soul and creating doubt as to his purpose to live. The police arrived and questioned him as he lay in his bed, and Carter was with him. The shooter was dead they reported, and the police needed the details of the event. Matthew told them what he could remember. Carter assured the police it was self-defense, and he would defend Matthew if the DA decided to press charges, which did not seem likely. Carter asked the police what had happened, and their theory was a robbery. In their assessment, the robber thinking the family was away broke into the house. Matthew and his family had shown up at the wrong time.

On the third day of his stay, Ashley talked with him about making the arrangements and said she would handle everything for the family, and she did. He was not sure he could attend the funeral. He just wanted to withdraw from life. It was not until the next day during the drive home from the hospital that Carter told him that the shooter was arrested and jailed for armed robbery of a convenience store years ago. He had shot the cashier and put him in a wheelchair for the rest of his life, along with a mother and a child that both survived after surgery. He was paroled six months ago after serving ten years for his crime. Matthew could feel himself rise from the dark hole that had consumed his last several days as the fire found in a new purpose of his life emerged. He looked at Carter.

"We are going to fix this so that this does not happen to others," Matthew said calmly.

"You're damn right, we are. Whatever it takes."

CHAPTER 8

C arter Hurst was one of the most influential people in the Supervisor's life. Not only was he there during the darkest period in his life, but because of him, he was standing in front of this committee today, presenting a program that was not possible without him. Carter just didn't know it. Shortly after the death of the Supervisor's family, Carter won his first election and headed to Washington, DC. Matthew remembered when Hurst asked him to join him there and work in a relatively new field called Artificial Intelligence. Carter had told him that he was a good engineer, but a great manager and leader that knew how to get things done. Carter had told him over a glass of bourbon that he had never met anyone that possessed a vision for the new technology and ability to manage large programs like he possessed. Matthew was grateful for the offer and moved to Northern Virginia. The funding from Congress started with an Army organization called the Army Research Lab; and it was not long before Matthew had his first breakthrough in AI technology. Matthew's ideas for AI's future occupied many of their conversations and it was not long after that he saw the opportunity to build VLS.

Initially, Matthew worked diligently to share the technology and breakthroughs with other government agencies leading to the creation a unique classified research facility. Over the years and successful elections that followed, Carter championed funding the AI research in Congress and was able to get the Justice and Defense departments to contribute dollars to the organization. It was not long after Homeland Security joined the organization and they became known as "the Coalition" around the beltway. Soon, new requirements and specifications were pouring in from the Departments to develop new AI technology. One such requirement the government wanted built, was the capability to identify the numerous names of terrorist individuals and connect them with biometric physical features allowing their identification to be admissible in court, much like DNA testing. Matthew did the impossible and built a working prototype almost overnight. The technology was there, now it would be up to the courts to allow the evidence. The success of the prototype strengthened his reputation as a doer around the beltway.

As Matthew invested more time into VLS, he began to adopt his title of the Supervisor and less of his real name. His cover identity provided the invisibility he needed to build VLS and distance Matthew Boyd from the program. He used the title of Supervisor to conceal his use of dollars for VLS and was successful, since he was given the funding to build these new systems without program oversight. His namesake, Matthew Boyd reported research findings to executives in all three departments and kept them from asking questions about how their money was used.

When he achieved technology breakthroughs, Matthew provided them to everyone in the coalition, which made each Department believe they were getting a return on their investment. Unknown to each was that much of the money was used to develop VLS without any direct involvement from their Departments. Breakthroughs were frequent, which kept the executives happy. The remaining funds were applied to VLS by the Supervisor's team. The Supervisor found this to be fortunate because had any Department of the government created a program to build VLS as he had done, it would have gotten mired in bureaucratic process and politics and taken twice the number of years and money. Without oversight, the Supervisor was able to develop his program "below the radar" while Congress and the White House remained oblivious. For him, this was the only way VLS could be created; and today, he was presenting the government with its newest asset to solve a significant problem: a gift of his life's work to help prevent the death of innocents.

It was time for the Supervisor to reveal his accomplishment. Building a prototype and demonstrating it worked was one thing. Now he needed to bring this capability into formal oversight to protect its continued funding and give it political top cover. The program would need this if it were going to expand and be maintained. Even his friend Hurst did not know that the prototype existed. Hurst only knew that he helped facilitate the funding from each of the three departments for AI research. He suspected a new capability when the Supervisor asked him to work the program in Texas to assist with sending inmates to DC instead of the state prisons. But like most politicians, Carter did not want to know about the details; which, if discovered, would need to be covered up or face being involved in something that could cost him an election.

Dr. Sandra O'Neil was the real genius behind the technology and was the public face for the AI coalition. When she took over the AI research from Matthew, his namesake disappeared into the ranks of early retirement, taking his name with him. From that point forward, Matthew Boyd no longer existed and the "Supervisor" would create VLS. Later, when Dr. O'Neil joined the VLS team, she was the only one on the team without a protected identity by intent. Her involvement in Artificial Intelligence development in no way connected her with VLS. This enabled her to contribute her incredible intellect to several classified programs under development, something she could not have done by adopting a cover and working only one program. Her impressive credentials, knowledge, and ability to sell her newest ideas, were instrumental in keeping the funding needed for each of these programs, which included indirectly supporting VLS. Until today, a couple of members on the committee knew her but not her involvement with the VLS program. Only Carter Hurst knew she was working with the Supervisor, and Carter was unsure what that even meant.

The committee members re-entered the chamber and took their seats. The Vice President called the committee back to order. The expressions on each lawmaker's face showed that the committee was not in total agreement with the provided information, but each was maintaining an open mind. *The second hour should go smoother*, the Supervisor thought. He took the initiative and began the conversation.

"The three challenges we face today with our existing prison system are first and foremost that society wants protection from criminals and their activity. Secondly, Americans, while wanting protection, no longer favor the death penalty and want criminals punished; but also want them to still have a life. Thirdly, informed citizens do not want to pay the rising costs associated with incarceration. VLS is that answer for all three challenges. It's the first time in history that we have an incarceration solution that protects society, maintains a continuous life for its inmates, and is much cheaper for the taxpayer.

Today, our prison and rehabilitation system is designed to force criminals to live without the rights possessed by the rest of society. Denying rights is done to create a life experience that over time, generates remorse by the very hindrance of those freedoms. This remorse is supposed to lead to acknowledging their wrong and create a desire to return to society where their freedoms are restored, or becoming a better person in prison for the rest of their life. So the theory goes."

The Supervisor paused to make sure the body language of the committee was positive and then continued.

"The only problem with this theory is that it no longer works. Our prisons create a culture of brotherhoods and sisterhoods, where inmates are bound together by their common conditions. Our prison systems, while not a picnic, still provide many freedoms not found in others around the world. Additionally, our society penalizes the individual after they have served their time by attaching the stigma of convict on their record. This stigma prevents reintegration into society without prejudice which leads them back to choosing the only life where they are accepted; prison. Mr. Vice President, ladies, and gentlemen: this, I believe, contributes to the high levels of recidivism, and while prison serves as a deterrent to crime for the average citizen, it has become a way of life for the worst of our society. I believe we have to admit that we are not as successful as we would like with the results of reforming our inmates. When we are successful, it is a mistake they carry the rest of their lives. Given our rise in population, changing national demographics, and failure to assimilate our inmates back into society, we believe that our existing prison system is not sustainable."

The committee erupted in opinions and sidebar discussions that were again silenced by Carter Hurst, raising his voice to surmount the committee's noise.

"Let him speak, please, ladies and gentlemen."

The room slowly returned to normal.

"We are the world's leader in prison inmates," the Supervisor continued. "We know that as our population grows, so will the number of people in prison. Eventually, conditions will force honest citizens to the conclusion that committing a crime will not result in jail time because we will no longer have the funding and facilities necessary to house them. Then what are our nation's options?"

The question was intended to be rhetorical, but Senator Hurst provided an answer.

"Our judicial system fails."

The Supervisor nodded in agreement and to let Carter know he was grateful for his support in making his point.

"I discussed our operations earlier. Placing the inmate into VLS represents the first and third components of our prison system: protect society from criminals and affordability. You've heard about the processes and technologies we use, inmate biological sustainment, death, post-death procedures, and the projected funding to build a complete system, but we have yet to describe the SOUP in detail. Dr. O'Neal will explain this portion. It involves the creation of the artificial environment, which comprises the humane portion of the prison system: how our inmates will live their lives."

"Thank you, sir," she said and looked to the presentation assistant and gave the go-ahead by nodding her head once. The TV screen snapped back on, and the presentation showed a screen saver of various, multicolored flowers.

"Advances in medical science and technology give us the solution today to place people into comas and remove them from society. While this will protect society, it is not humane by anyone's standards. Most voters will not support this approach. If we place criminals into a coma, this condition robs them of their right to continue to live a normal life and the hope of reform. We might as well bring back the death penalty; but unfortunately, that idea won't win elections either."

Dr. O'Neil cut straight to the heart of the matter that each politician understood; votes.

"For the first time in history, technology gives us both. Our program creates a life every bit as real for the inmates as our world around us. VLS manages the physical body, and the SOUP component provides the virtual reality that makes VLS more than a coma. When in the SOUP, inmates cannot tell the difference between their everyday life in Real Space and the reality provided by VLS. The VLS uses existing archetypes to create the mental images and symbols that are familiar to us all in Real Space. We do not put goggles on them and show them a different reality like a video game, rather we have mapped the response centers in the brain, which receives information and provides it directly to the location that will process the emotion or image."

Dr. O'Neil paused to ensure the Committee members were following her explanation, received a nod from the Vice President, and then continued.

"The SOUP environment is created by a combination of software induced images provided by our program; which, when added to their existing subconscious, create experiences of their life in our reality. We do not remove any of their memories. Rather, we start their new experiences beginning with their last real memory. As a reminder, we call this Jump-starting. Each experience builds upon the next, much like Algebra II builds upon previous knowledge of Algebra I in high school."

This example solicited smiles from the Committee.

"As the Supervisor explained, the only experience we provide them is a reaffirmation that the SOUP is real. This false experience or dream convinces them the SOUP is a continuation of their world. The last event they remember is likely their last crime, or their time in the courtroom, anything significant that they can recall. While in the SOUP, this memory is the starting point, and we believe it will be the memory that forms at CT. What is important from this point forward is *our inmates can create any life they choose*. Reform no longer is tied to removing individual freedoms behind fences and serving time. Being in the SOUP means they live life as they choose. There may or may not be remorse or redemption, but these objectives are now irrelevant."

"Why would you say they are irrelevant?" Katz asked.

"Because we no longer need to reform them. If they choose to murder, it is done 70 feet below a funeral home in DC, not to a real person. This means protecting society and paying for the program becomes the only components of a successful prison system. Because the paradigm for incarceration changes, VLS provides the way for a justice system to administer justice from the bench, keep this nation's laws, all while providing ample resources for those found guilty to be incarcerated, at a fraction of the price we pay today."

"Are you saying that the reality they live in is like the movie, *The Matrix*?" Hurst asked, referring to the popular science-fiction film.

"In terms of the world around them, our inmates are not aware that they are in the SOUP, which would be similar to the movie. I can't say whether VLS functions like the matrix or not, Senator. That was a movie. I can say that the SOUP reality creates every detail for them by drawing from their memories and the lifetime of images stored in their minds. If I understood the science fiction in the movie, humans were born having no life experiences of their own, and their environment existed around them. The movie environment, by the way, was created by machines to use human bodies as batteries for their energy needs. The SOUP is real. It was created by us, not machines, and serves a real purpose. The SOUP uses their individual life experiences, to create their reality."

Dr. O'Neil's explanation of the Matrix brought smiles from not only the committee members but the program support staff too, who were impressed with her knowledge of the movie.

"How do they build upon their memories to create their life?" Sheldon asked.

"Our brains are amazing Senator, and in many ways function like a computer. We have all heard the analogies about computers and humans having many similarities. It should be this way since we created them. Both accept input from their surrounding environment, both we and computers process this information and provide output in the way of verbal or written conversation for us, visual representations of information for the computer. The SOUP is programmed to facilitate continuous input for the brain to process, and when the output is released, this becomes part of the inmate's record. They build upon this record from other memories to continue their reality."

"Can you explain the inmate record for us, Dr. O'Neil?" Morrison asked.

"Yes, Mr. Vice President. Let's start with a basic definition of how we view virtual reality. We all have memories. As we explained, the inmates keep theirs as well. Each memory consists of an experience in our life and an emotion tied to that experience. For example, smelling apple pie can trigger memories of your grandmother baking. If the pie tasted good, you remember the positive emotion associated with eating it. A song can do the same thing for us as it transports us back to when we heard it. The feeling can be good or bad, depending upon the experience. So it is in the SOUP. New memories created by each inmate are placed in what we call the community record. Once in the community, other inmates can access other inmate memories, apply their own memories to the experience, and create a new record, and so on *without* our input.

Think of it as someone you hear on TV. It could be the news, a commercial, almost anything. Millions are listening to that same message as it is broadcast. As humans, we take the information and process its meaning through our minds. We create a memory tagged with an emotion to recall the experience. Now, if what you heard was sound advice about your health, for example, you would build upon the information and then personalize it in a way that is relevant to you. You could potentially alter your life or change your career because of what you heard. If it was significant, you might tell others that would do the same thing.

We all share as humans. We subconsciously filter what we hear, process the information, and then respond in some way. Our inmates do the same. We build a bridge between our reality and theirs when we Jumpstart them; afterward, it's all created by them. There is a difference in the realities. Some of us in Real Space may wish to hold on to what we heard and make it personal, never telling anyone. In the SOUP, everything that is processed becomes a community record for others to use. There are no secrets in the SOUP."

"So the community record is a database of life events,"

Sweet commented.

"Yes sir, but not a database as you might think of it; like plane travel schedules tied to records in normalized tables. The information is stored as energy waves and accessed differently. What is relevant to our discussion today is that we can read each community record. We know what experience each inmate has created, and if we wanted to, we could tie each record together and watch their life like a TV reality show. To them, their life has never stopped from the last recalled memory of this reality to their present reality in VLS. In essence, they are living their lives the way they want to, creating them from other inmates around them."

"Have you sampled the community, Dr. O'Neil? If so, what did you find?" Sheldon asked.

"We did sample the community record, Senator. Our inmates are murderers and terrorists, and so they continue to build their lives around what they remember how to do best. Death and destruction. To them, their new attacks are very real, life-fulfilling if you will. But fortunately for us, their hate and destruction are confined to the SOUP and the community records."

"You can watch their memories from their mental images? This is unprecedented. Do you have any examples to validate the statement you are making?" Sweet asked.

"I do Congressman, but I would ask the Committee to decide if they would wish to view the video. The content is disturbing."

The Vice President looked around.

"Any objections?"

There were none. Dr. O'Neal continued.

"The technology to transfer the image to a visual picture for us is not completely refined for our resolution. It will appear grainy and is in black and white – but you will get the idea. This video is inmate 35 or I35 as we refer to him. I35 is a high school English Literature teacher turned serial killer. We have edited the sequence to three minutes of the event. The victim we identified is an actual person, Mrs. Connie Parker, who today is alive and well, completely unaware of what our inmate intended for her. Run the video, please."

As the images of Parker and I35 appeared on the screen, the Supervisor could see the looks of horror on each of the faces of the Committee members as they witnessed the numerous rapes and Mrs. Parker's vivid murder and mutilation. The video ended, and all sat in their seats, stunned at what they saw. The TV screen returned to black – thankfully for several of the members.

"And this is real to the inmate?" Sweet asked.

"It is, sir. We have nearly 70 videos of this type that were created by our inmates to date, many borrowing from the community experiences of the others to create their unique events. From the VLS team perspective, we would rather have these events recorded in our system than acted out in our society."

There was unanimous agreement.

"Have you done any analysis of these events?" Katz asked

"We have, which is another reason our team is committed to the VLS program. While there is inherent bias in the system by putting a group of murderers together, we are working initiatives to introduce new input that can change their reality to something more aligned with a normal life, much like our prison systems today. Our goal is for each inmate to transition to a more peaceful reality.

However, there is one other benefit I would like to discuss. Because these are terrorists and criminals, we are analyzing the records they're creating and having real success with building profiles of behavior. These profiles are now assisting with creating threat scenarios for crimes that have yet to happen. We analyze their behavior and see what they would do by what is acted out in their minds. From their new community records and videos like you just witnessed, we develop countermeasures that we pass along to Defense,

Homeland, and Justice. The intelligence value is exceptional as these criminals are giving us insight into the deepest part of their thinking that no amount of interrogation would be able to reach."

"This just all seems too fantastic to be real," Katz said.

"I assure you, Congresswoman: it is all quite real."

Sensing the moment and seeing the small amount of remaining time available, the Supervisor stood up and looked at the committee. "Members of this Committee. I want to make the following points about VLS for you to consider as you decide about taking oversight of this program:

1. The most dangerous members of our society are now TRULY removed from harming society any further. Protecting Americans should be our number one priority.

2. The technology now exists to create and use VLS to solve the significant political and fiscal issues of capital crimes in our judicial system. While we cannot predict the mass shootings at Las Vegas, numerous churches, and synagogues, Sandy Hook, the El Paso Walmart, the bombings of US embassies, or even attacks on our homeland, we can make sure that the evil that did these things never does them again. We can also learn from them. With our intelligence analysis, we are feeling confident that we can prevent some future incidents from occurring. VLS allows that opportunity.

3.   VLS maintains the rights of these inmates by creating a reality that is indistinguishable to them from the reality in which we are living. A reality where they can live their life as they choose, regardless of their destructive nature. The conditions and quality of life for the inmates are far better than that of our current prisons, and the argument made that their life span is longer doing the things that they choose to do. It is more humane.

Ladies and Gentlemen, I know this is testing the limits of reality as you see it – and that's just the point here. It is about reality."

He paused and watched his audience. All eyes were on him.

"Justice depends upon the welfare of the inmate as well as society as defined by Americans today. It is our way as humans. VLS is the way to serve the needs of society and the inmate by separating our realities made possible by the technology."

The Supervisor paused, looking at the floor as though organizing his next words and then continued.

"What we see, experience, and feel creates our reality. In our circumstances, reality is created by reflected light that is captured by our eyes and sends the information to our brain for processing. Our mind applies this information to what we see and creates a picture. We compare this picture with images in our memory. When they match or come close to matching, we define and label what we see. This interpretation then creates this room and everything in it as a picture in our mind. Our understanding of these things known to us in our mind's view validates this chamber, and we accept it as real."

At this, he leaned over the table and rapped it with his fist sending dull raps and their echoes into the chamber.

"The table we are sitting around, this is our reality. We hear, we feel, we see, we touch, and we taste. The artificial reality created in the VLS is no different in its basic implementation. They too can experience the five senses just as we do, and to them, it is just as real as us standing here today except with one major difference. Society-is-protected-from-what-they-create-and-do."

The Supervisor began to walk deliberately behind his team while talking and now positioned himself behind Dr. O'Neal.

"But Mr. Vice President, ladies and gentlemen, unlike

VLS, which is defined and regulated via stimulating portions of the brain, our reality can sometimes be perceived in different ways. Nature occasionally plays games with us. Our perceptions allow us to experience life from many different views of the same event, which does not always serve our best interest. Within the SOUP, they have a controlled and defined community to create their experiences created by our technology. In our reality, what we see and how our mind interprets the events can be incorrect, despite what our eyes tell us. I want to thank Dr. O'Neal, for her presentation and her ability to distill complex science into basic understanding."

The Supervisor pulled back the chair. Dr. O'Neal stood and walked to the end of the table.

"Thank you, sir," she said, but the voice came from behind the group.

The lawmakers were surprised and turned in their chairs to look behind them and saw Dr. O'Neal walking in from the back chamber door. And when they turned their gaze quickly back to the end of the table - that Dr. O'Neal was gone.

CHAPTER 9

T he Supervisor entered the Russel Senate Office building two days after the VLS presentation to the committee. He was confident his program would be funded and supported by the highest levels of the government, despite only five of the government's top leaders knowing the full details. He received a call last night from Carter Hurst, who said, "Come by and see me tomorrow at 10 am. We need to talk." So here he was, walking down the long halls flanked by state flags and offices, each with the senator's nameplates attached to their doors. He had many conversations with Hurst over the last three years, but this was the first time he was visiting his office.

It was 9:45 a.m. when the Supervisor arrived. He opened the door to Hurst's outer office. Behind the desk was a young man in his mid-twenties who greeted him.

"May I help you, Sir?"

"Please tell Senator Hurst that his 10 o'clock is here."

The Supervisor could not help but survey all of the pictures of prominent Texas politicians and business people hanging on the wall, each one smiling and shaking hands with the senator. Sprinkled around the office walls and on end tables, each holding a federalist style lamp, were various state awards or memorabilia from speaking engagements that formed a tapestry of the senator's service to his home state and nation for over 20 years. Between the two windows that looked out onto a view of trees from the upper Senate Park hung a picture of the State Capitol in Austin. To its right, a framed, smaller version of the Lone Star flag signed by what looked to be the signature of Bush 43.

The young man looked at the daily schedule on his computer, saw the time was blocked out in red, and said, "The Senator asked that you wait in his office through that door there."

Pointing to his back right, he added "Can I get you some coffee, tea, or water, sir?"

"Coffee. Black, please."

"The Senator is finishing up another meeting and will be with you shortly. And I will bring that right in."

The Supervisor walked around the desk and into the Senator's office. The office was furnished as he expected for someone from Texas. There was a large desk in front of a wall turned into a bookshelf. Behind the desk was a tall back leather executive chair that could swivel and rock to and fro. Two big, dark leather Queen Anne chairs faced the desk for personal conversations. In the center of the office was a rectangular cherry table with six more conference chairs spaced around it. There were more pictures on the walls of Hurst, but this time with presidents, vice presidents, and other foreign dignitaries.

Additionally, there were basketball and debate team pictures at the University of Texas and fishing trips with members of Congress. On the back wall was a large black bass mounted with a lure attached to his mouth and on the sidewall, a 12-point deer rack with a bronze plate that was engraved with "Ft. Pickett, VA – 2017." Surrounding his desk, he recognized various pictures of Hurst with his wife Ashley, and their two sons on vacations and other personal moments when he was fortunate enough to break free of the Washington, DC rat race. There was a knock at the door, and it opened as the young man walked to the Supervisor with his coffee in a Lone Star State mug.

"Your black coffee, Sir."

"Thank you," he said, accepting the mug with steam rising off the top of the hot liquid within.

"The Senator will be right with you."

The Supervisor acknowledged the young man with a nod as he disappeared into the main office. He could hear Hurst's voice as he joked with his staff walking through the outer office right at 10:00 and then said, "Hey Mike – please get me a cup of coffee and bring it into my office."

"Sure thing, Senator."

In the next moment, Hurst was in his office.

"Have a seat at the table. We've got lots to talk about."

The Supervisor walked over to the table but did not sit as Hurst came over. The two looked at each other, shook hands firmly, and then briefly embraced, patting each other on the shoulders. The brotherly hug ended when Mike walked in with the Senator's coffee. The Supervisor took his seat, and the Senator joined him as the aide placed the coffee at Hurst's left elbow and put a US Senate coaster underneath to protect the wood from the mug's heat. He procured a second one and handed it to the Supervisor with a causal "sir," meaning take this and use it.

"Close the door on the way out, will you, Mike? No calls or interruptions unless it's POTUS or the Speaker."

"Yes, sir," and he closed the door with an audible click of the latch as it caught. Hurst started the conversation.

"We've come a long way since our days at the university together. Did you ever think we would end up here?"

"I always knew you would, Carter. I just wanted to get through differential equations."

The Supervisor smiled, recalling some of the best times of his life with the man across the table. They became good friends the first time they met in Austin on campus. They were attending one of the numerous parties during rush week. Both men quickly realized they shared a realistic view of serving this nation and that their futures would lie in pursuit of finding a way to contribute to history. Over the next four years, they forged a bond and common purpose, each finding their niche, which would become their life's pursuit. While Carter chose to practice law and then politics, his life began in the government as a civil servant, working as an electrical engineer starting at GS-9 pay and through grit, and at times, pure genius became one of the most successful managers of government programs – so he was told. He was not ashamed to admit that he had a stack of performance reviews which touted his ability to see the future potential of the United States and the world filled with the AI technology that he built.

"That was quite a show on Monday. I have to say the hologram of Dr. O'Neal was pretty impressive and removed any doubts from the committee members about supporting the program. Almost 30 minutes of conversation directly with her and nobody on the committee knew she was a hologram until she walked in the door at the back."

Both men laughed at the memory of seeing the Vice President's face when he realized that the Dr. O'Neal doing the presentation was not real.

"I hated to resort to parlor tricks, but I believed it was the only way that the committee could see a demonstration of just how real AI technology has become. She was a hologram to us, but 'inside,' our system creates her to look just as real as you and me. I know each member is concerned about the human experience for each inmate. It's the difference between living in a coma and living a life with free will. Even I believe the coma is unacceptable for what we are doing."

"Speaking of living, I picked up on your comment that one of the inmates died. You passed by the information very quickly and I did not want to ask in the meeting. What happened?"

The Supervisor hesitated.

"Do you really want to know?"

Hurst nodded his head.

"We had a transport problem. One of the Boxes dropped from about five feet. It broke open, and when I went to inspect the damage, the Crown was damaged and had disconnected from the junction. The damage to the junction was pretty bad as well, and I could tell the 'contents were already starting to spoil.' They were either going to be a vegetable or die shortly. Rather than see them suffer, I moved things along."

The Supervisor stopped. Hurst noticed the event had an impact on his friend.

"I don't need to hear anymore," Hurst said.

Both men were aware of the surroundings and lack of protections involving their discussion and guarded their conversation accordingly. The Supervisor moved off the topic and focused on the business at hand.

"So, let's talk about where we go next."

Hurst was relieved to end that topic and move on as well.

"POTUS trusts the Vice President and despite having only Top Secret knowledge of the existence of the program has given the Executive go-ahead. I have to say, you impressed the hell out of the VP. I briefed the Speaker at the Top Secret level as well yesterday. Katz and Sweet were with me. The Speaker was hesitant at first, but when he saw your funding request, the associated cost savings, and that the White House was on board, he was all in."

The Supervisor smiled again, knowing that the funding was the icing. At the core, every politician has looked to put away forever the evilest people impacting the country's citizens and turn it into political gold. Now, technology had produced a humane solution, and the nation's leaders possessed the will to act and cash in on their investment.

"So, let's start with the basics – what's the reporting chain?" The Supervisor asked.

"The five-person oversight Committee you briefed is now your Board of Directors. I chair the Committee. The Vice President, in his role as President of the Senate, will be the focal point for all things involving the executive branch. We collectively felt that Congress needed to lead this program to ensure its funding and minimize operational exposure to the Executive. Any problems with me being your boss?"

The Supervisor shook his head.

"I was hoping it would work out this way. What about Defense and Homeland? They funded a lot of the effort?"

"The VP will handle this with the Department Secretaries personally. This program, as of today, officially belongs to Justice. You will still co-operate and share your technology with Defense and Homeland, but all requests from the Departments will pass through the Committee first. Their funding support as of today ends. This will free them up to perform their own research using the AI you have developed to date."

This also means we don't owe them any more break-throughs, the Supervisor thought. *Very smart, given the Defense Department would have other applications for the technology. In today's political environment, the Department of Justice can't be perceived as being involved in those efforts. Smart move.* The Supervisor concurred by nodding his head.

"What about the Attorney General?" The Supervisor asked before taking a sip of coffee and burning his lip and recoiling slightly.

"Up to Morrison, he will read on members of the cabinet as he needs to, but never above the operational level. Same as POTUS and the Speaker. We will keep the technology and methods to ourselves."

Again, the Supervisor nodded in agreement. Hurst continued.

"A little over two years ago, when you approached me about using Texas to prototype portions of the program, you also suggested the postings of the key members of the House and Senate judiciary committees. Your recommendations are the reasons for implementing the next steps. Selecting representatives of high crime cities was pure genius. You've built quite a committee to provide your top cover."

Hurst looked at the Supervisor with admiration. They had played chess many times over the years and Hurst always lost in each game, none of which were ever close. The man possessed a gift for seeing the big picture, then pulling everything together and pointing the effort in the right direction.

"The Committee has approved your requested funding for new facilities to begin in Chicago, New York City, and Atlanta. This should make Morrison, Sweet, and Sheldon very popular. Each will be bringing about a billion in new contracts to their states this year alone. These three facilities will handle the maximum-security inmate transfers from around the country. We will start closing our existing facilities once these three have reached their operational state, and transfers are complete. Dallas will come online after these three and handle the overflow from DC and international terrorism. DC remains the flagship facility, but as you requested, all research and development facilities are moving above ground to Arlington. This made Katz happy. She is all in. When completed, the government should save roughly 50B per year on incarceration and the judicial process. Not bad for about ten years of work. It's good to see an investment made by us actually paying off."

"Jobs, jobs, jobs," The Supervisor said with a smile.

It was no secret that substantial federal funding and projects brought to a state guaranteed a long career in public service for the politician that brought them. People with work voted for the person that created the work. Carter mastered this over his 20-year career with Congress rising to the position of President Pro Tem of the Senate after serving in the house in the early years. More importantly, he was the power wielded by the one with the dollars. This was the hidden secret behind the "jobs" mantra. Congress got things done by making deals with dollars and votes, and the two in many ways were connected. If you held the dollars, you applied leverage, which meant a place at the table to negotiate your policy position.

Everyone wanted to know who was paying the cost of supporting new ideas. If you had a policy and no money, you provided your vote in support of an effort owned by a colleague with additional funds. This was called a compromise to the public. Those with the money and no policy ideas discovered everyone wanted to be your friend, and you could get them to vote on issues you picked in exchange for funding. This was great for getting votes for your colleagues for their policy and bills, and now they owed you as well. If you worked the system long enough, you acquired clout behind your name, and you neither traded votes or money; things just came your way. But with power, there was always a catch. Nothing was free in Washington, DC. It was how the system worked, and the Supervisor understood this better than some of the politicians.

"What about the Los Angeles facility. Did the Committee approve that one as well?"

"Yes, but we think that it will come after Dallas."

"Ok – I can see the rationale for staggering the Dallas and Los Angeles facilities."

"When will the transfer of the new dollars occur?" the Supervisor asked.

"Give us a couple of days since we ended the Defense funding. We'll use reserve or black accounts this year and push the rest through regular appropriations as Infrastructure Investments over the next two years. By then, it will be routine and automatically in each of the future bills. We need to do this as openly as possible with the public without compromising the program. The funding for your program was never in question, even before the hearing. What you were producing in AI alone justified the dollars. But now... This is your program, and you are to develop a solution for a specific national need. You don't have to serve many masters who control your funding anymore. We are going to move ahead with VLS as a single program under the committee's direction."

The Supervisor looked at his friend with gratitude and greatly respected the integrity he used in doing business. Hurst saw the look, stood up, and walked behind his desk. He leaned down and opened the bottom door of the bookshelf and produced a bottle of Texas made Ranger Creek Whiskey, looked at it, and put it back, substituting a bottle of Gentleman Jack in its place.

"Time to celebrate," Hurst declared.

He walked back over to the table and sat down. Both men took another drink of their cooling coffee to make room for the brown liquid that would take its place. Hurst poured them both a shot in their coffee mugs, and they used their fingers to stir the whiskey and coffee together. The Supervisor raised his cup and said, "To changing history," as the two clinked their mugs.

"To changing history," Hurst responded, and each took their first drink.

"Not bad," Hurst said. "For mixing coffee and whiskey at 10:30 in the morning. Just don't tell anyone that I chose Tennessee over Texas."

The Supervisor coughed slightly and nodded his head in agreement.

"You know," Hurst hesitated and then continued, "Elizabeth and the boys would be proud of what you've accomplished."

"Thanks, Carter."

He raised his mug to Carter as though offering cheers to the air.

"For everything."

"Well," Hurst said, dragging out the word. "Don't thank me yet. There's one more thing."

Here it comes, the Supervisor thought. *Nothing is ever easy.*

"Okay, what's the one more thing?"

"What you have done is truly amazing. You and your team have built a system by pulling together AI breakthroughs and integrating them on the fly into the VLS. You've made your program operational by funding your efforts from different projects across the government without anyone knowing about it, including me! You've secured some of the leading experts in the field and developed cutting edge technology to make our solution happen without the bill payers understanding they were paying for the system. You have also gotten DC to cooperate, though they may not have known they were doing so."

Hurst took another drink as he prepared himself to deliver the real reason for their meeting.

"Come on, Carter, don't soften me up – you know better."

"As I said, you impressed the hell out of the Vice President. When he briefed POTUS on the cost savings and what you have achieved, well…"

"Oh, you can't be saying what I think you are," the Supervisor said, disbelief in his voice.

"Next year is a big election year. The President wants a second term, and we have key guys running for Seats. We need some domestic wins that can hold up. Look, this is huge! This nation now has a working solution to our maximum-security prison system, and it works! It's not promises and wishful thinking. I don't need to tell you that Americans are pissed. They don't feel secure anymore and haven't since 9-11. Our press is ramping up mass hysteria with every event that brings domestic and criminal violence into the mainstream. I know because my phone didn't stop ringing when the shootings happened at a Walmart in MY STATE."

The Supervisor looked into his coffee and began to shake his head. He could not believe what he was hearing and what his friend was asking of him.

"Then the shopping district in Ohio and now the newspapers are building up conspiracy stories about Epstein and blaming his suicide on a lack of guards and lax conditions in prison. All this has put pressure on people. This administration is never going to compromise on guns, which most of America thinks is the problem, and frankly, neither will Texas. Look, we need this. We need to tell the American people that we have a solid answer to crime."

"So why not stick with the dollar savings as the win and say the achievements were the results of using new AI technology to find and apprehend criminals? Tell them we have better cameras and identification systems in law enforcement. Why do we have to talk about the program?"

"I wish it was that easy. People want the government to save dollars, but what they want more is security so they can pursue *their* American Dream. Why do you think most voters bitch about the overall government spending but support our defense budget or law enforcement costs? Your solution saves billions and provides a huge amount of security to its citizens. You know better than anyone else why bad guys need to STAY in prison. However, staying in prison means money for physical buildings, oversight, and continuous management. This country no longer supports the death penalty, but they want justice, so the only option we could offer until now was life in prison. You have given us a new solution."

He knew Carter was right but was still not happy with the decision.

"So, you want to blow the cover off one of the most classified programs we have ever developed and tell everyone?"

The Supervisor, ever calm, was now starting to heat up. Carter lowered his voice.

"Of course not, but this is all part of the deal. The Committee made promises to close the agreement with both parties and the White House. You know how this all works."

Yes, he knew how it worked. It was one of the main reasons why nobody knew he was building this capability until now. Oversight for dollars and the program's protection in Congress is one thing, but now politicians using the program to score political points? *What have you gotten us into, Carter? This is never good!* He calmed down and resigned himself to the inevitable. His program was a new capability for the country and knew this day would come, but he had not expected its arrival so quickly.

"How deep do we go?" the Supervisor asked, bringing the level of his anger down a couple of notches.

"You have full discretion on content. Locations are out – no one wants a riot at a funeral home or someone busting in to rescue their old cellmate. No disclosure of technology, other than that, it's up to you."

"Where does it print – internet blogs, professional publications? Who writes it?"

"Mainstream newspapers like the *New York Globe* and the *Washington Guardian*. The internet and major channels will pick up the story, and it will be everywhere. *Fox, MSNBC,* and *CNN* will analyze it in-depth, and after a week, no one will talk about it again until it's brought up as part of the campaign."

"Who is the writer?"

"POTUS named the guy personally. Alexander Richardson."

"Alexander, wait, do you mean Alec Richardson?"

The Supervisor felt the anger start to return.

"Yes, do you know him?"

"No, but I know OF him. Pulitzer Prize winner, does occasional pieces for *60 minutes*, leans *very* left politically. What the hell is POTUS thinking?"

Cuss words in the Supervisor's vocabulary were almost non-existent. The word shocked Carter and gave him insight into the depth of anger that was brewing. It was clear he needed to diffuse his friend, but these were the facts of the situation. The Supervisor would have to accept them as a condition of moving forward.

Carter said nothing and let the silence of the question speak for itself and allowed his friend to regain his composure. The Supervisor's mind was already in overdrive, figuring out courses of action and the pros and cons of each, filling out the checklists he was visualizing. Carter Hurst, his best friend, stood up. He knew the meeting was over.

"One more thing," Carter said as the two men faced each other. "The Speaker asked an interesting question when we were briefing him. He wants to know how families and friends visit the inmates. I told him you worked out a solution, and someone would get back to him."

The Supervisor looked at his friend in the eyes.

"I'll get back to you."

Hurst smiled.

"Okay."

Both men walked to the door of the office, and Hurst opened it while proclaiming for his staff, "Well, that was a fine meeting. It's always good to see you, and I will consider everything we discussed."

The Supervisor, understanding the cue, replied, "Thank you, Senator. It is always a pleasure to see you, as well."

The two shook hands for all to see.

"I will talk to you soon about our next meeting. I will set it up for the Monocle, and we can grab some lunch."

"Sounds great," Carter replied, flashing his election-winning smile. "What's next on the schedule Mike?"

The Supervisor smiled at everyone in the office as he exited. The walk down the corridor was longer than he remembered at 9:40 that morning. What a difference an hour makes. He made his way to the exit, deep in thought. As he walked past the security station at the main door, he nodded to the guards and reflected. *We both have our role to play in keeping people safe. I just wish I had yours today.*

He exited into the bright sun on Constitution Avenue and strolled over to a bench in the Upper Senate Park, pulled out his phone and dialed the number from memory. A male's voice, on the other side, answered, "101".

"U-T – assemble the team. I will be there in about 30 minutes."

"How did it go?"

"We are cleared and hot, but we have some things to work out."

"That's great news, boss."

"See you in 30."

The Supervisor ended the call. This was DC. "Great news" was never "great news." He placed a second call. It was connected but not answered.

"I'm in the park near the main entrance where you let me out," he said, then ended the call.

Two minutes later, he recognized his black SUV pulling up and walked to the curb. The car stopped in an area used by taxis, and he got into the back seat.

"Let's go to the office."

The car pulled away and entered the morning traffic pattern on Constitution. Carter Hurst was his best and probably only friend, but he just laid a couple of big problems at his feet in exchange for keeping the program going. *Maybe the old saying is correct*, he mused. *If you want a friend in DC, get a dog.*

CHAPTER 10

Alec Richardson awoke to sun streaming through his window, filling each space in the room with an angelic white hue. The place was quiet and still. No sounds filled the streets outside his large townhouse in Old Town, Alexandria. There was no one slamming car doors, no people speaking loudly on their way out to start their day, nothing to disturb the quiet tranquility he was feeling. It was going to be a gorgeous day.

Lying next to him, still asleep in her crumple of blankets was the latest surprise to enter his life. He met Adelle Hall at a CBS event two years ago and knew immediately she was different. She was aloof at first, but Alec began a conversation that lasted three minutes, almost an eternity in the busy surroundings of network gatherings where continuous interruptions were normal. She called him "charming" as she was whisked away by the arm and directed to her newest introduction. Adelle had flashed a smile that told him to find her later when the crowds thinned out. He did find her, and unlike any women he'd invited into his life, they spent the evening together talking about more than work. The Newseum closed around 9:00 for their event, and they were asked politely to leave. She suggested a drink, and the two walked across the street to the Capitol Grill, their conversation swirling from their professional lives, then diving deeply into their personal thoughts on politics and hobbies. He looked at her approvingly when she ordered a glass of single malt Macallam 18 neat, and she looked at him disapprovingly when he ordered the same on ice, and then both laughed. The pair clinked their glasses together in a toast to "new friendships" and enjoyed their Scotch as the night melted away before them like the ice in Alec's drink. The evening ended in two Uber rides in different directions, but both realized their next meeting was a foregone conclusion. The chemistry between them was real.

Their careers and travel kept them apart by day, but nothing prevented the nightly Facetiming and closeness that built as they discussed both personal and professional topics late into the evening. Both lived in New York, but Alec was considering moving to his place in Alexandria, Virginia, full time. He won his Pulitzer at age 36 for his series on Afghanistan and the corruption within its government. His Pulitzer opened many doors, and Alec chose to freelance for *60 Minutes* while writing for the *Washington Guardian*. He decided, if you were going to write about government corruption, Washington, DC, was where you needed to be.

Adelle continued to travel. As a marketing executive for her network, she spent considerable time building up miles on her credit card. As a product of Ivy League Princeton with a Warton MBA, she was indomitable in the board room, and the network wanted her everywhere closing deals. Unless you knew her background, you would never suspect the power behind her smile. After many late-night FaceTimes, both agreed that if they wanted to have a chance, they needed to be together. Adelle pulled some strings with the network and was assigned to DC. She rented a small place in Georgetown from a professor friend that had received a year sabbatical from American University. It was not long before both owned duplicate wardrobes and the essentials in two locations.

Two years later, Alec looked at her peaceful stillness as she lay next to him barely breathing. His decision to wake her required no thought as he used his hand to pull back the cover from around her shoulders slowly. Her skin was smooth to the touch with only freckles from sun filled summers in her childhood to add color. Her shoulders were bare from the previous night's lovemaking that continued into the morning hours, the result of which was unidentifiable mounds of clothing strew around the room, creating small piles wherever it landed. He leaned down to place a tender kiss at the base of her neck and slowly worked his kissing to the top of her shoulder, each kiss an expression of the feelings deep within him. His delicate alarm clock awakened Adelle.

She rolled over to look at him and said softly, "Good morning."

As Alec looked upon her long brown hair, deep dark eyes, and perfect smile, he felt overwhelming joy within his heart and a kaleidoscope of powerful emotions, all created with a simple greeting. There was no doubt anymore. For the first time in his life, Alec was in love, and it scared the hell out him. He leaned down, and both their lips barely touched, but the connection sent clear messages removing doubt of any feelings they had for each other. As Alec began to kiss her long and passionately, she stopped him, concerned about how the night of sleep might have caused the need for a toothbrush.

"Alec, I have morning breath. I can't kiss you." Alec knew the comment was Adelle's way to tell him that he needed the toothbrush, but also knew he was not going to let this ruin the mood.

Undeterred but still considerate, he placed his hands under the covers and pushed them away, moving his mouth to her right breast where he continued his delicate but passionate advance. She responded with a low moan, and placing both her hands on his head gave him a clear signal to go lower, to which he willingly obliged. Minutes later, her body lifted and shook as the orgasm moved through her body, curling her toes. Her heavy sighs broke the silence of the morning. As she laid there breathing heavily and coming down slowly from her body's response to his affections, she felt his hand gently apply pressure to her left hip. Following the subtle lead of a partner on the dance floor, she rolled over on to her stomach, anticipating her lover's next move.

She willingly opened her legs, sending the covers and a small pillow into a slow slide off the bed into yet another heap on the floor. She felt his hot breath on the nape of her neck, and his kissing began once again along the width of her shoulders. His strong arms pushed into the bed, creating divots in the mattress on both sides of her head. She could feel him rise over her, adding to her excitement. Closing her eyes, she bit into her pillow and felt the gentleness with which he entered her. She had waited all her life for a man like this. Passionate and loving, he respected her sexual boundaries but had no problem taking charge. Their lovemaking intensified as Alec reached his climax. He yelled out loudly as emotion overtook him and was swept into the very soul of Adelle, where the two were joined briefly by more than just their bodies. It was his turn to fall to the bed gasping for breath as he withdrew himself from the women he loved. She looked into his eyes that sparkled back at her and knew that he loved her, as she did him. She broke the lover's trance abruptly.

"Let's get some coffee."

Both laughed hard as they rolled off the bed and dug through the piles on the floor, looking for a shirt and pants. Moments later, Alec had the Keurig producing its first cup for Adelle. She emerged from the guest bathroom in his white collared shirt from their dinner event last night.

"I'll make your cup," she said.

Alec took the hint and headed for an appointment with his toothbrush, admiring her in his shirt with the upper two buttons left undone to provide him a view of her ultimate femininity. It worked for as he passed her, he felt himself stir again. He joined her at the breakfast table, where both cups were steaming.

The breakfast nook was perfect for these types of mornings. The curved-out window provided a picturesque look into his courtyard below. Alec called it his own Royal Gardens.

It was a perfect balance of the natural color of green plants and perfectly positioned perennials. The ground places not reserved for plants and flowers were covered with brick creating a formal hard surfaced patio large enough to host about 70 people. Enclosed by more red brick, the back yard had a wall about 6 feet high, finished with black iron fencing on the top. While it was not the Governor's Mansion in Williamsburg, it was his castle. In between, he and his neighbor's almost mirror garden was a small gate that connected the two properties at the very back. Trees planted years ago by previous owners provided shade throughout the day, completing the finishing touches on the perfect blend of nature and red brick. This garden is what closed the deal for him when he bought the house, and at this moment, the morning sun illuminated the garden in just the right way to make the colors explode.

Adelle picked up her mug and wrapped both her hands around it, savoring the heat provided by the hot coffee. She inhaled the steam rising from the coffee deeply, letting the aroma fill her senses and add its pleasure to the morning's previous activities. They sat in silence as they drank their coffee, each keeping to their thoughts but exchanging smiles and looks that bound the two in their intimate moment. As they enjoyed the presence of the other and the view of the garden, both found their peaceful center in the Zen of their Sunday morning hazelnut coffee. The sky expectantly began to darken, and it appeared a late morning storm was inbound. Thunder sounded in the distance to confirm their suspicions.

"No walk this morning," Alec said, faking disappointment.

"Guess we'll have to take a rain check," she responded.

The silence was interrupted by the ringing of a cell phone from the bedroom. "Yours or mine?" she asked.

"I'm not sure, isn't that your ring?"

"Not getting it if it is," Adelle replied, finishing her mug and placing it on the table.

Alec stood up and headed upstairs to the bedroom at a

slight jog. As the fourth and final ring sounded, she heard him say, "Richardson."

She had left instructions with her assistant that she was not to be interrupted unless World War III started this weekend. She was relieved to know that the world was safe and that the Democracy of the nation was intact.

"Yes, yes," she heard him say from the bedroom.

"Sounds like last night," she said out loud and giggled. "Now it's just more serious and not as loud."

She was quite impressed by her quick wit and enjoyed the humor as she remembered the previous night and the flurry of clothes flying.

"Ok, got it, thanks."

The call ended. She put her game face back on. Alec walked out of the bedroom, down the stairs and back into the nook, a puzzled look on his face.

"You are not going to believe this. That was a Mr. U-T from the Justice Department. He said he had an interesting, life changing story for me."

"U-T, that's an odd name. Did he give you any more information?"

"Not really, his number was blocked. He asked if we could meet at a restaurant named McCormick and Schmick's at the National Harbor tomorrow around 2:00."

He retrieved his mug from the table, placed it under the Keurig, and loaded a new cartridge from the cabinet. He pressed the start button, and his cup began filling with the sound of a steady pour as the machine did its job.

"Are you going to meet him?"

"He sounded credible. My intuition tells me I should. Leads like this are how big things start."

He looked out the window, and raindrops were beginning to fall. All indicators showed it was building into a long rainy day.

"Want to put on some rain gear and head out for some breakfast?"

Adelle stood up and walked over to Alec. She reached down, gently took his hand and placed it on her breast, introducing him again to what she had in mind, and then started to lead him to the bedroom upstairs.

"It's a rainy, lazy Sunday morning, Alec. Let's not waste it."

He agreed and did not care that his coffee would get cold.

CHAPTER 11

T he sun started its trip to the west as Alec Richardson boarded the water taxi in front of the Torpedo Art Factory in Old Town, Alexandria. Dozens of tourists loaded on to the converted fishing boat for a summer ride to the National Harbor and other destinations on the Potomac River. Children were running around on the deck with parents in pursuit, enjoying the perfect summer day. One brushed by him, chasing his sister and smeared his dripping ice cream cone on his khaki pants. The trailing parent apologized profusely for the mishap and provided Alec with their bottled water, and a couple of napkins intended to clean up their kids when the ice cream was gone. Alec wet the napkin and rubbed. Thankfully the ice cream washed out. He walked over and sat on one of the empty benches on the bow of the boat and waited for the sun to complete the job of drying the spot.

The ice cream accident was so random, Alec thought. He realized from the incident that he had little control in avoiding the running child and acknowledged he felt the same way going to this meeting. Before the phone call he felt that his life was stable and had started to enjoy its predictability. His relationship with Adelle was near perfect. Had she changed his life that much? Now, uncertainty loomed and his life could change, significantly because of that call, and he felt once again that he had little control over the outcome. *I guess Afghanistan had a bigger impact on me than I thought.* Or was he nervous because for the first time in his life, he had found someone to share it with? *Get ahold of yourself Alec, you live for this kind of story. It's what you do! Take a couple of deep breaths and enjoy the ride* he told himself.

August in DC was typically associated with "dog days," where the temperature reached into the mid-90s with close to 100% humidity. Generally, if you walked outside, the feeling was oppressive like standing in a hot bath; but yesterday's storm front moved through and dropped the temperature to a pleasant 80 degrees, a perfect number for being on the water.

The horn blew twice, signaling that the boat was getting underway, and kids squealed in anticipation of their new adventure. The boat backed out of the dock into the channel of the Potomac River, turned south and headed for the National Harbor already visible on the horizon. The Woodrow Wilson Bridge, a vital component of the 495 beltway, loomed in the distance, and Alec could see the traffic zipping between Maryland and Virginia. In another three hours, that traffic would come to a halt as the DC area entered 'Rush Hour,' which represented the four hours or so where everyone crammed onto the highways and headed to work in the morning and home in the evening. Every driver and passenger collectively hoped the sun position was just right and prayed that no one hit a deer, no police were parked checking radar for speeding cars, or God forbid a fender bender or worse. Commuters could find a 30-minute ride turn into two hours. Rush hour was the reason he opted for the river ride to his meeting.

As the water taxi churned through the river, its engines rhythmic sound began to mimic "I think I can, I think I can." The boat passed under the bridge and turned slightly to its left, the National Harbor now in clear sight. Sitting as the crown jewel on the hill overlooking the river was the Gaylord National Resort & Convention Center, one of the original buildings of the Harbor and now home to conferences and political events year-round. One of the newer features added after the harbor's construction was the massive Ferris wheel.

The cars were enclosed, and climate-controlled, providing comfort to the riders as well as a beautiful look of the Potomac River, Alexandria, and the harbor activity in any weather. One day he would take Adelle for a ride, to say he had done it, and then the two of them would head to one of the numerous restaurants or nightspots.

He was already glad he elected the water taxi as the traffic coming into the harbor was beginning to back up to the off-ramp. Much of the new traffic pattern was due to the recently built MGM Casino, a full-on gambling and entertainment facility which attracted thousands daily to try their luck or watch a big-name entertainer in the casino's large venue. Normally he would divert to enjoy some time with the slots or at the Black Jack table, but not today.

The water taxi initiated its final approach and reversed its engines. The boat eased into the slip, rocking slightly back and forth on the small waves it created on its turn and bumping the bow into the rubber dock protectors. The crew scrambled into action to tie the boat to the moorings and position the gangplank to offload the anxious passengers already lining up at the boat's exit.

Alec checked his watch. It was 1:45 and could see the McCormick and Schmick's just off the pier. He waited until almost everyone disembarked before leaving the boat and entering the hustle and activity of the National Harbor. He'd done some checking with friends in law enforcement and contacts in the Intelligence Agencies, and there was no reference to a Mr. U-T in Justice. It was not all that uncommon for people to use false names in this business, and even his friends would never tell him about anything new in the agencies if the information was classified. He felt uncomfortable going into the meeting with no information and remembered the ice cream cone – unpredictable but survivable. This thought put him at ease. Alec arrived at the Restaurant on time and met by the hostess behind her stand by the entrance. While no line was at the door, the place was busy despite the 2:00 time for lunch.

"Table for one?" she asked.

"My name is Alec Richardson. I am meeting someone here at two."

She checked the many sticky notes on her stand.

"Ah yes, your guest is waiting in the back. Please follow me."

She guided him around the bar and through a door that led into a dining area with numerous seats and booths positioned to look out large windows with a view of the water. The guests were not as numerous in this section; that was good. She continued walking to the back of the restaurant to what looked like an area set up for private parties. There was a lone guest, a man of about 40 with graying hair and glasses that sat in one of the booths drinking a beer and checking his cell phone.

"Here you are, Mr. Richardson," the hostess said.

Alec nodded and smiled a thank you. At the sound of his name, the man put away the cell phone and stood up.

"Hello Mr. Richardson, it is a pleasure to meet you."

His handshake was firm but welcoming.

"Mr. U-T?" Alec asked.

The man nodded, and both sat down on opposite sides of the booth. A waiter appeared in a white shirt with his ten or so black pens lined up in perfect order above the second button, looking like an organized quill of arrows.

"Can I get you a drink, sir?"

Alex looked at Mr. UT and asked, "What are you drinking?"

"Blue Moon with an orange."

Alec turned to the waiter and said, "I'll have the same."

As the waiter disappeared, he mentally checked off his first verification. The voice on the phone matched the one of the man across from him. So far, so good.

"So Mr. U-T," he began and then stopped. "Is that really your name?"

"For purposes of our discussion today, 'yes;' and hopefully we can discuss that in more detail at a later time. For conversation though, it is pronounced as its letters U-T as you have done, much like you would a nickname or an abbreviation for the University of Texas."

"Ok, thanks for clarifying."

Alec filed away the information for future reference.

"So you mentioned on the phone that you had a story I would want to hear. How would you like to proceed?" Alec asked, getting straight to the purpose of the meeting.

"Tell me, Mr. Richardson, what's it like to win a Pulitzer Prize?"

Alec was asked that question on every talk show after winning the prize, and each time he gave the same answer with minor modifications. He decided on the standard one.

"It's a great honor to be recognized and have your work acknowledged by the best in the business. Winning the prize though is really about-"

Richardson was interrupted as the waiter returned with his beer and a tray of oysters, the smell of cooked bacon immediately recognizable and creating a small growl in his stomach where his skipped lunch should have been.

"Here is your beer," the waiter said, placing it on the table in front of Richardson with a coaster.

He turned and picked up two other items off his serving tray that were on a folding stand nearby, "and for the table, Oysters Kilpatrick and fried calamari."

The waiter placed a pewter colored plate with oysters on the table along with a bowl of fried calamari.

"Can I get you any fresh baked bread while you decide about lunch?"

UT looked at the waiter.

"I don't think we will be ordering lunch today, and we're fine with the beers. I'll look for you if we need anything else or when it's time for the bill. Sound good?"

The waiter looked at UT a moment and smiled.

"Yes, sir" he replied, reading the signals to leave them alone.

He folded up his stand and exited.

"You were saying Mr. Richardson, winning the prize is really about?"

But Richardson didn't finish. Alec also picked up the routine, small talk until the beer came, get rid of the waiter, and then on to business. If he were right, UT would take the lead in the conversation. He did not have to wait long to confirm his thoughts.

"Help yourself, Mr. Richardson, I thought you might be hungry when you arrived," he said, pointing to the appetizers and then continued. "I represent the Department of Justice and am working a program that we think your readers at The *Washington Guardian* would be interested in knowing about. It involves a new incarceration system for maximum security criminals."

Alec had already taken care of one oyster and was spooning Calamari on a small plate while listening to UT.

"Can you elaborate a little more?" he asked.

In his years of experience with this type of source, Alec had one general rule. In the initial meeting, ask questions to get the source to tell as much of their story as possible. He would analyze the content later.

"Mr. Richardson, I can tell you that this program is classified and that I am not a whistle-blower. I can confirm that I have authorization from my department to release portions of the program to the public."

He had Alec's attention, and he leaned forward slightly with interest.

"What type of information do you have that you wish to release? Do you have a briefing or plans for building this new system?"

Alec expected UT was going to turn over something classified that would become public knowledge when the story broke. UT surmised by his question that Richardson thought this would be another of Washington DC's infamous leaks finding its way to the evening news and causing a ruckus in the media.

"No, Mr. Richardson, I don't have any information to provide to you."

"I'm afraid Mr. UT that I don't understand the purpose of this meeting. Is there something you want from me before you release the information? Payment perhaps? A special favor?"

Negotiating the information release was the part of this process that Alec hated. Someone on the inside of the government agency leaking the information was designated the messenger. The messenger was directed by their boss to leak sensitive information to the press. There were a variety of motives for leaking information. It could be an honest citizen wanting to do the right thing; or an unnamed senior official wanting to politically embarrass an opponent to make good on a threat made when meetings turned into power struggles; or his favorite, to apply leverage to get the upper hand in negotiations by disclosing the information publically. For Alec, he would only write a story once he knew the motive. If the leak revealed the truth, then the story was written. If it was a power struggle between two titans in Congress, he passed. Regardless, this routine to leak the information, at whatever location in the world, never came without something in return. The messenger was taking the risk and never delivered information for free. Unbeknownst to their boss, the messenger always wanted a favor or money before turning over the delivery.

"I'm afraid that you have misunderstood me, an easy mistake to make around the beltway for sure," UT said with a chuckle. "I came here today to deliver an invitation?"

"An invitation? For what? Or better yet, to where?"

"Mr. Richardson, you've been personally selected to visit a new incarceration facility."

The warning bells in Alec's head rang. This was starting to sound unreliable. He knew nothing about a new facility, not even a rumor of one existed as far as he knew.

"I'm afraid I'm having a hard time buying this? Why not just slip me information as an anonymous source that I could use to write the piece?"

"Because Mr. Richardson, leaking anonymous information is not the way we would like to proceed. Think of it this way; you've been selected to be the person to report a significant new technology advancement to the public."

"Selected?"

Alec leaned aggressively into the table towards UT, encroaching on his personal space.

"Who selected me? Some deputy undersecretary that's looking to get political points for showing me a new method to lower recidivism and change inmate behavior. Is this about giving everyone in maximum security HBO *and* Cinemax? Is that the new system we are talking about here? New cable channels?"

He paused and slowed his delivery.

"Well, I'm not that guy. Select someone else."

UT remained silent and used his fork to spear a couple of calamari bites and put them in his mouth, using the appetizers as a way to remove the emotion from the conversation before proceeding. *Pretty good flavor*, UT thought and took a drink of his beer to wash them down. He set his glass back on the table gingerly, adding more seconds to the response to let Alec know he was controlling the pace of the conversation. Alec, sensing he might have overreacted, leaned backward. UT observed the change in body position and knew he could continue.

"I assure you, Mr. Richardson that is not the case. You were selected because there are people that think you can tell this story correctly. Much will need to remain classified that pertains to technology, methods, and procedures, but the overall story is going to be unclassified."

Alec thought for a moment about the story's potential impact if written his way. *This must be something big*, he thought.

"Say I agree, what comes next?"

"First of all, so there is no misunderstanding: no classified information is to be written or released. Do we agree?"

Alec understood what UT was saying. They wanted this story in the open and where possible, transparency of facts. More importantly, they wanted this story linked to this administration. That meant if he compromised information, they would prosecute. He would need to play this very carefully. Alec nodded his head to UT's question.

"Yes, I agree."

"Very good, then we could start as early as tomorrow. We would ask that you allow us to put you under while we travel to the facility. The location is classified."

"What do you mean, put me under? Are you talking about knocking me out with some drug for a couple of hours?"

"No sir, I'm talking about four hours – two there and two back."

"That's a lot to ask for something that could just be a high rock wall with a guard tower."

"Oh, I assure you, Mr. Richardson, this facility is quite real, and different."

UT locked eyes with him, and Alec could feel the energy of the discussion just below UT's calm demeanor. The last time he sensed this type of excitement, Alec was in Afghanistan, where his driver and friend set up a meeting with informants to provide information about the Afghani government. Alec allowed the blindfolds to be placed on them by their informants while driving to the meeting as a sign of trust. A day later, coming home from a stop at the market, his friend was abducted. Alec received the note delivered by one of the street kids stating his informants had taken his friend and the location in the desert where Alec could find him. They also indicated they provided information to the Afghani government that Alec was writing his story about their corruption. It ended with a clear message to stop investigating the government.

Alec immediately left for the desert location. What he found was gruesome. His friend's wife couldn't recognize what they brought back and buried, and Alec had no way to locate where the meeting occurred to try and find justice for his friend. It was only logical he ask UT, "Why should I trust you?"

"You have asked a good question, Mr. Richardson. Let me be candid here. You were selected because you showed some balls and impressed some people with your Afghanistan reporting. Your series of stories hurt this administration politically since we supported the government you proved corrupt."

"You're not asking me to apologize, are you?" Alec asked.

"Quite the contrary - in a rare instance of government collaboration, everyone involved in supporting the Afghani regime moved on from their mistake because your articles provided solid facts unknown to our people but later confirmed. These facts became the basis for teaching valuable lessons to our side, from State to CIA. You earned some respect with your reporting despite causing a lot of embarrassment."

UT stopped to spear a couple more calamari pieces and looked at Richardson. Alec took the hint and did the same. Both washed them down with another drink of their beer.

"Somehow, based on the stories I've heard, I don't think you are worried about being in danger, are you, Mr. Richardson?"

UT was right. Reporting was a dangerous business, and you decided to play or not. Alec was more concerned about how he was being used. There was no question that he was; that part was obvious. However, how high did this go, and why was it important for Justice to take credit for this story publicly? Did this tie into the election? A new incarceration system? Just what had his government developed? Was his article supposed to be political? Was he going to be part of keeping the current guy in the White House next year as well as the others in his party in Congress? Most importantly, despite all those political questions, could this help the American people and the country if they knew?

UT watched Richardson closely. He had some idea of what was going through his mind. He and the team war-gamed out many of the questions that they suspected he would ask when the Supervisor returned from his meeting with Senator Hurst. They could take no chance of being caught off guard. The Supervisor would not allow that to happen. It was time to close the offer.

"Mr. Richardson, are you in or out? You have an opportunity here to be the writer who tells the world about something new. I can assure you this story is not a different angle on the old topics of war, disease, and corruption. You can tell a story about something that will better this nation and potentially humankind. So I ask, where does your desire to be an impartial member of the press end and your desire to try and influence politics with what you write begin? Are you a reporter looking for the truth or another media guy looking to score points for your team?"

UT took a drink of his beer. He picked up one of the remaining two oysters, dropped it in his mouth, chewed a couple of times, and then washed it down with the final drink of his Blue Moon.

"Did we pick the right man, Mr. Richardson?"

"What guarantees do I have that I will have the exclusive on this story?"

UT slid his glasses down his nose and reached into his padfolio next to him and pulled out a sheet of paper, handing it to Alec. Alec was surprised. The paper was top quality and embossed with the Vice Presidential Seal. Handwritten on the paper was the following note:

Dear Mr. Richardson,

Please accept this note as my affirmation of your sole selection to perform the task asked of you by the Department of Justice. You will have exclusive access to the information

*required by you. You have my greatest respect and fondest ap-
preciation for your consideration to serve our nation and its
people.*

-Harold "Trip" Morrison.

UT pushed his glasses back up onto the top of his nose.

"Take it with you. Have it checked out to validate the handwriting. I assure you, it is who it says it is."

He recognized the Vice President's handwriting immediately. Alec knew the note was an excellent forgery or authentic. If this all was a hoax, Alec wanted time to talk with Adelle and try to put the proper precautions in place. She needed as a minimum to know what he agreed to and the details about when he would leave. He rolled the dice as he did in Afghanistan.

"Let's go the day after tomorrow."

"Outstanding Mr. Richardson. We will pick you up at 6:00 am on the corner of Prince and Strand near the park in Alexandria. Dress comfortably and eat breakfast."

"I know where it is," he said.

*They picked the location knowing where he lived and that he
could walk to the spot. This group did their homework.*

"If I change my mind?"

"We called you once; we will call again to confirm that morning if you are not there."

"If I don't go?"

"Then Mr. Richardson, you lose the story of the century. That last oyster is for you."

CHAPTER 12

Officer Jefferson Grant sat at his computer in the precinct office and stared blankly out the window. Grant had researched this mystery funeral home for four hours and had nothing to show for his efforts. There were no records that anyone other than the original family still owned the business. He looked into all the public records to include DC tax payments, and there was nothing that raised his suspicions. He thought he must be missing something: some obscure link, maybe to the murder involving the man Maggie told him about. He researched that for another hour. Nothing, just a dead-end. And it looked like things were starting to come off the rail in other parts of the investigation as well.

Three days ago, he left a quarter under the mall sign at the Kiosk. He had not received the verification text. He visited the Washington monument for two days straight around the time set to meet with Maggie. She never showed. He checked the funding used to make payments to his sources, and the money was still in the account from their last meeting. He was starting to worry. It was not uncommon for sources on the street to go missing for days, if not weeks at a time. They had their lives on the street that were real. Drugs, petty crime, and various other illegal schemes were all a part of a source's life. Without access to that activity, they would never have valuable information to men like Grant.

But Maggie was different. She was the neighborhood

grandmother who comforted the drug users. She knew where the children were that needed medical attention or food, locked away by their abusive parents. She was friends with hookers and the homeless. She used her ears and compassion. These activities included Maggie in some of the worst aspects of street life in DC, but never did she participate in the hard stuff, as best as Grant knew.

And now, she was not answering the messages that he was sending her. In their last meeting, she told him that her one source that witnessed the unloading activity at the funeral home disappeared. It was unusual, she said, for her source not to be around. She thought he was scared not of what he had seen, but what the people who saw him might do. She mentioned that the home used security cameras. Maggie said that she was seen and approached by the men working there as well. Did they take her because they could ID her with the cameras?

He acknowledged that he, too, was there. Did his image show up on the camera footage? Was the heavy rain the only thing that prevented them from getting a good look at him? Was it only a matter of time before they came for him?

Grant was still wrestling with his decision to report the shooting at the funeral home. But if he did, what would he say? He did not have a body. Grant had no proof that the man in the casket was alive when he was shot, let alone that he even witnessed the shooting. There was no one there but him, and even Grant could not convince himself that a crime had occurred. They would think he needed a long vacation if he came forward with evidence as flimsy as this. *No,* he thought, *he was going to have to solve this one on his own and bring in proof before he mentioned this to anyone at the station.*

His cell phone rang, making him jump slightly in his chair. He checked the caller ID. His wife was calling. He put on his best Barry White, low voice.

"Hello baby," he answered.

"Hey babe, it's seven. When are you coming home? I've

got Michaela here and was hoping we could sit down together. Wouldn't that be nice? You mentioned today was an office day."

He looked up quickly at the clock and realized the time.

"Sorry, I got involved in doing some paperwork, and the time got away from me. I'll be home in about 30 minutes."

"Ok, baby – looking forward to seeing you. Bye."

And the phone call ended. Grant was not a sentimental guy, but one place where his buddies could get him to tear up was his family. There was no doubt that his wife LaShanda was the love of his life. They met officially at their church when they were both 19. He admired her every Sunday. She possessed a beautiful voice and sang in the choir. He had never thought he had a chance with her. On a high spirit day when the church rocked, she could challenge the vocals of Patty La-Belle or Whitney Houston as the choir got to praising Jesus through song. As a young man, he couldn't wait for something to stir the pastor; and knew that as the organ keys started to dance and play the background for the pastor's message, his angel was going to take them all into heaven before the service was through.

He decided the only way he could make his move was to get her to see him. Once she met him, he knew her heart would be his. To do this, he needed to join the choir. Encouraged by his personal assessment to sing Earth, Wind, and Fire and Ohio Express, he showed up for practice and informed the choir director of his intent. Grant remembered the choir director looked at him with uncertainty.

"Let's hear your pipes, brother," he'd said, and started playing the old spiritual hymn Wade in the Water on the organ. "Jump in anytime."

This was an obvious joke to the choir members, who started laughing at his comment about jumping in the water. Distracted and thinking they were laughing at him, Grant missed the key and started too low.

"Wade in the water, Wade in the water, Children. Wade

in the water God's gonna trouble the water."

The Choir director continued to play despite Grant sounding like a dying frog. Just as Grant was about to stick to pop music, he heard the voice from heaven. He looked into the choir, and LaShanda locked eyes with him, smiling and now walking to him from her seat, and picking up the next verse and making a duet out of the audition.

"Who's that young girl dressed in red, wade in the water? Must be the children that Moses led. God's gonna trouble the water."

Grant found his key, and his notes blended with his angel's. When they finished, the choir applauded, and Grant realized she was holding his hand. The choir director turned to him and said, "I think you're in the bass group."

Grant responded, "I have a falsetto too."

The Director smiled.

"Not at this church, brother. Our pipes don't play that loud."

That was one of the best nights of his life. LaShanda later confided in him that she, too, started watching him from the choir loft and also planned to meet him.

"Your courage, not your voice won me that night," she once said. "So be a cop and not a singing star."

Prophetic words from the love of his life. As he now walked down the stairs and out the door to his car singing "Roller Coaster, of love – SAY WHAT!" He was instantly reminded by the "SAY WHAT?" While researching today, he popped in on his daughter's Facebook page and saw she was in a new relationship. A quick check of the guy showed he had a Facebook page as well, and Grant did not like what he saw. There were numerous pictures of young people with gang references and the whole hip hop gangster stuff in others. Fortunately, his 22 year-old daughter Michaela was not in any of the pictures, yet. He knew that Facebook was there for your parents, and the real stuff was happening on something he heard about called Snap Chat. Why do kids respect the wrong things today? He made a mental note to talk with LaShanda about it. The two of them working together could fix anything that life threw at them.

CHAPTER 13

At 6:00 am, Alec Richardson entered the black SUV at the intersection of Prince and Strand Ave. Adelle was parked in Alec's white BMW 5 series further west on Prince St. She could see everything from her vantage point on the hill overlooking the intersection. Once Alec was inside, the SUV pulled away from the curb and drove past her.

Uh-oh," she thought as she ducked down onto the seat when the SUV drove past. She was expecting them to turn on Strand and head north. She put the car into gear and did a quick U-turn at the next four-way stop that existed at almost every intersection in Old Town. Once turned, she saw the vehicle driving ahead of her. She accelerated slowly. Adelle did not want to look like she was chasing them and stopped a block away at another four-way. Up ahead, she could see the SUV turn right on Washington St. which was one of the two North-South roads that took motorists through Old Town. Washington Street was lined with some of the premier restaurants and shopping in Alexandria. It seemed to her that each street corner contributed to history through its building architectures or because an event occurred nearby marked by a historical sign. She had used them to become familiar with the city when she moved from New York. Now they were helping her monitor her progress up Washington Street.

Adelle was careful to remain several car lengths behind and would have no problem fitting in with the number of cars starting to flood the roads as people began their morning commutes. She and Alec discussed their plan for today, and Adelle insisted that she follow them as far as possible. Neither had any illusions that she would find where the facility was, but following as long as she could was necessary to piece together some of the landmarks and general directions. Alec was still not sure that he could trust the offer, but as they talked through the facts together, they both realized that the government did not need a ruse to harm him if that was their intent. After weighing the alternatives with Adelle, they decided to take the offer by Mr. UT.

Washington Street had a stoplight on each block, so the traffic moved slowly, allowing Adelle to keep the SUV in sight. As they passed the last of the traffic lights heading north towards DC, the thoroughfare turned into the George Washington Parkway, and the speed of the SUV increased. She ran through a light that turned red to keep pace and not lose her target.

The SUV was among a handful of cars on the road and was increasing its speed. She watched as she passed the Dangerfield Island Sailing Club on her right, a landmark for all the locals with its restaurant and marina sitting directly on the Potomac River. Every land mark she knew was becoming part of her route that she would need to recall later to help reassemble the route she took. As they approached Regan National Airport, the SUV began to slow, and it was apparent that the airport was their destination. She slowed her speed until the SUV took the exit and began to close the gap. As she exited the parkway, she saw the SUV turn into the General Aviation section of the Airport, where private aircraft of corporations and individuals were serviced and maintained. She found a small service road and pulled off to observe the tarmac. As she watched the activity below, a white-topped, dark green bodied Huey helicopter rotors began whirling. As she observed the activity, two men emerged from the vehicle, and between them was Alec. Nothing appeared to indicate that he was in trouble or under duress. He was helped into the back of the helicopter, and then the sliding side door was closed by one of the ground crew. The helicopter rose into the air, turned to face the Potomac River, and headed into the eastern sunrise and out of sight. She knew this was the right thing for him and that risks came with the big stories, but that did not prevent the tears from filling her eyes.

◆ ◆ ◆

Inside the helicopter, Alec was flanked by an agent and Mr. UT. Alec rolled up his sleeve as instructed on the ride to the airport, and Mr. UT administered the sleeping sedative that would have Mr. Richardson out for the next two hours. Alec collapsed slowly into his seat.

The helicopter continued east until reaching Annapolis and then headed North over Washington DC until sighting the United States Naval Observatory on Massachusetts Ave. The pilot finalized his clearance instructions and landed on the grounds. As the Huey landed, the pilot cut his engines, and the rotors began their slow spin to their final resting position. Another SUV pulled up next to the helicopter and brought a small liter. UT ensured that Alec was transported to the SUV and placed him into the rear seat between him and the agent that accompanied him in the helicopter. The driver waved to the police escort, and they began their commute to Benning Road as officials representing the Vice President of America.

Law enforcement temporarily closed the roads to allow the VIP visiting the Vice President unimpeded travel to the heart of DC, causing delays and traffic backups around the city. As they passed each blocked intersection, each barrier was taken down, and normal traffic patterns resumed. One block away from their destination, their police escort left them, and they became just another car on the road and traveled to their destination as a regular commuter.

CHAPTER 14

Alec Richardson had a gritty taste in his mouth as though he had eaten a tube of toothpaste with baking soda. His eyes blinked once, and for a brief second he detected a dull white light shining into his eyes. Panic set in as Alec momentarily forgot where he was and why he was there. He seemed to be floating in midair, but he knew that was not possible. *This is good,* he thought as his rational thinking was starting to return. Then like a busted dam gushing water, his mind filled with the information he was looking for; he was in the facility. He remembered meeting the SUV this morning and entering the vehicle. UT was there along with two others that looked like federal agents in their suits and short haircuts. UT explained the process that was to happen and what he would experience waking up and asked if he was ready. Alec remembered saying "I am" as he volunteered his arm. UT had injected the sedative.

As he focused on his surroundings in the dim light, he could make out a desk, bookcase, computer, and chairs. He was in an office lying on a couch; and as he turned his head could make out a digital clock on the wall. Its luminous numbers read 04:45. Wait, UT told him he would be out for two hours. The time was before he left. Where was he? Middle America? West Coast?

The door to the office opened, and the motion detector turned on the overhead lights. The bulbs came to life slowly from a low dim and eventually brightened for which Alec was grateful. He looked up, and UT was standing next to him with his hand extended outward, holding a cup with an orange looking liquid.

"Here, drink this. It will clear up the pasty taste immediately."

Alec sat up, took the cup, and swallowed it in two gulps, a familiar orange taste touching his taste buds as he felt the paste disintegrate in his mouth. "Good stuff. What is this?"

"Tang – the breakfast drink used by Astronauts," UT said, quoting the 60's commercial.

Alec felt great. No headache, no burning in the eyes, no lethargic feeling in his limbs. Quite the opposite, he felt stimulated and ready to go as though he just worked out. His mind felt sharp. Things he observed had instant clarity. UT looked at him.

"We gave you the good stuff; a special sedative we've developed that increases perception and awareness as an after effect. Are you ready to stand? The team is assembled in the briefing room."

Alec stood up without difficulty.

"Ready to go."

"This way," UT said, pointing out the door. "Straight across the hall."

Alec walked out the door and emerged into a brightly lit hallway about 15 feet wide. Across from where he was standing were two transparent glass doors with handles. Midway up each entry was a frosting-like covering that looked very much like the doors found in corporate board rooms around the world. The hallway was empty of any pictures, but painted on the walls were different directional signs. Covering the walls was a substance that made them look like white metal that reflected the recessed LEDs above to provide maximum visibility in the hallway. As he looked left, he saw two separate doors that looked like the inside of a submarine or Navy ship, each embedded into transparent glass that connected the walls of the hallway, with one access door at each place. Each contained a card swipe on both sides restricting access, and they looked like they could be hermetically sealed to hold someone or something on either side.

Alec opened the door to the conference room, and a man and a woman stood up and moved towards him. The woman was in her mid to late 40s, tall, trim, and attractive with blonde hair that was pulled into a bun. The man was late-50s, graying and looked like he spent most of his time behind a desk despite his 6'2" height and trim physique. UT followed Alec through the door and positioned himself between the two and Richardson. They met halfway down the long glass-topped conference room table.

"Welcome, Mr. Richardson. I trust your trip here was uneventful," the man said, extending his hand.

"If you say so," Alec said, shaking his hand and smiling. "I don't remember it."

UT began the introductions.

"Mr. Richardson, this is the Supervisor. He is the Program Executive. And this is the Warden."

The Warden and Alec shook hands.

"Coffee, Alec?" and pointed him to the Keurig.

Even in one of the government's most top secret facilities, a familiar coffee maker was available. Alec was handed a light blue mug with no markings and selected hazelnut from the variety of K-cups stacked in a decorative box. He grabbed a coaster from the stack and chose a seat near the other mugs already on the table. At one end of the conference room was a large TV, controlled by a remote positioned by the Supervisor's cup.

As UT was filling his mug, Alec asked, "Why the names and what do they mean?"

The Warden fielded the question.

"This program has code level clearance. I take it you know what that means."

Alec nodded his head. He was very familiar with

the government's security classification system. Most people thought that "Top Secret" was the highest. Technically it was, but security was also based on a "Need to Know" basis. Information and even programs were compartmentalized and given additional levels of security; and within those levels, code names for the nation's most closely held secrets. Only people with 'special' access could receive information and only specifically for that topic. Most of America thought the President had access to everything, but in many cases, he only possessed a working knowledge and not the details. He suspected this was the circumstances here. The Warden continued.

"Each of us with descriptive names have made a commitment to this program. We do not work anywhere else and we don't use our real names. Our functional names protect us and keep our identity unknown. Even false names can lead to identification via public sources. We have extended families who are also protected by us assuming these identities. Our lives, for the most part, are here at work, minimizing our interaction with people. When our work requires us to interact like this, names describing our roles on the project become our persona."

"Something like a super-hero, I suspect," Alec said, looking at the Supervisor, who returned his comment with an emotionless stare.

"Something like that," the Warden commented. "Let's move on. As the Warden, I run operations for the facility and oversee all activity involving the cell block. And Mr. UT whom you have conversed with the most is the Undertaker. It's a dark name, and while his job is not to prepare any dead since our inmates are very much alive, there is a transitional process that he oversees as part of our solution. He is the inventor of numerous medical patents, which include sedatives and their derivatives for the medical procedures we use."

Alec shot a look at UT. He shrugged and looked back at Alec.

"So now you know," UT said.

Alec took a big drink of his coffee.

"And you Ms. Warden, can you provide any more information on yourself for the article?"

"Like what Mr. Richardson?"

"Like, how do you qualify to be the Warden at a place like this?"

"Without going too deep, I have a law enforcement background with the Department of Defense."

"Well, I guess that's helpful," Alec said, disappointed by the response. "Mr. Supervisor, how about you?"

"Mr. UT will provide some limited background information later. Let's get started," the Supervisor said as he reached for the remote and turned on the TV monitor. The lights in the conference room dimmed, and the cover slide of the presentation filled the screen. Three words were on the monitor, and they sent an unexpected chill through Alec. It read, "Virtual Life Solution (VLS)." The Supervisor began, appearing to choose his words carefully.

"You are most likely aware of the state of our current incarceration system or at least the information that is available in the public domain."

He clicked the next slide showing numbers, pie charts, and graphs.

"If you look at this information, Mr. Richardson, you will see that the state of our current incarceration system is much different than what Americans believe. This data shows that our prison system is no longer sustainable. We are running out of two things: prisons and the money to build, operate, and maintain them."

The Supervisor paused while Alec processed the numbers. *If this chart is to be believed,* Alec reflected, *then things are much worse than what I thought.* He had contributed to stories about the nation's prisons but not seen numbers quite this compelling. He understood the country needed to act; but like so many problems, it was a matter of priority and funding.

This information already made this a story worth writing.

"Ask questions at any time, Mr. Richardson," the Warden stated.

Alec nodded that he understood. The Supervisor clicked the next slide of information for Richardson, and it was labeled "History." It showed several graphs and their correlation to historical events, each with arrows moving in a generally downward direction.

"I would like to talk about this information with you, Mr. Richardson. We all know that you are here for a specific reason. The last chart showed numbers that until now were classified. Before you ask, they were classified because the American public did not need to know the condition of our incarceration system. Your article is an attempt to be honest with the American people. The information on the screen tells you why. Each of these graphs shows historical events that world governments faced when dealing with their criminals. As you look at the timelines, each government has taken actions they hoped would protect their society. Look at the top timeline. England, facing a domestic population explosion and shrinking resources in the late 18th century, sent their criminals to Australia."

The line identified England, and a quick click expanded the timeline.

"What most Americans do not know is that England took its worst convicts and misfits from Ireland and Scotland and sent them to America first beginning in the early 1700s. For decades our country filled up with the worst of Europe's rejects. Historians estimate approximately 10% of immigrants coming into the US from around 1710 until 1776 were convicts of some sort. Fortunately for us, this practice of sending convicts to the US ended when our revolution started in 1776. England had to find another place to send them, and it was around 1783 that they chose Australia."

"Well, that explains why Americans are always looking

for free cable," Alec said, trying to keep his mind sharp and relax the atmosphere with a little humor.

No one in the room reacted to his comment. Another click of the remote shrunk the England timeline and highlighted the remaining two underneath it. Alec decided not to use humor during the remainder of the stay.

"The second and third timelines show the Brits were not the only ones looking to remove criminals from their countries. Every major power, like the Soviet Union and France, had penial colonies. They shipped their criminals to these places to preserve and protect the best of society for future generations. France had Devil's Island in Guiana, the Russians, well they always had Siberia.

"History shows us that during a time when the land was abundant, and oceans and travel times protected civilizations, this solution worked. Mr. Richardson, today, we are out of land, and nations of the world do not want our criminals immigrating to their countries. The era of Global expansionism and colonialism is over. Our forefathers thought they solved the problem, but they just postponed it.

"So now we face a unique situation. If the land is no longer available, and political power is not used, how do we solve this problem?"

The Supervisor clicked the next slide. It read, "Civilization requires law and order to exist and be applied equally to all citizens."

"Our constitution states that our government exists to protect our liberties and our property; and if done correctly, our nation will prosper. Stability and government go hand in hand. A stable society means a stable government and vice versa. While many Americans may not support the administration in power, over 85% believe that our Republican form of government is the best."

Richardson nodded his head in agreement. While Americans complain about the country's democratic system, most acknowledge that it is still better than other governments around the world.

"So I ask you, Mr. Richardson: what happens when our government can no longer exercise a justice system fairly by incarcerating its convicted criminals because there is no place to put them? What then is the purpose of our judicial system? What happens to the government? What happens to society? It's a pretty bleak picture, wouldn't you agree?"

It was evident to Alec the intent behind the questions. If our judicial system was unable to punish criminals justly, then society could react in ways that led to significant changes in government. History documented revolutions and government changes because they no longer served the needs of the people. Could this happen again? He believed it was a mistake to think these things only happened in developing countries.

"Which is why we built the VLS," the Supervisor added as he clicked to the next slide.

The chart read, "Our incarceration system has two simple principles that serve this nation: Criminals are locked away to protect society, and while locked away, Criminals lose many of their rights and freedoms as a method to reform behavior.

"It is this second one that that comprises our belief in justice and hope for the future." Alec read the chart and the Supervisor continued.

"Unless receiving the death sentence, time spent in prison and the loss of freedom is intended to make the inmate remorseful or regret his harm to society. It is this process that is intended to reform the individual so that they are reintegrated into society or at least accept the reason they are spending their life in prison."

The Supervisor made this comment to clearly reinforce the content that he wished Alec to address in his article. He paused, letting the information sink in with the man that would carry his program's purpose to the American people. He wanted to make sure the message was correct. If the White

House wanted the facts revealed, then they were going to be the truth. He clicked the next slide. It read 'Recidivism.' The Supervisor went on.

"Our system is not working. Inmates released are arrested and end up back in prison. Sixty percent of those re-arrested occur during years 4 through 9 after their release. An estimated 68% of released prisoners are arrested within three years, 79% within six years, and 83% within nine years. Why is it so high? No one knows, but we can agree: the numbers ARE high. Experts quote the references, 'it is likely due to a combination of personal, sociological, economic, and lifestyle factors.' The bottom-line, Mr. Richardson, is that *our system no longer works, whatever the reason.* Reformed inmates are supposed to be reintegrated back into society and contribute. Instead, they add their weight back into a system that is already stressed."

"What about space? You know, up there?" Alec pointed to the sky, implying off-planet.

"This too has the attention of senior people but currently is a costly proposition. Besides, history has shown us, as we've discussed, Mr. Richardson, that eliminating convicts by deportation only postpones the problem. It does not solve it."

Alec agreed with the logic he was hearing.

"To exasperate the problem, as our nation has aged, the views of society changed. Today, the death penalty is looked down upon as being un-American and not in line with our values. Unfortunately, the people that feel this way and vote are not receiving this presentation that you are today, nor are many of the politicians that wish to keep their job and respond to the wish of those voters. Presidents in our recent history have dealt with prison reform and tried to find space in over crowded prisons by letting lesser criminals out into society. This approach frankly is short-term thinking and has done nothing but allow criminals back into the general public before they were ready to contribute, inflicting even more harm on the people we are supposed to protect.

"Your role here is instrumental in educating our nation and the world. If people knew what was happening, they would understand that every life or long-term conviction adds additional weight to a system that is ready to break at any time. Put another way, returning criminals, and newer criminals with life or multiyear sentences, are maxing out the system and the dollars available. VLS makes these problems go away. It provides space and provides a life for each inmate. It also provides an experience that frees society of expectations of reform."

Alec asked no questions but made a mental note of his comment "expectations of reform." The Supervisor took his cue from his body language and clicked the next slide. It read, "Protect Society."

"Our society today is preyed upon by many elements of illegal activity from the elderly victimized in phone scams to businesses creating the newest health crisis. Everywhere, people feel like victims. When you feel this, you recognize the inequities in the system, which leads you to begin to weigh punishment against crime. Today, even good citizens contemplate committing crimes to fix the injustice. What happens when honest citizens feel they can act illegally without fear because the law will not punish them? We have all faced the moral question, 'Is it wrong to steal bread if you are doing it to feed your family?' We need to get our criminal element away from society so that we do not have to answer this question. So how is this done? Medical advances allow us to do this. Criminals could be placed into medical comas, but there is no quality of life; this is unacceptable to the American people."

The Supervisor clicked the remote again. The next slide read, "Life without Expectation of Reform." It was evident to Alec that the Supervisor was making an effort to drive home each point of his program and provide the framework for his story.

"VLS is built upon virtual reality and artificial intelligence. An environment so realistic that the inmate cannot tell

TOM DEWITT

the difference between our reality or what we call 'Real Space,' and their reality. We call their reality the Special Operational Unfenced Prison or SOUP. In the SOUP, the inmate creates the world they wish to live. Our role is to monitor, not reform."

Richardson's mind was whirling. *My God, have we created something like this?* Mr. UT was right. This was a game-changer. Alec was all-in.

"The real difference between life in the SOUP and life, in reality, is no different for the inmate. The difference resides in society's expectation of reform. Put bluntly – there is none. The nation's worst criminals to include terrorists, are placed in the SOUP. Only the worst criminals, with little chance of reform and a high probability that they will commit equally egregious crimes again, are selected for VLS. Lesser crimes are still placed in our existing prison system because their chances for reform are higher."

"Who decides if the inmates come here or go to an existing prison?" Alec asked.

"Our criminal justice system. VLS replaces the high-security prison system and our methods of incarceration only. We are not rewriting the law. VLS is the next continent of Australia, but one created by technology. We anticipate that the quality of life for inmates and their length of life is extended because even our criminals are protected from the evils of the outside world." The Supervisor paused and looked at Alec for questions. He had none.

"VLS not only provides the facilities and a life for its inmates more closely aligned to what they would choose, but the cost to incarcerate is a fraction of what we spend today. We estimate savings of $50B per year once the program is up and running. What could we do with $50B a year and a society that can focus on advancement? Pay for educating our citizens, create new job programs? Feed the hungry? These are all ideas that, in turn, lower crime."

The Supervisor advanced to the next slide, which showed a drawing of the facility layout.

"Ms. Warden, your slide," the Supervisor said, indicating that she would now field the questions.

The Warden began. "Our facility is approximately 50,000 square feet in comparison to acres of land needed by prisons that are enclosed by fences and concertina wire. As a comparison, Alcatraz was 22 acres and held a little over 1550 prisoners. We can hold 1500 in a little over an acre. Alcatraz had about 50 guards to keep inmates in; we can operate on three per shift to keep the public out. We don't have escapes or prison riots and many of the other issues associated with housing maximum-security inmates. In essence, Mr. Richardson, you are sitting in the new Alcatraz."

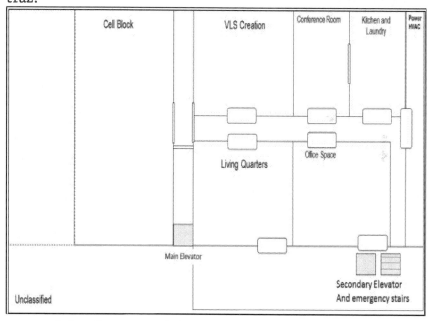

Richardson noted the quiet that permeated the facility. There were no sounds. It reminded him more of a library than a high-security prison. She waited a moment, then resumed.

"On our left and down the hall is the cell block."

She produced a pocket laser from her jacket and used the thin beam of light to point to the cell block on the diagram. "This is where our inmates reside. Also contained in the cell block are all the supplies and equipment needed to maintain our inmate's physical spaces as well as their care and feeding."

"How many inmates do you currently have?"

"We have 100. The remainder of the facility exists for the support personnel. We have our office spaces, living quarters, mess hall – sorry kitchen," she corrected, betraying her link to the armed forces.

I wonder which branch of service she was, Alec thought as the Warden finished her sentence, "and all the essential services."

"Do you live here full time?"

"That depends on the operational tempo, but the short answer is no. Each of us has a home and regular lives, not unlike wardens and their support staff in existing prisons."

"What are the special doors between the cell block and the rest of the facility?"

"These are high-security doors preventing access to the cellblock. In the event the facility is compromised via the main elevator, the three doors protect the staff. This one here in the main corridor," the Warden said, pointing with her pocket laser at the thin door depiction, "and this one here by the living quarters and this one on the cell block."

"How about the Secondary entrances?"

"They also have high-security doors much like these, but at their entry points located away from the facility. This allows the staff to leave the facility without dealing with security protocols until they are at the doors providing access to the outside."

"The main corridor looks bigger, I assume, for shipping and delivery."

"Correct, Mr. Richardson."

"How probable is an inmate escape?"

"We assess that it is impossible."

"What assurances can I write about in the story that inmates cannot escape?"

"First of all," the Warden began, "the inmate would have to overcome the physical containment restrictions inside their 'cell.' If for some reason they were able to do this, they would have to deal with these doors. But I ask you, Mr. Richardson if you are creating your own reality, why not just orchestrate your escape in the SOUP? The experience would be the same. The bottom line, they can't get out."

"If an inmate wakes up – what happens?"

The Supervisor cut in.

"Sorry, Mr. Richardson, that question will not be answered."

Understanding that he hit a dead end with his questioning of the VLS, Alec moved on. This would be worth exploring later.

"Are we underground?"

"Yes"

"Why?"

"For several reasons. The first and primary is security. We do not want the locations of our prisons known to the public. Once your article is published, we become targets if they know locations. There will be no towers or fences."

Alec nodded.

"The other reasons? You mentioned several."

"Out of sight, out of mind. People feel safe when they don't see the threat that exists within their county or neighborhood, especially a maximum-security facility. Alcatraz was on an island not only to keep prisoners from escaping but keeping the public informed, knowing they were safe from that likelihood by high walls and a shark invested Pacific Ocean.

"Lastly, prisons take up valuable real estate space and impact local markets. There is a good example outside of DC called the Lorton prison. Lorton incarcerated every level of prisoner and crime. Crumbling infrastructure and encroachment of new neighborhoods toward the prison resulted in its eventual closure. The community was pleased when helicopters no longer circled houses during the night because of escaped inmates. Today, neighborhoods exist very close to the old prison buildings; some communities look at old guard towers outside their windows that remain standing. The prison buildings are now an Arts Center for local artists. The prison is part of the community and not something to be avoided. Prisons can free up land to build new homes or retail for expanding populations and renewed safety for the community."

This was all making sense to Alec. They had thought this through. The example of Lorton was a nice touch.

"How deep are we?"

"About 40-80 feet."

Alec wanted to know more about the VLS, so he tried a different angle, hoping to get the information he was seeking.

"Is this a connected facility? In other words, does your VLS network interface to the outside world?"

"No," she answered. "This is a self-contained facility. Our VLS is on a closed network and will never connect to the outside world for security reasons. Our network in the office spaces is a physically different network which enables us to work as though we were in any other office building."

"How much did it cost to build this facility?"

"About $1 billion; or $3.4 billion less than one of the Navy's newest ships in the fleet. We will save about $5 billion per year, Mr. Richardson, on this facility alone in operational costs. We will provide you with the cost savings and break down of how we reached those numbers for your story."

"Thank you, Ms. Warden. I have no further questions."

"This ends the information portion of the presentation and our discussion," the Supervisor said. "I trust Mr. Richardson that you understand everything we discussed may be written in your story. I would like you to focus on the information you just received. This is the story the American people need to hear. Change to our system is required, and for once, we are ahead of the problem. We have an answer."

"How much freedom do I have to write this story?" Alec asked.

"Much of this, including the existence of the program, was classified, but decisions were made for sharing this with the American people. Because we have not allowed you to take notes, Mr. UT will provide you information after your visit. Additionally, several photos are available for your use. Also declassified for your article is the facility diagram you were just shown. Do you have any more questions before you see the facility?"

"What if you are asking me to lie and cover-up even greater truths?"

"Your visit here should answer all your questions. As I've mentioned, other than classified information that the public should not know for National Security Reasons, the story is yours to write. I want the final editorial rights before publishing."

"What guarantees do I have that you will not remove or alter the truth of what I write?"

"Mr. Richardson, we can approach this two ways. The first way involves the promise of prosecution if you reveal classified information by choosing to go around me to publish the article. The second way involves building upon the trust you've developed on both sides of the aisle and with this administration. This trust allowed you access to this facility, and there could be many more opportunities such as this for a man with your talents. Ultimately, we want the truth revealed to the American people for many of the reasons we have discussed, and not just for this program. I prefer the second approach, Mr. Richardson. Which one do you prefer?"

Alec acknowledged the silence of the facility for a second time. It became very apparent as he considered the Supervisor's question that working together was the right approach. He had never seen or heard of anything like this before.

"Ok, you have my word. Everything will go through

you."

"Thank you. I have to leave Mr. Richardson. Other duties call, but the Warden and UT will take you through the rest of the facility."

He stood, as did everyone around the table, and shook Alec's hand.

"I look forward to reading your article."

The Supervisor exited the conference room and headed towards the secondary elevator. Alec was still in awe at the engineering and marveled at the achievements he'd seen.

"Well, Mr. Richardson, would you like to see the facilities and what your tax money has built?" the Warden asked, pointing the way out of the conference room doors.

"Let's start with the VLS creation facility if you don't mind," Alec stated.

He was very interested in how the inmates created their reality. As the three walked down the hall, Richardson made a note of the office space behind the same type door as the conference room as well as the sign marking the living quarters for the facility personnel. At the end of the hall was one of the two doors he noticed earlier. Before reaching the door, the Warden directed Alec into the VLS Environment room on his right. UT swiped his security card hanging on the lanyard around his neck, and the door buzzed open.

As they entered the room, Richardson was disappointed. He expected to see an engineering marvel but instead saw a facility that appeared to look more like a standard command center. At the front of the room were seven different large screen TVs that were turned off for security reasons. Inside an environmentally controlled enclosed area on the room's right side were approximately 30 tall white cabinets, each encased in an outer shell cabinet, and a door providing access to the contents inside. Various colored hoses and cables protruded from the top of each housing; an obvious give away that each contained the servers that were hosting the VLS environment and processing each inmate's thoughts. By his estimate, there were approximately 15 per cabinet for a total of 450 to 500 servers contained in this portion of the facility. It reminded him of nothing more than the inside of some of the data centers he visited in Ashburn, VA, many years ago when companies like Amazon and Facebook began to consolidate their processing power in huge buildings and connected everything by the internet. As he looked around, he noticed there was no staff on duty. Everything was strangely quiet. It was surreal.

"Where is everyone?" he asked.

"We are operating with minimal crew while you are here, but even when fully staffed, it's not much more than you see today," The Warden said. "There are two security guards on duty in the facility and about 20 technicians that rotate through in shifts. That's all we need. Many of the monitoring systems are off, and their functions are classified. Sorry. Have you seen everything you need to see in here, Mr. Richardson?"

Alec nodded.

"Let's go to your domain, Mr. UT."

"This way, please."

UT swiped his card, and once again, the buzzer indicated the door was unlocked. They walked out, turned right, and stood in front of a high-security door. UT stood on the right side of the door and swiped his card through the reader. Richardson was surprised to hear a male's voice speak from the door in the silence on the facility.

"Enter access code."

UT entered eight digits onto the keypad attached to the card reader. A small audible click confirmed each entry on the keyboard.

"Stand by for biometric scan," the voice once again spoke.

UT leaned his face forward to the door, and a beam of yellow light entered UT's eye and flickered.

"Bioscan confirmed, access granted."

The door opened to their front as did the one locking access to the cellblock.

"This way, please, Mr. Richardson," UT stated and walked through the first door.

As Alec followed, he looked to his left and saw the hallway and primary elevator to the facility. As briefed, both were larger to accommodate the transfer of prisoners and noted that the appearance of the entire facility was the original white looking paint that he had seen when he first awoke. Mr. UT entered the second door and welcomed Richardson with a warm and hearty, "Welcome to the cell block."

As Alec walked inside, lights came on automatically to illuminate the area. What he saw now surprised him. It was a room, a big one but a room none the less. As he stood with his back to the wall, he felt as though he had walked into a giant mausoleum. There were places on his right side for 100 containers on the bottom row. Above the bottom row, four more rows reached up to about 20 feet high. "500," Richardson counted as he looked at the wall. This number repeated for the wall in front and on his left. "1500," he said as if to confirm the briefing he received. On his right, about 100 of the containers were active. A green light glowed on each of the doors, and data streamed across a front panel even as the three stood in the vast hall. In typical government fashion, there was a yellow line painted on the floor approximately five feet from the container doors for each wall creating a "buffer zone" around the room. Painted at 10-foot intervals in yellow within the zone were the words, "Caution, loading zone." UT began the conversation.

"This way, Mr. Richardson. I am authorized to show you the information on the doors and share a little about the inmate."

Alec and the Warden walked over to where he stood. Each door contained a digital number designating the inmate's assigned position in the cell block. Some things remain the same, Alec thought. Our prisons today provide numbers, as well, to take away the individual identity of the inmate. He was sure that was not the case here, though, since the prisoners would never interact with the staff.

"So let's begin with Inmate Number 1," Alec said.

UT began his presentation. "As you have already noticed, each door has a number that corresponds with our inmate database. The information contained on the outside shows us that the connection to the VLS is functioning. The green light here verifies that everything is working correctly," he said, pointing to the indicator.

"The information on the door provides the physical wellbeing indicators, heart rate, pulse, all very similar information that you would find NASA monitoring during a space flight or an intensive care hospital room. All the readings on the door indicate the physical condition of the inmate. We can view different information by swiping the screen like so."

UT touched the screen with a swiping motion, and a new one with different information replaced it, much like swiping through screens on your smartphone.

"We can monitor every aspect to include vitamin levels and urine composition since each is fed intravenously. These information screens serve as a quick check when the staff is in the block. All this information flows to the VLS Environment room, where it is correlated and analyzed. In many ways, Mr. Richardson, our inmates receive the best health care on the planet. We care for and monitor every aspect of their biological systems. It would be safe to say that they are in better condition in the SOUP than if they were still in our world. We expect their actual lifespan data to validate our models eventually — Ms. Warden?"

The Warden swiped the screen again. New information presented as a graph displayed in the center of the screen with four lines moving as though monitoring the heartbeat.

"This screen is the inmate's brain activity function. Information on this display lets us know that the inmate is creating and living in their reality. We view this through the brain wave indicators. Please make note Mr. Richardson as we go to each inmate, the degree of activity that is occurring within each inmate's mind. We monitor for the four basic types, beta, alpha, theta, and delta, located here in the center of the screen. Beta waves indicate an alert and creative mind. We are very interested in this wave; and trust me, Mr. Richardson, when I tell you our inmate's minds are very active. Alpha gives us an indicator that our inmate has completed a task and taking some satisfaction in doing it well. Theta waves equate to daydreaming, another active component of our inmates and delta normally indicates sleep. Our analysis of our current inmates all show a normal rhythm of all four types and how their brain is working. While we may not experience their world, we are very much engaged in monitoring their reality."

"The Supervisor said that the inmates create their own reality and you monitor the activity. Can you tell me how they do this?" Alec asked.

"Without going too deep into the classified information, I can say that each inmate keeps their memories from Real Space. We can identify their last memory and build a bridge into the SOUP with a procedure we call Jumpstarting. Jumpstarting allows their brain to create their first new memory in the SOUP by associating it with their last real memory. When they wake up, they see no difference in the reality they perceive. It's like they took a nap."

"I understand this part, but how do they create their present life if they have no memories but past ones? You don't keep feeding them their new memories do you?"

"Not at all," the Warden replied. "We have something called the community. This technology allows the inmates to create their new present reality. They do this by sharing other inmate memories, personalizing them, and then placing them back into the community. These new memories are, in turn, shared by others in the community, much like when you go to a new school as a young person. You have no memories of that school or the people in it, but as you interact with new friends, you build them. New memories created by our inmates are stored the same way. These new community memories are shared with others. In doing so, this creates new experiences that are shared and so on. Every memory created can be used by inmates to create their new lives because they draw upon the experiences of others."

"How do you know they perceive reality as we do?"

"Sorry, Mr. Richardson, methods, and processes."

"Fair enough, but I am still looking for the way they *create* their life."

UT interjected.

"Are you familiar with Quantum Mechanics, Mr. Richardson?"

"I've done limited reading if that's what you mean."

"Imagine that our community consists of electrical energy associated with our brain activity. As we have shown, we store brain activity in waves, and you will have to trust me when I tell you that we store memories the same way; they too are waves of energy. Each wave is also associated with another energy wave, which allows the inmate to 'feel' the thought instead of seeing it. Do you follow?"

"Yes, experiences and associated emotions are energy and stored as waves," Alec said, quite positive that his statement was right but not quite sure he had the correct concept.

"While in the SOUP, the inmate searches for different senses or waves of energy that allow him to "feel" what he wishes to experience. We call these feelings quantum tags. Because our inmates are looking for a certain mood, we can assign probabilities to them for selecting events that they wish to create. This is like a child's probability of choosing broccoli over ice cream. The chance they will pick broccoli is minimal, less than .009 as a matter of fact since the primary desire is for ice cream. Once our inmates can sense the emotion of the event that they desire, the inmate's consciousness 'sees' the combined waves."

Alec finished for him.

"Then the wave collapses and becomes a particle forming larger particles and eventually his reality. Is that correct?"

"Sort of, but you are on the right track. But because of our second attached wave, the particle becomes numerous associated particles that combine to create an image and the emotion associated with that image. This creates the reality of that moment in the inmate's mind, much like when you wake up in the morning and see your bedroom for the first time again. Billions, if not trillions of electrical functions, are happening in the brain to create the image of the bedroom, interpret the other four sensory inputs, and any emotion at that moment. We call this an experience frame."

The Warden chimed in.

"And then, much like an old filmed movie or flipping through a book of characters in slightly different positions on each page, individual experience frames are combined with the other experience frames to create movement. When movement occurs to produce motion, we create the perception of time passing. Experience plus time equals reality."

"Out of my league, but I do see it. I will rely upon your help to write this, Ms. Warden."

"Glad to help, but this is all quantum mechanics. We have done a 'few things' to tailor it for our use, but most of this is in public sources journals in the scientific community. I would not elaborate too much on this in your story if you want your readers to finish to the end."

Each laughed and broke the silence of the cell block.

"So, what happens to the inmate's memories when they die?"

There was an awkward pause for the Warden and Mr. UT as both looked at each other, wondering who would answer. It was the Warden that proceeded.

"The memories created in the SOUP are no longer 'connected' to the inmate. They remain in the community."

Alec nodded his understanding.

"But what happens to the inmate?"

"In the final 30 seconds of their life, their VLS memories

will disassociate from the inmate's minds. To them, it looks like a picture that de-pixelates, much like a picture that someone has applied special effects to that causes it to come apart before your eyes. It happens bits at a time and then completely disappears. Their mind recalls their last memory from Real Space, which is our reality, as the last thing they see, and then they pass."

Alec began his next question, "How does..."

"Methods and techniques Mr. Richardson," the Warden said, anticipating his next question. "Let's move on."

Disappointed in not continuing with his questioning, he turned his attention to the inmates.

"So what is the story on Inmate Number 1, Ms. Warden?"

The Warden paused as though searching for the right words.

"Inmate Number 1 is a terrorist; at one time, the most wanted man in the world."

"What country is he from?" Alec asked.

"Let's just say he was apprehended in Pakistan and leave it there."

"Pakistan? Are you telling me that..." and he trailed off.

His brain started whirling, as he contemplated the facts told to the American public about Osama Bin Laden. Shot dead by Seal Team Six, buried at sea all very quickly. Could this be possible? Is Bin Laden inmate number 1?

The Warden stated in her official-sounding voice, "Mr. Richardson, we have discovered with this facility that by studying our inmates and their brain wave activities, we learn much about their human behavior. I can surmise what you may be thinking. Please don't state this as a fact in your article. Many people will not take it seriously. The article is intended to be factual and not a conspiracy theory, if you get my meaning."

He got it. Play by the rules. Write an acceptable article for the Supervisor, and he will have exclusive additional information. With this article, he will generate trust with this

Administration as well as the American people. His new trust will provide him access into some of the darker parts of the government and will expose those truths when the time is right.

"How about the next several?" he asked.

The Warden walked down the loading zone lane, describing each as though she was reviewing personnel files.

"Inmate Number 2, murderer that killed his family and three neighbors that witnessed him. Inmate Number 5, serial killer transferred from death row and responsible for 24 confirmed murders. Inmate Number 6, convicted for rape three times, murdered two of his victims by... I will spare you the details. Inmate Number 22, terrorists responsible for killing 132 foreign nationals including women and children, and 12 Americans in a marketplace bombing in the Middle East."

Alec remembered that event coming across the wire. He was not aware of the American fatalities. What else was omitted from the story?

"These 100 are the worst of the worst, Mr. Richardson. They represent pure evil that walks among us. Preying on the innocent and taking their lives without remorse. Their motive, some higher calling or for just pure pleasure and enjoyment. This is what we want you to tell the American people and the world about."

"How long before you anticipate having this facility filled?"

"That depends upon our justice system; and that is above my pay grade, Mr. Richardson."

"Will there be more facilities built?"

"Above my paygrade Mr. Richardson."

It was apparent to Alec he was finished with the visit. The Warden confirmed this suspicion.

"I do want you to take one last look around before we prepare you for your return trip. You are in a facility that is roughly the size of three floors of an office building. In this facility are some of the worst criminals in the world, and today, they are guarded by three men. You are completely safe. Think about that, Mr. Richardson, and marvel at what this country has built."

He did think about it and had to admit: this was pure genius.

CHAPTER 15

"They are using you, Alec!" Adelle exclaimed as the two of them sat at the breakfast table in Alec's Alexandria house.

"Yes, they are!" he shot back at her in affirmation, "but you didn't see what I saw. This information has got to get out, so why not me? If I don't write this story, someone else will."

"So what if the American public goes along with this idea? Do you realize that 'our friends' are going to view you as compromising your integrity as a journalist as well as setting up this Administration for the next four years, if not further?"

"Look, Adelle. This goes beyond politics. This project was developed over the last 15 years or so. That means both parties get credit for this success, and I can write it that way. I don't see where this country has a choice, and we can't wait for our person to get elected. Look at these charts," he said, passing over the printed slides with the pie charts and statics. "Our prison system is in terrible shape and may not make it through the next 20 years. If the prison system goes, the justice system goes, and we both know what that means."

Adelle scanned the information in front of her. True to his word, the Supervisor provided each of the charts he presented in the conference room to UT; who in turn marked them all "Unclassified" and gave them to Alec at their second meeting at the National Harbor McCormick and Schmick's a week ago. Alec recounted that after a brief conversation involving nothing but small talk while having a beer and oysters, UT slid the manila envelope across the booth to him. Alec had shared with her the details of the meeting looking for anything that would give them a clue about the government's real intent. Alec had said UT was professional and efficient in the exchange. She recalled the conversation Alec relayed to her but could not find anything nefarious in their meeting. She played the words through in her mind quickly now, as she sat with all the details in front of her.

"Here is the information we promised you. Now Mr. Richardson, fulfill your promise to us. I will call in a week to check your progress."

"How do I get hold of you, UT?" Alec had asked.

"You don't," he said, standing up. "I think it's your turn, Mr. Richardson."

With that UT departed, leaving Alec to pay the bill.

It appeared to Adelle to be straight forward. The government wanted this story written and had provided the information. In addition to the charts, she observed that UT also marked "Unclassified" several pictures, including a picture of the full Cell Block and two more of the door information showing the indicators of the inmate's welfare. Adelle had to admit to herself, the facility was very impressive. Along with the photos were several pages of spreadsheets containing cost information and the projected savings; or, as the government calls it, cost avoidance. The supporting numbers were transferred to Department of Justice letterhead memos, all official looking and signed by The Supervisor using nothing more than a capital "S" swirling the bottom of the S line almost into an "8."

Adelle jumped back to the present as she scanned the charts just passed to her and came to the same conclusion as Alec. If these numbers were true, then America had little choice about this. She still would not confirm their authenticity, but if they were true, Alec was right. Something needed to be done soon. This small bit of truth helped her to calm down but she still had questions.

"You've shown me these numbers," she said. "They look good on paper, but what makes you think you can believe them?"

"We have to start believing someone. When I was there, it was a legitimate facility, and never once did I think that I could not trust what they were telling me. These people are professionals, and they have solved a major problem. What they've done could change the world. This is big!"

"I don't like that this story could ruin you. I don't trust these people!"

"Adelle, we take chances in our business. If this is done right, I will have access to programs that are truly corrupt and could fix those. I won my Pulitzer Prize for writing about corruption in another country. Now, I want to make a difference in mine. Work this with me and where you think I might be compromising my integrity, tell me, and we will figure something out."

She could not argue with his passion or commitment to write this article and by all indicators she could find no warning signs. That meant that he was going to write it no matter what she said. Part of her felt the pride of having this man with this type of integrity in her life, but part of her knew the way Washington politics could play. She had no choice. She looked at him and smiled. She loved him so deeply. She reached across the table and put her hand on his.

"Ok, how can I help, and when do we start?"

"We can start by laying all this out in a way that Americans can understand the problem. We have to get them to understand it first before we can talk about the solution."

Adelle nodded in agreement but could not forget the apprehension she felt waiting for him to come back from the facility. Things were happening so fast. *Are we doing the right thing?* She thought.

♦ ♦ ♦

It was two weeks since Alec had visited the facility. Adelle remembered receiving a phone call from a hidden number after Alec came back. When Adelle answered, she was told a helicopter would bring Alec to Reagan National at 4:30. Adelle was to park at the private aviation terminal. The voice told her she would know which one, since she watched it depart earlier that morning. Adelle did not know if she should be upset about being identified while following them or relieved that Alec was coming back. Adelle did as instructed, and at 4:30, the "whop whop" sound of the Huey passed overhead. She opened the car door, got out, and walked around to the passenger side and opened that door as well. Adelle waited nervously, checking her watch every 30 seconds. As she checked for the 5th time, the doors to the terminal opened, and Alec emerged, being helped by two men in suits.

"Is he ok?" she said, running to the two men and looking at Alec's eyes and body for indicators of harm.

"He's fine, just coming out of sedation so a little weak on his feet," one of the men said.

The other man helping him carry Alec said, "Let's get him to the car."

As they approached the vehicle, they slid Alec into the front seat. One of the men reached in, fastened his seat belt, and started heading back to the terminal doors. The remaining man stood in front of Adelle.

"Did you bring the sports bottle with water?"

"Yes, I have it here," she replied while reaching to the center console.

"Here," the man said, "mix this with the water. As soon as he says something, have him start drinking it."

Adelle took the packet. It read "TANG" on the outside. "What is this?" showing the man the package and looking at him with contempt. "Is this some kind of joke?"

"It's TANG, the breakfast drink," the man commented. "It will help him transition out of his sedated state and clear up any of the grunge he has in his mouth from the sedative. He is going to want it. Trust me. Also, if he experiences heightened awareness, this is normal for about the first 30-45 minutes after he wakes up. I will call you in two hours to make sure everything is okay."

The man turned and walked through the terminal doors and was gone. Adelle returned to the driver's seat and mixed the TANG with the bottled water. She had just placed it in the center console when Alec awoke and looked over at her.

Through hazy eyes, he said, "Hey, baby."

"You're back now. I've got you with me," Adelle said, emotion filling her voice.

"TANG?" he asked.

She lifted the bottle and let him drink through the straw, draining about half of the container. He returned it to her.

"Oh, that's the good stuff!" he said, his voice already close to normal but still speaking slowly. "You would not believe what they have done! So much to tell you."

She felt the tears start to rise in her eyes. Alec was back and safe with her. She shut her door and started the car. Turning around in the parking lot, they exited the airport and headed south on the George Washington Parkway back to Alexandria.

CHAPTER 16

Johnathan Wilkes, Executive Editor of the *Washington Guardian*, stood up from behind his desk when he saw Alec Richardson through the glass wall in his office. Wilkes was finishing up a phone call and motioned for Alec to come in and sit down.

"Fine, fine, that will be great. Talk with you soon. Give my best to Monique."

He concluded his phone call with his left hand and shook Alec's with the right, smiling the whole time. Wilkes respected Alec's writing as well as his investigative skills in connecting dots in his stories. He had blown the lid off the can of worms with his piece in Afghanistan, and the resulting explosion covered this administration in some of the deepest trouble he had seen in a long time. Payoffs, bribes with tax-payer money, compromising National Security with business interests: all the good stuff that the American people had a right to know about. It was the same story repeated through-out history, but it never failed to sell papers. Americans love a good scandal and the smell of blood in the sand. He loved this business.

"Have a seat."

Wilkes pointed to a couch, a couple of comfortable chairs, and a coffee table in the corner of his office. Alec took one of the easy chairs, and Wilkes took a spot on the sofa. On the coffee table was a blue paper binder with a copy of the story that Alec sent to him a couple of days ago as a read-ahead. Wilkes leaned forward and opened the folder. Getting down to business, Alec started.

"What did you think of the story?"

Wilkes looked down at the folder then up at Alec.

"It is well written, as is all your work, but I have some concerns, Alec," he said, shaking his head. "Where did you get all of this, or should I even ask?"

"Believe it or not, I can tell you. Someone in Justice contacted me. That person became my source for everything that is in there."

"Don't you think it odd that instead of using 'anonymous sources,' you give names, but they are just as cryptic like 'the Supervisor,' 'Warden,' and what the hell is a 'Mr. UT?'"

"U-T, like the University of Texas," Alec responded, "not UT."

Wilkes pressed on. "There are incarceration numbers and statistics here that I've not seen before, and frankly, the whole AI stuff is a little advanced for me to believe. You validated this information, correct?"

Wilkes knew he should not doubt the man across from him; he was a professional but had to ask the question. Alec nodded his head.

"Yes, I validated this information. I know you have doubts, but this story is solid."

"How solid?" Wilkes asked.

"I've been to the facility. I have met these people. They have shown me all of this."

Wilkes stared at him for a moment, processing what he just heard.

"You're kidding!"

"That's right. It was one of the conditions of writing this article, one of THEIR conditions, not mine. They wanted this in the open and were willing to show me the facility to back up their information. I guess they anticipated this conversation."

"Why would they want this in the open? All of this is usually Top Secret as a minimum."

"VLS is ready. I saw the inmates. I saw the facility. I saw the proof of what I've written. They showed me all of it. How they did it is still classified, but the results are clear, and they want them out there. They want the public to know it exists, and they want them to know it is the Justice Department that created this solution."

"If this is as good as you write that it is, then this administration is going to try and use this politically for the election next year. They need to show progress with some of their domestic programs after getting hammered in foreign policy. Some of that was thanks to you."

"I know," Alec admitted. "I have thought through all of this. But this administration did not create this in three years. There were two previous administrations involved representing both parties."

"You know that they are using you, right?"

"So I've been told."

"And through you, they are also using the *Guardian*. I don't know if I want to be used to keep these assholes in office. They've pushed so much crap under the carpet in the room it looks like you are walking the Himalayas."

Alec smiled at Wilkes. He used such descriptive metaphors, the benefit of being a newsman for over 30 years. He had mastered the English language and was starting to develop his own derivation of the spoken lingo.

"No one has said that the American people will agree with what they have built. It's their litmus test. It could backfire."

Wilkes thought about that a moment.

"Maybe the story could be written a little differently to emphasize the downside, you know, guys in boxes losing personal liberties, that kind of stuff."

"That's not going to happen," Alec responded, leaning forward over the coffee table. "The facts here are as I have stated. I am not going to create innuendo or any other thoughts for readers to understand this any differently than I have reported."

This was is a little different than I had anticipated. Wilkes thought. *When Alec first told me about this story, I assumed Alec had an anonymous source leaking a document. Now it looks like not only does he have a source, but the source is him!* That's the angle Wilkes decided to play. If Alec were the source, then he would be responsible for the editing and content. It was a no lose situation for Wilkes.

"What did you have in mind?" Alec asked.

"Let's try a different approach. Nowhere in this article does it say you were there. Without you stating you were there, this is just a bunch of hearsay, another leaked story from some document. As you know, leaked stories are nothing new in DC, but those stories do get people fired up."

Wilkes smiled again. He loved selling newspapers whatever the cause.

"But this one is different. There IS some journalism here that reports facts... but only if you and your reputation are the eyewitness to the event. You have to provide credibility to the story. Are you willing to do that?"

Alec looked at Wilkes.

"What if I just take this to the *New York Globe*, or run it on 60 Minutes?"

"Without video and interviews, you don't have the 60 Minutes story."

"Who says I can't get them? The titles offered in this article are protecting my sources, but both you and I know that I could get them in black-out on camera and do the interview."

He's bluffing, Wilkes thought. In his best scenario, he did not think Alec could pull that off.

"But if I can't get them on 60 minutes, that still leaves the *Globe*. Want me to take the story to them, Johnathan?"

Wilkes knew, but would never admit, that his newspaper's last great victory was several years ago when they scooped the industry and broke the news with their series of articles on election fraud and cover-up. His paper received the credit for uncovering the story and the reputation as a paper fighting for truth. Since then however, the news business had not only become more competitive, but had just "changed". The *New York Globe* scored a couple of wins on their own but had shared credit for most of the significant scoops in the news business with his paper. Wilkes was not going to let that happen with this opportunity. Alec had to be there, which meant he was no longer just the writer but also a source. Being the source put a big target on his back, and his girlfriend Adelle's as well. Wilkes figured Alec was used to death threats for his work in Afghanistan, but he wondered if the kid thought it worth starting them all over again in the US. Time to roll the dice and either sink or swim with the story. Wilkes pressed ahead.

"Sure Alec. You could take it to the *Globe*, but I am telling you: if you are not an eyewitness, this story has no fact. It does not matter where you take it. Others will publish it because of who you are, but without you vouching for the information, it's just a fluff piece to get people riled up."

Wilkes watched Alec's facial expression and knew he had him. *This kid wants to make this story count. He knows he has to be an eyewitness.*

"Do we have a deal if I get approval from my source to make me an eyewitness?" Alec asked.

"If you are willing to stick your ass out for this, we will print it."

The two men stood and shook hands.

"Get me your new copy, and we will run it within 48 hours."

This was a significant win. Wilkes knew that Alec could take the story to the *Globe*, but Wilkes needed this. There was too much competition in the news business, and his paper was losing subscribers.

"One more thing, Johnathan."

"What's that?"

"You have to print what I give you. No changes, no last-minute editing."

Wilkes eyed him over. *What the hell have you gotten yourself into Alec,* he thought. *It must be serious.* "You have my word," he said.

They shook hands again. Alec let out a short sigh of relief.

"Sort of makes me feel like we are doing business old school, the way journalism is supposed to work," Alec commented, looking Wilkes in the eye.

"How is that, Alec?"

"We tell a story based on eye-witness facts and observation. We report, and we don't tell people what to do with the information or spin it."

"Good luck with your idealism. And for your sake, I hope no one decides to make this ugly."

"Thanks, Johnathan, I know you will always have my back," Alec said sarcastically.

Alec opened the office door and walked down the hall. The exchange with Alec made Wilkes think of the days when he started his journalism career. Putting it all out there for the story. The truth does not serve everyone's purpose, but it does relay the facts if the reporter does their job. And doing your job well was the ultimate compliment from your editor. The truth. That's why newspapers like this one started. To inform and educate. Let people decide. It was different now. No one disputed or argued that point. *What happened that changed the press into what it was today?* He wondered.

"Well, one thing for sure, that guy has balls," he said aloud.

The phone rang, and Wilkes walked to his desk, not realizing he answered his own question.

CHAPTER 17

Alec Richardson's cell phone rang, and the words "unknown caller" shone brightly in the darkness of his study. He knew who would be on the other end and was expecting UT's progress call.

"Richardson," he answered in his usual tone.

"Mr. Richardson, this is the Supervisor. I hope you don't mind talking with me instead of UT. I wanted to see what progress you were making."

We must be getting close to the final product if I am getting a call directly from the Supervisor, Alec thought. Either we are at the finish line, or he is getting pressure to complete this story. Either way, he was in an excellent position to discuss the changes asked for by Wilkes.

"How was your talk with the *Washington Guardian*?"

"We have to change the article," Alec said. There was silence on the other end of the phone. He continued, "The *Guardian* will not publish unless I am an eyewitness in the story. I have to be the source."

The silence continued, and Alec could sense that numerous mental calculations were being performed to incorporate this new development. To prompt a response, Alec spoke.

"Sir?"

"I'm here, Mr. Richardson. I understand why he would want you to do this. You realize that you are no longer a reporter telling the story provided by sources with functional names, but are now *the* identified source. Are you ok with that?"

"Yes."

"How soon can you have the next draft here for review?"

His appointments with UT had discontinued when he provided Alec with the information and pictures. Instead, he was given an obscure Justice Email address at their last meeting. He was instructed to send his edits there. He suspected the email messages were routed from the mailbox to the facility on their connected network, or else someone logged into the inbox periodically and checked.

"I can have it drafted tomorrow by noon. The editor has agreed that if I am a part of the article, he will publish within 48 hours of receiving my copy. He will print what we give him with no changes. I have his assurances."

"UT will call with authorization or new edits. Anything else?"

"No."

Click. Silence filled the study again, leaving Alec only with his thoughts about the changes he would make.

◆ ◆ ◆

The Supervisor entered a number from memory into his phone and pushed connect.

"Yes?" was the response from the other end.

"It will be out in 72 hours, Carter. Time to let your folks know."

"Ok, I will pass this along."

"By the way, Carter, I am beginning to see why POTUS likes this guy."

"This is a big gamble. Cross your fingers and grab your ass," Carter said.

"Good talking with you, too, Carter."

The Supervisor called the Chief of Staff next and provided the same brief update. While the Supervisor was updating the White House Chief of Staff, Carter Hurst called the other three members of the Committee and then the Vice President, who, in turn, called the Attorney General Mr. Franklin Pierce.

The AG found out about VLS two weeks after the Vice President's Committee meeting. It was not even on the Justice radar of programs because, he had to admit, the real genius behind the program funded it from three different departments as AI research. Pierce liked that kind of initiative. However, knowing nothing about the program made him less than enamored with the decision to take the details public. Pierce found himself scrambling to put the right response team in place and build the necessary scenarios to handle the barrage of questions that he knew would be coming his way. This was DC, and people wanted blood if things got screwed up. He stayed up nights wondering why in the hell he wanted this job but realized in the end that his time as Attorney General was golden with the private sector whether this administration won a second term or not. He had one of the rare jobs in government where even if things did go wrong, his knowledge of the law and special status in the Executive Branch could be used to pass along the blame to any Department he wished. This made him very powerful in DC and loved the thought that people he dealt with knew this little power fact as well. *The law was a wonderful thing.* But when his phone rang, and it was the Vice President, Pierce focused on serving the President, a man he admired and respected. The Vice President started the conversation.

"Franklin? This is Trip. This thing is going public in 72 hours," he said. "Don't deny anything in the article and find something you can get behind to support the positive efforts of each administration to get us to the finish line. Have you finalized your contingency plans that we reviewed to deal with the backlash if this goes sideways?"

"Yes, Mr. Vice President, everything is ready."

"Good, did you decide on your front man?"

"His name is Jennings, sir. He is one of my deputies, and I trust him completely. He will be our face in the press and Program Executive, if we need him to be. He's been getting the drafts of the article as Richardson has written them from someone in Hurst's office. We are both up to speed with the program. The White House council and I have approved his initial message and his communications plan."

"I may need you to step out front as well, Franklin. This Program belongs to Justice, so own it. The White House has no official role in this at this point, understood? Our response to questions about the program will be to point the press to you."

"Yes, Mr. Vice President, understood."

"Ok Franklin, in 72 hours or so, we are going to know if we have jobs for four more years. Make it count."

"Yes, Mr. Vice President," but the response was unheard by Morrison. He was already making his next call.

CHAPTER 18

As the sun rose in the east over the Nation's Capital, phones started ringing, emails filled inboxes, and text messages started popping up on smartphones everywhere. The front page of the *Washington Guardian* began with the lead story: "Federal Government Declassifies New Maximum Security Incarceration Solution." The author was well known to many in the government, and they recalled less than fondly the last major series he wrote to win his Pulitzer Prize.

As the early morning progressed, those in influential positions took to twitter supporting the story as well as those appalled and surprised by the article's contents. The major news channels, including Fox, MSNBC, and CNN, began the debate by lining up their expert panels and guests to discuss what the story really meant. These panel members were called first by the networks because they received the story the day before from insiders at the *Washington Guardian* and prepared their talking points. As members of Congress entered their offices, staffers provided them with summary reviews and sound bites, in the event they were approached by the press. By mid-morning, the article made it to the rest of social media, and all politically-minded Americans began to offer their opinions in the numerous comment sections on webpages.

The article was laid out in succinctly ordered points and addressed each in perfect prose as only a Pulitzer author could do. The highlighted points were:

1. The maximum-security incarceration system was unsustainable and supported by new data.
2. Through the vision of previous presidents, all administrations had worked diligently over their terms to wrestle with this problem leading to this solution.
3. The government had a functional prototype site that was less than a city block in size but housed the equivalent prison population of Alcatraz.
4. Inmates and technology were combined to produce the new "prison cell" of the future that was escape proof and underground in undisclosed locations.
5. The technology was used to provide the best health care in the world to inmates.
6. The technology was used to create a virtual world for each inmate.
7. An estimated cost savings of $50B or more per year with the new system.
8. These savings could be applied to free college or other domestic programs benefiting all of America.
9. The author witnessed it all and could vouch for it being real.

The terms VLS and SOUP entered the American lexicon. By noon, Richardson completed 30 minute interviews with CNN and FOX and would be appearing again for the evening shows. He would be on the Sunday talk shows that weekend, and if America was still interested, continue his appearances on the network news channels. Richardson and UT selected professional organizations designated for visits and speaking engagements and anticipated an education campaign. The Department of Justice would continue to keep the article in the public's view by references on its website, mentions by the AG at his engagements, and Jennings would act as the Program Executive, handling the unclassified settings with Congress and the press. Any approved classified briefings to Congress would be handled by the leadership of the House or Senate Judiciary Committees. If all went according to the Supervisor's recommendations to the Committee, VLS would be a household name by the New Year and everyone in Congress an expert touting its merits to the public 11 months before the election. This had played well with Carter Hurst. Carter knew that he could rely on the innovation and creativity of the American law enforcement agencies to run with the idea of VLS as a deterrent to crime. A few well-placed federal dollars to Law Enforcement Non-Profit Organizations lit the advertising fires at the grassroots level.

Adopted slogans by Organizations such as "This is not your mom's SOUP – don't do the crime," showed up as a New Yorker cartoon and posters covered the worst crime sections of major cities. "Crime is not the way to free health care," ranked highly among the major media stations.

Carter's favorite was a cartoon run in the *New York Globe* that used an old cannibal theme he had seen as a kid. It showed several convicts in a large pot with a fire burning underneath and NPD officers watching with their arms crossed. The caption read, "You do not want to end up in this SOUP."

As expected, the backlash from Human Rights organizations, businesses that would lose millions in government contracts to build or administer the maximum-security prisons, and general portions of the population that oppose everything associated with the government rose up with one voice creating the ultimate squeaky wheel. Lobbyists for each of the organizations descended on Congress, creating a swirling abyss of confusion in the capital. Numerous segments of airtime were provided for the opposing side to state their case. Inmates on death row were portrayed as victims in the media as the debate began to prevent the implementation of VLS.

It was during a cold November afternoon, three weeks after the published article hit the streets that CNN was broadcasting one of the numerous demonstrations live on location. These events were occurring near prisons as protestors marched in solidarity to condemn the government's oppressive measures and highlight the need for prison reform. It was no surprise to Carter Hurst that his phone rang. It was the Vice President.

"Hurst," the voice began on the other side without waiting for Carter to speak, "Trip here. Are you watching CNN?"

"No, Mr. Vice President, I am away from my office."

"They are showing protestors outside of Big Sandy in Kentucky and they are shouting 'Murderers have rights too.' Can you believe this?"

"It is hard to believe, but Mr. Vice President, we knew we would have some of these types of elements, and we knew there would be a backlash."

"Look Carter, we have seen some positive effects from the article, but the press is using our announcement to move away from the VLS message and highlight the conditions of the existing prisons, which we all know are not good. They could take this win and turn it into a minus for us! We need to do something! We are on the clock. The election is only a year away. Do you have any ideas?"

Carter knew Morrison was right. He also knew the White House might have pulled the trigger too soon on the article. Going public with a story like this was always tricky business. Too close to the election and the intent of the article would be played as resume stuffing for the incumbent as a way to convince last minute voters still sitting on the fence. Too far away, and the press would have the time to spin the story. They were beginning their response by turning the story into the real and tangible conditions of the prisons today and asking this administration, "What have you done to fix them in the last three years?" Hurst believed American voters were shortsighted and did not care about investments like VLS; just what the government was doing for them today. This could be a problem.

"Do we know the score yet with the American people and where they stand on VLS, or are we reacting to the news in the press?"

Carter already knew the answer but asked the question anyway.

"No. I don't think we have polled yet to get the numbers."

"I would recommend that we get the numbers and then decide. If they look good, then we can accelerate the VLS schedule and report our progress publicly through the media. If we keep showing progress for the next year, this could work well for us and pull the narrative back to VLS and not the overall prison system."

"Hmm. I like the idea, Carter. Let me get this rolling on my end. Can the Supervisor work with this?"

"Yes, Mr. Vice President, I don't see any problems."

"Thanks, Carter."

Click. He'd just lied to the Vice President. The Supervisor was going to see all kinds of problems with this. Building new facilities, transferring existing prisoners from high-security facilities into the SOUP, and now providing progress reports to the press. He was not going to be happy. Each story had the potential to turn into the next crisis that could throw mud all over the White House and his colleagues. Never a good thing in an election year.

CHAPTER 19

Robert Bennington looked out of his office window on the New York City street of Madison Ave., 25 stories below. The holiday lights were up in Manhattan and brought a warmth to a city with a reputation for being welcoming but cold. He loved this time of year. He enjoyed the time with family; and, more importantly, the reduction of work that came during the holidays. This always allowed him the time to view the city from his office perch.

That was not going to be the case this year. His firm was recently hired by the White House to assess the American public's opinion of the current administration and their electability in the November election. As part of the polling about their domestic policies, critical questions about the Virtual Life Solution were asked and designed to correlate with the President's strong position on law and order. Results from the poll were to be used to begin building a nationwide media campaign highlighting key successes, among them the VLS and its benefits. Bennington had the results in front of him.

His firm orchestrated phone campaigns in all 50 states but was asked by the White House to provide immediate results from New York, Florida, California, Pennsylvania, Texas, Michigan, Georgia, Illinois, Iowa, and Vermont. It was an odd mix of states. He understood some of these were big count or swing states in the Electoral College with Iowa and Vermont as bell weathers representing traditional values of the nation, and a couple states were just interesting choices.

The White House selected his firm because of the new algorithms they pioneered in the 2016 election that uncovered voting and opinion patterns from social media sites. He prepared those data results as well. The data from the phone polling fell outside the standard 3% of error for some of the critical questions analyzed, but his social media data was pretty solid. He expected as much since the social media algorithms showed items that the phone polling missed. He reviewed the results one last time, felt confident in the procedures and analysis underlying the results, and pushed the release button on his computer screen. The report was immediately made visible to several of the key executives via the company's software that managed the firm's essential reports and documents.

Two hundred and thirty miles away, a computer in the company's DC office dinged. Rachael Harding was one of those executives anticipating the report's release and turned her attention away from her sushi lunch that had turned into early dinner. Her eyes quickly grasped the meaning of the numbers. Reaching for her cell phone, she pushed number 7 on her speed dial and connected with Aaron McAllister, the White House Chief of Staff.

"McAllister," he said, answering his cell phone.

"I've got the numbers for the top 10 that you wanted us to evaluate."

"What do they say?"

"You are going to like them."

McAllister looked at his calendar and then the one for POTUS.

"8:00 tonight in the Oval Office and use the secure email to send me an advanced copy."

"I'll be there," she said. The phone call ended.

McAllister yelled for his Secretary.

"Robin!"

"Yes Sir," came the immediate response as she looked in

the door to his office.

"Call the VP and let him know we have poll results and are meeting at 8:00 in the Oval. Ask him to reach out to Senator Hurst and the AG and invite them as well."

Robin disappeared to her desk to begin making the phone calls.

"Anything else?" she said to McAllister's office door behind her.

"Yes, I have a report coming in, and I will need six copies for the 8:00. I will send it to you when I get it."

McAllister checked the clock on his bookcase. 5:47 pm. He had plenty of time to prepare. His secure email list of messages showed an addition as the email popped into his inbox from Rachael. He forwarded the email to Robin.

"It's in," he yelled.

"I see it. Six copies on the way," came the response.

He opened the report and viewed the executive summary. This is all he would need for now and printed the page on his personal printer and slid it into a folder. He stood up and knocked on the door to the Oval Office. He anticipated POTUS was alone. He liked to take the time between 5 and 6 PM to catch up on some of his briefing books.

"Come in."

"Mr. President, the results of our polls are in for the top ten," and walked to the resolute desk and handed the folder to the President.

"How do they look, Aaron?"

McAllister locked eyes with the President and smiled.

"I have the team coming in at 8:00 tonight."

The President opened the folder and looked at the numbers in the Executive summary.

"Outstanding Chief. Outstanding."

CHAPTER 20

Betty Ferguson, gatekeeper to the President and senior secretary buzzed the intercom into the Oval Office at 7:56 p.m.

"Mr. President, your eight o'clock is all here, should I send them in?"

Instead of pushing the intercom switch, the Chief of Staff walked over to the Oval Office door and opened it, welcoming everyone into the office and then closing it behind the group. The President walked around the desk, greeting each of them, starting with the Vice President. When he reached out to shake Rachael Harding's hand, he said, "I have seen the executive summary. I am looking forward to the details of your report."

She nodded and calmly said, "Thank you, Mr. President."

POTUS pointed to the couch and chairs, and each member knew which seat to take except Harding, who just waited for everyone to claim one and took the place that was left. She looked over at McAllister, who smiled broadly, trying to make her feel welcome in a room that intimidated so many of its visitors. Carter Hurst began to evaluate the room. Attorney General, Chief of Staff, Vice President, and him. Include Ms. Harding into the group, and it made sense. But these were early numbers. Why was POTUS here? This is not a meeting that he would be involved in this early in the process – the

Chief could brief him on the results. His senses told him something happened, or POTUS was managing this effort personally. He suspected the latter. POTUS looked to the Chief and gave the nod to get started. The Chief began.

"The President and I have reviewed the executive summary of the polling report. The results are in for the top 10 states for which we wanted immediate numbers. Ms. Harding will supplement the report tonight with additional state results that are still coming in."

The President looked through his report as McAllister talked. The Chief reached down and retrieved the copies next to his chair for each attendee and placed them on his lap.

"Ms. Harding will brief the methods and results." Looking in her direction he nodded as her cue to begin.

"Our firm was selected for this effort because we've done polls over 15 years for the GOP. More importantly, we also pioneered the algorithms that allow us to mine social media information and translate it into relevant indicators. We proved this in the 2016 General Election, and because of each algorithm's reliability and accuracy, we have used them in this poll as well. I wanted to explain this in advance because there are certain questions for which we can only guess at the disparity in results."

Everyone nodded that they understood the set-up, and Harding smiled at McAllister, who passed the report copies to Franklin Pierce on his right. Pierce took one and continued passing the rest.

"If you turn to the executive summary, I would like to walk you through our results. I want to say that this is early in the campaign season, and we all know that these numbers are soft, but the remaining state's results are being tabulated in New York as we speak, and those appear to support the numbers in our report."

"The first question pertains to the President's job rating. You can see a clear disparity between the phone polling and the social media analysis."

"30% approval rating at this point of the campaign is a great floor to build on," Morrison said, sounding upbeat. "But I like the 56% from the social media."

"Don't get too excited, Trip," the President said, "that one is always a roller coaster."

Everyone smiled and offered brief comments on the fluctuation of polls numbers and the President's job approval by America. Rachael waited until the comments and affirmations to cease before proceeding.

"We are all familiar with the next question of the President's leadership."

Everyone saw the numbers – polling 45% versus 62% in social media.

"Our firm views the disparity between the two significant; however, we believe the social media portion indicates the real strength of the question."

There was a little Presidential ego boost, Hurst thought, but he let it go without expression. He reviewed the numbers and did not see anything to dispute what Harding was saying, but he was cautious and did not view them as anything more than a benchmark from which to compare all future evaluations. And then his eyes caught the next three questions, and his stomach rolled and could not help but feel vindication for the last four months.

"See something that caught your attention Carter?" the President asked.

"Yes, sir. I did not expect the numbers to be so close."

Harding watched, and the President added nothing further. She continued.

"Mr. President, your crime numbers, I believe, took us all by surprise at the firm. There is a strong correlation between the polling and social media numbers. Given your position on law and order issues, we expected you to rate highly in these areas. 58% and 60% are strong numbers this early in the campaign. As to the Virtual Life Solution, I think America has spoken, sir. The question is 'Do you agree the VLS should be used in the United States to incarcerate murder and other high crime inmates?' 81% poll, 84% social. 'Will the VLS make America more secure if implemented?' 87% poll, 90% social media. 'Do you feel that VLS inmates will be treated humanely when incarcerated?' 72% poll, 75% social medial. These are incredible numbers, Mr. President."

"Any insight as to why the numbers show that we have a high number that says Americans will be more secure yet less feel inmates will be treated humanely?" Pierce asked.

"We assess that the numbers are different because 90% of Americans agree the solution makes us safer, but 75% feel it is humane. Americans like the solution, but they also have a conscience. We expected something along this line would occur," she responded.

"Hell, yes, they like the solution," Morrison chimed in. "People want to feel safe. These numbers are pretty good this early in the campaign!"

"On page 22 of your report, you show that of the responses, 75% knew about VLS when questioned, so your results of VLS are based upon only 75% of the respondents," Hurst commented. "I understand the statics used to reach your numbers; but in your assessment, if the additional 25% were educated on VLS, would you expect the numbers to decrease the popularity of the program by 25%?"

"All of our numbers indicate that 25% more knowledgeable respondents may push the numbers down slightly, but given the numbers, even if you lose the full 25% off of a 90% response, you still have strong numbers approving of your program. Like all areas, these are also soft. We are working to put together the educational material to strengthen our message during the campaign. I think we can count on these to hold. VLS is designated a top domestic priority with our firm. We will make sure the numbers stay consistent."

"What is the break-out of women to men?" the AG wanted to know.

"53% of women, 47% men. A relatively strong sampling, our phone bank polled over 2500 respondents in each of the states. Social media was much higher."

"Ok, we've seen the VLS numbers, and I feel confident that this a solution that America can live with. Where do we go from here?" the President asked.

Morrison immediately pounced on the question.

"Mr. President, I think it is time for you to start including VLS in each of your public comments where you can work them in."

"I agree, Mr. President," Pierce said. "But sir, I feel you should strongly give credit to the administrations before you and their commitment to this effort. That way, VLS becomes an American Solution and not just something pushed by this administration. Each President that sat in this office while VLS was developed needs to be given credit for working VLS as part of their crime solution, even though they were probably surprised when the story broke."

"What do you think, Carter?"

"Mr. President, you are the one executing the solution. History will remember you for transforming our incarceration system and making our nation safer. We all know how the current system was built, but we have an opportunity to restore confidence in the people that this was a thought-out strategy by each president and not the work of civil servant with incredible vision. Give credit to the previous administrations and build the story of how both parties are working for America."

"Ms. Harding, your thoughts?"

"Mr. President, I believe we will see a measurable increase in your popularity numbers if your rhetoric with the American people is bi-partisan. An American solution works well in election years, and let's face it, Mr. President, there are not many programs like this one that can be declassified and have such an impact on society. If you take the 'win' sir but are generous in providing credit from now until the election to both parties, which also includes Congress, then you come across as humble and collaborative, something America thinks is missing in politics today."

The president looked at his Chief of Staff who nodded agreement.

"What else?"

Morrison retook the lead. "Mr. President, I believe that we also have to build on the VLS message by informing America of progress on the project. We have released the information, and the people are in favor of the solution."

"Your leadership numbers would see improvement with this approach, Mr. President," Harding added.

Morrison looked over at Carter. Carter knew that the hot potato was his now, and he needed to take it from here.

"Sir," he began choosing his words carefully. "We have seen the press downplay VLS and focus on the current state of the prison system. We need to counter this messaging. I would recommend we provide periodic, most likely quarterly VLS information to the media. These stories could highlight the number of new facilities built, the number of prisoners transferred, and dollars saved as we head into the election. This approach does the two things we want to accomplish. It keeps the story fresh in the minds of the voters and shows them real progress in capability and dollar savings."

"Who do you have in mind for providing the updates?"

"Mr. President, I would recommend keeping Alec Richardson at the front of the story. His reputation is solid, his name is associated with honest reporting and" Carter paused here knowing the next comment would give the President credit since Richardson was his choice for the first story, "he leans left, which means if he convinces his readers, their opinions will support our position." There was an agreement by all. The President smiled approval and nodded his head.

"Ok, Carter, make it happen."

The President looked over at McAllister.

"Alright, sounds like we have the direction to move towards based upon these numbers. Unless there are other questions, we're done here," McAllister said.

Everyone stood and almost together said, "Thank you, Mr. President," and exited the Oval Office. McAllister stayed behind as was typical for this type of meeting.

"Mr. President," he began. "I appreciate you allowing Ms. Harding to be part of the conversation. We will need her more frequently in our meetings as the campaign continues, and it's important to me that you can work with her."

"Aaron, I have confidence and trust in you. If you trust her, then so do I. You've never let me down. Anything else on the schedule?"

"No, Sir."

"Then go home. There will be plenty to deal with tomorrow."

"Goodnight, Mr. President."

The President looked at McAllister.

"Goodnight, Chief."

Aaron exited the Oval Office and headed to his desk. The President was finished for the night, but Aaron had about three more hours of work to do. You don't earn the President's trust and confidence by going home early.

CHAPTER 21

It was 8:17 p.m. when the Supervisor's cell phone rang, making an eerie noise in the silence of the facility. It was Carter Hurst.

"Do you have access to a TV?"

"Yes, just a moment while I turn it on."

The Supervisor was working at this desk in the Admin section of the facility. He clicked the icon on his desktop to open his TV application. His monitor transferred the display immediately to a large TV in his office.

"What channel?"

"CNN, Fox, MSNBC – just pick one. They're all running it."

One click and he had the live broadcast. On his screen was a local station, their show host talking to a woman in a remote studio with an ocean scene behind her. As the host asked his next question, the view of his studio dropped away and was replaced with a full shot of the women and a caption under her that read, "Katie Wilson, distressed wife of convicted felon and mother of three." The woman on his screen was mid-thirties, Caucasian, and her arms were wrapped around a young child sitting in her lap, aged somewhere around four – more to keep him from squirming while she talked, but the image of a desperate, protective mother was hard to mistake. Sitting next to her was a suited lawyer whose caption also ran under the screen and displayed Melvin

Perkins, esteemed defense attorney from Baton Rouge, Louisiana. Perkins looked at the mother and child very tenderly and then at the camera with professional grit as though he had a vendetta against the world. The Supervisor was able to deduce the question that he missed while turning on the TV. He knew immediately by the woman's response that there was a problem.

"I last visited my husband about six months ago. They said he murdered a man and his family. A jury put him in jail. We talked about this, and I forgave him for his sin. I told him that what he did was between him and Jesus. I know he wronged those people, so he is in prison to pay for his sins."

She started to cry slightly, the camera moving in just enough to see her tears and then catch her, wiping them away with one of her hands. The camera pulled back enough to see her lawyer, gently touch her shoulder to provide comfort while the tears fell.

"And what did you talk about the last time you saw him?"

"We talked about our family and how the boys missed their daddy and how I was dealing with not having him around to put food on the table. You know, family stuff like we always used to."

"And how often do you get to visit?"

"I try and get there to see him about once per month. More if my work lets me."

"And what happened last month?"

"When I showed up to visit, they told me that Ricky, that's my man, started a big fight with a guard and messed him up and that he was in solitary, and I couldn't see him."

"Did they tell you how long he would be in solitary confinement?"

"No, they didn't tell me anything. They were nice and said they was sorry but no one would give me any information about when I can see my man next. They said they could not tell me."

"And you went back yesterday, and what did they tell you?"

"Said he was still in solitary. Didn't know how long he would be there and that I should call before I come to the prison to check if he is out. Look, I know how prison works, but no one spends two months in solitary."

"Mrs. Wilson, prisoners have been known to spend long amounts of time in solitary, some as long as 35 years if they cannot conform with prison rules or are a threat to the guards," the host said.

"My husband ain't no threat to no guards!" She said, "They are keeping him from me for some reason. I need to see my husband. He needs to see his boys!"

Melvin Perkins took this opportunity of heightened emotions to first sooth his client's demeanor and then state, "This is highly unusual for this man's record of internment," he started, his Louisiana accent filling The Supervisor's office. "I plan to file the proper documents to get some answers for my client. If it turns out that this man was placed in VLS without my client's approval, we will be taking action against the federal government!"

"Jesus Christ!" Carter swore into the phone. "Did you hear that? Some bastard set this up to derail us. Tell me how you find the one woman in her circumstances and put her on TV to paint the problem as being bigger than it is. How in the hell are we going to deal with this?"

Carter was rambling. The Supervisor knew to let him finish his thoughts.

"Everybody with someone on death row or serving life is going to want to talk with their incarcerated loved ones because of this."

He paused for a moment as another phone call interrupted and signaled call waiting.

"That's the Speaker calling in now," Carter said. "He asked about this months ago. You told me you had an answer. He is going to have to wait!"

The call was sent to voicemail.

"Carter, I do have an answer, but like all things," the Supervisor said, slowly trying to diffuse his friend's temper. "You can't apply the answers we have to everyone. I am prepared to come in and brief my solution. When we can put the Committee together?"

"That's not going to work. Schedules are all over the place for the holidays, and next year is closing in fast."

"Okay, when can you come to the facility? I can have the team here, and we can lay it out for you. You can let me know what you think after you canvas each of the Committee members after we give you the information."

"So, what do I tell the Speaker tonight? He is going to want some...wait another call," he checked his phone. "It's the VP. I'm sure the Attorney General called him."

"Carter, tell them all that her husband is in solitary and that this is a one-off story. This story is staged. If you saw it was fake, then they saw it too. We will confirm here if we have the man as an inmate. In the meantime, have the VP direct the Press Secretary to encourage the public to visit their loved ones in prison. I am pretty sure the response will not be overwhelming for this group of people. For God's sake, they're in a high-security prison for a reason. You can stall the lawyer with normal government regulatory compliance for months. VLS has no precedent in the law. Look, this is a perception problem that translates to politics. YOU can handle the politics. When we meet, I will explain how we can keep this from happening again."

"Makes sense for the short term and answering the questions tonight. Sorry about the temper buddy. This is a high priority. How does tomorrow at 8:00 a.m. at the facility work?"

"You coming here?"

"I think it's time for a visit," Carter replied.

"8:00 is fine. Don't worry about your temper; you've been there enough for me."

The phone call ended, and the Supervisor was very glad he was not a politician. So far, politicians had screwed with his program, had him feeding information to Richardson for his article update, and used what should be a classified program to help win an election. Now, this. As he sat back in his chair and took a deep breath, another quote appropriate for DC came to mind as he contemplated his talk with Carter in the morning: "Power tends to corrupt, and absolute power corrupts absolutely. Great men are almost always bad men." He couldn't recall the source, but whoever said it, nailed it.

CHAPTER 22

O fficer Grant was getting nowhere with his search for Maggie on his own. He made a couple of inquiries with people around the station, but nothing that would indicate to them that he was missing a source. It was best to find the answer first and then bring it to the leadership.

Then finally, a break. Grant received the text from the phone that he and Maggie used to communicate yesterday at 11:03 am, and his relief was overwhelming. She was back from wherever she had been. He would be glad to see her. Grant assumed they would meet at the Washington Monument since that was his last signal. He pulled out his favorite Washington Capitals hat and placed it on his head. Maggie could always spot him coming when he wore his hat.

The day was overcast but mild for December, very typical for DC. "Jacket weather," he called it. The National Mall was unchanged, but around the fringe, buildings were conservatively decorated for the holidays. The Capital staff had decorated its People's tree two days ago. The White House tree in the Ellipse across the street, encircled by smaller trees with ornaments from each state, was visible from his vantage point on the north side of the monument. Tonight, this area would be alive with activity and lights as the Ellipse washed Washington in holiday colors from each of the trees and their thousands of tree lights. Grant loved the holidays.

It was 11:02, and Maggie still had not arrived. Tourists

passed by chatting about holiday plans, but otherwise, he owned the monument. And then he saw him. A tall black man dressed in a dark suit and wearing an overcoat began to walk

to the memorial from the direction of 14th Street. He felt his heart race, increasing the blood flow through his body, and he could feel the sweat accumulating under his arms and on his back. His mind sharpened as Grant began to scan his surroundings for a second man. He could not see one, but he knew the routine if they were going to take him. The first would make contact and engage him with a conversation, and a second would join them shortly afterward. Then the two would explain their real purpose and carefully walk him to a waiting vehicle. He looked for a parked car and saw none that stood out, but knew it could always drive up when they approached the street. His mind began to analyze every piece of information as his police training came into focus. The monument area did not possess trees or shrubs to conceal a second man, so he would have time to see him coming. He touched the breast of his jacket to remind himself that he was armed. They would be armed as well. Even though both sides would be carrying, Grant knew there would never be a shoot-out on the mall.

The man was getting closer, and with each step, Grant became cooler; more resolved to deal with the developing situation. One last check showed there was not a second guy. As the man got closer, he knew by the man's physical size that he could take him if it came to that. Confidence returned. He was back in control.

Grant turned to face the monument as though examining its construction when the man approached. Grant watched him closely with his peripheral vision. Ten feet away, five feet, and then he passed behind him. Grant turned his head to look at his back. The man stopped and looked at him and asked, "Officer Grant?"

"Who wants to know?" Grant asked in his deepest, most

threatening voice.

"Darnell Washington," he said.

"So, who are you? I don't know a Darnell Washington."

"I'm Jada Washington's son. You call her Maggie. She said you would be wearing a ratty old Caps hat if I ever needed to meet you. She was right about the hat."

Grant was shocked by the man's comment and disrespect to his hat. He looked closer at Darnell, standing in front of him and could see her features in his face. Grant was convinced this man was who he claimed.

"Don't take this the wrong way, brother, but why the suit?" Grant asked as the reality of who he was talking with started to relax him.

Washington turned and pointed to the African Museum.

"I work there. I'm a manager. They like us to wear a tie."

Grant nodded. He surmised that Maggie was still missing, but had other questions first.

"How did you know to find me here?"

"Mom told me she was working with 'the locals.' That's how she referred to you. She said if anything ever happened to her that there was a special place in her bedroom closet that would have instructions for how to reach you. I found a box right where she said it would be. It had the cell phone and her notes about how to contact you. I picked up the coin by the Kiosk yesterday. Here I am."

"Any idea where she could be?"

"Mom worked in a lot of places around the city. I thought she might be staying at one of them or be sick and in a hospital. She still may be at one of them. I just don't know. I did check the hospitals, but I didn't find anyone with her name."

"How often did you see her?"

"I never knew when mom would visit; she would just be knocking on my door or sitting on the stoop when I got home from work, maybe six times a year."

"Any other way that you and your mom communicated.

Did she call you, email, anything that we might be able to build a timeline from?"

"No, she was not much for technology or reaching out to me. She told me once that using a cell phone to text always hurt her brain."

"Yeah, I get that. Maggie told me the same thing."

Both men enjoyed the moment of imagining her figuring out a text message emoji on the phone and sending the message and laughed.

"So, what do you know about her visiting a funeral home in South East?" Grant asked, getting right to the point.

Washington looked at him a moment as if deciding to get to know Grant better before saying anything. Grant picked up on his apprehension and said, "If we don't talk, we can't find her."

Darnell, nodded his head in agreement. "She told me she received a tip from someone on the street that strange things were happening at a funeral home that she knew. Mom said that she went to check it out and watched guys offload new caskets for the home. Then one of the guards with a gun told her to leave."

"Does it strike you as odd that the home would offload their shipment at night?"

"Not really, Grant. I have seen stranger things, but..."

And they both finished the sentence together, "but not with armed guards."

"What was in those coffins?" Darnell asked.

Grant thought about withholding his part of the story but considered otherwise. If he was going to find Maggie, he needed to share it all.

"Look, Darnell, I don't want you to think that I am crazy, but I went to the home and witnessed the same thing your mother did with one exception."

"What was that?"

"It was raining hard the night I was there. I saw the fork-lift and the caskets just like your mom. But then one slipped.

I guess things got wet, and the coffin slid off the lift. It hit the ground hard and opened."

He paused, contemplating one last time if it was wise to tell Darnell.

"So, coffin hits the ground?" Darnell said. "What happened?"

"There was a man inside, wrapped in a weird suit with lights, and it looked like there were some lights in the coffin as well. It was tough to see with the rain. So when the coffin opened, this man rolled out, and this other guy doesn't hesitate at all. He walks over, pulls his piece, and puts three rounds into the guy's head on the ground."

"What! No way, man. Did anyone call the cops? Someone must have heard the shots."

"I don't know if the guy had a silencer or if the rain covered the sound, but even where I was, it was hard hearing the shots. And no, the cops did not show up."

"Are you telling me someone is shooting dead people?"

"That was the same question that I had. I have not told anyone at the station because they will think I'm crazy, and my boss doesn't like a problem without an answer."

"I get it, I get it."

"She mentioned that one of her people came to her with this info about the home and the armed men. She said he disappeared. Your mom said he was afraid that he'd witnessed something he was not supposed to and that someone was coming for him."

"Aw, man! So you think my mom is all tied up in this somehow?"

"There is a good chance, Darnell. I have been doing research and trying to track down everything I can on the home, owners, strange things happening in the surrounding neighborhood, and nothing comes up, either on the net or through our police databases."

"You say you saw what looked like lights inside the coffin?"

"Yes, but again, it was raining hard, and between the rain and the lights from cars passing by out front, it could have been anything."

Grant looked over at Darnell, and he was staring into the monument, thinking hard about something.

"Let's go sit down, Grant. I might know what's going on. I want to talk you through this."

Grant nodded, and the two men walked around and found one of the many benches that lined the mall and took a seat.

"Okay, what are you thinking, Darnell?"

"Now it's my turn to be crazy. There was a lot of press a while back that talked about a government program that was for the worst criminals. I read the article in the paper but didn't think much about it."

"I must have missed it. I know some of the uniforms are talking about some new badass system for prisoners, but I haven't given much thought to it."

"I think that's the one, Grant. If I remember right, this new prison would take something the size of Alcatraz and crunch it down into something smaller than a city block. Supposed to save all kinds of money…"

"And what?" Grant asked.

"Supposed to use some new technology. Something about putting murderers into something called the SOUP. Hold a second."

Darnell reached into his pocket and pulled out his cell phone, launched the *Washington Guardian* app, and searched for the word SOUP. "Yea, here it is. 'Federal Government Declassifies New Maximum Security Incarceration Solution.'" This was all over social media and the news a month or so ago. Name of the program is Virtual Life Solution, or VLS."

"Can I see that?" Grant said, reaching for the phone.

Darnell handed his phone to him, and Grant scrolled down the pages cussing to himself that he did not bring his reading glasses. He had a tough time making out the article's text and handed the phone back.

"Read me that part about the technology."

Darnell scrolled down.

"Advanced Artificial Intelligence will provide the backbone for the Virtual Reality of each inmate. Each inmate will exist inside a world created by them for the remainder of their time on earth in what is called the Secure Operational Unfenced Prison or SOUP."

"Does the article say where this place is located?"

Darnell swiped up and down the screen like a ninja master, keying on highlighted words and quickly swiping down to review each paragraph. After a short moment, he shook his head.

"Nothing."

Grant cussed to himself again. The answer to Maggie's disappearance was related to this VLS stuff, and it was in the paper of all places, right in front of him! He just missed it. This had to be the answer. That was Grant's only logical conclusion.

"How would my mom be involved with a maximum-security prison system, Grant?"

"I don't know, Darnell; but I think this is the missing piece. I was so busy focusing on the funeral home. I missed it! Damn!"

"What are you saying, Grant? That the feds have a prison in a funeral home in DC?"

Grant's head was starting to hurt. His brain felt like it was running at top speed, but he still was getting no answers that added up.

"Could be. I know it sounds crazy, but this whole thing is crazy from the start. Here, let me give you my card," Grant said, reaching into his back pants pocket and pulling one from his wallet. "Use the phone number there to reach me if you find out anything more. We can get rid of the coin contact stuff for now. This is no longer about a drug bust and gang shootings."

"What would you like me to do?"

"Look for anything that will help us find your mom. This case has taken a different twist and given me a new direction to pursue. Call me with anything new about VLS, whether you think it's important or not."

Darnell agreed.

"One more thing Darnell, you knew your mom was providing me information? You know I am a cop, so I need to know: did she ever tell you why she did it?"

Darnell smiled as he thought, then looked Grant in the eyes.

"She told me it was her way to help the people in her community. The press portrays our culture as rappers, gangsters, and professional athletes. Our celebrities come off that way, but 'that is not all of us' she used to say. Blacks are also school teachers, scientists, and in just about every honorable profession available to any person, regardless of color. We don't hear about those jobs much, so we are sending the wrong message to our kids. Keeping drugs out of the home and off the street was her way of making life better for others so that they could have opportunities in life." Darnell paused for a moment, reflecting on his mother's life choices. "She always said you were one of the good ones, and she trusted you. Your relationship was an important part of her purpose in life. I always used to tell her that she would never end up with a display in our museum, but she should. She is a real hero to me."

Darnell's story was close to what Maggie shared with him once. This final confirmation is what Grant needed to hear. He reached out and shook Darnell's hand. Grant knew he could trust this man. Darnell possessed many of the traits that he admired and knew Maggie was the reason.

"We are going to find your mom. Don't give up hope."

"Mom was right about you, I can tell. I'll be in touch."

The two men parted company. As Darnell headed back to work at the African American Museum and Grant headed to his car near the Red Cross building, the clouds opened up, and the rain started.

"I hope this is not a sign of things to come," Grant said as he quickened his pace to reach his car before he was soaked.

He entered the vehicle and threw his ratting Cap's hat in the seat next to him, and then a stray thought crossed his mind, "I wonder if he has a girlfriend?"

CHAPTER 23

C arter Hurst was impressed with the facility. The Warden gave him the tour before bringing him to the conference room. Now that Carter had witnessed the facility first hand, he was in awe of his friend's accomplishments.

"This is quite a marvel you've built here," Carter said, fixing himself a cup of coffee.

"We are very pleased with the facility and the integrity of the systems we've built. Each day continues to prove that our concept is technologically reliable. We've encountered zero problems with the inmate's or maintaining the VLS environment," the Warden responded.

Carter acknowledged the comment with a head nod and said, "Very impressive indeed," and chucked his wooden stirrer in the trashcan. "Ok, let's get down to business."

As if on cue, Dr. O'Neil and Mr. UT walked into the conference room.

"Dr. O'Neil," Carter said, "Good to see you again" and reached out with his hand and touched her shoulder to validate she was not a hologram as was the case the last time he saw her.

"Always good to see you, Senator," smiling as she spoke to confirm she understood the shoulder touch.

"Senator, you remember Mr. UT, our Chief Scientist and geneticist."

Again, Cater nodded and shook UT's hand. UT looked

Carter in the eye and calmly said, "Senator," then took his seat.

The room darkened, and the TV blinked on. The TV worked through its turn-on cycle displaying its mode and HDMI connection for any that were interested and then snapped the first slide into view for all to see. It read, "Inmate Visitation – Courses of Action."

"Senator, would you like to give the team some background on the topic?" The Supervisor asked. He knew his team understood the context of the discussion, but he was hoping that Carter would share additional information from conversations he had after the media report on TV.

"Sure," he said, slightly surprised by the opportunity to speak. "The Program has approved funding for four more locations: Atlanta, New York, Chicago, and Los Angeles. You probably know that all R&D will move, if not already, to Arlington. This funding came with a couple of strings attached, one of which was a question asked by the Speaker of the House about how we would do visitation after moving inmates into VLS."

Carter surveyed the room and saw that each person knew this information.

"I thought I would be able to give you some time to find a solution for this basic question, but as we have confirmed, an organization that does not want VLS implemented was able to get the media to provide coverage for an event they staged. You confirmed the inmate was not here, nor in any prison and we passed this information to the major news channels via back channels. When they found out the event was a hoax, they retracted the story. While everyone on the Hill and in White House knew it was staged, it created a public backlash to the program by focusing on the human side of our incarceration system. Americans want bad people in jail, but they believe they are entitled to see their families. This got everyone's attention because people vote based upon these types of issues. I want to emphasize that the program is not in jeopardy. Your funding and transfer schedule is intact, but this administration wants an answer to this question. That's what brings us here today."

The Supervisor said, "Any questions for the Senator?" and paused.

Dr. O'Neil took up the offer.

"Senator, any indication of how the public feels about VLS? I am sure that there's been sufficient time now to put a least one poll in the field."

"The public is very supportive of the program. Americans believe it improves public security, and a clear majority stand behind VLS. However, people still want inmates to be treated humanely. Our latest polls still show strong numbers for the program, but we don't want to take a chance that something like visitation could cause a problem for us on Election Day. Any other questions?"

No one had any. The Warden took control of the remote and moved to the next slide. It read, "Option 1 – New Policy." The pie chart showed the percentage of high-security inmates as well as a historical line chart showing the average number of visitation requests made per year by facility. The third graph showed the number of visitations made for the previous year. The Warden took the lead.

"Our first recommendation is intended to not only answer the question but serve as an additional deterrent to crime. We believe that there is no legal precedent for VLS in the courts, and we need to move quickly with the public to establish how our system will work. We recommend that we announce publicly that because of the technology used, and the unique way in which we incarcerate, that we set a policy to deny visitation to inmates in VLS. It's simple, and it's clean."

"You do know Ms. Warden that we are about to enter into an election year and want this program showcased as a major domestic success. That agenda is what was used to justify much of the funding you have received," Carter said.

"Yes, Senator, we do. But we also have the factual data behind the number of personnel that visit inmates in high security. It's not that large a number, and the administration's messaging could focus on a new future that highlights the program's advantages, each of which the public knows about as well. We believe that candidates can emphasize that people who murder will not receive this benefit anymore, much like inmates in federal prisons are denied conjugal visits in but a handful of states. Who passed that policy, Senator that sex was not allowed in prison between visiting spouses or partners?"

The Supervisor grinned slightly as his friend was thinking about how to answer the straightforward question posed to him.

Carter looked at the Warden.

"I truly don't know Ms. Warden; but whoever did, surely did not make that policy during an election year."

Carter's answer provided a short break from the seriousness of the discussion as everyone laughed, knowing the power of the image in an election year.

"Next option, please," Carter directed.

The Warden clicked the remote, and the next slide appeared. It read, "Option 2 – Notify people on the visitation list before terminating visitation rights."

It, too, contained additional information that showed timelines before VLS transfer and a chart of costs for counselors and social workers to prepare and educate family members about VLS.

"This option, Senator, gives the public a period; a visitation window if you will, to visit before the inmate enters into the SOUP. This option introduces counseling and education as part of the process to prepare family members for the inmate's transfer as well as the inmate. This option prevents the 'rip the Band-Aid off' in option number 1. We believe this is the more humane route and gives everyone a chance to say good-bye. The deterrence message is evident. We can present VLS as the most positive of the life options for the inmate when compared to regular incarceration. It provides the health care in Richardson's story as well as a new life that the inmate can decide how to live. This, we believe, will give comfort to the family. The risk is that non-incarcerated people with terrible lives will see the SOUP as a place for them and begin to commit serious crimes. This phenomenon is something that we have started to study."

Carter ran through the option in his mind. If the media could be used to show a distraught women missing her husband because he is in solitary, then leading to the election, he could see the horror as screaming children calling for their father with outstretched arms and tears streaming down their little faces as they are ripped away by federal guards leading their parent to be put in the SOUP while the mother cries in grief. Carter had to live through separating kids from parents at the border facilities. He witnessed enough of family separations with heart-wrenching scenes. They made him doubt the policy even though he understood its merits completely. Option 2 would not work in an election year.

"Option 2 shows the compassion that we want to show for our inmates. Unfortunately, where compassion exists, so does the opportunity to exploit the emotion that builds as families know the separation day is coming. The press does not take an interest in normal incarceration nor show on TV the emotion of an inmate entering a normal prison. This is because Americans know that inmates can be visited, even the worst of the worst. This option will be like providing a death sentence to the family. With foreknowledge that they will never see a loved one again, even though the inmate's sentence is life," Carter paused. "Not in an election year. This option would be tough in any year."

"But again, sir, there is the message of deterrence. If criminals know that this is where they will end up, it could deter criminal activity," Dr. O'Neil added.

"Ms. Warden commented that this could come back on us. People with no hope could begin committing terrible crimes because they know they will go into the SOUP, be cared for physically, and be able to create a new life for themselves. That's going to be the next problem you will have to solve." Unwilling to discuss this option further, Carter asked, "What's the next option?"

The Warden clicked the remote, and a new slide appeared. It read "Option 3 – Do nothing," and the rest of the slide was blank.

"What this?" Carter asked.

The Supervisor weighed in. "Senator, every course-of-action discussion considers the status quo. In many cases, it may be the best option. I used to ask my teams long ago, that if we were in the mouse removal business, why take years and resources to create a new mousetrap and build a new engineering marvel? Why not just get a faster cat that can catch the mice? It's cheaper and gets the job done quickly."

The Senator had to smile. He understood the message. Stay the course and continue to act as though there is no problem. To hell with the politics and weather the storm. Unfortunately, his friend and he both realized that politics was the storm. If only this program were still classified, but he couldn't think that now. The toothpaste was out of the tube and not going back in. They needed another option. The Speaker would demand it.

"Senator, if we did nothing, what would be the impact on the campaign?" the Warden asked. "The American people know about the program. They approve of the program. Instead of providing an answer to the question about visitation, why not delay the transfer schedule? Allow visitation until after the election, then implement one of the new policies."

The Supervisor interjected himself.

"Your idea is a good one, Ms. Warden, but there is a way to maintain our schedule and still handle visitation. Our new facilities will be online this summer, and inmates will begin transferring. We can prioritize those in supermax facilities. These prisoners are in solitary most of the time. Then, those in high-security that have received no visitations to date. We can rank order those that are visited from less to more frequently at the end of the transfer. By law, an inmate gets about four hours of visiting time per month. We can work with facility wardens to start shortening the length and number of visits. It's not perfect, but this will all help."

The Supervisor paused.

"However, we are building enough capacity to house 35,000 more inmates," he remarked. "Currently, there are 22,000 incarcerated in high security. We WILL have this whole population transferred by the end of next year. We may not have time to delay. Ms. Warden, look into this."

The Warden had already looked into transfer delay impacts and knew there was no time in the schedule. Her boss was leading up to something. Carter responded to the approach.

"Prioritizing inmate transfer sounds right, but the risk is still high for more negative coverage. The press will know when we close the facilities. Disgruntled guards out of a job will go to the media as well unless we find them other employment. All of the short-term negatives of a new program like this will surface during the campaign without anyone realizing that the problems will work themselves out in a year. We cannot afford that exposure. We need a solution that the press cannot use. We need a solution that is invisible until we get through the election."

The room was silent. Dr. O'Neil looked at the Warden, and then the Supervisor. UT studied the look on Carter's face, which was starting to show desperation. The Supervisor looked at the Warden, and she handed him the remote; a clear signal to all in the room that whatever happened next, the Supervisor was going to lead it personally.

"We have one more option, Senator." *Okay Carter, here it comes*, the Supervisor thought. *I've offered you three plausible solutions and here comes the one that we shouldn't adopt.* It was controversial, but it could be executed and meet the objectives that Senator Hurst wanted, like keeping the press in the dark about it.

"Let's hear it."

The Supervisor displayed the next slide. It read "Family Protection Program (FPP)."

"Senator, Option 4 is what we call the FPP. It's an option that focuses on the future development of the program while also keeping the press uninformed."

"What do you mean, the future of the program?" Carter asked as he leaned forward in his chair and put his arms on the conference room table.

"The priorities of this option are as follows," and he clicked the remote for the next slide. The slide displayed the following bulleted phrases, and The Supervisor continued:

"1. Create a second community with inmate records not generated by murder or crime.

2. Improve methods for jumpstarting the new reality.

3. Finalize Testing and Implement Cause and Effect Scenarios (CES).

4. Develop Last Memory Jumpstarting (LMJ)."

"What is this?" Hurst asked, the skepticism in his voice evident.

"It's a shift in priorities Senator," the Supervisor responded. "If we have to find a solution to visitation without press awareness then this accomplishes your objective."

"How?"

"By removing the visitation problem."

Carter Hurst looked intently at the screen, reading each line waiting for the next explanation of the program.

"I would like to start by discussing the research into improving our Jumpstarting methods," the Supervisor began.

"Wait," Carter interrupted, "what do you mean Last Memory Jumpstarting?"

The Supervisor paused as though offended that Hurst had interrupted him, then continued.

"At present, each inmate retains their last memory in Real Space when we put them into the SOUP. This memory is what they see at their death during CT because we erase the

VLS memories when the crown is disconnected," Dr. O'Neil answered.

"Okay – I remember that from your brief to the Committee. If I heard you right, you are looking for ways to change their last memory. Why?"

The Supervisor responded.

"If we can Jumpstart them with a memory that formed before they committed a crime, then if we ever bring them out of VLS..."

Carter finished for him, showing comprehension of the concept to the team.

"Then, in theory, you could reform the inmate by having his reality in this world begin before their criminal activity. A process like this would allow them to leave VLS with no memory of committing any crime in their life. They will have served their time and debt to society in VLS but have no memory of any of their crimes in Real Space. From their perspective, they re-enter society years older but as a crime-free citizen. It's as if they were in a coma and just lost the years or traveled backward in time and erased their crimes."

"I would not jump to time travel, but I understand your analogy, Senator. We have a variety of scientific and psychological challenges to overcome before we get there, but that's the general idea," Dr. O'Neil said.

"This opens up the possibility of all sentences and all inmates," Carter said slowly, letting the words he just heard filter into the right processing centers of his mind.

"But it will only work if we can provide them with memory scenarios that reinforce positive cause and effect events. We believe that if we use these scenarios, we can introduce memories that will TEACH them how to live a better life. They may lose each of their VLS memories when they return to Real Space, but their minds will remember the concepts taught during the experience. I am referring to the auto reflex of the hand and other body functions programmed into our subconscious. When we teach the brain, it does not require it to remember how it learned, it just does. Imagine the world we could live in, Senator, if all jail time resulted in 90-100% reform of the inmate?"

Carter got the idea, and then he understood what was actually being proposed.

"Wait, let's go back to what you said earlier. How did you say it? 'We remove the visitation problem'. It sounds like you are telling me you need new, non-criminal people to go into the SOUP to build a new community and make your trials work! What the hell are you thinking? We can't police up people in this country and put them in VLS! This is not Nazi Germany."

"You wanted a solution that did not involve the press, so we are giving you one," the Supervisor said, a steeled focus in his voice as he responded to his friend's accusations. "Hear me out, Senator!"

The team in the room was shocked. They never heard the Supervisor raise his voice. Usually frosty cool, he let a momentary spike in frustration cause him to reveal his inner passion. The Supervisor quickly regained his measured and calculating temperament, aware of this momentary breach.

"The mission of this program is to protect society from its worst criminals while providing a humane existence for those criminals as they repay their debt to society. The FPP is an extension of that mission."

"How so?" Carter asked, still simmering from the last suggestion.

"Mr. UT – could you explain the science behind our ideas?"

"Yes, sir."

It was apparent that his role with the program now brought him front and center in discussion with the Senator. It was also evident by observing UT's body language that he did not favor this option.

"Studies conducted as early as this year show that there are two main reasons why science believes people will commit terrible crimes. The first is related to their environment, with some studies suggesting that child abuse plays a major role in creating criminal behavior. The second is genetics."

"Are you saying that people are born to commit murders?"

"No sir, what I am saying is that science has identified several genes that they can correlate with violent behavior disorders in children and adults. One is called the Warrior Gene or a derivation of Monoamine oxidase A called MAOA and another called..."

"Mr. UT – Warrior gene is good. My degrees are in Political Science and Law."

Carter smiled, now visibly cooled after the outburst with the Supervisor, and UT received the message about explaining the complexity of the human genetic code.

"Yes, Senator. We believe that a combination of gene sequences produce many of the violent and anti-social behaviors leading to crime. Behaviors like Antisocial Personality Disorder (ASPD) diagnosed in adults over 18 years old, and Conduct Disorder (CD) found in children help to predict criminality. Some believe that children with CD will evolve into ASPD when they become adults. When behavioral disorders combine with a negative social environment, there is positive evidence that individuals with these genes commit the most terrible crimes."

"Thank you, Mr. UT," the Supervisor said and continued the brief. "Senator, this last option is to identify family members of our inmates and place them in the SOUP. This accomplishes several things. The first involves the press. Those most likely to make a legitimate complaint will no longer be accessible to the media. This move will drastically reduce the number of incidents involving the media like we experienced with the fake story."

He waited to gauge the reaction of Carter. There was none. Carter was looking straight ahead into the dim room, letting his mind absorb all that was said.

"Secondly, the genetic information contained within each of these people will assist us with our research and our ability to understand how their genes link to criminality. We would do this by assessing the data in the FPP community. If large amounts of crime records begin to emerge, we will have stronger evidence that genetics causes the behavior. The downside will be if they come from an abusive home in Real Space. This could prevent us from isolating the cause of genetics, but we *can study it* in VLS better than any scientist in Real Space. Think of the contribution we can make to eliminating crime because we know what causes it. We will know for sure if it is the environment because, with Cause and Effect scenarios, we can CREATE the environment.

Lastly, we need data on how to re-integrate back into society. This test group could create huge breakthroughs for us and allow us to formulate a solution for reform. One day, each of these people can be re-integrated when we possess the right solution to do so. I know what you are thinking, but we have the tools and an incredible solution at our disposal to create a free and safe society for the world. Imagine what we could do as a species if we did not fear crime or lose some of our brightest minds early in life because of violence."

The Supervisor made his last point and stopped. He looked over at Carter again, and the two men locked eyes.

"I would like to talk to you alone," Carter said.

The team understood Carter's reluctance to discuss this with the group present. They stood and departed the conference room. When the door closed, Carter began.

"We are moving down a very slippery slope here."

"Carter, think about what we can achieve. We are only dealing with a couple of hundred relevant people. Their lives will be better in the SOUP."

"Children too! I mean, how could we ever justify something like this?"

"We are not dealing with the tip of our society here."

"Bullshit! They are people! Are you so obsessed with

215

avenging your family that you would put innocent people in the VLS?"

"Don't start that, Carter. My family plays a part in what I do, but this is about numbers and solving your political problem. Most of these kids will be on the streets, rolling the homeless before they are 15 to get cash for weed and booze. Then they start the armed robbery, and then it goes from there. You know the numbers. We are helping them."

"Really? What is my political problem? Tell me, smart guy – what the hell do you know?"

"I know that the President doesn't understand this as we do. He wants to use this to get elected while pretending that there are no bumps with this thing. POTUS cannot have it both ways, and you are trying to give him that. The VP is breathing down your neck because he wants something to carry into his Presidential campaign five years from now. Then there is the Speaker that wants an answer to his question about visitation. I'm an operator, not a politician. You and your group on the Hill and the White House are making my life a living nightmare. You want solutions so your people can win elections. Well, this is the best we have. This would not be my answer, but it's the one I am offering to resolve this situation. So let's minimize our risk by taking away the media that can cause those bumps and recognize the scientific benefits to this program. If we have to do this option, let's focus on the benefits to the program."

Hurst nodded his head in agreement.

"Tell me the VP would not be indebted to you if we could solve the crime problem in this nation and get him elected. Wouldn't the Speaker appreciate an answer to his question? Think about what it means to this country. I do not want to see civil unrest and anarchy in my lifetime. Our government, or at the least justice system, is going to change if we do not act! You know it as well as I do."

Hurst heard his friend and could not dispute his conclusions. "Why do we have to take the whole family? I understand the genetic tie with the children, but the mother is not going to have the same genetics as the kid?"

"It has to be both. We can't take kids *from* their parents. Look, I know this sounds cruel, but look at what we can DO with VLS. Is the elimination of crime worth a couple hundred people that will be reintegrated into society anyway? They will LIVE their lives, Carter. It just won't be in our reality."

"You're a bastard; you know that."

"No, Carter. Your political problems are forcing me to offer recommendations and make decisions that I would never consider. You call me a bastard, but here YOU are looking for an answer from me."

Hurst knew his friend was right. He wanted him to just make this problem go away without having to get involved. The Supervisor went on.

"Let me put it this way, Carter: 'Great men are almost always bad men.' You've heard me say this many times before and it has always guided us. We've had to make tough decisions before but still found a way to do our jobs and not compromise our integrity. This time it's different. So which way do you want it? You can't be a part of history without getting dirty. If you want to make sure your leadership has four more years, then you are going to have to get in the mud with the rest of us. You are not going to pawn off this decision on me. You have a problem, and you are coming to me to fix it. To achieve the greater good, Carter, someone has to make the hard decisions. This one is yours."

"Don't tell me what I have to do!"

"We all have to do something that will alienate the few that do not benefit, and then let history judge us. Can you make the decision now that I am asking you to make, not for me but for America? I ask again, isn't the lives of this small group worth wiping out crime in our country?"

"If I remember your quote, there is also something about power and corruption that comes before your platitude. You are letting the power of your program and desire to fix the wrongs of years ago cloud your judgment," Hurst spoke through his anger.

"Well, Carter, I assure you, I am not the one corrupted by power; that's for you to figure out. I am trying to be a patriot and do something for this country. The science and what we can solve is the only way I can justify recommending this option."

Carter was not going to fence with his friend any longer. He knew that he would lose the battle of intellect with him. It was time to leave.

"You have given me something to contemplate. I need to talk with a majority of the Committee members and solicit their ideas. I will get back to you with an answer in about three days."

"Thank you, Carter. I look forward to hearing from you. One of the guards will take you out."

Agent Willis escorted Carter Hurst out of the facility via the main elevator. The Supervisor sat in the conference room and contemplated his next moves. He knew the answer would come back to execute. There was too much riding on this program; and there was even more VLS could accomplish. The Committee would see the numbers, and the decision would be academic. One thing about Carter he could rely on: he understood that decisions like this were not always easy but that his is the way you made history. The Supervisor could trust his friend to do the right thing for America. This was the only workable option for Hurst, and they were working to save their government. Progress was being made.

CHAPTER 24

It was a beautiful February morning as Andrew Cheatham drove to Harris Middle School in Shelbyville, Tennessee. He loved his job as a school Principal and found great personal satisfaction in watching his middle schoolers grow into young adults. Andrew was especially proud of how his students were performing in the classroom and the staff of teachers that led them to success. The sun brightened up his little paradise and reflected off of the school windows sparkling like a diamond cutting light as he turned into the parking lot. He turned off the engine and sat for a moment, reflecting on his joy filled life and offering a short prayer for the morning and his day ahead.

He was met by a cool breeze when he opened his car door and felt himself fill with happiness as he acknowledged his place in God's world. He was very content as he walked to the entrance of the building. The students were still at their bus stops, waiting for their bright yellow taxis to pick them up and bring them to another day of learning. His secretary Margie Cooper was already in, leaning down and hidden below the counter that separated the students from Cheatham's office. She was preparing for the day when he walked into the outer area of the central administrative office. For many students and their parents, sitting on the other side of the counter with butterflies in their stomachs waiting for Cheatham to call them into the Principal's Office was the ultimate reward for his hard work. He was a benevolent principal and always thought about his student's and community's best interests. Andrew still enjoyed the idea that "going to the Principal's office" was something that could work magic as well. He used that magic and his pleasant demeanor to fix problems. It was a combination of authority and forgiveness, just like the Good Book taught. He took pride in knowing that he set many on a path to doing the right thing.

"Morning, Mr. Cheatham," the voice from behind the counter said.

Then Margie Cooper stood for him to see as she finished arranging her desk. She was wearing her winter colors, he noticed: black pants with a brown tweed jacket and conservative white turtleneck.

"How did you know it was me?"

"Who else would it be this early in the morning? Coffee is almost finished brewing. I will bring you a cup shortly."

"Thank you, Margie."

He retrieved his keys from his pocket, unlocked the door to his office, and walked inside. His office was filled with sunlight, pushing through the upward facing Venetian blinds in a way that allowed him to see his computer screen in the early morning. He sat in his chair and watched the dust particles float through the air, reflecting in the sunlight. Margie walked in with his coffee and placed it on his desk.

"I can tell that you love this morning, but you need to focus, Mr. Cheatham. It's seven-thirty now, and we know what happens in fifteen minutes," she said, smiling.

"Ten more minutes to enjoy the quiet. Thanks for bringing in the coffee."

"You are always welcome. Been bringing it for 4 four years, and every day you say, 'Thank you.' It makes me feel appreciated," she said as she bent down and pushed the start button on his computer hidden under his desk and then exited.

Cheatham turned in his chair and stared out the window. The machine fan started to whirl to life, and the computer beeped once to indicate everything was working correctly. Then the hard drive began its morning routine to load the operating system. When he turned in his chair, his login screen was displayed. *Okay, time to work*, he thought and took the first drink of his coffee. He clicked the mail icon on the bottom of his screen, and his mail opened, taking the five seconds or so to load his new messages. He scrolled down the screen and saw a new arrival from one of his parents and opened it first. It read:

> *Dear Mr. Cheatham,*
> *I am sorry to tell you that Franklin and I are moving from Shelbyville and heading to be near relatives in Virginia. This was a decision I planned on making a while ago. Things in my family are not good, and they need me there now. I will put Franklin in school there, and my sister has given me the address so you can send his records. Please send them to Jefferson- Houston School 1600 Cameron St, PO Box 35 Alexandria, VA 22314. Thank you.*
> *Amanda Davis.*

Cheatham sat back in his chair. He felt this was all very sudden. But these things do happen, especially with women like her. Ever since she arrived in Shelbyville about two years ago, she was a woman waiting for a scandal. It was no secret that she was married to a man in prison. Some said her husband was in for murder. Looking at her, he could understand why he might have been driven to kill a man. She would show up at his PTA meetings in those low-cut shirts and tight shorts, long red hair, and those twinkly eyes. She tried hard to fit in and even volunteered for some of the PTA events, but the other women did not care for her, and behind her back, she was labeled every name from the Bible that applied to fallen women. With some difficulty, he admitted to himself that he always tried to sneak a peek at what was under those shirts. When Andrew talked with her, he had to make an effort to stay focused on her eyes, but even her eyes would make him think things. *Satan will tempt us all,* he told himself. *I am sorry that she had to leave. I'm going to miss her.*

He moved in his chair, uncomfortable at the new thoughts running through his mind, and took another drink of his coffee. Amanda's son was another matter. He was a hellion beyond what normal boys are at his age. Always in trouble in class, unable to sit still, disrespectful to his teachers, and picking fights with other boys on the playground. The boy could claim a middle school rap sheet as long as your arm. He had gotten to know Franklin more than he liked and spent many hours in his office with the boy trying to get him to understand the straight and narrow ways of life. All to no avail. When Amanda would come in for a meeting with him, she would always bring her beauty and the smell of lavender. During the first meeting with her, he was alone; so it was just the two of them. That was a terrible night for him as Andrew recounted the temptation he fought. After that, he always asked Ms. Cooper or the teacher who was having a problem with Franklin to sit in the office during the meeting. This development now presented a mixed blessing: Franklin was no longer his student to try and teach, but he would miss his mother. He clicked the print icon and took another drink of his coffee. When done, he walked it out to Ms. Cooper. *I could have just forwarded her this.* Well, it didn't matter now.

"Ms. Cooper, I am sad to say that Amanda Davis and her son have moved due to family problems and are now in Virginia. Here is the forwarding address for sending his records."

"That will be a big file to send. That poor school has no idea what they are getting with that mother and son."

"No doubt, Franklin was a handful; but I thought his mom tried hard to raise him right," he offered.

Margie Cooper looked at Mr. Cheatham for a moment, her eyes focused and narrowed as though she needed to pray for his soul. *Maybe she is right to look at me that way,* he thought. It's hard to eat good cookies when Satan's hand is in the cookie jar. Cheatham blushed.

"Well, good riddance to her son and to that Jezebel," Margie said.

Neither of them noticed the address number was not correct. Franklin's records would never make it to Jefferson - Houston Middle School. Instead, they were bound to an obscure looking building with a personal post office box in the neighborhood. The records would be collected and taken to a facility in Arlington, VA, where the information would be scanned and become part of the on-going research conducted there.

CHAPTER 25

Jefferson Grant was laid back in his reclined chair taking a midafternoon nap when the kitchen phone started ringing. The sound started first as an intrusion to his sleep, and when Grant recognized the noise as a ringing phone, hoped that he would not have to get up and could return to his nap. Much to his delight, he heard LaShanda answer. As he was returning to his sleep, LaShanda came in and woke him.

"A Mr. Darnell Washington just called. He was very nice and apologized for interrupting your Saturday afternoon. He said to tell you he found something and needed to see you immediately."

"What did you say to him baby?"

"I gave him our address. He was polite and said he would be here in about an hour. Time for you to get up and get moving."

"No nap this afternoon," Grant lamented, stretching his arms above his head.

"What's the matter Jefferson, getting old?"

"Recharging the batteries baby, recharging the batteries. Got to keep up with you."

"Good luck with that," she teased. "Who is Mr. Washington?"

"We are working an investigation together."

"Is he the young man you told me about?"

"That's the one."

"I got some work to do." She leaned down and kissed Grant affectionately. "Your batteries are just fine old fool," and walked off to the kitchen.

A 2017 Kia Forte pulled up to the house and parked out front of his home in North West about 50 minutes later. Grant watched as Darnell got out of his car and thought, *nice car - conservative and not flashy.* Grant waited at the door until he was about to ring the bell and opened it to greet him.

"Damn," Darnell said, stamping his feet and shivering while holding his arms across his chest. "February is here for real!"

There was a briefcase at his feet.

"Good to see you again, Darnell. Come inside."

Grant opened the door wide enough so Darnell could enter.

"Thank you, Sir." Darnell moved his case inside and removed his jacket. He hung it on the coat rack as he surveyed his surroundings, taking in the smell of a cooking pot roast coming from the kitchen.

"Very nice house you have here, Mr. Grant."

"Thanks. Let's go into my office," and pointed to a room off the main living room to their right. "We can work in there without a lot of interruption."

Grant led the way, and Darnell followed with his briefcase in hand. The room they entered was large enough for three people and had a desk with a computer in the center. A small chair sat at one end of the office, allowing a second person to observe the screen, perfect for a husband and wife team working on projects together.

"What do you have?" Grant asked as he took the chair behind the desk.

Darnell sat in the remaining chair and opened his briefcase. He removed several manila folders and laid them on the desk.

"When we last talked, I felt pretty sure that mom had gotten involved in this VLS program that we read about in the

Washington Guardian. I have done some research of my own and found the articles about VLS in the *New York Globe*, a variety of smaller magazines, online papers, and all across social media. This story had pretty wide coverage."

Grant nodded and felt like a rookie for not catching any of the press on the program until they had met. But since then, he researched and read many of the same articles that Darnell just shown him.

"I went down this road, too, but came to a dead-end," Grant said. "I still couldn't find anything that connected your mom to the Program."

He looked over at Darnell, who looked like he could not wait to reveal what he discovered.

"Okay, Darnell, show me what you found."

"So, the first thing I did was start to think about what this program was all about. What came through loud and clear to me was that this was really about the worst criminals we have in America and how they were going to be transferred to the SOUP when we build enough facilities. Like you, I dead-ended on trying to find out more about the facility and the technology. The information is just not out there. But then I realized there would be a lot on the criminals themselves."

Grant nodded. He was following Darnell's logic.

"And there was. I found trial cases, names of top 10 criminals in America, who is on death row, where they went to prison, and, most importantly, their hometowns. All this came from the internet or TV. You would be amazed at the number of documentaries and YouTube videos that talk in detail about some of these cases. America's Most Wanted and a couple of other crime shows had stuff too. Everywhere there was info on these guys, and ladies too. Some badass ladies out there, Mr. Grant."

"Tell me, I know. Had to deal with a couple myself over the years."

"Really, Mr. Grant, did any of them kick your ass?" he said, smiling.

"Only one, and that one is cooking the pot roast in the kitchen. If she asks, LaShanda got me; but in reality, my moves won it."

Both men laughed.

"All right, Mr. Grant. Give me some dap," and reached out for a fist bump.

Grant did not respond in kind, and instead looked him in the eyes.

"Enough wasting time, let's keep it rolling."

However much he wanted to proceed forward, Grant could not deny that he was taking a liking to this young man and should be talking about sports or cars; not his missing mother.

"Let me show you a list I put together."

Darnell pulled a printed spreadsheet out of one of the folders. The list organized each criminal's name, current place incarcerated, and their hometown. Next to this information were columns that showed the inmate's marital status; and, if married, the names of their spouse and children."

"Good detective work, Darnell. But what does it all mean?"

"Pick a criminal name," he said, pointing at the spreadsheet.

"Anyone of them?" Grant asked

"Pick one with a family."

Grant selected one.

"Let's try 'Mario Flores, incarcerated in Allenwood, PA.' His spouse is Juanita. They have three daughters Alma 8, Francesca 5, and Lilian 2."

Darnell reached into a folder that said Flores on the tab and pulled out an article that he printed and gave it to Grant. Reaching into the top drawer of his desk, Grant pulled out his reading glasses and put them on.

The headline of the article read, "Tragic Deaths of Local Family." It was dated two weeks ago. Grant continued reading aloud.

"A family tragically died in an automobile accident this past Saturday. Eyewitness accounts saw the mother driving with her three daughters along the Susquehanna when suddenly, the car swerved out of control and plunged into the river. Recent storms caused the river current to be swift, and the levels of water were much higher than normal for this time of year. The automobile was found several miles downriver, but no bodies recovered. The car was registered to Mrs. Juanita Flores. She and her three daughters were Alma 8, Francesca 5, and Lilian 2 are presumed dead..."

Grant looked up – "Ok, the family died. Tragic, but I don't get it."

"Pick another one."

Grant selected another one.

"Jose Lopez. It looks like his sister Isabella, 27, was raising his two boys: Mateo, 8, and Samuel, 4."

Darnell pulled out another printed article from the folder labeled Lopez and handed it over. Grant started reading, "Tragic Boating Accident Contributes to Four Missing." This one reported that this family was doing some winter fishing on the water with a male friend of Isabella's at Sabine Lake in Texas. The article stated the family had fished until after dark and had not returned. Witnesses said that they thought the family decided to stay on the water for the night since the weather turned warm. The next morning, other boaters observed the floating hull of the boat. There was no one on the capsized hull or in the water. It went on to report that the bottom had a massive scrape mark at the bow, and a piece of the hull was broken. Authorities were investigating the cause of the accident and conducting a search but no bodies were found. The missing persons were listed as Isabella Lopez, age 27, her unknown male friend, and two nephews Mateo, 8, and Samuel, aged 4. When asked about the incident local authorities commented that the boat most likely hit something in the water at high speed causing the craft to eject the people and capsize. Despite the warm surface temperatures, the water temperatures were below 55 degrees. Unnamed sources stated that the night time air temperatures, the possibility of injuries when ejected, and hypothermia were reliable indicators that the family is lost."

Anticipating Grant's question, Darnell pulled out yet another article and began to read.

"Here's another one. The wife of an inmate in Atwater, CA, goes missing while hiking in Yosemite. Here is one from Florence, Colorado – family goes missing in the Rockies while hiking. All of these missing families, Mr. Grant, have something in common – they go missing, and their bodies are not found. Also, notice that none of these articles are printed by the actual local paper but are articles published by local internet newspapers."

"So you think these stories are just there to explain the family's disappearance?"

"Yes, none of the articles have a law enforcement official mentioned by name. There are no reliable sources for the events."

"How did you know that the families belonged to the inmates?" Grant asked.

"My position at the Museum allows me access to others that are serving in law enforcement or at the Justice Department. I provided the names of the inmates, and I got the family names from them. I have 10 of these types of articles that map to the ten inmates I have researched here. Each of these events happens in towns where there are federal high-security prisons."

They validated the remaining names on the spreadsheet, and each family or spouse of an inmate had met with tragedy. No bodies were found.

"These people are being taken," Darnell stated.

"But why?"

"I don't know Mr. Grant, but I bet this points us to where mom could be. What do you think we need to do next?"

This was fantastic. Darnell was on to something. Could

it be that the government was taking the family members of these convicts? He would need more proof, but this could explain Maggie. If they were taking family members, then making an older woman disappear who discovered their operations in DC was also possible. This was big.

"I think it's time to pay a visit to the guy who started all this, Alec Richardson. He is the author of the *Washington Guardian* story. He lives in Old Town, Alexandria. The article says he was at the facility. Let's see what he knows."

Darnell nodded in agreement.

"Nice job, Darnell. If you weren't already in a job, I would offer you one."

"Thank you, sir, but I'm fine."

"Ok, I think we are done here for today," Grant said.

He cleared his throat loudly.

"Let me show you out, Darnell."

Darnell looked at Grant. *What was that all about,* he wondered? As the two men walked out of the office and toward the coat stand, they heard a voice from the kitchen.

"Jefferson, is that you? You finally done with your work?"

"Yes, baby. I will be right-"

He never finished. LaShanda Grant, about 5'7 inches of brown eyes and beauty, walked out of the kitchen.

"Jefferson, you never told me you were meeting with a fine young man. I thought it would be one of your old cigar-smoking fools you call friends."

"Baby, let me introduce you to Mr. Darnell Washington. We are working on a project together."

"Not any more tonight, I have a pot roast that needs to be eaten. Mr. Washington, there is a bathroom right around that corner. I am sure you will want to wash up before dinner."

"Ma'am, I don't want to be rude, but I need to be going," Darnell replied.

However, this juggernaut was not going to back down.

"I won't hear any more of you having to leave. It's Saturday, and you are staying. I make some of the best biscuits in DC. You always need something good to go with the gravy. Have I tempted you enough, Mr. Washington?"

"I am not sure temptation would be the right word, ma'am."

"Just say 'Yes' so that I can eat in peace, Darnell," Grant commented.

"You old fool, what makes you think you are going to eat in peace anyway?" LaShanda said as she smiled at her husband and disappeared into the kitchen.

Grant shrugged his shoulders.

"Make this easy on me," he whispered to Darnell. Then in his normal voice, he added, "Dining room is through the kitchen; we will meet you there."

Darnell accepted his fate and headed to the bathroom to wash up. *These folks are great people*, he thought. Mom knew what she was doing, getting connected with Grant. He liked him and the way he worked. Grant let him lay out his info and listened intently before deciding the next step. Grant had taken what he found seriously and appreciated the efforts behind his research. That meant a lot to him coming from an experienced police officer. As he approached the kitchen, he heard the noise of final preparations for the meal. Darnell rounded the corner and immediately saw the ambush. Setting the silverware was the most beautiful woman he had ever seen in his life. LaShanda caught the look and grabbed Darnell by the arm and led him into the dining room. It was apparent by the stare coming back to him that he was not the only one ambushed. The woman stopped, and then smiled.

"Michaela, this is Mr. Darnell Washington," LaShanda said. "He is working on a project with your father. Mr. Washington, this is our daughter Michaela who agreed at the last minute to join us tonight for Saturday dinner. Why don't you sit there?"

Pointing at the narrow portion of the table across from Michaela, her implication was apparent.

"Jefferson, please go get the biscuits," she added.

As Grant walked by her, she gave him a knowing wink. She approved of Mr. Washington. When she saw Darnell get out of his car, LaShanda called Michaela and convinced her she needed to eat dinner with the family. Using a combination of guilt and home cooked food, LaShanda applied 'motherly pressure' to her daughter and talked her into canceling her plans for the evening with the loser on Facebook.

"So, Mr. Washington, why don't you tell us a little about yourself? Hurry up with those biscuits, Jefferson. You need to bless this meal so we can get started."

She turned her eyes back to her daughter and Darnell. "Started," she thought. Based upon the looks happening across the table, this has already started, and I need to catch up.

CHAPTER 26

Officer Grant found himself sitting in his car once again, but this time, he was not staking out a location. Instead, he sat in his mini-van outside Alec Richardson's house in Old Town Alexandria, waiting for any sign of movement in the early morning. Normally, Grant would have expected a bedroom or downstairs light to come on and watch for motion, but that was not the case this morning. He did not have to wait long. He saw a bedroom light come on, followed by a downstairs light and then one at the doorway. Alec stepped outside for his morning run with Adelle. Both were wearing matching stocking caps. They walked to separate trees to complete their last-minute warm up, each leaning on the tree and stretching out their hamstrings and calves. Grant chose this as the moment to get out of his car and approach them. The sun was beginning to rise over the Potomac, so the two could observe him walking across the street in the morning nautical twilight.

"Mr. Richardson," Grant said, holding his DC police badge out so that Alec could see.

Alec and Adelle stopped stretching and looked in his direction. Grant crossed to their side of the street, walking cautiously toward the couple, still holding out his badge with one hand and holding a briefcase in his other. Alec did a quick check of his surroundings for others, a technique he learned in Afghanistan, and did not see anything that looked threating on the street.

"Who are you?" Richardson asked without confirming his identity. "And stop right there, you are close enough."

Grant stopped about six feet from the couple on the sidewalk.

"My name is Officer Jefferson Grant. I work for the Washington, DC Metropolitan Police Department. I am here to talk to you about VLS."

"You are a long way from your precinct, Officer Grant," Adelle said.

"If you want to talk about VLS, call the editor at the *Washington Guardian*, "Alec said, moving closer to Adelle.

"How did you get this address?" Adelle asked.

Officer Grant looked at them and held his badge out again.

"Not hard to find an address when you work for the police."

Adelle and Alec looked at each other. Adelle gave a sheepish grin, and her face flushed red.

"What do you want, Officer Grant? Are we in trouble?"

"No, not even a late parking ticket. You two are clean. Can I come closer? I am who I say I am. I am carrying a police standard pistol under my jacket. If I were going to harm you, I could have just shot you. It's a little cold out here."

"Throw me your badge," Alec said.

Grant shook his head in disbelief that he needed to prove his identity, but he figured if he was as popular as Richardson was for writing the article, he would do the same thing. Grant tossed his badge to Richardson, who caught it. Alec looked and convinced of the badge's authenticity showed it to Adelle to verify. She nodded her head.

"Ok, Officer Grant. Come on in the house," Alec said.

Both he and Adelle headed back to the door with Grant following.

"Can we trust him, Alec?"

"Let's hear what he has to say."

"Thank you," Grant said as he walked behind them.

When he approached the door, Adelle followed Alec, and she held it open for Grant but blocked him for about 5 seconds.

"Sorry," she said and turned to get in front of him. "Please follow me to the kitchen, Officer Grant. I will make us some coffee."

Grant started to follow her when he heard the unmistakable sound off to his right of a bolt on a .45 pistol pull back and slide forward, chambering a round. He turned and saw Richardson pointing the gun at him. Then Grant heard a second .45 bolt being pulled back and sliding another round into its chamber. He looked to his left and saw Adelle pointing her pistol at him from the kitchen. Both were steady and seemed ready to shoot. Alec moved to where he could cover Grant from the side.

"Slide your briefcase very slowly to the lady, Officer Grant."

Grant did as instructed. *Holy crap*, Grant thought. *These folks are very cautious*. Adelle took his briefcase and placed it on the kitchen table.

"Now take off your coat."

Grant apparently started to do so a little took quickly for Alec.

"Slowly Officer Grant," he said.

Grant removed his coat and held it in his hands.

Then Adelle said, "Throw it on the couch."

Officer Grant complied.

"Ok – now the pistol."

Grant unsnapped his holster and pulled out his pistol.

"Slide that to the lady as well," Alec instructed, which Grant also did.

"Ok, Officer Grant, will you please come into the kitchen and have a seat?" Adelle said, picking up his pistol and motioning to the table. Acting as though nothing happened, she then asked him, "How do you like your coffee?"

Alec followed Grant into the kitchen and waited for him to sit down, then took Grant's pistol from Adelle and placed it on the counter at the far side of the room.

"Sorry for being paranoid, Officer Grant. Things are not as they seem these days. No trouble so far, but we're not taking any chances."

"Please call me Jefferson. I take my coffee black."

"I am the first one to ask you about VLS?" Grant asked.

"No Officer Grant, but fortunately for us, most inquiries are online, along with the shouting comments and occasional death threat. No one has shown up to the house, until you." Alec said.

"What would you have done if I pulled my gun outside?"

Alec raised his shirt to show a .38 snub nose in a removable holster in the small of his back. Grant raised his eyebrows.

"I see."

"Learned to pack in Afghanistan," Alec said.

"And you, ma'am. That's a lot of gun for a woman," Grant said.

"Please call me Adelle. I spent a little time in Iraq and Syria so know a little about weapons. I like the .45. It makes a bold statement." She said, smiling.

Both Alec and Adelle placed their .45s with Grant's pistol on the counter. Alec pulled the .38 out of the small of his back, and set with the other handguns, then took a seat with his back to the firearms, but within arm's reach. The coffee maker signaled it was ready by making a sucking sound as the last ounce of water pushed through the k-cup.

"Tell me, Jefferson: what do you want to talk about?" Alec asked.

Jefferson took a drink of the coffee given to him.

"Thank you, Adelle."

Grant paused, deciding how to proceed.

"I believe that the government is taking innocent people and putting them in the SOUP," he said.

Adelle looked at Alec. He could see the contempt this

comment portrayed in her face. She was opposed to his involvement from the beginning.

"How did you come to that conclusion?" Alec asked.

Grant recounted his conversations with Maggie about the home but never mentioned the location. He told them he suspected federal agents took Maggie and her source.

"So why do you believe that innocent people are being taken and placed in the SOUP?" Adelle queried.

"Maggie's son, Mr. Darnell Washington, has connected family members of some of the high-security convicts with news articles placed online. If you look here, you can match up the convict and their family with the stories. Notice that in each of the pieces, the bodies are still missing.

During the time that Grant was explaining the connections that Darnell showed him, Adelle reviewed one of the news articles and said under her breath, "Son of a Bitch." Alec and Adelle sat in silence for a moment absorbing the information and not wanting to speak about the obvious conclusion. Alec broke the silence.

"Very compelling, Jefferson. So what do you suggest we do? Other than this lady Maggie and her source, we don't even know the location of the facility."

It was Grant's turn to be confused.

"I thought you went there."

"I did, but they sedated me going and coming back. I have no clue where the facility is."

"But *I* do," Grant said emphatically. "I was *there.*"

Alec and Adelle looked at him.

"So tell us! Where exactly is it?" both asked.

"I didn't mention it because I thought you knew. It's in Southeast DC."

Both looked shocked.

"What do you mean? In Washington, DC?"

"I was there; not inside but there based upon one of the tips that Maggie gave me," Grant said. "It was raining hard, but I could still see men transferring what looked like coffins to the funeral home. I saw one of the coffins fall, and when it opened, I saw what I believed was a dead man fall out."

"What do you mean? What you believed was a dead man?"

"I saw lights in the coffin, and a man wrapped in some kind of net that also had lights on it. He looked like a lit-up Christmas tree."

"What happened?"

"When the guy fell out, one of the men walked over and emptied three rounds into the guy's head."

"What!" Adelle gasped. "Oh my God!" and tears formed in her eyes caused by her anger. "Those bastards! Alec, we have to do something."

"We will. But we have to figure out what that will be."

Alec placed an arm around her that she coldly pushed away.

"Our government can't do this!"

"Adelle, we don't even know if it is our government! This could be street crime. Come on, this is not the time for building up conspiracy theories!"

"Well, I can add a little more to the notion of conspiracy," Grant commented.

He reached into his briefcase and pulled out another group of manila folders and laid them on the table.

"Here is some additional research I did. I was able to find out my information using our police systems and calling in favors. Once Darnell made the connection, this next step was logical to follow. It provides the rest of the story."

Alec looked at Adelle. She was clearly angry but engaged in the conversation.

"Ok, Jefferson, walk us through this," she said.

"We knew that VLS was designed to handle high-security inmates, and that's what led Darnell to find the group of missing family members and the correlation with inmates. I assumed that they only built one facility."

"I think that's true," Alec said. "The Program Executive

has provided me information to write my next article. He provided inmate transfer numbers and progress on facilities. So far, there is only one built according to the updates."

"Good, then that provides further credibility to the other info I have collected. I believe family members are being sent to the facility, and that they were doing so in coffins transported by the airlines as human remains."

Alec was not sure he could believe Grant's story. It appeared to Alec that Adelle already decided to trust Grant. Grant continued.

"Otherwise, the guy's coffin that opened would not have the setup I saw. If my hunch were right, then there would be an increase in the number of remains flying to DC. And there was! It appears they are flying them into BWI. I found over 65 remains shipped via different airlines in the last month alone. This number is more than four times the average for a month."

"This may sound morbid, but how do you prove that there just aren't a larger number of people dying and shipped home?" Alec asked.

"I thought that too. But the numbers were too high, so I dug a little deeper. There are only four airlines that ship remains as far as I could tell. Normally, human remains sent have burial certificates and other documentation from funeral homes on this end. Airlines require this validation on the shipping end before putting remains on the aircraft. So, I followed the paper trail."

Grant paused, and Alec and Adelle looked at him.

"And?" Alec asked.

"And, of the 65 remains shipped, 42 of the remains were placed in the care of a company called 'Supervisor Shipping,' and the company used all four of the airlines to send the remains."

Grant placed the documentation on the table for each shipping document containing the origin of the remains.

"I can't believe this!" Alec exclaimed.

"Did they really think no one would connect the dots,

especially after your article Alec that talks about the Supervisor?" Adelle asked.

Alec agreed with Adelle. "You have got to be kidding me. Jefferson, did you verify the company? Are they legitimate? Do you know where they are doing business?" he asked, reading quickly through the shipping documents.

"Nothing showed up anywhere; it's like the company doesn't exist."

"This is amazing! Why aren't they using government flights, shipping in with normal cargo into Andrews?" Adelle asked.

"I suspect they are operating on some time constraints to get the people back to DC," Grant said. "They might very well be shipping on government flights. We just don't know. Here is the final straw: not all, but many of the bodies sent through Supervisor Shipping came from an airport closest to the town housing a federal prison. When you look at the missing family members, tie that with the phony news articles, and track the remains from origin to BWI, it all adds up to me. And one last thing. It's a straight shot down the Baltimore Washington Parkway to get to the home I visited in SE. It makes a pretty tight transportation solution."

Grant showed them a map from the Airport to the funeral home location.

"This is pretty compelling information, Jefferson," Alec said.

Alec looked at the table, continuing to validate all the information.

"Ok Jefferson, what's next? Without proof, I can't write any of this."

"Write. Write what?"

"Instead of the story the Program wants, I am going to write what is really happening. I..."

He then looked at Adelle and changed his sentence.

"We did not sign up for any of this."

"So, how do we get proof?" Adelle asked.

"That's what we police do. In this case, I find out the date of the next shipment of human remains coming into BWI, stake it out, and follow the coffins. I figure out how I can get into one, use a nice portable gadget we have for taking finger-prints from one of the shipments and then match it to a federal database. If the prints are not a convicted felon or better yet match the family members of one, then I think we have our proof."

Alec and Adelle both nodded.

"We're in," Adelle said.

"Whoa, hold on. You two are not going with me. I said this is police work. I'm trained for this."

"I've seen some rough stuff collecting evidence in Afghanistan. I lost a good friend. As Adelle said, she has been in Iraq and Syria. I think we can handle this; and besides, you are going to need some help. Add to it that we got the jump on you today."

Grant thought a moment. These were not your ordinary civilians for sure. Maybe they could help, at least drive the car.

"Okay," he said, standing up and shaking both their hands. "Looks like we will do this together. I will send you the next shipment dates, and we can meet back here and lay out our plan."

"How do I know you won't just do this on your own?" Alec asked.

"I came here to see you. I brought the information. You have confirmed that my info is correct. And you are right. I can't pull this off on my own."

Alec still eyed him suspiciously. "Let me give you my cell phone number so that you can call me direct. What else do you need?"

"You could start by returning my pistol."

CHAPTER 27

The sun dropped below the horizon, treating the Baltimore Washington International airport travelers to one of the most beautiful sunsets of the winter. Officer Grant found his perfect observation spot at the corner of the BWI Marshall Airport short term parking building. From his vantage point, Grant could see the northeast side of the entire airport and each of the associated cargo buildings located at the north end of the cargo plane runways. Grant's position was perfect for observing all wheeled traffic coming and going from any of these locations.

"Are you set?" he said into the mouthpiece on his walkie talkie that he borrowed from the DC police department. He liked this equipment because it allowed him to talk while keeping his hands free to use the binoculars that he also acquired for the night.

"All set here," said Adelle into her mouthpiece.

She was sitting in the Delta terminal, observing each of the incoming planes. Grant checked the inbound schedule and found that several flights containing human remains were being shipped in on Delta flights that would arrive between 8:30 and 11:30 pm.

"Me too," Alec replied from his location at the aircraft observation area at the south end of the airport.

His job was to identify vehicle traffic east-west along HWY 176. Between the three positions, they had the majority of roads that encircled the airport, the interior tarmac, and the northern cargo areas covered. Alec was not sure what he would see with the Glen Bernie Maryland State Police station down the road to his right. If he were a bad guy, he would stay clear of the place, but Jefferson told him that was not always the case, and he should pay attention.

"Okay," Grant said. "Welcome to my world. We have about an hour before the first flight arrives. Everyone get comfortable and watch everything around you. We're lucky tonight. We have a full moon to light things up. Next time we talk, it will be because we see something or it's a bust. Out."

Alec got out of the car and walked around the observation area. There were several other cars parked filled with families or dating couples that came to watch the planes land. The parking place was an oblong circle of parking places that afforded an unrestricted view to landing jets. He noticed there was a playground near the parking lot. It was hidden in the woods at the bottom of the parking places, far enough away to keep the kids from traffic. He was sure the area would be packed during an early summer evening as jet after jet from unknown origins with their loud engines and low altitude thrilled them all as they made their final approach before touching down. He pulled out his binoculars to observe an inboard jet and noticed that several other watchers were out of their cars with binoculars as well. He was glad that he fit in as he trained his set onto the road to observe the vehicles passing by. The ambient light from passing car headlights, combined with the landing lights in the field next to the observation area, illuminated the area enough for him to see most of the surrounding roads and the vehicles on them. Alec walked back to his car, which had a thermos of hot coffee and its warm heater. He could at least be comfortable while waiting for the remaining hour to pass.

The extra time gave Grant a chance to think through some of the decisions he'd made within the last several days. Most importantly, the one to keep Darnell out of harm's way.

TOM DEWITT

Since "Pot Roast Night" as he and LaShanda called it, Darnell and Michaela saw a lot of each other. He was becoming a regular at the house and Grant enjoyed watching the Darnell and Michaela build their relationship. Darnell was a young man with ambition that did not involve street gangs or drugs, and that was paramount to his daughter staying focused on her schooling and church. It was way too early to guess about their future, but the kids had something between them. Darnell was not happy when Grant told him that the meeting with Richardson was a dead end and that the two would continue to find his mother on their own. Grant hated lying to the young man, but he did not want him on the streets dealing with the stuff they were tonight. Part of it was because Grant was selfish. He wanted grandchildren, and he knew that he could count on LaShanda to keep the two focused on the good things that were happening in their lives. It was an excellent decision to keep Darnell out. *He could handle this with Alec and Adelle. Grandkids*, he thought and felt warm despite the cold winter night.

Inside the Delta terminal Adelle checked the flight status board for the flights that interested them and found the first one. The flight's status was listed as "On Time," and the time of arrival was 8:35. She walked over to a Sports Bar in the terminal and sat down and ordered an iced tea. She would want the extra caffeine tonight, and she could kill 20 minutes or so while getting caught up on the news. She had to hand it to Grant for his commitment to this type of work. Stakeouts were not her way of solving a case and were boring as hell.

In contrast to Adelle's experience, Alec enjoyed the heavy jets flying close overhead and occasionally shaking the ground under his car as the pilots throttled between slowing down and speeding up to maintain the perfect mix of speed and altitude during landing. He wondered how many of the jets landed with that feather touch down the passengers don't feel, given the amount of changes that occur when landing. Letting his mind wander, he identified the family cars. They were the ones that kids rolled down the windows and cheered as the jets came in, merging their voices with the engine roar and screaming at the top of their lungs, which was permitted by their parents under the circumstances. In contrast, the cars where couples were parking contained the steamed-up windows.

The alarm on his cell phone went off. Game time! It was 8:20. Alec stepped out of the car to see if he detected the approaching flight Grant identified. As he scanned the sky with his binoculars, he saw the flashing signature lights of an incoming aircraft and started to track its approach. It was not long before Alec made out the Delta logo on the tail, helped by the moonlit night. As the jet lumbered above his head and towards the runway, he swung his binoculars to HWY 176 in front of him and was startled as he observed two limousine hearses drive past his location, timed perfectly with the jet's passing.

"Movement," he said, calmly into his microphone.

"What do you have?" came Grant's voice.

"I have two black limousine hearses traveling east on 176."

"What are they doing?"

"Just a minute."

Alec opened the door and stepped up on the runner board of his car to get a better view. He watched the vehicles travel up the road through his binoculars. He watched for about 15 more seconds.

"Looks like they are slowing down. Wait- I've lost them."

"I can't see them yet," Grant said from his perch in short term parking. "Adelle?"

"Let me move to the south side of the terminal."

Adelle returned to her gate seat as a waiting passenger after leaving the bar and calmly walked down to the end of the gates to get a better picture of the southern approach.

"Nothing yet," she said.

Alec lost the view when the vehicles looked like they were making a turn.

"Grant, what's on the map?"

"There is an access road across the highway. Yes! There is a fence gate there with a road through the woods that will take them to the terminal. Adelle, be watching. If they come that way, then they have special access, which points to our guys. Alec, get your car heading west. If they come back the way they came, they will drive past you. I will stay here until Adelle has them at the plane, just in case they have to come around to the cargo access gates."

"Got it!" Alec exclaimed.

It was time to leave the observation area. Alec jumped into his car and pulled out onto HWY 176. He drove east and found a spot to make a U-Turn, did so, and headed west, checking his rearview mirror.

"Just checked behind me," he said. "Nothing westbound."

Seconds, and then a minute passed of silence before it was broken by Adelle.

"Got them!" Adelle whispered into her mike. "They just came out of the woods using an access road. They are heading to the Terminal. The flight is making its final taxi to the gate."

"Most likely, they will let the passengers off and get the baggage out. Then, when they are re-fitting for the next flight, they will unload the coffins, Adelle," Grant said.

"Ok, the jet just parked at the gate." More time passed, and a flight attendant appeared at the doorway to the gate. As passengers exited, she stated, "Does anyone need connecting flight information?" The flight attendant assisted an elderly couple and a young woman carrying her baby, directing them to their connections. After a flurry of activity by unloading passengers, the gate was instantly quiet. She looked out the window and saw the hearses directed by the ground crew with flashlights. They waited for the remaining baggage to be offloaded on to the portable carrier, which was whisked away by its mini cart to make room for the first hearse. A small cargo door dropped at the rear of the plane to provide the crew with easy access to the cargo.

"They have started loading. One is going in. There is a second one sliding in back as well."

"Two into one hearse? Are you sure?"

She looked hard to see inside the back of the vehicle.

"Yes, it looks like they are configured only for transport, no seats."

The loaded hearse moved out of the way, and the second one took its place following the waving flashlights.

"Two more," Adelle reported.

The rear of the automobile shut, and the first began to drive away. The second vehicle followed.

"They are heading back to the woods!"

Adelle rose from her chair to follow the hearses as long as possible. Grant scanned the woods with his binoculars now that he knew where to pick up the vehicles.

"Ok – I see them now. Alec, be ready. They will come back by you and head west. Follow them, but not too closely. Adelle, come to me in short term parking. You did great. Wait for me to come down and pick you up. I want to make sure they don't double back towards the cargo warehouses."

"Heading your way."

"On it," Alec said.

Alec stared hard to his left at the incoming traffic. He found a place to pull off the highway near an intersection near Matheson Way, where he could see the West Bound traffic.

"Bingo!" Alec reported as he observed the two hearses coming.

"Ok, Adelle, I'm moving. Will pick you up in five. Alec, use your phone if you need to, but stay on them! We might lose our range on the Walkies. Call me when you can."

The hearses passed by Alec. He pulled up to the highway and turned right. He let the vehicles get about 200 yards in front of him. His only concern was making the light with them at the intersection of HWY 170. Stay sharp. As the intersection approached, the light turned red, and all traffic stopped. He continued forward and applied his breaks about 20 feet from the trailing hearse. He immediately reached for his phone and began to look like he was texting and left the gap of 20 feet between them. He dared not look up into the back of the vehicle.

The light turned green, and the procession continued. Alec hung back to let the vehicles get further in front. He jumped abruptly as the car behind him laid on his horn, and he saw the driver show him the universal sign of impatience in the rearview mirror. Alec accelerated through the intersection and kept his gap. Fortunately, traffic was not heavy this time in the evening, and he was able to keep an eye on the trailing hearse. Just as Alec was beginning to close the gap, he saw the brake lights and watched as both vehicles turned into a large warehouse distribution center.

He continued to drive past the complex, looking for clues for where the hearses would drive to as well as any other information about the location. He found a turnaround spot and headed east, slowing as he passed the complex again. He saw the last of the taillights drive around the right side of the building. He searched for a place to link up with Adelle and Grant. Then he saw it on his left: St. Luke's United Methodist Church. He put on his blinker and turned into the parking lot. The lot was empty, and only the night lights of the church were on, shinning dimly and lighting the sanctuary building and administrative offices.

"Grant, can you hear me?" he said into the microphone. "Grant?"

No answer. He picked up his cell phone and hit the speed dial for Adelle.

"Hello, Alec. Where are you?"

In the background, he could hear Grant cussing at what appeared to be the parking machine to let them out of short-term parking.

"I am at a place called St. Lukes's United Methodist Church. Come down 170 and turn right onto 176. It will be on your right. They've stopped."

"Ok – we are on our way. Maybe."

He heard the smile in her voice.

"'Bout damn time you took my credit card," Grant said while cussing at the parking machine.

Alec grinned.

"See you soon," he said and then hung up. He unhooked his seat belt and took a deep breath. It was going to be a long night.

CHAPTER 28

Alec checked his watch. It was 10:18 when he recognized Grant's car pull into the parking lot. Grant must have seen his vehicle because he turned off his headlights and drove straight towards him, pulling up into the next parking spot. Grant motioned for Alec to get into his car. Alec exited and climbed into the back seat where the heat started to warm his face immediately. Adelle turned around to look at him and flash him a smile. Grant began the conversation.

"Ok, Alec, where are they?"

"About a half a mile up in what looks like a warehouse complex. I didn't see any signs for company names or anything else that would help to ID the place when I rode past. We can get there straight through the woods on foot."

Alec pointed to the woods behind the parking lot that connected to the warehouses. Grant nodded in agreement.

"How do we know where they are?" Adelle asked.

"There is another flight inbound tonight around 10:45. That gives us less than half an hour to move through the woods and see if the limos leave. If they do, then we have our answer."

"If they don't, Grant?" Adelle asked.

"Then we get to do some snooping around," Alec finished.

"Ok, Grant, what's our plan?"

"It's pretty simple. I get the fingerprint reader. Alec, you get your .45."

Grant looked at Adelle, and she patted her jacket.

"We walk through the woods real quite like. When we get to the building, Alec, you go left towards the street. Adelle stays in the center, and I go right. Walkies will work again. Just keep your voices low. If something happens, we develop our plan as we go. Any questions?"

Adelle shook her head.

Alec said, "HUA!"

Grant gave him a blank stare.

"What the hell was that? Some Marine thing?"

Adelle looked at Alec in disbelief like he just said a word that was trying to make him sound hip with the kids.

"No, I learned it from the Army Grunts in Afghanistan. It means Heard, Understood, Acknowledged: HUA!"

"Well, HUA, your ass over to your car and get your pistol and hand me that fingerprint reader in the back."

Alec reached over behind the passenger seat and retrieved a small carrying case and strap. He passed it forward to Grant, opened his door, and walked to his vehicle to retrieve his .45. Adelle watched Alec take off his jacket and strap on his shoulder holster.

"Do you think we will need these?" she asked Grant while patting the pistol under her coat.

"Let's hope not. Sometimes you don't have to shoot the bad guys. Guns make an excellent bargaining chip – like in your kitchen."

"Sorry about that whole thing, but we had to be sure."

"Water under the bridge. Let's go."

Both got out of the car. Alec was finished with his holster and put on his outer jacket.

"Let me take the point," Grant said. "Single file behind me."

Grant looked along the edge of the parking lot and found a small path into the woods. He was right: the full moon made seeing everything easy, but now it could work to their disadvantage. The foliage was off the trees, and if someone were looking in their direction, they would be detected despite their black attire and dark wool caps. He turned to face Adelle and Alec.

"Okay, taking a path is not my best idea, but if we walk through the woods, the fallen leaves and stuff will make too much noise. The moon will light up our way but watch your step and avoid twigs and stepping on things that will snap."

Both nodded.

"From here on in, let's stay very quiet."

Soon after they began walking the path, lights from the building could be seen through the winter forest and served as a perfect guide to their objective. They kept about five feet between them as they cautiously hiked onward. As they approached the building, Grant placed his arm out to his side and brought it back to his body in a movement that told the group to get down. Grant bent on one knee and motioned for his group to come close to talk.

"My time says 10:30. We are about 100 yards out and should be able to see vehicle traffic in and out. I've been watching and not seen any activity or headlights since your two vehicles, Alec. Adelle, you stay here. I'm going to the back of the building and Alec, head about 50 yards to your left. Questions?"

There were none.

"Ok, stay quiet as you move Alec."

Alec kissed Adelle on the lips. They were cold, but he could still feel the warmth inside him as he looked into her eyes.

"Stay safe," she said.

He gave her the thumbs up and headed off to her left. She laid down on the dirt path and focused on the building to her front. Alec was able to make his way almost to the road. He had perfect visibility, and then he too laid down. He had just gotten into position when Grant announced, "Movement!" His breathing increased, and his heart raced, reminding him of some of his time in the Middle East.

Adelle reported, "I see it, one hearse moving to my front."

Then Alec confirmed, "I have it too," as the hearse passed him and turned left on HWY 176 and headed to the airport.

"Alec, rejoin Adelle and come to me. I am about 500 feet from you."

"Moving," Alec said and quickly returned to Adelle.

The two started making their way to Grant, and when they arrived at where he thought he should be, they saw him motioning from behind a fallen tree to come to him. They joined him and crouched low. Grant pointed to a place on the back of the building.

"Use your binoculars. You will see what I am pointing to."

Both lifted their binoculars.

"Ok, focus on the back of the building closest to us. See the waiting hearse?"

Both nodded.

"Up from the hearse is a set of stairs onto the loading dock, and you will see a door. That's where the driver came from that just drove away."

Both nodded in affirmation.

"I see it," Adelle said.

The back of the building contained a high loading dock for trucks to pull up and offload at level. There were stairs close to their position to walk up from the outside, and the door pointed out by Grant. There was one truck parked in the back that was painted green with no other markings to identify it with a company or business.

"See the truck. I think that is the same type of truck I saw at the funeral home," Grant said. "This building has got to be part of the operation."

"So now, what do we do?" Alec asked.

"We sit tight until the hearse comes back. When they start to offload, we take out the guys, I get in, get the fingerprints, and we get out of here."

Adelle and Alec looked at each other. Neither were buying the plan.

"How about we find another door, pick the lock and get to one of the coffins transported earlier? Then get out?" Alec suggested.

"There are going to be four agents, if not more, and unless we want to start shooting, that means you and Alec get two each to knock out. You ready for that?" Adelle asked Grant.

Grant realized that none of them could handle trained agents at those odds in an open fight.

"Okay, maybe a little hasty in my planning, but you know this place will have the doors alarmed. As soon as we enter, we trip them. We need a better plan."

"How about we get into the hearse and wait. Where do you think they park these things for the night? Inside?" Alec suggested.

Adelle looked at him like he was crazy. Alec continued to explain.

"Two of us get inside the hearse. If they park it inside, then that's how we get inside. Once in, we find a coffin, get the prints, and get out. If the vehicle takes off down the road, then we 'convince' the driver to stop."

"If we have to confront the driver, that will blow a second chance of getting back inside," Grant said. "They will know someone is trying to get information about their operations."

"You said it, Grant. The doors are probably alarmed, and so are the windows. Unless we hitch a ride, we don't get inside the building. That vehicle is our only way of getting in. We better decide quickly. The second one will be back from the airport soon, and they will move them when they offload the second one."

"Too late!" Adelle whispered. "Look!"

The second hearse was pulling around the back of the building as they were talking.

"Shit!" Grant exclaimed. "That run was much faster than the first one."

As the second hearse drove past their vantage point, they heard people walking out onto the loading dock. The vehicle parked nose in with its back door towards the woods. It did not come close to having the height to offload on the loading dock. They heard a voice yell, "Jansen, get the folk lift!" and watched as a body sprinted across the parking lot to a shed, opened both doors, and started a vehicle inside. A forklift emerged from the shed and spun around with its tongs pointed menacingly at the three hiding in the woods.

"We are calling an Audible," Grant said. "I think we have a way in."

"Better be quick, Jefferson," Adelle said. "They have this routine down."

As she watched the action in front of her, the first coffin slid on rails inside the hearse and on to the forklift, which backed away from the vehicle and moved to the dock. The arms elevated the coffin above the loading dock and then drove forward. The men slid a dolly under the arms, which slowly dropped until the casket was in place. A small cable was attached to the coffin and taken inside by the men.

"I've seen this before. When the last coffin goes in, the team will follow, leaving the forklift operator to park the vehicle, close up the shed and join them inside. We take the driver out, get their credentials, and go inside. It's our only shot at this, but we will have to hurry."

A second coffin was taken out of the hearse and was loaded on the dolly as they were talking.

"It's on us, Alec, to do this," Grant said.

"Why just you two? What about me?"

"If this does not work, Adelle, you have to get out of here. Go to the *Guardian*. Wilkes will listen to you. Tell him what we know and how we got this far."

"Here, take this," Grant said, handing Adelle the portable fingerprint reader. "Alec, they are finishing up! The forklift is heading to the shed. Let's go!"

Without further discussion, Grant and Richardson took off at run for the shed, remaining as much in the woods for cover as possible. They were almost to the shed when the forklift disappeared inside. They reached the small building, breathing hard as they heard the operator kill the engine and get off the vehicle. Alec moved around to the other side to approach the driver from two different attack points. The operator came out of the shed quickly and reached for the door on the right to close it. Grant grabbed the arm and landed a punch to the operator's face.

The blow pushed the driver backward, and Grant realized as the person steadied themselves that a woman had taken his punch. She shook her head to clear the cobwebs from the hit, and without warning, stepped forward and kicked Grant in the stomach, knocking the wind out of him. He collapsed onto the grass. Alec went into action and brought her to the ground with a tackle from behind, pushing her face into the grass next to Grant. In one smooth move, she flipped Alec around and was ready to punch him squarely in the face when there was a quick motion, and the operator fell forward on top of him, unconscious. Alec looked up, and Adelle was standing there with her pistol drawn, holding it by the grip from where she just stuck the driver with the barrel and knocked her out. Grant groaned slightly and rose to his knees.

"Damn, I am getting too old for this."

"Come on!" Adelle said. "Drag her around back of the shed."

She grabbed one of the driver's limp arms and started pulling. Alec assisted with the other, and the two pulled her into the grass behind the shed at the edge of the parking lot. Grant pulled out a pair of plastic "quick cuffs" from his jacket pocket and with a smooth zip, cuffed her hands together. Then he moved to her feet, placed them together, and repeated the process. He pulled a small handkerchief from his other pocket and put it in her mouth and to finish his efforts, produced a small roll of duct tape and taped it across her mouth to secure the handkerchief. Adelle was impressed with how much Grant had loaded into his jacket. Alec lifted the driver's back slightly and removed her lanyard from around her neck. The cord contained various ID cards and was going to be their ticket inside. Adelle did a quick look through her pockets and patted her down. She found nothing.

"Ok, get the doors closed and locked. They will know something is wrong if they see them open."

Alec moved in front of the shed, saw the keys on the ground next to where he tackled her, closed the doors, and secured the shed.

"Grant, are you okay?" Adelle asked.

She handed the fingerprint reader back to him, and he placed the strap around his neck.

"Never better," he said unconvincingly, "Let's go!"

She knew he was lying, he had taken quite a blow but no time for that now. The three raced across the parking lot to the door, praying no one would come out to move the vehicles. Alec picked a solid white pass with no markings from the collection on the lanyard.

"Here goes nothing," he said as he swiped the card through the reader.

The door buzzed and clicked. The three all sighed as the door moved slightly inward. Alec opened the door slowly and peered sideways inside. He looked into a hall that opened into a large gymnasium sized room at the end. At the far end of the room were offices, with glass windows looking into the open space, most likely used by managers to observe activity in the loading area. The three quickly moved inside and stood in the darkness of the short hallway and let the door close behind them with a soft click. The entrance had two large glass panes on the right side of the wall facing the loading dock's interior.

On their left was a doorway that looked to lead to an office or closet of some sort.

All three were sweating, their hearts beating swiftly, and could feel the adrenaline pushing them forward into danger. As their eyes grew accustomed to the dimly lit building, they saw a room, more of a container storage area to their right through one of the windows in the hall, yet another place to observe activity in the loading area. It was black inside, but they could see the contents. There were six coffins, each on top of their portable dollies lined up across the room. No one was with them. Adelle was the first to see them and pointed them out. Both men nodded as they too focused their eyes and saw them.

"Find the door in," Grant said.

All three stared into the darkness around the coffins.

"There," Adelle whispered. "On the far side."

"That means someone has to go out into the open area and around to the door," Alec said.

"Time to earn my pay," Grant replied.

He slid the fingerprint recorder around to the side of his body and repositioned the straps under his coat collar. The three moved forward and observed the enclosed loading dock area.

"This must be a special room used for keeping the remains until transported. Everything else is open in here," Adelle commented, scanning the open space for any movement.

"If we are going to do this, you two have to cover me until I get into the room. If they see me before I get to the room, we all get out. Agreed?" Grant asked.

Both nodded again.

"One, two, three!"

Grant moved past them and around the corner. No shouts or alerts filled the building, just quiet. Adelle looked through the window. Grant was in the room.

Grant surveyed his surroundings in the darkness, letting

his eyes readjust to his night sight. To his left was the large loading door that was used to bring the coffins in. Next to the door was a large green knob that said "Open," and a red one that said "Close." *Good to know I have a quick way out,* he thought.

He took off his gloves and placed them in his jacket pocket. He pulled his portable fingerprinting machine out of the carrying case and turned it on. The inner lights behind the transparent glass in the device lit up, creating an eerie glow in the coffin filled room. He could see Adelle watching him through the glass window, and Alec's body faced outward, looking for any signs of movement. He moved to the first coffin and used the light from the reader to survey the top. These were not standard coffins. There were instructions for proper lift, external wiring harness connectors, and the casket was cold to the touch. He read the instructions on the top of the coffin using the light from the reader, slid his fingers along the seam of the top and bottom of the casket, and found a small latch. Lifting the reader above so he could continue to read, he shook his head, and with his other hand, moved the small lever forward. The coffin hissed as it opened slightly, breaking a seal and making available a small hook latch that he pulled back to him. The top opened automatically.

Grant stared into the coffin and was shocked at what he saw. There was a small Hispanic boy, wrapped inside of a wire mesh that glowed with blinking lights surrounding his body. Again, he thought it looked like a lit Christmas tree. On the top of his head was another ring of lights that blinked yellow and white connected into a box. The boy was dressed in skin-tight fabric, and his head was shaved. Grant fought to keep the small amount of vomit in his throat down and to control the anger he felt as he watched the boy's chest rise and fall as he took each breath. Shaking slightly, he reached into the coffin and took hold of the boy's arm and lifted it so that he could place his fingers on the reader. Grant already knew the answer the fingerprints would reveal and immediately struggled with his feelings, knowing his country could do this to people. Young boys were not inmates in high security! Darnell was right. They were taking families. The device beeped twice, indicating that the fingerprints were made correctly and accepted.

The instructions read that there would be a small button inside on the top left of the coffin. He was to press this to close the lid. For a moment, Grant hesitated, wondering if he unhooked the boy if he could free him but knew that he could also kill him. He was way out of his league. Grant felt the tears move to his eyes as he pressed the button, and the lid began to close down until it connected with the central portion of the coffin. He watched, feeling helpless as the lid seated itself and was drawn down tightly by some invisible force, and heard the small whine of gears and locks inside the box as they secured the body from the air outside.

"Shake it off, Grant," he said aloud. "You've got to get through this now, to help these people later."

He moved to a second coffin and repeated the procedure with a young man of about 12. He had just opened the third one and dealt with the emotion of seeing a young woman inside when he heard a small knock on the window. Adelle was pointing to the door they entered.

Outside the room where Grant was working, Adelle and Alec heard talking on the other side of the door. They made their decision in a split second as the door buzzed, and the lock clicked open. They were out into the hall and around the corner making their way to the room where Grant was when they heard a small pop fired from a pistol to their left, and the wood beam above their head exploded into tiny fragments that sprayed everywhere.

Oh my God, Alec thought. They were shooting! They rounded the last corner and opened the door. It took them just seconds for their eyes to adjust. In the center of the room was an open coffin. The women inside peacefully slept wrapped in small blinking lights, oblivious to the mayhem occurring around them. Grant moved to the loading dock door and was pushing on the open button without success.

"Alec, help me here!"

Alec moved to assist Grant and hit the open button flat with his hand. The door refused to move. He pounded it again without results. Adelle moved to the center of the room and was staring at the women in the coffin when she saw two men carrying the bound woman they assaulted in their arms looking in the window.

"This doesn't look good, Grant!" Alec said with urgency. "They were shooting at us outside."

"Guys, they found the forklift driver," Adelle said. "I think this is over."

It was a calm but knowing voice that provided the opinion.

"Bullshit, nothing is over while I can still fight!" Grant exclaimed, pulling his pistol and moving to the side of the door. "We are getting out of here one way or another!"

Alec was preparing to agree with Grant when all around them, noises like closing rattling doors quieted their conversation. Alec moved to be with Adelle, who was standing rock solid as her mind searched for what was happening around her. Some outer material instantly covered the windows. He looked into her eyes, and she looked back and smiled.

"I love you. I will never let anyone hurt you. Trust me," he told her.

She nodded her head quickly up and down and stared into his eyes. He pulled her close, running one of his hands through her hair in an attempt to comfort her, and she hugged him back.

"My ears are popping!" Grant exclaimed, and each of them felt the air in the room change, and their ears pop to adjust to the higher pressure.

"What's happening, Grant?"

"I wish I knew."

And then they heard it. A loud pop and then a hissing

sound like someone turned on the gas to their stove. Each of them produced a couple of coughs, and all three crumpled to the ground unconscious.

◆ ◆ ◆

Alec awoke with his hands handcuffed behind him, sitting in a wooden dining room chair in the middle of the loading dock. His surroundings were blurred as he looked through the haze caused by whatever knocked him out. He could feel Adelle next to him and Grant on the other side. He heard Grant cough.

"Adelle? Are you alright?"

"Right here, Alec."

Grant coughed again. Alec looked up, and there were three men dressed in suits standing in front of them.

"Welcome back, folks. Sorry for the short nap, but it was necessary to keep anyone from getting hurt."

"Who the hell are you?" Grant said as he tested the strength of the handcuffs that held him to the chair.

"My name is Agent Willis, Officer Grant. I have to admit. I've been waiting to meet you in person."

"What the hell? Been waiting for what?"

"We couldn't get a good picture of you the night you were outside the home in SE because of the rain, but we did see you. It only makes sense that the guy who showed up in all our video would also be the one to break in here."

"So then, if you know who I am, what do you want?"

"I don't want anything, Officer Grant; but my boss wants to ask you a few questions. He should be in shortly."

Alec looked over at Adelle's watch on her cuffed hands behind the chair. 2:15 a.m. That stuff put them out for a while. It was far from a short nap.

"While we are waiting, though, I want you to know a couple of things about our facility. These are important facts for you to remember the next time you want to visit. Number one, we identified your car when you followed our hearses, Mr. Richardson. Each of our cars has backward-facing cameras that scanned your license plate, and despite the darkness, identified you driving the car."

"How could you do that?"

"Mr. Richardson, our program has made significant breakthroughs in Artificial Intelligence for the Justice Department and others. *It's what we do.* Cameras and rapid identification is nothing new for us, given we have invented most of this type of technology. After you were identified, the three of you tripped Nanosensors in the woods. You could not tell, but the woods, especially this time of year, are covered with infrared cameras in our trees about the size of acorns, so once we saw that you were not deer, we monitored your movements. You did take us by surprise by assaulting our forklift driver. You'll be happy to know she needs a couple of stitches but will be back to duty in no time. Nice work, Ms. Hall."

"Sorry it was only a couple of stitches," Adelle said, staring straight into Willis's eyes, the contempt evident in every feature and expression from her eyes to her tightened jaw.

"Alright, you saw us coming for miles. Nice story!" Grant exclaimed. "So, what now?"

"I can take it from here, Agent Willis," the Supervisor said, walking across the loading area to stand in front of Alec.

"Mr. Richardson, I thought we had an agreement. I am surprised to see you and Ms. Hall here tonight. Agent Willis, the handcuffs are no longer needed. Take them off."

Agent Willis and his agents walked behind the group and removed their handcuffs. Each of them pulled their arms around front and rubbed their wrist to get the blood moving again.

"Okay – that's better. We can talk now."

"I'm not sure I have anything to say to you," Alec said, the venom unmistakable in his response.

"What gives you the right to put innocent women into the SOUP?"

"And children," Grant added, standing abruptly and moving towards the Supervisor. Agent Willis moved quickly in front and said, "Sit down, Officer Grant. We still have a rifle trained on you."

Grant sat back down.

"Yeah, well, he can't hit anything," Adelle dug.

"He does if he wants to, Ms. Hall. The shot was fired high to get you into the room where we could control the situation," the Supervisor calmly said. "The last thing we wanted was people shooting at each other." The Supervisor paused for a moment, looking at the three sitting in their chairs. "So, why are you here?"

"Isn't it obvious?" Alex questioned.

"Maybe I should rephrase my question. How did you find this place?"

"You think we would tell you?" Grant said. "Go to hell!"

"Come now, Officer Grant. Civility, please."

"Look, Mr. Supervisor, what happened? We had an agreement about providing press for the program, but that did not include anything that included taking civilians off the street and putting them in the SOUP. Tell me what THEY did wrong?"

The Supervisor paused for a moment.

"I can't answer that question for you. But one day, you will understand."

"Well, it's going to be un-fucking classified when we write the next article," Adelle retorted.

"Come, Ms. Hall, I understood from your reputation that you were aggressive but always the lady."

"Screw you! There are women and children in there!"

Adelle pointed to the room and rose to threaten the Supervisor, but Alec grabbed her arm and pulled her back to her chair.

"Please, Ms. Hall, do not make me use force to keep you seated. You three have caused me some real headaches tonight."

"I'm sure it's nothing like I am feeling right now, ass-hole!" Grant said, coughing again loudly.

The Supervisor ignored his outburst and continued.

"The effects of the gas are temporary. They will pass in an hour more or so. However, the headaches I am referring to involve shutting this facility down and moving our operations. Additionally, you have also threatened to write an article about what you believe is happening here. This will not do."

"Why not? The last time I checked, this was still America," Alec replied. "I can write whatever I want."

"Unless you want to violate our National Security Laws, then I have every right to prosecute under the full weight under those laws. Being prosecuted as a spy never goes well for anyone. Which is exactly the deal I am willing to make with you, Ms. Hall, and you, Mr. Richardson? I will treat you as spies if I ever determine you are going to release this information or write about what happened tonight."

"How can you call us spies? We have done nothing except act under our 1st amendment rights. It is not illegal to investigate government corruption."

"Yes Mr. Richardson, you can investigate but as soon as you publish and our adversaries are aware of this evening and your assumptions about what we are doing, you might as well work out an elaborate system to place coins on the mall to set up meetings with those adversaries, right Officer Grant?"

This struck Grant deeply. The idea that this son of a bitch understood way too much about him shook him to the core. How and the hell could he get that info? Darnell?

"So, what do I have to do to walk out of here tonight?" Grant asked.

"You, Officer Grant, are a proud father and loyal husband. And no, Darnell does not work with us," the Supervisor said, anticipating what Grant was thinking. "A fine young man, though. Is he dating your daughter?"

Grant remained silent.

"Your family is my guarantee," the Supervisor concluded.

Grant rose out of the chair and went straight for the Supervisor.

"You bastard! If you hurt my family-"

Agent Willis stepped forward and took Officer Grant to his knees with one blow to the back of his neck.

"Come on, Jefferson. You are too old for this. You said it yourself," Willis said.

Officer Grant coughed and regained his breathing again and slowly rose up. Alec thought, *Grant is one tough SOB*.

"Here, have a seat," Willis said, pointing to Grant's chair. "You are getting close to retirement. Why cause these kinds of problems in your life now?"

"I think we're done here," the Supervisor said. "Consider this a warning to stay out of my program. Mr. Richardson, can I count on you to continue to write for us?"

"As my beautiful partner stated, 'screw you.'"

The Supervisor smiled.

"I will take that as a 'yes.'"

Alec knew the Supervisor held the advantage and that he had no leverage against him. Not yet, anyway.

"Agent Willis, they are free to go. Let them out the way they came in. We will keep your weapons, however. Officer Grant, we know losing yours would cause you many difficulties at work and too many questions about how it happened. So, we will make arrangements to bring it to your house within the next day or so. The fingerprint reader will stay here as well."

Agent Willis looked at one of his associates.

"Nichols, show them the door."

The three rose to their feet and followed the agent to the door. He opened it and said, "Have a good evening." And let the door click shut behind them.

The Supervisor looked at Willis.

"I want daily updates on what they are doing and where they are going. Understood?"

"Yes, sir."

Outside, Adelle started to talk.

"What just happened?"

Grant looked around, still unable to see the cameras.

"Not here, Adelle."

They walked in silence back to their cars. When they reached them, Grant pulled out his keys and opened his door. Sliding into the driver seat, he looked up at his two partners. Adelle had never seen him this emotional.

"There are kids in there!" Grant exclaimed.

"We are not beaten yet, Jefferson. We are going to do something, but now is not the time." Alec said. "I've been to this point before in Afghanistan. We are going to make that guy pay."

"We'll be in touch with you, Grant. Are you ok to drive home?" Adelle asked.

He nodded and turned on the ignition. Alec got into his car, and Adelle heard their car start as she watched Grant drive out of the parking lot and head for home. She stood there a moment thinking and then got in the passenger side and shut the door. The car heater was still blowing cold air, so she rubbed her hands together.

"I love you, Alec. I don't know what I would do if I ever lost you."

"You would live on Adelle and make the best of your life."

She nodded her head, knowing it to be the truth but never wanted to face those circumstances.

"Hey, by the way, where did you get those moves with the .45? I thought that Amazon was going to kick my ass."

"She probably would have," and smiled, "Let's just say when I was in Iraq with the network, I spent some time learning to defend myself with the help of one of the Special Operations teams. They used different small arms but thought the .45 would be a good one for me. So they 'found' me one. They were right. The .45 became a really good friend of mine. A little heavy and kicked like a mule, but as the team told me, it was an excellent pistol for just about everything, especially when the bad guys were close. They also showed me the knockout move I used. I thought I would shoot someone before using it as a club, but I guess you never know."

He looked over at her eyes, looking at him.

"Thank you."

"Any time, Alec. I have your back. You have mine."

They rode in silence, letting the closeness of their evening connect them. Alec broke the silence as they crossed the Woodrow Wilson Bridge into Virginia.

"It's almost 4:30. It will be close to 5:00 when we get home. How about we stop for breakfast along the way."

Adelle looked at Alec like he was nuts.

"Who can eat after the night we just experienced?"

"Sooner or later, we are both going to have to get past this and eat, or else we die from lack of nutrition, right?" he said, smiling, trying to bring her back to him. "I prefer to do it with some pancakes and sausage. Plus, I have this ratty taste in my mouth."

"Me too," she said, twirling her tongue over her teeth. "Do you think we need some Tang?"

"There is a 24-hour grocery store down the street from the pancake place. Let's see if they have any."

This man was solid, Adelle thought. She never relied on anyone but herself for years, but for the first time, she felt sharing her security with him fit with her personality perfectly. There was no resentment and no negative feelings of losing herself to a man. She was happier now than she had ever been. She leaned over and kissed his cheek.

"I guess that means yes," he said as he turned off the Alexandria exit.

It was 5:00 am, and the traffic was already starting to build for the morning rush hour.

CHAPTER 29

"**S**o why all the secrecy?" Johnathan Wilkes, Managing Editor of the *Washington Guardian*, asked Alec as they walked down a pathway on the National Mall. Alec called Wilkes and asked for a meeting out of the office. This was not unusual for Wilkes since he was always having conversations that were best outdoors and away from employee ears. The sky was overcast and threatened rain on this April day in Washington, DC, as they walked past the National Air and Space Museum on the way to the nation's Capital Building, dominating the view in front of them.

"Is this about the quarterly updates you are giving me to your VLS story?" he asked, the irritation very clear in his voice.

Wilkes was still upset at the idea that the Administration was gaining momentum in the polls based upon his newspaper's coverage of VLS.

"What I have to tell you Johnathan could mean the VLS story turns into something much different than what I've reported to date."

"About time you decided to quit carrying the water for those losers. What do you have?"

"Not so fast. I need to know something first before we talk about the changes. I want some assurances from you."

Wilkes stopped walking and looked at Alec.

"Okay – like what?"

"Like what kind of legal support can the *Guardian* provide me if I bring something to them that could cause all of this to go off the rails."

Wilkes stopped walking and looked at Alec, who was searching for the right words to describe his dilemma.

"I could be charged with espionage when the story breaks," Alec confessed.

"Damn, Alec. You've really hit a nerve with someone. How do you know they will pursue you for espionage?"

"Because they told me they would."

Wilkes put the pieces together. Alec has found something big and already had a conversation with the government about their exposure. This would make the story even more valuable. If he played this right, this could be the next big story for the *Guardian*. Derailing this administration would make many of his well-connected, wealthy friends very happy.

"To answer the question, the *Washington Guardian* will not officially defend you, nor can the newspaper's money be used to defend you."

"Even though the *Guardian* prints the story," Alec confirmed.

"We're just the messenger Alec. We seldom are the one shot."

"Come on, Johnathan, I thought we knew each other. That's a BS answer and the party line. I know the *Guardian* will not cover me, but what about the money behind the *Guardian*? You know as well as I do that there are high-wealth people that would rather not make a political contribution to a candidate and would rather see their money used for something like protecting me. This article could be your October surprise."

Alec was alluding to the phrase used for stories released to the press in the waning days of October that politically damaged a candidate and provided no response time to change public opinion before the November election.

"This story is that big? What made you change your mind? I thought you were a big supporter of VLS?"

He is sitting on top of something big, Wilkes thought, *and knows it could ruin his life if he publishes.* Wilkes concluded that Alec was an idealist willing to provide the truth to America regardless of the information and consequences. But that thinking comes with a price this time. This guy is scared. They have threatened espionage, and once that threat is made, they do not back down. He was right, though, about the money. He had numerous rich contacts that would pay for his legal defense with a story like this, especially if that story brought this administration down.

"How is this as a teaser?" Alec said. "This story is as big as, if not bigger than, Snowden and the NSA. As to changing my mind, VLS has moved from genius idea to abuse of power".

Wilkes whistled.

"Welcome to DC, Alec. Our government routinely snatches defeat from the jaws of victory."

"Do you want this story, or should I take it to someone that can work with me and provide some protection?"

"Look, we can make the legal protection work. It's going to take a little thinking about how we line up the bill payers."

Alec had made his point, and it appeared Wilkes was going to help. "I want this for Adelle AND me. She will be pulled into all of this if they come after me."

Wilkes thought through the numbers again. This case could go into the tens of millions if both of them needed defending. His information was going to have to be good to get his people to buy-in and support the idea.

"Can you give me an idea of the headline? The people paying for your defenses are going to want to know where their money is going."

"Tell them; Federal Government puts innocent Women and Children in the SOUP."

"What!"

"I told you it was big."

Alec felt good to say the words out loud to someone other than Grant or Adelle.

"How do you know this? How did you figure all this out? What the hell?"

Then Wilkes paused and started laughing.

"Wait, this is some kind of joke. You son of a bitch. You led with that story to get the drop on me because you need a favor for the next VLS article. This is all a joke, right?"

Wilkes did not see the humorous response and admission from Alec that he was hoping to see. Instead, Alec stared at Wilkes, his eyes piecing Wilkes' so deeply that the smile quickly turned to a tight lip. Wilkes shivered slightly under Alec's intense stare, the assumed humor broken by the seriousness of Alec's expression. His silence was a final condemnation of the joke that Wilkes thought it was.

"Wilkes, it's all real. You did not see what I saw, so can you be serious about this? This is my ass on the line."

Wilkes put on his professional face again.

"Alright, Alec, you have my attention."

Smartass Pulitzer punk. Wilkes was tempted to let him flounder in his own problem but knew this story would be huge for the paper and big trouble for the administration. "I'm just trying to ease the tension. You just dropped a bomb in my lap. Do you know how many favors I will need to call in for this?"

"I really don't care Johnathan. It'll be worth it to you."

Wilkes thought a moment and never to let newspaper sales slip by said, "Okay, what did you see?"

"I was at a warehouse with witnesses. We saw women and children ready for transport to the VLS facility."

His memory of the night haunted him since it happened. He had to get this story out to clear his and Adelle's consciences.

"I am prepared to give you locations as well as the research we used to prove our story's facts. In exchange, I want the best legal protection in this country and the funding to pay for it, for both of us. In return, you get the exclusive on this story for the *Guardian*."

Both men knew the *Guardian* could gain a lot of political points with an article that showed they still showed hutzpah in the newspaper business and would publish a controversial article intended to sway an election, a piece with real facts behind it.

I really would like to see this group get booted from the White House Wilkes thought. *This just might be what is needed to make that happen. I think the people I know would be willing to support this idea.*

Wilkes looked at Alec and moved his head to look at the Capitol.

"How do you think the first Congress would have felt about this kind of abuse of power?" Wilkes asked.

"Just like Congress today. If there are political points to be gained that they can leverage into power for a later day, they would be all for it. I don't think much has changed in that building for a long time."

Wilkes paused to reflect on the magnitude of the story he was preparing to publish. *If this story prints*, he thought, *a lot of people will lose their job in this town. Good riddance to all of them.*

"A story like this could guarantee control of the house and senate as well," Alec commented, trying to add more convincing points to his request. "Americans will be outraged and will blame the party in power. The real question is, once power changes, will the new administration abuse it too?"

"You sound like a pessimist, Alec."

"Maybe I am, or maybe I'm just a realist."

"Sounds like one and the same when you talk politics Alec."

"Okay Johnathan, if we work this out, what are the next steps?"

Wilkes turned around without a response and started

walking, retracing their steps on the pathway guided now by the Washington Monument to their front. *Ironic*, Wilkes thought, *that they would be standing between the Nation's seat of government and the monument symbolizing the man and his positive values he lived by while discussing this nation's abuse of the people's trust to gain power.* Alec turned and walked with him.

Wilkes liked this guy. Alec was learning how to work the system and would be a great asset after the election for writing the types of stories the paper would need to overcome the several digital rags taking their subscribers. Internet newspapers were popping up everywhere that covered DC politics and were taking a bite out of his paper's business. Wilkes decided it was time to provide a little mentoring to build a relationship for the future and help put Alec's mind at ease. He did not need Alec to fold when he was sitting on a story like this.

"This is how we do it, Alec. We start by publishing the story anonymously."

"What will that do, they already know I am the source?"

"That's true, but in the legal world, the law and time are used to ensure the defendants are not rolled over by the justice system. So, we publish anonymously. That means the government has to prove that you wrote the article before they can charge you or Adelle. That is the first stepping-stone, and every defense we build that they have to overcome takes time. See where I am going with this?"

"But, they had cameras and have a video of us."

"That's right. The government knows you were at the facility. They do not know you wrote the article. You could have passed the info off to another writer that published because of the threat they made to prosecute you. You could be implicated, but they have to prove your involvement in the story. Just because you were at the facility does not mean that you wrote the article. It's flimsy to us here, but in court, they need something to connect the two. It buys us time."

Alec acknowledged this was true, and Wilkes continued.

"For you, each point in the article has to be proven by them using the espionage law. This means they have to prove damage to national security. Here is where they have a problem. If they go after you, they have to decide what portions of abducting citizens they have to admit? You can see they are going to have to pick and choose carefully what parts of the article they want to use to prosecute, and even then, there is a lot of gray areas and high standards of proof in those laws."

That was a good point, Alec thought. To prosecute, they would have to admit what they abducted US citizens or make something up to charge him and Adelle. Wilkes read his mind.

"They may have to charge you with lessor statutes not making it worth prosecuting at all. Lastly, this is still America. In the justice system, you are innocent until proven guilty. It doesn't work that way with public opinion."

"Johnathan, I am a writer, not a lawyer. Tell me why I should buy what you are telling me right now."

"Because I have seen, reported on, or been involved in cases like this before?"

"Let's say I follow your advice, then what?"

"This case will take a long time between evidence gathering and appeals. Time for a high vis federal case like this one means administrations change, politics change, and the will to prosecute turns into a dropped case or a settlement."

Wilkes paused to make his next point and leaned closer to Alec.

"Especially when you have done the new administration a huge favor. This problem will probably just 'go away.' If you do settle, no one will publicly hear about it."

"What about the *Guardian*?"

"The *Guardian* won't be sued by the administration. They will either be out of power in January or not want the perception of going after a newspaper that printed a story that has yet to be proven in court. If they say the story we print is true, then they are guilty of abducting innocent

Americans. So while the legal system looks for proof in your case over the next two years, Americans hear and decide their truth when we print the article at election time. This is where publishing this story is powerful. It does not matter if you are guilty or innocent; Americans will assume the government abducted citizens because you will lay out a great case with proof in the article, and most Americans today do not trust the government. Voters will believe you today. The results of the court case could be years away."

Wilkes smiled. His options were all positive. He just had to make sure he published the story.

"Here is something the newspaper business has taught me about the law, Alec. The truth does not matter if the law cannot prove it. Innocent people get screwed, and guilty people go free not because of the truth of the case because they have a better lawyer that knows how to make the law work for the client."

"Maybe so, Johnathan, but I would still like to think the truth will ultimately win."

"It does, Alec; but not in the legal system. A proven axiom in the newspaper business is 'published articles like this one in October never result in court cases if we win the election.'"

Alec smiled. He knew that Wilkes was making this up as he was saying it, but his experience in the business still added credibility to his point.

"The American people determine the truth of what you write the day it's printed, not in court years later. You can take that to the bank."

What Wilkes said made sense. The Supervisor was between a rock and a hard spot. If the government went after them, they would have to explain taking innocent US citizens. Then a new fact emerged into Alec's thinking. The Supervisor would know all of this as well and would have walked through the same legal points that Wilkes was doing with him. The Supervisor was not going to charge them with espionage. He already judged them as spies. He said so at BWI. If this story were published, he would be coming for them and not in court! Time to go.

"I appreciate you taking the time to walk me through this. You, of course, can understand that I would like a lawyer to verify your advice as well." Alec said, trying to stay focused on the conversation.

"Sure, I get it, Alec." Wilkes chuckled. "I hate to use the saying because it came from a Republican, but I will, 'Trust but verify.' It's a damn shame Bill Clinton could not come up with something more eloquent than 'it's the economy stupid.'" Both men agreed on Wilkes' recollection of history.

"How soon do you think I can have a written agreement from a law firm along with supporting dollars placed in escrow?"

Alec needed to maintain the façade of a legal battle to conclude this meeting despite realizing that the Supervisor would make his threat stick outside of the courtroom.

"I'll make it happen as soon as possible. It's April now. I will make you a promise. This will be done by July. That should give you time before we publish the story in October."

Wilkes paused and then asked, "What are you going to do about the quarterly updates to your existing VLS story?" Wilkes asked.

"I intend to keep working with the program and provide the information they want to be published until we get this figured out."

Wilkes nodded.

"Okay, makes sense. I will continue to publish their crap. It makes it easier knowing that the real story will drop in October."

The two men made their way back to the Smithsonian Castle, the oldest building belonging to the Smithsonian Institute.

"I'll be in touch, Alec. Keep your head low and tell Adelle I said 'hello.'"

Keep his head low! Hell, he was thinking about disappearing, but he knew that Adelle would want this story written; and when it came down to the bottom line, so did he.

"Contact me when you have things together. I will start working on the article," Alec said.

The two shook hands, and Wilkes headed for the Smithsonian Metro not far from where they stood. Alec decided not to head home quite yet. He needed a little time to clear his head. A walk down the mall would help.

This was a big move. If he published, they would come after him and Adelle. Wilkes might joke around sometimes, but he did seem to know his trade and the impact of doing what they discussed. Perhaps instead of defending them in court, he could convince Wilkes to get his backers to protect him in other ways. Alec knew that the *Guardian* published many controversial stories in his lifetime, and the authors and the *Guardian* survived most of them. It would be an exciting conversation with Adelle tonight. He knew one thing for sure. This could turn sideways fast. He was going to have a plan B with Adelle, and they would do this their way. He would not turn over their lives to a bunch of lawyers.

CHAPTER 30

A delle and Alec sat on the couch in the living room, discussing his meeting with Wilkes. Adelle opened a bottle of wine, but neither touched their glass since the conversation began. Alec explained the agreement he made with Wilkes and the timeframe they'd set up. He also shared his revelation during the discussion on the mall and Adelle agreed that the Supervisor would come after them to prevent their article from destroying his program.

"Do you really believe that the Supervisor will try and kill us if we publish this article?" Adelle asked.

"That's his only move if we do. I listened to Wilkes walk me through some of the legal thinking for previous cases, and there is no way the government can charge us with espionage without admitting they abducted US citizens. Any charges less than spying will get dropped after the election. But as I said, I don't think there will be charges."

"Because someone credible in the government will deny the story, right? Denial gets us off the hook because if they deny the abductions, then we have revealed nothing compromising national security. The program is in trouble either way because a denial means that the story still is valuable to the *Guardian* because people mistrust the government. Despite the denial, most voters will assume the story is true anyway."

Alec loved this woman. She had an incredible mind as

well as a commitment to the truth and doing the right thing. From the first time he met her, she was always true to her values of right and wrong. This ability to see the proper moral path and take it was something that inspired Alec. He had the tendency to look at the overall situation and compromise small parts of what he believed to achieve his goals. Adelle remained true to her values and never compromised. Right was right and wrong was wrong. It had cost her some business deals she confided in him, but she always walked out "being able to look at herself in the mirror" and live with the decision she'd made. He was a better person when he was with her and frequently admitted that her moral compass pointed true north while his just pointed north.

"This story is all political which is why this is so strange. My impression of the Supervisor is that he is more of an operator than a politician. I really don't think he cares one way or the other."

Adelle nodded in agreement.

"Personally, I think it's the people he is working for that have the most to lose. Those are the real politicians and the people that would be concerned most about our story getting out. I think the Supervisor is caught in the middle between implementing his system and protecting some very senior people. If we print, then it's almost guaranteed that they will lose their election," Alec said.

"I get it. The value is in the truth of our experiences told in the story. Do you think the political pressure might put heat on the program to change what it is doing?"

"I don't know. If it does, and this isn't just about politics, then we are a real target. The program will come after us with a vengeance if we derail their operations."

"So Wilkes will do whatever we want until we publish? We need to think of other ways for him to help us as an ally while we are writing. After that, we better have our ducks in a row."

Alec recognized the phrase immediately as one used in

the military to mean, "Be organized and prepared."

"Ducks in a row? What kind of education did you get from that team in Iraq?" he asked, leaning towards her for a kiss but stopping inches from her face. "First proficiency in side-arms and now the lingo. Should I be jealous?"

"Maybe," she said, playfully signaling the conversation was over and that she was interested in him.

She closed the gap between their lips and kissed him gently. The kiss was perfect but interrupted by Alec's cell phone.

"Don't get that," she said.

Her eyes told Alec he should let the call go to voicemail. Alec picked up the phone and recognized the number. It was Grant's.

"It's Grant," he said, and the moment of intimacy ended. "I've got to take it."

Alec put the phone to his ear.

"Grant, what's going on?"

An angered and distraught voice answered.

"What did you do? What did you do?"

"Settle down and tell me what's going on."

Alec pressed the speaker button for Adelle to also hear the conversation. Grant tried to regain his composure, but Alec could detect the shaking in his voice.

"LaShanda called me at the office for dinner around 6:00. When I got home, she wasn't here. The table was set, food still in the oven cooking but she was gone! I called our neighbors, but no one said they'd seen her. Then I get a call from a hidden number."

Grant paused, searching for his next words, his emotional distress clearly heard in his voice.

"The guy on the phone said they took her! My baby is gone!"

"Who said they took her?"

"I don't fucking know! I didn't ask him his name. He said Michaela and Darnell were gone too! He said if I wanted to know why," he paused, fighting back the emotion, "to call you!"

Alec looked at Adelle. *Did they know about the meeting today?* Alec thought.

"Grant, come here to the house. Come right now!" Adelle said. "We can figure this out, and you can stay here until we do."

"You better have some damn good answers when I get there."

The call ended. Adelle and Alec looked at each other.

"Ok, Adelle, let's start thinking this through. What do we think happened?" Alec said.

"My God, Alec. His family. Everything in his life!"

"Adelle, we have to put that aside right now," he said, rattled by the news but trying to stay calm. "Let's think this through."

Adelle was thinking and looking into the darkness outside through the window. Her mind whirled as she processed what just happened. She could not focus as one scenario after another flashed through her mind demanding evaluation. She felt panic start to consume her as she was bombarded and betrayed by the information emerging from her darkest imagination.

"Adelle! I need you here with me. We knew this was possible."

He reached over and grabbed her hand and turned her to look into his eyes. She stared back, pulling back from her imagination's worst images and eliminating the panic she was experiencing.

"Ok – Alec. I'm with you," she said, shaken.

The thoughts of Grant's family in those caskets like those they'd witnessed at BWI still remained in her mind but started to fade as she focused on Alec's voice. She regained her rationale self. Alec handed her the glass of wine she poured hours ago. Alec grabbed his. They both chugged their drinks, and Alec poured another quickly, sloshing a couple of drops on the carpet as he emptied the bottle. They promptly downed the second round as well, and both took deep breaths when they finished. Alec knew Adelle was settling down when she looked over at Alec.

"That's not the way to properly treat a nice Pinot Noir," she commented.

Alec stood up and ran his hand through his hair, trying to relieve some of his stress.

"Ok, what do we have? Let's focus on the facts that we know. Let's start with what the Supervisor told us," he said, standing up before he started to pace back and forth.

"If we publish this story, he said he will pursue us as spies and charge us with espionage, or worse. As long as we don't publish the BWI incident, we have nothing to worry about."

"And then he threatened Grant that his family would be taken if he talked about the evening."

"You met with Wilkes today to discuss publishing the story. If we think the story will cause no problems with the program, why take the family? Maybe it's not about the program but really is about losing in November."

"Hell, I don't know. We covered this already. You think they took Grant's family to protect the White House? To get the upper hand and leverage to get us to back off?"

The real possibility of what was happening came rushing into Adelle's mind and her intuition confirmed it. Her mind yelled, *they didn't just take them to release them with further assurances, they put them in the SOUP!*

"They're in the SOUP Alec!" she shouted.

Alec shook his head.

"Adelle, we have no proof of that!"

"Do you think the Supervisor would do it?"

"I would have never imagined the Supervisor could act like this. It is a possibility. If he is putting innocent families in the SOUP, we have to assume he would do the same with Grant's family."

"Can they be taken out without damage? What did you see there?"

"I didn't see anything that will help us! The Supervisor would not answer the question when I asked him what would happen if they woke up!"

"Ok, Alec, now YOU calm down."

"God, I feel responsible for Grant's family." Alec continued to pace.

"Both of us decided you should meet with Wilkes. I am just as responsible as you are," she said, her voice dropping in recognition of the part she played that caused this situation. "What do we do now?"

"We come up with an answer. Grant will be here in about an hour."

Adelle stood up and walked over to Alec and put her hand on his shoulder.

"What do we tell Grant?" Alec asked.

"We tell him the truth."

It seemed like only minutes before Grant's mini-van pulled up and parked in the street out front. Adelle and Alec were relieved when Grant's knock on the door sounded like a regular visitor and not someone looking for vengeance. Adelle answered the door, and Grant stepped into the foyer. He dropped his overnight bag. Adelle moved forward, and the two embraced, and then cried. They supported each other as they struggled to stand upright, so overwhelming was the emotion of the event. Alec stood by and marveled at the strength Adelle showed as Grant's grief washed itself out with the tears he shed. Then as abruptly as it began, Adelle felt Grant's resolve replace his despair as his legs strengthened under him, and his back straightened.

"Enough of that," he said, whipping away the remaining tears. "Let's figure this all out."

Grant walked into the living room and gave Alec a huge but short bear hug ending with several hand pats on the back of Alec's shoulders. Alec knew that under the tough cop was a caring, loving family man capable of emotion.

"Before you ask about the whup-ass I was gonna bring on you," Grant started. "I realized I need your help to get them back. You are my family now. Shooting you solves nothing," he said with a smile.

"Glad to hear that Jefferson because I think shooting is our next step. Want a beer?" Alec asked.

"Thought you folks were Scotch people. Do you have some of that? I could use something a little stiffer than beer."

"Do we have Scotch? I think I could find us some," Adelle commented, walking into the kitchen. "Do you want it neat or with ice?"

"Straight up."

"Have a seat, Grant," Alec said, pointing to a comfortable chair in the room's corner.

Adelle emerged with a neat scotch and handed it to Grant. Grant tipped the glass and emptied it.

"Should I bring the bottle?" Adelle asked.

"No, that will be enough. Thank you."

Grant stared into his empty glass a moment, then looked up.

"So what the hell happened?" he asked.

Alec and Adelle took their seat back on the couch.

"It was my fault," Alec began.

"Our fault," Adelle corrected.

"Either way, I met with the *Washington Guardian* today."

"So, you brought this on."

Grant's voice started to rise as his emotions emerged again. He steadied himself and did as his police training directed him to do, get the facts, remain unemotional, and think.

"We did, and we're sorry," Adelle started.

"I don't give a...I don't care whose fault this is right now. Answer me this. Were you talking about publishing our story?"

"Yes," Alec answered. "You can't tell me, Jefferson, that what you saw did not affect you."

Grant looked them both in the eyes.

"I've not been able to sleep since that night. That image of that young boy still haunts me. I thought about payback but hit on nothing. I'm ashamed to admit it, but I did not want to risk my family for someone else's."

"We felt the same way but knew we had to do something. That's why I set up my meeting."

"What did you find out?"

"Charging us with espionage if we published was only part of what the Supervisor said. He said we were spies, and he is coming for us if we publish."

"So what the hell are you thinking? Let this story go."

"We can't Jefferson," Adelle said, leaning forward towards him. "Because what they are doing is wrong, and for us."

She pointed at herself and Alec.

"Wrong gets fixed even if it means putting yourself in harm's way or worse," she continued. "It's the way we have lived our lives, and I am sure you've been willing to sacrifice yourself to protect someone as part of your job."

Grant felt that way many times. His search for Maggie was similar. He always knew that LaShanda could continue without him. She had incredible strength inside of her, and because of that strength, Grant could take risks as part of the job. Now Grant had to face the reality that he could not match his wife's courage to persevere. He was not sure that he could live without her and his daughter. He was supposed to go first. But that's not the way it was. So now he had to dig down and fight.

"I want to know what we are going to do to get them back."

"Alec and I've been talking about this all night, and we have a plan."

Adelle did not have a plan; she just needed to keep a conversation going and hope that an idea would arise.

"I'm listening."

"Grant, you know the location of the facility, and you know how to work with the coffins."

She was grasping for ideas, but was sure something would develop.

"Alec was inside the facility and knows the layout. We thought that-"

Adelle welcomed the interruption caused by the vibration of Alec's phone. Alec checked the message, and his face turned pale. Alec put his finger to his mouth, signaling each to remain quiet.

"Look," Alec said, adding a huge yawn. "I don't think we are going to be able to plan anything more tonight. We are exhausted. It's been a long day."

Alec passed the phone to Adelle. She read the message.

"I agree with you. Let's get a fresh start tomorrow. Grant, we have a guest room, or if you would prefer, you can have the couch. There is a bathroom around the corner. Your call."

She handed the phone to Grant. He read the message and understood.

"I don't think I can sleep, so I'll take the couch. Before you go upstairs, do you have a copy of the first article you put in the *Guardian*? I want to read it. Maybe it will jar some ideas for tomorrow."

"Sure," Alex said. "Let me get you a copy."

Alec walked over to the bookcase standing in the corner of the room and opened the bottom drawer on the one of the supporting chest. He extracted his article from a folder and closed the drawer.

"Here you go," Alec said.

Grant handed the phone back to Alec.

"Jefferson have faith; we will find your family."

"I know," Grant responded.

Alec looked at the message one more time to make sure he read it correctly, and there were no hidden meanings. It was pretty clear. The text message read:

Stop talking. Your place is bugged. Don't try and find it. Come to our usual meeting place tomorrow at 1200. I will meet you out front. Do not discuss any plans with others until after we meet. Don't say **anything** when you see me tomorrow. UT

CHAPTER 31

Alec elected to drive this time to the National Harbor. The circumstances of the meeting were much different from the other times that he and UT talked about general topics like scotch and wine while passing information about the articles and their edits across the table in sealed envelopes. Over the last eight months or so, he and UT communicated frequently, and while Alec would not say that he trusted him, he did like him.

Alec turned his car into the multilayer parking deck closest to McCormick and Schmick's, took his ticket from the automated teller and drove three levels before he found a parking spot. He took the stairs down and exited into the street that intersected with the main road through the Harbor. The restaurant was across the street and filled with lunchtime patrons. It was a beautiful spring day, and it appeared a large number of people were skipping work to enjoy the weather.

As he crossed the street, he immediately identified UT sitting at a table outside the restaurant. Rather than approach him directly, Alec stood off to the side until UT saw him. UT would have to make the first move. His message was direct, but Alec admitted he didn't have the first idea about what kind of bug was in the home, but nothing surprised him anymore.

Alec found a spot to the left of the table, and it was not

long before UT was at his elbow. He put his finger to his mouth to signal quiet and removed a small lipstick shaped device from his pocket. UT pushed a switch on the side, which activated the device, making a sound reminding Alec of special effect sounds from an old Science Fiction movie. He moved the object up to Alec's head and down to his feet. He noticed a small light on the side turn from red to green when he finished with his feet. His action caught the attention of passerby's who stopped and looked for a moment. UT caught on.

"This will be perfect for our next movie," UT commented.

Hearing this, they walked away none the wiser.

"It's good to see you again, Mr. Richardson," UT said and stuck out his hand.

"You as well, UT," Grasping his hand and shaking it firmly. "You want to tell me what that was all about?"

"Sure, but let's walk over to the observation railing behind the restaurant."

UT pointed to a small deck overlooking the water that visitors could use to watch the Potomac River traffic.

"We can talk better there."

The two men walked down the sidewalk and up the gentle grade to the place UT suggested. UT stopped and leaned forward on the rail. Alec followed his example. Both men looked out at the river and not at each other. UT began the conversation.

"The device I just used debugged your clothes, Mr. Richardson."

"What do you mean, debugged my clothes?" he asked, still looking out at the river pretending to be interested in the boats sailing or fishing in front of him.

"We all heard about BWI. I am not surprised you ended up there. You always were a smart reporter. Your visit caused a lot of concern."

"Well, sorry about that UT, but it was something we had to do. You want to tell me about that device?"

If he was going to help Alec, he had to be honest with him. It all starts here. After a moment, UT answered.

"Yes. After you were gassed and brought to the loading dock, we used new nanotechnology created in our lab to bug each of you. We call them "dust mites" because of the double meaning for bugs. I'm sorry we could not be more original."

"I don't care about the name, UT. What are they?"

"Dust mites are surveillance devices, not visible to the naked eye. You had about 300 on you today that I just deactivated."

"300! How many were put on us that night?"

"Approximately 20,000. Each is an independent device integrating their information with each other. They send their audio signals back to our listening post. We've recorded all your conversations since leaving BWI."

"Wait, all of them?"

Alec leaned closer to UT.

"Even the intimate ones?"

"All of them, Mr. Richardson. And based on Ms. Hall's reaction during those moments, it seems that you have more talent than just writing."

Alec did not know whether he wanted to be embarrassed or smile at UT's comments. Part of him felt like he was just hanging out with one of his old friends, talking about guy stuff, but he had to pull himself back to focus on what UT was really saying. UT was not a friend, and his familiarly with him could be an attempt to lower his defense. Alec settled for pride and humility.

"That's good to know UT. Is there any way to turn them off during those special moments?"

"None. Each mite receives signals up to 500 feet. What makes them powerful is once they deploy, they associate with the closest smartphone. The mites use the phone to transmit their information. If you have a signal on your phone, we can hear you. Your phone gives you no indication that this is happening."

Alec recalled that TVs and other devices could be used by the intelligence agencies to eavesdrop, but using microscopic devices to piggyback off a smartphone was pretty ingenious.

"So, where are they?"

"You brought them into your house, into your car. Anywhere you've been, you have dropped them, and they have associated with the nearest phone. It's quite impressive technology."

"How long can these devices work?"

"A while, Mr. Richardson."

UT was not going to reveal more than necessary.

"For now, I want you to take this."

UT handed him a lipstick type device.

"Do not use it unless you have to and use it as I did. Those that monitor would notice your absence if you suddenly stopped sending information."

"How does this work?" Alex asked, inspecting the gadget.

"This device produces a small EMP signal that fries the internal circuity of the dust mites. Turn it on, wave it over the areas about six inches away, and the bugs are gone."

"And now? Will there be a gap in my monitoring?"

"I will take care of our time here today when I get back. You have to trust me, Mr. Richardson."

"So this technology explains my meeting with the *Guardian*. You heard it all?"

"With Mr. Wilkes? Yes, we did."

"And you took Grant's family because you heard I was going to publish?"

"Yes."

"Well, I guess that brings us to the point of our meeting today. So what do you want, UT?"

UT looked at the river and thought for a moment. He then turned to Alec.

"I want out."

Alec was surprised. He expected to be working a deal with UT for the release of Grant's family. Instead, the medical genius associated with VLS was telling him he was done with the Supervisor and the program. *How do you break that kind of loyalty?*

"Why are you doing this, UT? You are as committed to this program as anyone."

"You are wrong, Mr. Richardson. I am committed to the program that was in your story. The program that you visited. These recent events sicken me. A wonderful asset for our nation is being used for the wrong purposes because of powerful people. The Supervisor was an honorable and ethical man; and now, I am expected to put women and children in the SOUP. These people are innocent and have committed no crime! That is not who I am! Criminals in the SOUP, yes. Innocents no. They have taken this too far."

This was amazing. Alec would not have expected someone like UT to have a conscience. Most in positions like his were loyal to the program, whatever the circumstances.

"Ok, UT, I am willing to help you, but you have to help us."

"So, what do you want?"

"I want answers and the truth."

"I may not answer every question, but the answers I give will be the truth."

Good enough, Alec thought.

"Is all of Grant's family and a man named Darnell at the facility?"

"Yes, and Darnell Washington's mother. Grant calls her Maggie. She is there as well."

"What about a man that worked for Maggie that saw the facility?"

"Shot and killed in DC shortly after his cousin's funeral by the same people that killed his cousin. We never took him – but we were going to. It might have saved his life."

"Why did you take Maggie?"

"National Security. Our cameras at the home assisted with quick identification, just like they did with you at BWI. She saw the operation, Mr. Richardson. The decision was made to pick her up."

Alec could not believe what he was hearing. What kind of people pick up an older woman shooed away by one of the agents?

"Why didn't you just let her stay on the street?"

"First, Mr. Richardson, she tipped off Officer Grant; and that's what started this whole chain of events."

"And second?"

UT looked at him with resolve that Alec had not witnessed before with the man.

"We can talk about that later."

Alec caved. He knew there was information that UT would not share. Stay focused on the main objective he told himself. He needed to get Grant's family out and make his mistake right.

"Ok, UT – you get a pass on that one."

UT sighed, an apparent emotional weight taken off his shoulders.

"Can we take them out of the SOUP?"

"Yes. It's like coming out of a coma. They will remember their last memory in Real Space, but nothing else."

"Does it hurt them?"

"We don't know. We have limited experience with taking people out of the SOUP. But our data suggest there are no long-term effects."

"Then why did the Supervisor evade my question when I asked him about this?"

"The Supervisor is not going to give you an answer that is not factual. As a medical doctor, I can tell you I think they will be fine with some risk. As a manager, he is going to tell you only when he knows the facts."

Once again, that made sense to Alec.

"How do we get them out?"

"Grant was close at BWI. Opening the Box, that's our word for it, and disconnecting them from the Jacket and the Crown. Again, our terms. The procedures inside the container have to be followed closely. It involves pushing a couple of buttons only, but if they are not disengaged from the SOUP correctly and in the right sequence, you're going to have someone with no brain activity. They'll be a vegetable. That much I know for sure."

Alec listened to what he said. The information was believable, and he felt that UT was truthful with him. He had no reason to lie. He wondered briefly about how he knew about the possibility of making a SOUP occupant a vegetable, but did not think it would help to know the answer. Could he trust UT? If the Supervisor wanted them, he could pick them up, but then why release them from BWI in the first place? These facts fell in place for him. He trusted UT on his first visit in August of last year to visit the facility. He decided to trust him now.

"UT, they are not going to let us walk in and take them out. Have you thought about that?"

"I have. I also think I have a plan that will work."

"Ok, let's hear it."

"The Supervisor and the team are going to the Hill this Thursday to brief the Committee. That gives us three days to prepare. The Committee oversees the program policy and funding. And no, I am not telling you who sits on the Committee. All I will say is they are very powerful people."

Alec nodded.

"The briefing begins at 0800 in the morning, so the team will be out around 0700. That will leave only two agents in the facility and one topside in the home by the elevator. I can handle them with the same substance used on you at BWI. It will clear quickly so you will not be affected when you come into the facility."

"Alright. Where do we meet you?"

"Park about a quarter of a mile from the facility. Our

cameras will not see you with clarity that far away."

Alec understood.

"When you see The Supervisor leave, debug everyone, and come inside the home to the Funeral Director's office. The elevator to go downstairs is there. I will meet you in the office. The gas will keep the agents out for two hours. I will use my credentials to get you past the security doors and into the cell block. I know the inmates you want and will unlock the containers from the VLS Environment room. We have added some enhancements since your visit, so the higher containers do not need a lift to move them anymore. They will come to ground level."

"What do we need to do?"

"Until Thursday morning, I need you to deceive the program. I am going to have to add more dust mites to you when you leave. Write a script that you follow for the next two days that focuses on an internal discussion of whether you should publish or not. Keep them guessing and have them believe you and Ms. Hall have split from Officer Grant because of your differences to publish. Have Officer Grant go home for these days. The less you communicate, the better."

"How do I do that?"

"Look, Mr. Richardson, you have a Pulitzer Prize, write something! I can't solve every problem."

Alec smiled and looked at UT. UT had not noticed, but a few of the people close to them turned and looked at his last outburst but kept walking on their way. UT was obviously under pressure.

"Ok," Alec said, lowering his voice, "I will put together a script and list of topics to avoid. I'll show it to them when I see them. This way, Grant and Adelle will know what we are doing and why."

"Good. But under no circumstance remove their bugs until you are about to enter the facility. Now one last part of the plan. We have to leave the facility and be on our way by 0900, if not sooner."

"That cuts it pretty short, UT."

"We have plenty of time to pull your people out of the SOUP. I am more concerned when the effects of the anesthesia will start wearing off. The agents will make things very difficult if they catch us down below. While Officer Grant is home, have him procure protective masks for you. Standard police issue will protect you from the type gas I will use to flood the facility in the event I have to flood it again. We can get his family out, though we may have to carry them. Let me give you this as well."

UT looked around to see if anyone was watching him and pulled from his jacket two small, round devices about 2 inches in diameter. On the top of the device was a handle, that screwed into the top of the object holding a thin piece of gold metal. The gold metal and device were held together with a pin stuck in a small hole. The pin was flared out at the opposite end to prevent it from accidentally falling out and was the largest part on the items.

"Are those what I think they are?" Alec reached over and took the devices in each hand, marveling at their small size and simplicity.

"Yes, they are small nonexplosive grenades containing the mixture of gas that I will use to knock everyone out. We used these in a special bin connected to the office you were in at BWI. The room at BWI was pressurized to keep the gas from escaping into the facility. The effects lasted much longer at BWI because of the overpressure system in the room with the shipments. Your bodies absorbed a fairly concentrated amount which kept you out much longer than normal."

This answered some of the questions Alec had about that night at BWI.

"I will use larger versions of these little jewels to knock everyone out on Thursday. The grenades you have are small but powerful. The gas will put to sleep anyone within a 5000 square foot building. It works quickly, about 10 seconds, but wears off within 8 minutes, so if you use them, you must act quickly. They are made out of a special plastic alloy, so an added feature is infrared or metal detecting sensors can't see them. Put them away for safekeeping. If I do my job, you will not need them on Thursday."

"So, why are you giving these to me?"

"We don't know the future, Mr. Richardson. I have found when you are going to do what we have planned, you will always need something like these later on as well. Call it insurance for now."

"Thanks, UT."

He put them away into his jacket. Alec could sense there was something UT was not saying. He pushed for more.

"UT – is there something more you are not telling me?"

Silence. Alec could see that he was thinking through how best to explain what he was thinking or even to share the information.

"Mr. Richardson, we are technically making a prison break. The agents are authorized to use deadly force to stop inmates from getting back into society, AND once you are out of the SOUP, they will not put you back in. Do you understand what I am saying?"

Alec understood. The agents would shoot to kill. Alec could feel his blood start to pump harder. He looked at UT and could tell there was more.

"What else?"

"There is a Rapid Response Force of five more agents. This team carries heavy weapons and will activate if they suspect a problem."

"What kind of problem?"

"The Supervisor and the facility use a duress system. If the guards at the facility do not authenticate every two hours or the boss does not check-in 15 minutes after his projected arrival time at a new location, the Response Force automatically assumes the worse and deploys."

"What do we do about them?"

"I will gas the alternate elevator entry and tunnel as

well. The Response Force will come that way, but I can offer no assurances. We need to get in and out quickly. This is why I can only keep the facility out for two hours. The shorter it takes us to free the family, the more time we have before the two hours expire. Do you understand?"

Alec nodded his head in affirmation.

"Anything else?"

UT paused.

"Listen to me, Mr. Richardson, I want to go with you when we leave. I am not going back there."

Alec thought about it and expected this. Once they entered the facility, their digital data would be everywhere, and that included UT's. There would be no doubt that he was the insider that betrayed the program.

"I understand. Do you have any place in mind?"

"Off the grid – no technology. Once you get rid of the mites, the program will have no *immediate* way to know where you are. They will use normal procedures such as cameras and other surveillance devices, but as you saw, these are all made faster because of the AI advances we have made. When I say off the grid, I mean the middle of nowhere."

He stopped for a moment.

"Personally, I have always wanted to visit Utah. You work this out with your team along with the logistics for getting out west. I leave that part in your capable hands."

"Why do you trust me, UT?"

"Because you were at BWI. You know what they are doing is wrong, and you and your friends acted. You are also willing to risk your lives to publish your story and now, to save Officer Grant's family. That shows me all I need to know about you, Alec."

Alec did not miss the use of his first name.

"Okay."

Alec reached over and shook UT's hand.

"Thank you in advance. See you on Thursday."

"Thursday," UT repeated. "Oh, a couple more things.

Leave your cell phones at home. Pull any phone numbers off them you will need. Bring cash to sustain you for about two months; gold or silver, if you have it. For a while, we are going back to the Stone Age."

Alec smiled. Gold or silver was not in his portfolio.

"Now, let's get you bugged again."

UT pulled out a small container that looked like a woman's round compact with a small tube. He pressed the side, and a red glow came from within the box. When it turned green, he twisted the top, opening up a small hole in the side. He placed the small tube in his mouth and blew a quick puff. Alec felt nothing. UT looked at the device and gave him a thumbs up. The two men walked off in different directions. Alec had a script to write and a lot to think about before going home.

CHAPTER 32

The team sat a little more than a quarter of a mile away from the facility in South East, hidden in a small shopping center off of the main road in two vehicles. Grant was driving his 2008 Town and Country mini-van, large enough to carry his family, Darnell, and Maggie. Adelle and Alec were in his BMW 5 series.

The plan was to get Grant's family and head west on Benning Road to a local bus and limo company where a large white panel van was positioned, parked there the day before. They would leave their own cars, move everyone into the vehicle and head south down Interstate 295, then Interstate 495 West. Alexandria was the first exit over the Woodrow Wilson Bridge. Located in a parking garage near the Torpedo Factory in Old Town were two more rental cars loaded with the supplies and cash necessary to get out of Northern Virginia. They would swap the vehicles with the white van and start the trek west, heading south first to Richmond on Route 1 and then secondary roads to stay off the interstates as far as they could.

Alec felt awkward, asking his neighbor to contract the rental cars. He simply handed his neighbor an envelope with instructions to rent the vehicles for 30 days and $10,000 in cash. He promised $5,000 more when the cars were delivered to his neighbor's house that evening. Alec provided the key to a small shed with a strongbox where his neighbor could find more cash to cover the value of the cars if something happened. He explained all this in his written document instructions. Alec stated he was doing investigative work and could not be associated with or mention the transaction. His neighbor understood the need for a Pulitzer Prize winning investigative reporter to talk little and pay well for service. There were no questions, and Adelle helped Alec prep and position the vehicles when they arrived, occasionally talking about the BWI story but mostly about their fictional intent to marry. Alec had not realized the amount of detail that goes into wedding planning, and the conversation more than covered their time preparing together.

Grant spent his time back at the precinct, asking for favors the same way. A handwritten note to a friend resulted in procuring three silencers for the .45s they recently bought. Grant always believed you asked for more than what you needed. He bought one for his police revolver years ago, and he packed all four in his overnight bag as he said goodbye to his house, knowing he may never return. He also poked around the precinct and was able to get the police protective masks that Alec said they would need. He used the same philosophy as the silencers, and to his satisfaction was given five that had mysteriously fallen off the property book last spring. Grant didn't need to ask questions. He spent the remaining half-day in Alexandria with Adelle and Alec, prepping for the trip, positioning cars, and covering their activity by genuinely getting to know each other and discussing the pros and cons of publishing their story. As a precautionary measure, Alec had taken the extra silencer, .45 ammo, the two gas grenades, and two additional protective masks and put them in a small carry bag. He placed the bag inside of a cardboard moving box. Alec showed Adelle and Grant what he'd done, taped the box closed, marked it Christmas, and took it to the attic. He hoped he would never have to use them after today.

The three stood in their hiding place parking lot and observed the home through their binoculars. No movement yet, and none of them said a word to tip off the operation; despite their phones remaining at home. Alec looked at his watch. It was 7:10. All three were wearing light jackets and holstered their sidearm underneath, silencers were in their inside jacket pockets. Alec shared the details of the guard policy and the reaction force in his handwritten script that he had shown the others after his meeting with UT. None of them expected this to be easy, and they were taking no chances. Adelle touched Alec and pointed to the home. Two black government SUVs were pulling out of the parking lot and onto the main road. Alec acknowledged with a thumbs up. He removed the lipstick device that UT gave him and turned it on as UT showed him. Alec waved the device near Adelle until a green light appeared. He turned it off and back on and repeated the motions with Grant. Greenlight. Adelle did the same for Alec. All green.

"Ok, let's go," Grant said. "And drive normal. We have to move quickly, but let's not draw suspicion by driving crazy."

The two cars pulled out of their hiding place and headed up the main road with Grant in the lead and pulled into the funeral home's main driveway. They pulled around back to the parking lot and took the extra time to pull into the parking space backward, pointing toward the main road. They expected to be leaving in a hurry. All three exited their vehicles and headed for a doorway in the back that Grant identified.

"Come on, UT. I hope you have taken care of everything," Alec said out loud, crossing his fingers as he did so.

Grant jumped up onto the platform and pulled Adelle up. Alec followed.

"Alec, they built this platform for the facility. This is new construction," Grant said.

Alec nodded. Grant pulled on the two metal doors. They were locked.

"Now what!" Alec asked.

"No problem," Grant said, removing his pistol, attaching the silencer, and putting two rounds into the door before anyone could object. The right door swung open. There were no alarms.

"Let's go!"

Grant motioned to follow him. All three moved through the door in single file. Then Grant stopped at a hall intersection.

"Head to the Funeral Director's office," Alec said and pointed to a sign on the wall that indicated the direction.

As they turned the corner and walked into the office, an agent was sprawled out on the floor along with two other program employees that posed as funeral parlor workers for the local community. All three were unconscious. They surveyed the room and saw no elevator.

"Now what?" Grant said, looking for the main entrance.

"Give him time," Adelle said.

At that moment, a large bookcase on the wall in front of them slid sideways, revealing a freight elevator. In the center stood UT in a gas protective mask. He pulled it off and motioned to come.

"This way!"

The three rushed in. UT pushed a down button, and the bookcase returned to its initial place, covering the elevator entrance. The elevator descended to the facility with a smooth but quick drop. Everyone felt it in their stomachs.

"Any problems?" Grant asked UT.

"None. When we get to the bottom, I would like Alec with me. Grant, you and Ms. Hall go to the cell block and be ready to open the containers as they come to the ground. PLEASE follow the instructions inside. I assume Alec has briefed you?"

"Yes. I got it," Grant said.

"I have set the security doors to open when I authenticate with the first one."

The elevator stopped, and the doors opened on the opposite side of their entry, revealing the glossy white interior that Alec recognized immediately from his visit.

"Grant, you will also need this code, 1998S, to disconnect the crown. I will join you as soon as I get everyone to the ground."

The group quickly jogged to the first door. UT slid his ID card, punched in his eight-digit code, and responded to the biometric authentication. He added the necessary security code to open each of the doors from this authentication console. Each of the three doors opened, providing unrestricted access to the facility.

As they moved through the door, Alec pointed Grant and Adelle to the cell block. He proceeded with UT to the VLS Environment control room. It looked much different now. TVs were lit up with displays providing the core of information used by the three analysts lying on the floor near their desks. Their job to control and improve the engineering marvel of the facility was on a temporary hold. UT moved to a desk with a computer.

"Alec, help me move this person out of the way."

Alec grabbed the arms of an unconscious woman and pulled her away from the desk. UT immediately sat down.

"I am accessing the main inmate database," he told Alec.

A display list appeared with each of the names for the corresponding numbers on the container.

"Here they are!"

He pressed a "Maintenance" button next to each name on the touch screen, and an indicator turned green for each of them.

"Ok – we are all set. The containers should be coming down. Head to the cell block, Alec."

UT stood up, and as he did, an alarm on the console sounded.

"What happening, UT?"

"It's one of the containers, the one with Darnell Washington. The new loading device has malfunctioned. His container is not moving!"

"How do we deal with this, UT?"

"The container is on the third row. The door has opened, but the Box is stuck inside. Let me keep working this. If we need to, there is a manual extraction device to unlock the clamps. It's locked in a storage cabinet. Wake the others! If I can't get the loading device to work, I will bring it with me. Now go!"

Alec left the room and entered the cell block. Grant was beginning to wake the person in the first container on the first row. Two boxes were in various states of movement as the loading devices brought them to ground level. They operated through a series of motions that looked like mechanical arms that appeared from a bigger tube. These arms suspended the weight of the coffin in midair and then built a framework below it to lower the coffin to the ground. It resembled a painter's scaffolding to Alec. The operation produced a low hum and then loud clicks as connections in the arms locked together. Alec ran to Grant and Adelle at the back of the cell block.

"Cross your fingers!"

Grant worked through the procedure of opening the coffin as he did at BWI. As the top lifted, he immediately recognized his daughter.

"It's Michaela! Adelle, please read the instructions inside the lid for me."

Adelle scanned the long list of items under Emergency Actions.

"Found it! There should be a connection up near the crown, the device on her head, on the right side of the coffin. It is a keypad. Enter the code to disconnect the crown from the inmate."

"Code? What code?" Grant asked, lost in the emotion of the moment.

"1998S," Adelle reminded him.

"Found the keypad!" Grant replied.

He observed a small device with ten digits and five letters on a tiny keyboard. He pressed in the four numbers, and the letter 's' and nothing happened.

"Nothing's happening. Are you sure that's the right

code?"

"Positive," Adelle responded. "Let me look."

She did a quick observation of the pad and saw a small shift key. She entered the code again this time using the shift key before pressing the "s." The coffin began to hum as the local battery provided the power to move the gear assembly and start the complicated procedure of disconnecting the fiber optic cables from the crown assembly.

"Ok – it's working. What is the second step?"

Adelle read for all to hear.

"When the crown assembly is disconnected, press the button pad next to the jacket assembly interface on the right inside of the container at the container's mid-point. Press the 'release' button to disconnect the jacket assembly. Jesus, who writes this stuff?"

Grant ignored the question and focused on recovering Michaela.

"Ok, found that as well. How do we know when the crown assembly is disconnected?" Grant asked.

As if in response to his question, the crown emitted three beeps and separated with an audible click.

"It's done!"

Adelle pressed the "release" button. All three marveled at what was occurring in front of them. The lights on the jacket were the first to turn off, followed by pops as the feeding and waste extraction tubes separated from the connectors on Michaela's body and the Jacket assembly. Adelle could smell urine as one of the plastic tubes spilled its blue contents inside the coffin after coming free from the jacket.

"That's all. Let's get the jacket off. It looks like it's hooked to the sides," Alec said, pulling the snaps away from his portion of the outer mesh.

Grant and Adelle joined in, snapping and popping sounds reinforcing their progress until no connectors remained. As they lifted the Jacket, they could make out key places where her body and the sensors precisely matched the body function needed to maintain her life support.

"Grant, let's get to the next ones! We are running on the clock. Adelle, stay with her until she wakes up."

The two ran over to the next container on the ground, and Grant went to work to repeat the process. Alec noted that the door to the outer container housing Darnell was open, but the coffin had not moved. *Damn, that's going to be a problem*, he thought.

UT walked in to confirm Alec's assessment with a device under his arm and a bundle of lab coats and jogged to the coffin they were getting ready to open.

"We are going to have to pull it out manually. Can you drive a forklift, Alec?"

"I can try."

"Follow me," he said. "It's kept in the rear of the cell block. I have the keys."

"Grant?" Alec was looking to confirm that he could handle the coffin on his own.

"I got this. I know what I am doing now."

A shout went up from Adelle.

"She's awake and asking questions!"

"That's a good sign," UT said. "Hurry, Alec. We need to get this last one out. Grant, put them in these lab coats. It will help to warm their internal body temperature."

Grant was conflicted between running to his baby girl and working to free the next in his family. Adelle could take care of Michaela. He decided to keep working. He came for everyone, and he was leaving no one behind.

Alec and UT reached the locked closet. UT produced the keys and swung open the doors that were flush with the walls. Inside, a forklift vehicle was parked. Alec jumped in, found the start button, and pushed it. He was surprised when the lights on the dash came on, but there was no engine sound. Alec looked at UT with a perplexed look.

"It's electric," UT said.

Alec reached for the gear level and placed it in reverse.

The vehicle lurched out of the closet. Alec turned the wheel quickly and applied the brakes, causing the tires to squeal on the polished floor. UT jumped on and gave the thumbs up. *I have this*, Alec told himself. He placed the gear selector into drive and began the short trip to Darnell's container.

"Park in front of the yellow line. That will give us the distance we need to back the box out of the container. You are going to have to lift me to the third level so that I can disconnect the box from the inside locks of the deployment system," UT directed.

"Ok, but give me a couple of minutes to get the hang of the lifting controls."

"We don't have minutes."

Alec looked at his watch. It read 7:57. He was going to take a couple of minutes regardless of what UT said. The thought of the coffin bouncing off the floor put a pit in his stomach. He pulled up to the line as UT suggested. As UT started to step on the vehicle to be lifted by the forks, Alec stopped him.

"I want to try this first. Don't get on the fork."

The controls looked reasonably simple, and Alec began his trial and error phase of learning how to raise and lower the forks. He started the toggle motion of the controls with his hands. He was surprised when the forks responded and moved to the top position. Filled with confidence, he brought them back down, and they crashed with a loud "boom" that echoed in the cell block and caused everyone to look up at him.

Ok –move more slowly coming down, he told himself. He looked over at UT.

"Ready to go?"

"Why don't you practice the move one more time, Alec? After that last try, I agree we can take another minute."

UT smiled at Alec, but he did not have the confidence to let Alec lift him to the third level and bring him and the coffin down gently.

"Jump on the fork. I've got this figured out."

UT moved to the front of the vehicle.

"Get on, UT!"

UT reluctantly stepped on his new ride. Alec lifted the fork like a pro three feet upward, giving UT the space to sit down and straddle the device like a cowboy on his horse. Then he lifted him the rest of the way to the third level approximately 15 feet from the hard surface below. UT pulled himself up using the open outer door.

"Get me closer," he yelled down to Alec. He moved the vehicle forward.

"That's it. WHOA!"

Alec pressed the brakes pitching UT slightly forward.

Thank God it was not any higher, UT thought.

A 15-foot fall seemed less ominous than 20! UT reached down and moved a lever inside the lip on the outer container, and a three foot by three footpad emerged from the wall underneath the forks of the vehicle.

"Service platform!" UT yelled and stepped on the platform, freeing himself from the forklift. "Turn your vehicle sideways so I can slide the coffin onto the forks." And he pulled the unlocking device from a pocket in his lab coat. Alec looked at his watch. 8:10.

A smile broadened on his face as he saw Adelle, walking with Michaela toward Grant. Michaela was shaky on her feet but under her own power. Grant had the second coffin open and looked like he was getting ready to remove the jacket as he looked for the crown security pad.

Alec lowered the forks and maneuvered the vehicle into position to accept the coffin sideways when UT was ready. He just finished positioning the forklift when UT yelled, "Ok, Alec, the locks are released. I am going to slide the coffin out. Have the forks ready at the same height or as close as you can."

UT reached inside and using the platform for leverage pulled on the coffin. It slid easily out onto extended rails. UT held it, controlling the speed as the arms rolled it out until it extended fully. The forks were too high. UT signaled to lower the forks and closed his fist when they matched the needed height. He finished sliding the coffin out the remaining space and slowly nursed it onto the forklift.

"Take it down!"

Alec moved the lever causing the forks to drop suddenly, causing both he and UT to gasp. The coffin settled itself but was off balance, looking precariously close to falling. Without overthinking the problem, he brought the lift down, the coffin delicately balancing on one and a half of the forks. Six inches from the ground, the coffin slid and landed with a dignified but loud "clump."

Alec looked up. UT was unexpressive. He backed away and cleared the lift and raised it again to retrieve his reluctant passenger. UT stepped off the platform and on to the fork, this time standing and holding onto the steel frame of the vehicle. The lift touched down again, the better landing of the three, and UT jumped off toward Darnell's coffin. Alec turned off the lift and headed to assist Grant. As he arrived, Grant was at work opening the last coffin containing LaShanda. Maggie was already sitting up in hers, and Alec moved to her side.

"Let me help you out of this, Ms. Washington."

He looked over to Adelle and Michaela. Grant gave them a lab coat, and Michaela was looking much better already. Alec reached over for a lab jacket on the floor, helped her to stand, and wrapped the coat around her shoulders.

"Who are you?" she asked weakly.

"We are your family," Alec responded. "Lift your foot over the side. That's it. One at a time."

Maggie was out, and Adelle rushed over to support her weight.

"I've got you, Ms. Washington. Come over here with me."

Adelle guided her to where Michaela was standing. UT had his coffin open and was moving through the procedure quickly. Alec decided to help Grant and jogged to where he just entered the code to disengage the crown. He looked at his watch. 8:25. As he approached, tears were streaming down Grant's face as he waited impatiently for the Crown to disengage. Alec looked inside. Grant's LaShanda, the love of his life, even in these conditions, was a real beauty. The Crown disengaged, and Grant pushed the "release" button almost immediately. As the lights on the jacket faded, Grant tore into the device like a man possessed, sending pieces of plastic flying as he ripped the Jacket from her body. Alec freed the two clamps at the bottom and discarded the Jacket on the floor. Grant leaned in.

"Baby, baby," he said, slapping her gently on the cheek. "Baby, please wake up."

"Give it a couple of minutes, Grant. There is stuff going on here that we can't see. She is already on her way back to you."

While it sounded good as Alec said it, he had no clue what he was saying was true.

"UT," Alec yelled. "All ok?"

"He's fine. Give me a couple of minutes. His temperature needs to return to normal."

"See Grant? Her temperature has to stabilize."

He caught a quick look at Adelle, keeping control of Michaela and Maggie as they continued to walk in a daze. 8:31. Alec felt his pulse start to quicken. It was going to take them at least five or more minutes to load them in the Van.

Alec was startled as he heard, "You old fool!" come from Grant's direction. The officer broke into open sobs.

"I'll help you, baby, hold on."

Grant kissed LaShanda's cheek.

"I'm never letting you go again!"

Alec grabbed a lab coat and gave it to Grant.

"Here, put this on her when I get her to stand up."

He looked at LaShanda and said, "Mrs. Grant, can you stand?"

"You're damn right, I can!" she replied, defiant but weak.

"Grant, get her up. I am going to help UT with Darnell.

We gotta go!"

Alec looked in UT's direction. Darnell was sitting up, holding his head. Alec closed the distance, quickly bringing the last lab coat.

"My head hurts," Darnell said.

"Tough landing," UT said, looking at Alec.

"Any landing you can walk away from...you know the rest, UT. Darnell, we have to go. Can you stand up?"

Alec was helping Darnell to his feet.

"Yes."

Darnell used Alec to stand up, and UT wrapped the lab coat around him.

"Let's walk," UT commanded and gingerly moved Darnell out of his coffin.

Alec did a quick survey of his surroundings. Michaela looked the best. Maggie's color was returning fast. 8:37.

UT and Darnell were with Adelle and her group. Grant had LaShanda standing and shuffling toward the door.

"Let's go, Adelle, guide them out. UT, take Darnell."

The group moved out of the cellblock door and into the hallway. The secure doors were still open.

"Alec, I have a bag around the corner with some medical items. I can work on them while we are driving. Let me get it."

Alec took Darnell placing Darnell's arm around his neck.

"Lean on me, Darnell."

The two of them shuffled down the hall to the elevator.

"Come on, UT!" Alec yelled, positioned at the front of the open elevator.

Grant pushed the up button, the doors opened, and everyone moved inside. UT emerged from around the corner with a bag in his hand.

"Let's go. I just saw the analyst team start to wake up."

UT stepped in the elevator, and Grant pushed the "door closed" button. Nothing happened. Alec looked at UT. UT pushed the button, and the doors slowly closed, eating into valuable time. 8:42.

Alec reached into his jacket pocket and pulled out his silencer. This would be the time when they might have to use their pistols. Best to be prepared. He looked over at Adelle and motioned with his head for her to do the same. She did. Both screwed them on to the end of their .45. Alec's read Obsidian 45. *Beats the hell of him where Grant got them, but he hoped they worked.*

The front elevator doors opened, and the bookcase slid to the side. Adelle was the first to see the agent slowly standing, shaking his head, and reach for his pistol when he observed the group. She fired one shot and hit the agent in the chest, sending him backward and covering the furniture behind him with blood. His pistol dropped with a dull thud on the carpeted floor. The group shuffled out past the dead agent, each still too unsteady to take in what just happened. Alec reached down and grabbed the pistol.

"Head them for the side exit," UT said. "We can load faster."

"Grant, go get the van! Adelle, here are the keys. Get our car. I will stay here in the event the guards come up from downstairs. Go!"

The two moved out of the back door that they entered. UT and Alec shuffled the group down the hall. 8:50

The BMW drove by first and braked. Grant parked the van outside the door used generally by the funeral home and slid open the side door to the minivan. Alec kept watching in the direction of the Director's Office for more agents. Grant and Adelle loaded Darnell and Michaela first in the very rear and Maggie and LaShanda in the middle seats. Grant closed the door and got into the front seat. UT walked around the van and got into the passenger side seat. Adelle ran to Alec.

"Let's go. Everyone is loaded."

The sound of the bookcase sliding told them what they needed to know. Someone had just come up the elevator.

"We've got to hit them first while they are still not 100%," he whispered to Adelle.

Alec moved toward the Director's office. Adelle was right with him. As they turned the corner, two agents were in the room, one kneeling over their dead comrade and the other standing. Both were still shaking the cobwebs out of their heads. Adelle and Alec fired. They dropped both, firing several shots each, their silencers muffling the sound into "pops." They were not sure if they killed them or not. Both rapidly moved out of the office and down the hall.

"What happened?" Grant asked.

"Tell you later," Alec said, rushing by and jumped into the driver's seat of the still running BMW. Adelle got in. He put it in gear and pulled out of the driveway and turned left onto Benning Road. Another car approached, and Grant delayed a moment. Then he too pulled out and followed Alec. UT got up from his seat and slid between the two front captain chairs with his medical bag ready to assist each of the passengers back to this reality.

They rapidly approached Minnesota Ave and were caught by the light. Alec was first to stop. Grant was a car behind and observable by Alec. So far, so good. Not far to the transfer point. As the light turned green, Alec accelerated through as did the car behind him. As Grant entered the intersection, the vehicle behind Alec stopped abruptly. Adelle turned to see what was happening when a Black SUV pulled out of a nearby apartment complex, drove over the curb to avoid the traffic and plowed into the mini-van from the side, collapsing the sliding door.

"Oh, God!" Adelle yelled. "Someone has hit the van!"

Alec looked in his rearview mirror and saw the mini-van with a caved-in passenger side pushed into the eastbound lanes of the intersection. Grant opened his door and stumbled out of the driver's seat. The car behind them turned around and raced to the intersection to block off the northbound lanes of Minnesota. Two agents jumped out of the car and leaving their doors open, crouched behind them, and started to fire their automatic rifles into the van and at Grant. It was the

Response Force, called by the agents from in the facility before they shot them in the Director's office. Alec already knew the outcome. Deadly force, no one was going back into the SOUP — escaped inmates.

Alec pulled off the side of the road along with several vehicles as they watched the scene unfold. Many accelerated to leave, weaving around the cars and adding to the chaos. Grant returned fire at the two agents, and Alec saw one go down. The three agents from the SUV that t-boned the mini-van remained in position behind their van firing and riddling the mini-van with bullets from handheld machine guns almost at point-blank range.

They watched in horror as Grant was shot several times and crumpled to the pavement. The agents continued to fire until the side of the van was filled with bullet holes, and then one called for a cease-fire. An agent from the SUV walked cautiously to the vehicle, fired a short burst inside at one of the passengers, and threw what looked like a smoke canister under the back of the van. The grenade puffed then turned bright white. Alec knew it was a thermite grenade built not to explode into shrapnel but burn. It ignited the dripping gas from the collision under the van and blazed a new trail to the gas tank.

The tank blew, transforming the car into an inferno, sending shards of glass from the windows into the street. Alec watched, unable to move as he saw the body of one of their friends creating circles in the flames and heard their cries of agony, and then all movement and cries stopped. Alec looked over to Adelle and saw her drop to her knees and vomit, unable to control her body's response to what she just witnessed. He ran around the car to the other side and watched her as she retched again, her body heaving in massive waves of emotion.

"They murdered them like animals, Alec! They were not criminals!"

Alec grabbed her by her shirt and threw her into the passenger side of the car and shut the door, trying to keep himself from losing everything inside of him as well. He ran back to his side of the car as she continued to wretch with nothing left to exit, curled in a compressed fetal position in the front seat. Sirens from the local police and rescue vehicles began to sound in the distance as they responded to the incident. The remaining motorists were getting back in their cars and leaving fast, not wanting to be part of the imminent chaos as police cleaned up the carnage and tried to figure out what happened. Alec looked in his rearview mirror, the black SUV and other car were gone, sped off to some hidden location.

Alec put his car in gear and crossed 295. He saw the limo yard and the white van parked along a side road outside of the fenced lot. Alec pulled up behind it and turned off the BMW. He moved to the driver's side of the van, opened the door, pulled the keys from his pocket, and turned on the ignition. Alec quickly ran back to the BMW and opened the passenger side door. Adelle was sitting up.

"Let's go, Adelle" he said quietly while helping her out.

The two walked quickly to the van, and Adelle opened the passenger side and got in.

"Alec, get our weapons out of the car!"

Alec went back to the BMW and retrieved their pistols and a small bag in the backseat. Suddenly, he leaned over quickly, vomiting and wrenching next to his car. His chest was heaving as he recalled what just happened to his friend and family. He fought back the emotion.

"Today is not the day for payback, but your day is coming, and I will show you no mercy," he said, wiping the side of his face with his sleeve.

He returned to the van and got into the driver's seat. Adelle's awareness was returning.

"Are you OK," she asked.

Alec nodded. He pulled the vehicle forward and was on the southbound exit just as the DC police began to shut down the on and off-ramps to Benning as well as the northbound lane. He sped up to leave the scene, observing traffic on the north side building into a significant delay as their lanes closed. He just made it out. There was no traffic behind him as the southbound route closed as well.

"Where to Alec?"

They had a plan, and he needed to stick to the script. He was in no condition to improvise as he headed to Alexandria.

"We head west and disappear for a while, then come back and make this right."

"Damn right," she said.

CHAPTER 33

The Supervisor concluded his meeting with the Committee when Dr. O'Neil approached him in the large hall close to the security exit inside the Russell Building. Agent Willis had notified Dr. O'Neil of the escape attempt during the briefing. Rather than interrupt, Dr. O'Neil told Willis "Just handle it. Both knew the procedures and what action was required. Dr. O'Neil provided the Supervisor with only the information he needed.

"There was an inmate escape attempt this morning shortly after you left the facility. Officer Grant, Ms. Hall, and Mr. Richardson came after Grant's family and two others."

"Darnell and Jada Washington?"

"Yes, sir. All but Ms. Hall and Mr. Richardson were killed. UT provided access to the cellblock and died at the scene. Two agents dead, one wounded. The Ready Reaction Force left the scene before local law enforcement arrived."

"They removed them from the SOUP?"

"Yes, sir. They were successful. The new Crown and Jacket removal routines worked well from what we can ascertain. We do not know their mental condition as a result of removing the VLS memories, unfortunately."

The Supervisor did not respond to the apparent disagreement with the Deadly Force policy. His job was to protect society from the nation's worst criminals, and as far as he was concerned, this policy was working.

"Did all this come from the facility video?"

"Yes sir."

"Where are Mr. Richardson and Ms. Hall now?"

"Unknown, sir. They were able to remove the Dust Mites using our EMP device."

"Were you able to trace their car?"

"No, sir. It appears they used multiple cars as part of their escape. Mr. Richardson's BMW was found abandoned off Benning Road, but we have no clue where they are heading."

The Supervisor processed the information he was being provided and then continued.

"How could we lose them Dr. O'Neil?"

"It's a mystery to me Sir. I can get some people looking."

"No, – let's run this one out. I want you to stay focused on our next steps. Let's play their game and wait for them to resurface. We will find them."

"You don't want to bring in additional resources to search?"

"Not at this point. We need to handle this ourselves. I'm not sure how we would be able to explain our actions."

"Yes, sir. I understand. With your permission, I would like to implement Protocol B."

"You have my authorization to proceed with your implementation, Dr. O'Neil."

Dr. O'Neil turned and walked toward the building exit.

The Supervisor made his call and exited the building. His thoughts moved between the topic of the inmates and the additional funding he received to expand the number of facilities under the Program. Los Angeles was greenlighted, and so was Denver. That would require Carter to make overtures to Senator Barnes from Colorado and read him onto the program.

He wondered if the program access was starting to get too big but dismissed the idea almost immediately. He would work with Carter to restrict code name access to only the people that needed to be involved with their methods. Perhaps a different approach was required with Senator Barnes.

Anyway, Barnes would see little value in knowing the details of the program. He already knew about VLS, as did anyone in America that could read or turn on a TV. The progress on inmate transfer and new facilities was satisfactory, and the last update in the *Guardian* by Richardson was giving the President a boost in the polls. The politicians could fight over whose idea it was and what kind of bump they would get. Carter could handle how he wanted Barnes to be involved, he decided. He would call him tomorrow to discuss it. Frankly, he only cared about the success of his program. The political use of his program was disruptive to his schedule. He would be glad when the election was over.

He reflected on his recent testimony to the Committee. This meeting was different. Rather than facility updates and funding requirements, he briefed the Committee on their new breakthrough. Dr. O'Neil believed they found a way to introduce "Cause and Effects Scenarios" into the community database as a source for inmates to access beyond their own collective memories. He explained this to the Committee using the analogy of adding clean water to a muddy pond to decrease the amount of dirt per particle of water. This could produce great results for reforming inmates, he told them. The new protocol, in theory, allowed the program team to insert memories into the community to create more positive experiences and change the perception of their environment. He was looking forward to the testing results to see if these community memories could begin to transform the violent criminals that fueled the inmate's current community. This new procedure offered great hope for removing criminal behavior permanently. If this worked, the SOUP could now be an actual reform environment as well as a containment facility. It was the first step to expanding the program into medium-security inmates. The Supervisor's car pulled up to the same taxi spot as always, and The Supervisor got in.

"To the facility, sir?" his driver asked.

"Yes, let's go see what happened."

CHAPTER 34

Alec could not prevent the screen door from slamming as he walked into the kitchen with three bags of groceries that he purchased from Barrett's Food Town and set them on the counter. He had all the essentials that he and Adelle would need for the next week or so. Alec shut the door to keep the coolness of the window-mounted AC in the house. As he started to unbag his items and put them away, he realized they had almost completed their first month of their six-month lease in a cute little brick home that they found in Salina, UT. They picked the town because it seemed to have the essentials of any small town, and with a population of around 2500 people and both he and Adelle felt the probability of being identified was very low. The only security cameras were near the town bank, and they did not plan to be going there anytime soon.

A month had passed since the attempted escape from the facility. As planned, they picked up one of the provisioned rental cars in Alexandria and headed south on the back roads to Richmond. Neither talked much, each working through the loss of Grant and his family in their own way. They drove through the night on Interstate 64 and stopped somewhere in Beckley, West Virginia. Alec found a place behind a building to spend the night. They slept in the car, not wanting to risk a hotel. They discussed traveling west and decided to stay on back roads when possible and splitting the time behind the wheel. They would risk discovery if they used the Interstates and agreed to only go six hours a day, most of which they chose to drive at night.

As they moved further away from the east coast, they found that the back roads became less of an option, and the interstate was the only way to drive west. They both agreed to press on. They continued west on 64 until it turned into interstate 70 at St. Louis, keeping the course due west, further and further from the facility and its memory. It was outside Kansas City when it finally hit Alec that when he asked UT where he wanted to go, he said Utah. Alec connected his friend's name to the state abbreviation UT and realized the joke. They had driven halfway to a destination determined by UT's sense of humor. When Adelle saw him laughing while pumping gas, she asked him what was happening, and he told her. She joined in with him. It was the first time he felt they were a little like themselves again, though the memory of their friends still had a deep hold on them. They drove through Colorado and smiled at each other when they crossed the Utah state line.

They had not intended to settle in Salina and found it by accident as they turned off 70 and looked for a place to eat late in the evening. Adelle pressed him onward toward Salina, as it showed signs of being civilized. When they arrived in town, they liked the location, and both decided they were tired of running.

Alec also knew that their neighbor would be identified as the renter of the vehicles, and the Supervisor would not take long to begin the process of tracking them down. They paid cash for a used car and two nights later, took the rental deep into the backcountry, and left it in a canyon they found in the surrounding desert. Alec removed the plates and the VIN number, making the engine number the only way to identify the vehicle. They chose their location away from the numerous trails used by the local four-wheelers and hikers. From the looks of the hiding place, they bought themselves at least the six months they were planning to stay.

They were able to convince the local realtor to give them a lease when they paid cash for the full amount in advance. It wasn't until they signed their contract under their new names of Tom and Nancy Snyder, and were chatting with the real estate agent, that she explained the Salina history to them. Shortly after WWII ended, a soldier guarding German and Italian prisoners of war in Camp Salina opened fire with his .30 caliber machinegun, killing nine Germans and wounding 19. He was declared insane afterward, saying he "hated Germans and wanted to kill them." The soldier was sent to a mental hospital in New York. The realtor told them there was even a museum in town, and they should see it. They thanked her for the history lesson and left the office, both shaken by the closeness of their own experience.

Adelle came out of the bedroom and kissed Alec before helping him with the groceries. She was working the outline for the story on the computer they recently purchased. Both had no idea how much they integrated their lives into the internet with credit cards until they started paying cash for things. It was Adelle's idea to go to the local library and use one of their computers to search Craig's list for a laptop. Offerings were abundant, and since they were using it only for word processing, it wasn't long before they identified one. They met the buyer in a place called the Munch Box off Highway 89 in a small town named Gunnison. They promptly purchased their laptop and a couple of memory sticks. After booting the computer to verify it worked, the pair grabbed a burger and fries before returning home. It was on the way home that Adelle mentioned making a food run to Barrett's, saying that they could not continue to live on burgers and fries.

As they put the last of salad ingredients into the refrigerator, Adelle asked, "Would you like to see my outline?"

"Sure," he said enthusiastically.

She went into the bedroom and returned with the computer, placing it on the table so they both could see the 15-inch screen. Alec sat down next to her. The feeling of closeness reenergized buried emotions and revealed how numb he had become since the attempted escape. Adelle began to work through her ideas for the story structure and the organization of the article. Yet, Alec could not focus on what she was saying. He was torn inside about their lives and needed to talk to her, now. He stopped her.

"Adelle, could you put this on hold for just a moment. I need to ask you a question."

She turned her attention from the computer screen and looked at Alec. She could sense that this would be a serious discussion.

"Okay," she reluctantly agreed, not wanting to focus on anything but the story at this time.

Alec searched for the right words to fit the emotion in the room, carried forward from the prior month's events.

"It's been over a month now since the escape. I don't think either of us has concentrated on anything other than surviving. I think we are starting to get our heads back in the game, and we need to talk through what we are going to do."

"Going to do? What do you mean? We are going to write this article and burn those bastards for what they did," she said.

Alec was beginning to regret his decision to bring up the topic and thought about trying to find a way to postpone the subject a little longer but could not. He was committed.

"Adelle, then what?"

It had not come out the way he planned, but he asked the question. Adelle looked at him a moment.

"You mean, how do our lives return to normal if ever?"

Alec nodded.

"So, what is normal to you, Alec? After what we have seen and experienced, normal is a little hard to define."

Alec took a deep breath.

"Maybe. Which is why I think we need to talk through our options. Take a step back and look at where we are."

"You are not having second thoughts about printing the

story, not with everything that has happened, are you?"

"No, we need to print if nothing more than to highlight the wrongs with the program."

"Wrongs with the program, those PEOPLE shot innocent men and women and then burned them! Is that what you call 'wrongs of the program'?"

This conversation was starting to go poorly. Alec needed to refocus Adelle to think about after the story. He was all in now.

"I'm sorry. That came out wrong," he apologized. "So, let's say we print the story,"
Alec said, rising from the table and starting to pace back and forth in the kitchen.

"Tell me what happens."

"If the *Guardian* publishes in October, this administration loses the election. We have friends in power, and we can come out of hiding. How do you see it?" Adelle asked.

"I think if we publish the story, the current administration, not happy about losing because of our article, orders the program to come after us before they lose power. Or, if they win the election they come after us because they are still in power. Either way, we die, just like our friends did."

"Ok," Adelle said quietly. "I am having a hard time still believing that our own government could do such a thing."

"I would never have believed it either, but try and remember, it is not our government, just a small part of it, the part that needs to change."

"It doesn't matter who it is if you end up dead."

"I agree," Alec said, acknowledging her comments and sitting back at the table. "But stay with me here. If our side wins the election, they will think that they can revolutionize incarceration in this country. I hate to say it, but as much as this party has taken credit for the idea, our side will do the same. I think our friends will want us to stay quiet about any further abuses or, worse yet, turn on us because they will want to use it the way it's being used now. There is a lot of power for someone that controls VLS. We lose both ways."

Adelle nodded her head in agreement.

"Okay, I see your point. So, what do you suggest?"

"We have three options after we print."

"Okay, I'm listening."

"The first option is we disappear, but both you and I know that if we choose this option, we have to go overseas and even then with technology today there are no guarantees that we will stay off the grid unless we live in a remote mountain shack with no one around. That would be nice for a while, but…"

At this, Adelle smiled.

"I think you would agree, this is not a good option. Sooner or later, we are going to show up on a camera somewhere that will identify our location. They have too much information on us, pictures etc."

"If they want us badly enough to come oversees, I would agree. What is option number 2?"

"Option 2 is that we hide in the open, but doing so means we hire 24x7 protection. We do not have the choice to use the Secret Service, so we will have to settle on bodyguards. Bodyguards are expensive and will not protect us from real threats they could use if they want to get even. We end up the same way."

"You have such a way of explaining things. And 3?"

She smiled faintly.

"We go straight at them."

"You mean we go back to the facility, and what, start another gunfight?"

"No. Let's think about this. We have two stories to write. BWI is about the abuse of power and the SOUP being used to collect innocent civilians. The focus of the article will be on the current leadership which disregards God-given rights our citizens have as people. So, we write this story about the current leadership, the crimes they've committed, and write about how a new administration would ensure that these things would not happen if they are elected. It starts with a promise to review VLS and fix things that are broken. The new administration would offer transparency into the program, let's say, by creating a new Presidential organization announced during the campaign like an inspector general office. Doing this gives our side a way to get ahead in the polls and provides credible standing with the American people. I am pretty sure I can get Wilkes to print now and not in October to give our side time to introduce the idea into the platform."

"But if we publish, they still come after us."

"Maybe," Alec smiled.

Adelle made the connection.

"You are a genius! The second story. Neither party wants it printed. Without this story, the American people can forgive and forget BWI. They can also pin the blame directly on the current leadership. If we publish the second story, the American people will want the Program shut down. If this happens, our friends will be just as angry as the current administration, and that will be the reason for them to turn on us. We use it for security and leverage! Threating to print if they come after us."

"Additionally, we use our connections and our names to continue to write the stories necessary to keep the pressure on the new administration to follow through on the campaign promise to build true, transparent oversight."

"And Grant and his family?" Adelle asked.

"They're gone, and we can't bring them back. I believe Grant would want us to tell their story. I believe their deaths are the reason we stay alive to make sure what happened at BWI and DC never happen again. Maybe this is the best we can do for them."

She thought for a moment, recalling Grant's commitment to his family and for the innocents taken.

"I think they would be okay with that," she said, wiping away the tears forming in her eyes.

Adelle composed herself quickly, but as soon as her tears stopped, she felt the emotions associated with being close to Alec surface.

"So, Alec, you might have given us a way to return to a normal life, but you never answered my question. What is a normal life for you?"

Alec took his second big breath of the night.

"Adelle, I see the two of us back in Alexandria, me writing again, you are working with the network except I see a wedding ring on your finger; and mine too, of course," he added.

"Glad you added that that last part. Smart move."

They looked at each other, and Alec wrestled with the feelings he was beginning to experience again. He sat down in the chair next to her. For the first time since DC and the escape attempt, he was sensing things returning to normal. Adelle's eyes showed Alec that she had found peace somewhere in their conversation. She needed to be close to him again.

"Why do you want to marry me, Alec?" her voice was dreamy and innocent.

"I think it was all the talking about wedding planning we did. You seemed to enjoy the idea of being married."

"Oh, you got that wrong, mister," she said, becoming instantly animated. "I was enjoying the idea of a wedding day, not marriage for a lifetime."

She was moving closer now, staring into his eyes and letting him see the apparent sarcasm.

"Well, you can't have one without the other. I think that's the rule, anyway."

He could sense Adelle's love reemerging from whatever darkness it had traveled to the day they lost Grant. Alec could feel it too, a returning light to his soul from the night into which he had ascended. He leaned over and kissed her. Alec kept his face close to hers after the kiss.

"I also want to add that in addition to the wedding day you also get the wedding night. It's a package deal," he added in convincingly naïve voice of an overconfident salesman.

"Really," she said. "Well, if we are going to execute this plan, we better start rehearsing for the wedding night. We've gotten a little rusty."

"I agree," Alec said.

And that's precisely what they did.

CHAPTER 35

It was amazing how hard it was to find a payphone in Salina; but surprisingly, there were two. Adelle found the locations on a computer at the library by doing a Google search of payphones in Utah. She was surprised to find that there were still 100,000 in the United States kept available for Americans without any other way of communicating or for areas with inadequate cell phone coverage. Salina fit into category two. Adelle always loved bits of trivia, and her research this morning for a payphone produced an ample amount of little-known information for her to engage people during small talk at business functions if she ever attended one again.

Alec was waiting for her. When she pulled up in the car from her trip to the library, he went out to meet her.

"Success?"

"Hop in. There are two not far from us. We have to get a pre-paid card to make a long-distance call, but we can buy one at the Scenic Quick Stop. That's where the phone's located."

Alec got in and kissed Adelle.

"Great job."

"I know."

She put the car in reverse, and it was not long until they were pulling into the Quick Stop and parked.

"I'll get the card. You figure out what you are going to say to Wilkes."

Alec got out of the car and found the payphone. It was

outside under a small covering near the side of the building. He had not used a payphone in a while. Even in Afghanistan, he used a mobile phone. His life had changed so much in the last six weeks. Adelle came out of the store, saw Alec, and waved a card as she walked towards him.

"We got lucky! The attendant inside told me they are taking this phone out next week. They just put in a new cell phone tower to improve the coverage."

"How much time is on the card?"

"I bought a card for 30 minutes. It was the last one. That should be long enough."

"Great! How do we use this thing again?"

"50 cents into the phone. Dial the toll-free number on the card, then-"

She saw him smiling, knowing that he already knew.

"Aren't you the real comedian today?"

Alec made the connection to the toll-free number and dialed Johnathan Wilkes at the *Washington Guardian*. Adelle never cared for him. She always found him a little flippant about serious matters, as though he was untouchable under the umbrella of the free press. Alec agreed with her. It was only recently, Adelle softened because of the conversations that Alec shared with her. She still did not trust him but had told him that she respected Wilkes for how he was approaching their story.

"Hello, I'd like to speak with Mr. Wilkes," he said, putting a finger in his free ear to reduce the amount of noise from the 18 wheelers pulling in and off the freeway. "Is this Betsy?"

Adelle knew that Betsy Gibbons was Wilkes's secretary and general gatekeeper. She and Alec liked each other and always joked around when Alec came in to visit. Alec knew that keeping Betsy happy was the way to reach Wilkes and made a point every year to send Betsy something special for Christmas and on her birthday. While Adelle could not hear the other side of the conversation, she could imagine the routine of office telephone protocol that was unfolding for Alec.

"Betsy, I don't care if he is in a meeting, tell him it's me. He will want to take my call. Yes, yes, I will hold."

Three minutes into their precious 30-minute card, Wilkes got on the call.

"Alec, thanks for calling." Wilkes possessed one of those gregarious voices that boomed from a phone regardless if on speaker or not. His voice was loud and clear despite the background noise. "Where are you? I tried calling your cell phone and kept getting voice mail. Are you all right? Is Adelle with you?"

"Sorry about that, Johnathan. We've been doing some traveling."

Adelle knew that unanswered phone calls and Alec emphasizing the word "traveling" would tip him off that something the two discussed on the mall was already in motion.

"I understand. What can I help you with?"

"We have the story, Johnathan. It's done, but we need to discuss some things. A lot has changed since we talked last."

"So I surmised. I'm listening."

"We will send the article to you via email. We've set up a Gmail account. It will come from 84R85H@gmail.com. For God's sake, don't delete this and check your junk or clutter folder in case it gets placed there."

"I got it. I am looking forward to reading it."

"That's not all, Johnathan. I need you to do more than read it. I want you to publish it immediately."

"But we discussed late October. Polling is very close. This story could make a difference."

"I know, but all I will say is that Adelle's and my life depend upon publishing now."

"Hell, Alec, I can't make any guarantees that I can publish now. It's too early in the cycle; it gives this administration time to respond."

"Look, Johnathan, don't pull this crap with me! Did you hear what I said? Adelle and I are not in a good place right now. It could mean our lives."

"Okay, Okay. I got too far out front. I'm sorry."

Adelle knew that if Wilkes did not play this right, they would not send the story, and then Wilkes would have nothing for October. *Finally, a little leverage!* This would not play well since she suspected Wilkes already made promises to very influential people that an article was coming that could swing the election their way. Wilkes would need this in October.

"Are you ready to listen to me now? I have a solution for you," Alec said.

"Alright, I'm listening."

"The articles leaves no doubt in anyone's mind that the current leadership is to blame for taking innocent women and children off the street and putting them in the SOUP."

"Okay. Okay."

"I want you to talk with your friends and sell them on the idea that if you publish now, you can blame the current administration for the activity. Then, and listen to me carefully, tell them that the campaign needs to talk positively about the program."

"Do you want to tell me why?"

"Because the campaign is going to promise to make the program activities transparent and provide oversight through some new organization in Justice."

"New organization? What new organization?"

"It hasn't been created yet! That's the sell. Tell them something like a new Inspector General office will report to the Attorney General and Congress."

"Why would we want to do this?"

"Because your friends are going to want to keep the program. It is a game-changer, Johnathan. I have seen what can be done, and we are only scratching the surface with the technology that's being developed."

"So we don't want the program discredited? We want the current leadership to fail because of the article's contents, right?"

"They should fail, Johnathan! When I first saw the VLS Program, I thought these guys were geniuses; but since then, they have abused their power, corrupted the intent of the original program, and..."

"And what Alec?"

He was on the point of finishing with the phrase "committed murder" but stopped, knowing that Johnathan would start to ask more questions. Adelle was pointing to her watch, giving him the signal that the card's time was ticking away.

"Our country needs this program but not the current people running it. Take the time between now and November to build the party's case to make that point! When you read the article. You will know what to do."

"When did you get so political? I thought you were always looking for the truth regardless of politics."

"Let's say things have changed. I still believe in the truth, but not the people controlling this program."

"When will you be sending the story?"

"In the next two hours or so."

"How do I get back in touch? I know there will be questions."

"Use the email. Once we confirm you have the article, we will not be hiding anymore."

"What about your protection? The things we talked about on the mall?"

"We have something else for that now."

"Is that the part you are not telling me about?"

Alec ignored the question and knew by not answering, Wilkes would hear the answer.

The silence allowed Alec to move to his next point.

"Johnathan, I want you to use a by line. Both Adelle and my names. This story does not need to be anonymous. We both say we were there in the story."

He looked over at Adelle and smiled. He wanted to share as many possible moments from this point forward with her. She was at BWI and contributed in more ways than a by-line could portray.

"I will send you a confirmation that we are answering our cell phones again via text when we get set up again."

Wilkes pressed again, "It sounds like there is more to this story. Do we get that one as well?"

Alec bristled as Wilkes transitioned back to being self-serving. Alec was ready to light him up again, but the emotion attached to that story was still too raw.

"Let's hope not."

He could not hide the remorse in his voice. It was clear Wilkes picked up on the change in his voice immediately.

"Stay safe, Alec. I will be in touch."

Click. Adelle looked at Alec.

"I heard it all. It was a little hard not to. What are you thinking?" she asked as Alec put the handset back in its receiver.

"We might have to work harder on this than we thought. Wilkes has never liked change. It looks like he has talked up the October strategy to more people than I would have liked. Now Wilkes has to change the strategy. He is playing with a pretty powerful group that does not like change when the stakes are this high. Polling puts the candidates pretty close together."

Adelle kept the conversation going as they walked to their car.

"We can't solve his problems too. What do we do about ours?"

"We have the second story written. Let's figure out a safe place to keep it."

"And a way for us to send it to the *Guardian* or *Globe* if things don't work out the way we planned them. Do you think they will come here and strike a deal with us?" Adelle asked.

"I think they will. Especially when we email both the articles to the Supervisor and tell him we want to talk. Once we know that Wilkes has the story, we'll let him know that the BWI article will be published, but the second one is up to him. The first story gives us payback for UT, Grant, and his family. The second one, well, let's hope we don't have to publish."

"Like a doomsday strategy?"

She opened her door and got inside the car. Alec opened his door and sat down in the driver's seat.

"I guess."

He turned his head and looked at her puzzled.

"Doomsday strategy? Have you been reading Ian Fleming again or just Cold War books in general? Or is this another thing you learned overseas?" Alec teased.

Adelle just smiled and leaned in to kiss Alec. She kept her lips extra-long on his and then slowly pulled away, surprising him with her sensuality that caused his body to instantly warm. When he opened his eyes, Adelle was poised inches from his face, and purposely licked her lips. When his eyes widened, she moved back to her side of the car. She sent the message. The kiss always works.

"Hey, why did you pull away like that?"

"Don't tease me again, Mr. Bond. You are out of your league."

Alec slid the car into gear and raced back to the house.

CHAPTER 36

A lec and Adelle used the library computer to email their BWI article to Johnathan at the *Guardian* shortly after their call. They received an immediate response that he received it. Once Wilkes acknowledged receipt of the story, there was no reason to remain hidden. They spent the day in south Salt Lake City, no longer concerned about security cameras or keeping themselves hidden from technology. They calmly entered the Best Buy location in the suburb of West Jordon, bought new cell phones, and connected them to their old plans. They no longer had anything to hide from the invisible watchers that used every camera and remote sensor to collect and correlate the billions of data elements that flowed through America's networks. Both of them experienced a sense of freedom when they used their credit cards to make their phone purchases and reactivate their accounts temporarily shut off from missed payments. They spent the drive back to Salina listening to old voice messages with mixed emotions. Most were work colleagues reaching out; but Grant was also there, moving through the script of conversations they developed before DC. They decided to delete them all and start over before listening to any more. The living would call again, let Grant rested in peace.

Their next move was to forward both articles to the Supervisor. The following day, with phones in hand, they were ready. Alec sent the stories in the hopes the VLS team was monitoring the mailbox since UT's death. He provided contact instructions, and both he and Adelle crossed their fingers when Alec pushed the "send" button on his phone with the attachments.

Both were hungry and decided to walk up the street to one of their favorite places called Mom's Café. A small, but popular restaurant, it provided all the charm and homemade food required to keep Salina's citizens and travelers on the interstate happy. Numerous newspaper articles describing their culinary service to the community were hanging on the wall enclosed in a shadow box. Several newer pieces, one from the Salina Sun, were hung next to the shadow box tacked to the wall with white paper for their background. Known to host Chamber of Commerce meetings and a loyal crowd, Mom's reputation even included an article in National Geographic, proudly displayed in a frame above the booths along the wall.

The first time Alec and Adelle ate there, they marveled at the deep-fried scones, which were the size of a plate, and came with a generous amount of honey butter on top. The scones reminded Alec more of a funnel cake from the state fair than the hardened biscuit from the coffee shops back east. As they entered this time, they walked through the main dining room to the empty back meeting room and took a seat. This would give them the privacy they needed when receiving their expected call. The waitress, known for her kindness and efficiency, smiled as they came in. Adelle noticed the list of daily pies written on the front of a small cooling unit behind the counter facing the dining room, and considered getting apple. She and Alec decided on coffee and a scone. Adelle loved the simple living and the kindness of the people in this town. She almost hated to leave. They had spent an important part of their lives here.

An hour later, their hopes were confirmed when an undisclosed number rang through on their phone. Richardson answered, "Yes."

"Mr. Richardson," the Supervisor began. "I am glad to see you've surfaced. In Utah, I see."

"You received the message?" Alec said, keeping his voice low in the restaurant.

"Yes, we did. Fascinating articles. My compliments to you and Ms. Hall."

"I'm sure you did not call to congratulate us."

"I just wanted to confirm your note. The DC story stays buried as your protection, and the BWI story is with the *Washington Guardian* to be published. Is that correct?"

"Yes."

"Why publish at all? Why not use both stories as your protection?"

"Because…"

Alec's voice rose, and Adelle gave him the whisper sign.

"Because there has to be some justice for our friends."

"I understand. And I am sure that you have some plan in place for your protection with the second story, if anything were to happen to you and Ms. Hall."

"Yes."

"Very good. I just wanted to confirm the details. I think it best that you return to Alexandria, and we can continue our conversation here. I'm sure you are looking forward to seeing the color green again."

Alec could hear the sarcastic undertones in his voice, but let it pass. *One day he would get what is coming to him.*

"Under these conditions, I can assure your safety. Let's meet somewhere public as a sign of my good faith."

Alec thought a moment, and the perfect place presented itself.

"McCormick and Schmick's, the National Harbor, two days from now at noon."

"Done."

Click.

"You heard?"

Adelle nodded her head.

"I want to be there when we meet him."

"I don't know if he will come personally. Besides, don't you believe it safer if you are observing our conversation close by instead of both of us being together?"

"I am committed to being with you. We are going to work this out together. This is both of our lives. I am going to be there."

Alec knew she was right, but the thought of her being that close to death again did not settle well with him. However, arguing with her would not be smart either. Alec knew he would lose. She earned the right to be there, and it was her life too.

"Okay – no arguments from me."

"Good."

She smiled to close the deal.

They rose to pay their bill at the front counter when Alec's phone rang again. This time, the caller ID showed Johnathan Wilkes. Adelle took care of the bill, and Alec stepped outside to take the call.

"Yes."

"Alec. I have just read your story. Sorry, it took so long. This is great, really great! You have given me something to take to the people I mentioned before. Don't hold me to this, but I believe I can convince them to publish early."

"That would be great news!"

"I have a list of questions for you. Send them to your new email?"

"No, send them to my old email. Adelle and I are coming back to Alexandria. We are going to see about catching a flight tonight."

"Perfect! It will be good to have you back from- where are you?"

"Utah, in a quaint little town called Salina."

"What the hell is in Utah?"

"Good people and lots of natural beauty, which is why we came here. But that's another story. Maybe I will write that one."

"Great. See you soon."

Wilkes hung up. Adelle finished paying inside and walked up as the conversation was ending.

"That guy should spend a little time out here. It might give him some appreciation for real people not influenced by DC politics."

"Some people will never change, Alec. They can't see what's right in front of them," Adelle said.

"I did not miss these things."

She held up her cell phone.

"Me, either."

He looked into her deep brown eyes. He had to admit, these last several months had changed his life. The shared danger, their perseverance, the comfort and strength both gave to each other to prevail and emerge from their emotional darkness cemented their relationship into an unbreakable one.

"Last chance to change your mind and stay out here."

"Tempting," she said, then put on a serious voice. "But we have matters to settle."

"Yes, we do. Fortunately, we do not have a lot to pack."

"I guess that is an upside."

She stopped walking.

"Alec, let's take a later flight out tomorrow afternoon. I would like to see this town and some of the others on the route to Salt Lake City."

"Getting sentimental?"

"Not really. Life is so different here. I just want to enjoy it before we go back to Alexandria."

Alec agreed. While not possessing the plush green trees and grass of the east coast, the kindness of the people, the desert beauty, and the slower pace of life had won him over.

"Sure."

Adelle's cell phone rang. She reached into the back pocket of her jeans, pulled it out, and turned it off.

"I want 18 more hours of just us."

Alec reached in his shirt pocket, pulled out his phone, and turned it off.

"Done."

"Let's walk for a while and not head straight home," Adelle said, reaching out for Alec's hand and feeling the warm connection as he took hers. "Let's take some time to see where we've been living."

CHAPTER 37

Their plane touched down at Reagan National Airport at 10:12 that evening, and they taxied back to their home in Alexandria. The house was untouched as though they had taken an extended vacation. They were both thankful for the "bill pay" technology at their bank that kept their utility accounts current. This allowed them to experience a hot shower at home, with lights; an unexpected luxury. There were a couple of angry notes from their neighbor about the rental vehicles taped to their door. Alec would take care of those problems tomorrow.

Adelle removed the lipstick device from her travel bag and swept the room. Everything was green, the power sources on each of the mites exhausted after months of spying on an empty house. She put the device in her drawer, trying to remove that element of her life for a least the evening. She did not know if it was the idea of being home, but for some reason she was content and felt safe. Part of that feeling was the man in the shower. Together, they had overcome challenges that might have broken others. A combination of her thoughts manifested into desire.

Alec emerged from the shower, his towel wrapped around his waist.

"You're overdressed for the occasion," Adelle said walking up to Alec. She pulled on the side wrap that held the cloth in place, and it dropped to the floor.

In response, Alec lifted Adelle off her feet and carried her to the bed.

"Oh really," he said, his voice strained while lifting her.

The lift caught Adelle by surprise and she started laughing. "Alec, for God's sake be careful. You'll pull your back out!"

Alec ignored her playful warnings, and Adelle wrapped her arms around his neck for extra support. Walking gingerly to the bed, he put her down gently into a sitting position on the warm comforter, her legs hanging off the bed. Alec took his right hand and slid it up her back, reaching the tie behind her neck that held her silk pajama top in place, and pulled the bowstring. It fell forward, no longer a barrier between them. He pulled the fabric away and she laid back on the bed, her smile inviting him to join her there. As he felt their physical closeness, he looked into her eyes and sensed their souls connect in one rhythmic heartbeat.

After they made love, Alec was not sure whether he liked having reports of his bedroom activity known by others as UT had explained.

"You made sure there were no bugs in the room, right?"

"Yes, aren't you glad that I did?"

"Well, maybe. I'm conflicted on this matter," he said teasingly.

"You are such a man!"

"Lucky you!"

"Yes I am," she said, moving closer to place her head on his chest. They said nothing more and listened to each other's breathing until they fell asleep.

The alarm woke them at 8:00, and they both headed for their morning coffee. Adelle did another sweep for mites in the kitchen and living room and found the same results. All green. They spoke candidly about how they saw the day progressing, and by 10:00, they were walking to breakfast before heading to the National Harbor. It was a couple of blocks walk to King Street and Jackson 20, their destination for morning breakfast. As they turned the corner at Pitt and King, Alec's phone rang. It was Johnathan Wilkes.

"Yes?" Alec answered.

"Alec, do you have time to talk?"

When Wilkes asked this question, it was never good news.

"I do. I am walking to breakfast. What's going on?"

"I sent the article out to my group last night. I'll give it to you straight. They want to wait until October to publish."

"Why?"

"This is explosive stuff. Our people agree that releasing in October works to our advantage."

"It's going to work to their advantage now if we publish."

"I got the message loud and clear from them that they are not interested in modifying the platform to talk about transparency, blah, blah, blah. Our people believe that hitting the current administration with a leadership failure in the program will do the trick."

"Don't they understand this is their chance to take the moral high ground?"

"They do and feel they can have that in October without having to make changes to the platform. Easier to attack when your opponent is down and deliver a knockout punch, than to try and influence the American people with noble ideals. The second way takes money and commitment. The first, just a bunch of angry Congressmen raising hell about needed change as we get closer to the election."

"Is this a done deal, or do you believe you have a second opportunity?"

"Alec, you know our candidate this year is not the quickest on their feet. Frankly, I believe they don't want to put them out front and risk it backfiring. If they can't make the case you are proposing, this could cost us votes. I don't see a second chance."

"So what about Adelle and me? Do you just leave us hanging here?"

"I thought you had that covered Alec. I didn't even re-visit that part of the conversation with them."

"Thanks for nothing, Johnathan."

Click.

Alec thought about what Wilkes was saying. The party was expecting to win an election without having to work for it! *Since when did you not talk about issues and take a case to the American people for why your ideas were better than your opponents? When did election strategies shift from earning the win with a platform about issues to a platform that emphasized your opponent's incompetence, which somehow justifies you being elected? Why would you then tell the American people if they voted for your opponent, they were stupid?*

Experts would tell you that platforms and issues were becoming too complicated for the American people. The real question here was: were the voters unable to comprehend, or was it the candidates? It seemed neither party could articulate the issues, giving the American people little in the way of choice. Alec's party wanted the election to be about popularity. Several states already changed the way the Electoral College would work by casting their votes for the winner of the popular vote and not each state's results. Welcome to high school! *We might as well make the Presidential race an election for homecoming king or queen.* Alec was pissed, both at the political system but mostly for allowing himself to get so far away from what he believed.

"Shit!" he exclaimed.

"Is the *Guardian* backing out?"

"No, they want to publish in October."

"Why?" Adelle's asked in disbelief.

"Our candidate cannot handle what we suggested, and they don't want to spend the money to change the platform."

"Are you going to try and change his mind?"

"Wilkes is going to go with the funding. He will not rock the boat when the dollars are in favor of waiting."

"What are you going to do?"

"I'm thinking, I'm thinking. Do you have any ideas?"

"Maybe one. I don't think you are going to like it, but it accomplishes the same outcome for us. I think it might help us fix our problem as well as change the program leadership."

"I'm listening," he said, opening the door to the restaurant and letting her go first.

They discussed the idea over a simple breakfast of omelets, and Alec admitted, Adelle's solution might work. They paid their bill and requested an Uber to take them to the National Harbor. They arrived at 11:45 in front of the restaurant and sat at an outside table waiting for their meeting. It was a perfect September day, and the sun felt warm and welcoming on their faces in contrast to the skin-penetrating feel of the Utah sun at noon. They did not have to wait long. Alec recognized the Warden as she and an agent walked towards them. The Warden approached the table first.

"Hello, Mr. Richardson. This must be Ms. Hall. You both know, Agent Willis."

Alec and Adelle locked eyes with the Warden and said nothing.

"Now that introductions are finished, let's find someplace a little quieter to talk."

"All down to business," Adelle whispered to Alec as they rose from the table.

"So are we," he whispered back.

They walked down the pathway towards the water and walked out onto the docks where the water taxis arrived. While the taxis still made their trek from the torpedo factory across the river, they were less frequent this time of year as the tourist season waned and families returned their children to one of the many schools across the region.

When they found their spot, Alec took a center position with Adelle on his left. The Warden was next to him with Willis on her right. The Warden looked out over the water.

"Mr. Richardson, I want to pass along my condolences for Mr. UT. I know the two of you were close."

Alec felt Adelle start to respond but touched her leg with his hand, a signal to let it go. He wanted to focus on why they were here and not be led into an unbalanced position by digging into the emotions associated with the DC event.

"You must feel his loss as well," Alec responded.

"You'll understand if I don't agree."

He did. The program would perceive UT as a traitor for helping Alec. Alec remembered him as a man of conscious that did what he believed was morally right. He knew they would not share the same opinion.

"So, let's get down to it." The Warden said. "What do you want?"

"You've seen the articles?"

"I have."

"One will be published shortly. The other will never be published as long as we are safe."

"When you say safe, you mean from us?"

"Yes. And any other people associated with the program. Make sure you share the article with them as well. Anyone that works with you needs to know what we agree to today."

"I have to compliment you, Mr. Richardson. The power of your pen is truly compelling and persuasive. I don't think that I have ever felt at a disadvantage by anyone not carrying a weapon. You have the leverage. You aren't carrying a weapon today, are you? The last time you did, you killed several of my team."

Alec let the comment slide. He felt Adelle start to respond but touched her leg again.

Instead of responding to the Warden's last comment Adelle said, "So let's hear you say it, Ms. Warden. You will NOT seek retribution against us for publishing the BWI article. You WILL leave us the hell alone?" Adelle said, leaning slightly over the rail and talking into the water, but heard by all four.

"Yes. You have our word. The BWI story is a set-back, but we know you could shut down the program with the other. We are not naïve, Ms. Hall. Nor do we seek revenge. We, too, want to avoid losing the program."

"Listen to me, you piss ant of a shrew. You have no idea what you have put us through," Adelle spoke in an even but vehement tone.

"I am sure I don't, Ms. Hall," the Warden said, also wanting to avoid the emotional baggage associated with recent events.

The Warden paused a moment.

"You have some items that belong to the program that UT gave you. I would like them returned."

"I don't think so," Alec said. "While we heard your assurances that you will not do us physical harm, I don't like my every word monitored and analyzed."

"You do realize that eventually, your device will no longer work."

"Well, then you won't mind us holding on to it," Adelle sniped.

Alec suspected that the Warden had an agenda too. He was not surprised when she asked the next question.

"Mr. Richardson, do I have your assurances that you will not leak the second article anonymously or otherwise to the press?"

Alec looked at Adelle, and she nodded.

"You have the article Ms. Warden. You will know where it came from."

"And you did not give it to the *Guardian* or any other media partner for safekeeping."

"You have our assurances that no one in the press has the second article. But you know, we do have a failsafe if something happens to us. If you go back on your word, the article prints."

"You do realize Mr. Richardson, that one day the value

of the article will diminish. I can make no assurances for that day."

"Let's hope for all of us that that day does not come anytime soon."

The Warden gave him a pencil-thin smile.

"Is there anything else we need to discuss?"

Alec looked at Adelle a final time, and she shook her head no.

"We're done here," Alec stated.

"As are we. Mr. Willis, let's get back to work."

The Warden and Willis walked off to the parking garage, and when they were out of sight, Adelle looked at Alec.

"We did it!" she cried while wrapping her arms around Alec.

The joy was genuine and overwhelming as the two of them felt the burden associated with the constant fear of death, lift from their shoulders. The idea of having a future with Alec, the trauma of DC, and the loss of friends brought the tears rushing forward as Adelle let loose her emotions. She buried her head into Alec's chest to conceal her tears. Alec could feel her release everything inside of her. She looked up at him, whipping the tears away.

"I believe I've screwed up my make-up."

"You look great," he lied. "Come on, we have the breakfast thing to do. Let's go handle it."

"Ok, you get the Uber, I am going to go into the restaurant for a moment and see if I can get things cleaned up."

"I'll be right here when you get back."

"You better be mister."

And she walked up the small hill to the restaurant, looking back at him twice to make sure he was.

CHAPTER 38

A delle stepped closer to Alec and kissed him sweetly on the mouth as he was getting ready to exit the house.

"Good luck," she wished him.

Things were moving quickly, and after yesterday's trip to the National Harbor, Alec made his phone call and secured his meeting for 3:00 today.

"With a kiss like that, how could my luck be anything but good?" Alec responded.

He opened the door and stepped outside into the autumn weather. There was a light rain falling as Alec made his way to their new BMW parked on the road in the front of their house. As he approached, his car picked up his key's electronic signature and unlocked the doors for him. He got inside, applied his foot to the brake, and pressed the start button. The engine purred to life. He was on his way to meet an old friend, Aaron McAllister, the Chief of Staff at the White House. He met Aaron about 15 years ago while he was working a story for the Department of Defense, and the two men formed a great relationship. McAllister was impressed with Alec's reporting integrity, and through his influence in the Defense community, pulled some strings to give Alec access to the right people at the right time. Today, Alec was going to return the favor. When he called Aaron and told him it was vital that they meet and that he had something to discuss of importance to the campaign, McAllister reluctantly agreed. A combination of trust and loyalty convinced Aaron to see him despite his schedule and Alec's political affiliation.

It did not take long for Alec to travel the George Washington Memorial Parkway to the 14th Street Bridge and into DC. He arranged to meet Aaron at the Willard Hotel bar, not far from the White House. The Willard, so history "as told to him," offered a plush and cool lobby during the Washington summers for both government officials and solicitors to meet during the Grant administration after the Civil War. The number of business discussions and Congressional influencing that occurred at the Willard led to the use of the phrase "lobbying" as a way to describe the "cigar filled backroom meetings" where citizens and businesses influenced and changed the future laws for America. Some lobbyists have met there ever since Alec noted.

Alec arrived at Pennsylvania Ave. and pulled his car into the street-side entrance to the hotel. Attendants that managed the valet parking hovered, waiting to serve. The building was impressive with its old column architecture accented by the French Parisian entrance that decorated the doors to the historic building. He turned his keys over to a young valet that turned dreamy-eyed upon seeing his car.

"Only to the parking spot, young man."

His comment snapped the young boy out of his daydream.

"Yes, sir," he said crisply and provided Alec his valet receipt.

Alec reached into the passenger seat and grabbed two sealed 8x11 manila envelopes. Alec walked inside and marveled at the hanging chandelier that accented the long hall to the opposite side of the building and its exit onto a new block. The lobby was incredible and transported him back to the 19th century with little difficulty. He was in the "lobby." He missed this place. *Adelle and I should come down here more often.*

He walked straight ahead and made a hard right into a side hall that delivered him to the main bar.

The bar was one of Alec's favorites in DC. Round in shape, the bartenders operated out of the center of a dark marble ring seated on a beautiful dark wood frame. On the bar was an unlimited supply of spicy Chex mix found in small serving bowls that exhibited the class of the bar by its freshness. The walls were dark wood with pictures of serious-looking men placed against a white matting that made them come alive in their frames. This place brought back great memories to include the first time he ever ordered scotch. He was hooked on both the bar and scotch from that point forward. The bar could hold about 45 people, and he scanned for McAllister. Alec observed he was the first to arrive, and took a seat at a small table on the non-entrance side of the bar to get a little more privacy for this discussion; ordering a Scotch on the rocks as he passed the bartender. Technically it was a scotch on a rock since Alec always instructed only one ice cube be used. As he sat down, he pulled out his cell phone to check for messages. So far, so good. There was nothing from Aaron saying he was canceling. The bartender brought his scotch, and he let the ice begin to melt before he took his first drink. He was enjoying the second sip when McAllister walked in. Alec stood up to draw McAllister's attention.

"Alec," he said, walking toward him with his hand extended. "It's been years."

"Close to 10, off and on," Alec said, shaking McAllister's hand.

"I have followed your progress in the press. Congratulations on winning the Pulitzer."

Alec knew that was a bittersweet compliment since his stories had shined a very negative light on this administration.

"Thanks, Aaron. You do not seem to be doing so bad yourself."

"Some days, I wonder," as both men shared a brief laugh.

The bartender showed up, and Alec's old friend ordered a bourbon straight. Not one to mince words on a Chief of Staff's schedule McAllister asked straight out, "What can I do for you, Alec?"

Alec passed him over one of the sealed envelopes. "Inside of that envelope, you will find a story that an associate and I wrote. If you agree to what we talk about today, you will win this next election."

The bartender brought McAllister his drink. McAllister stirred the straw for a moment, thinking about if he should walk away from this conversation now given Alec's past and political leanings or stay and listen. McAllister chose trust over suspicion.

"I'm listening."

A group of about twelve walked into the bar, intent on moving their previous party to this location. Alec saw McAllister tense and appear uneasy as the noise from their boisterous conversations filled the room. Alec sensed McAllister would not focus on his discussion or worse, chose to leave. He stood up and walked up to the bartender. "Do you see the man I'm talking with?"

The bartender nodded.

"I know who he is."

"Good, be so kind as to keep the party on the other side of the bar and keep the noise down. There is a big tip for you, if you can."

The bartender acknowledged Alec and said to the new arrivals, "Ladies and gentlemen, please choose any of the seats around you on this side of the bar."

Alec returned to his seat. Seeing the crowd contained and safely out of earshot of the conversation, Aaron let a smile escape him.

"I'm comfortable with this. Thank you, Alec. Continue."

"I provided this story to the *Washington Guardian* several days ago. I don't want to go into detail, but you will see this published in the latter part of October."

McAllister knew the impact of the story immediately.

"Why are you giving it to me?"

"Because I want you to have a response when it prints."

"Alec, don't take this wrong. I respect your integrity as a journalist, but what makes you think I would trust you with something like this? Your political views and contributions to the *Guardian* put you and me on opposite sides of the table."

"I still believe in doing the right thing. I might vote differently; but at the end of the day, you and I agree on the same things for America: and it starts with truth. This article will be damaging to your campaign. If you don't act on this, you will not have anything to counter with when it prints. Look, Aaron. Doing the planning and getting your message right burns no political capital. It's just time spent with your staff. But you won't have that time if this prints in late October. I'm asking you to take a look and be ready."

"What's the high-level picture?"

"You know I did the piece on VLS, as well as the updates."

"Yes."

It was McAllister's recommendation to POTUS that he be the writer, but he would not admit that here, nor would he ever. Alec lowered his voice.

"There were innocent women and children taken as well."

"Jesus, are you kidding me?" McAllister said.

"I was there along with a DC police officer and my associate. It's real, Aaron."

Alec could not tell if Aaron knew or not. His reaction appeared to be sincere, but experience had shown him that professionals in DC lie with sincerity if you do not have the right security clearance level.

"All of the details: how we put the pieces together and followed the trail to their facility. It's all in the article."

"What do you want in return for this?"

"It's important to us that the *Guardian* publish this for

many reasons that I won't discuss. I want some assurance that if you win this election, you will ensure that the leadership of the program is changed, and your administration is transparent with the American people when the change is made."

"I am not sure I follow."

"Read the story, and you'll understand my request."

"They are really going to publish this in late October?"

Alec nodded his head.

"I thought you were here to return a favor. If we win because of this, I will still owe you."

"No, you won't. We're even. I'll even pick up the tab today," Alec said, pointing to the drinks.

McAllister stood with the envelope in his hand. "I'll read it. Thank you."

He extended his hand and Alec shook it. McAllister then noticed the second envelope.

"Something else, Alec?"

"Just a second copy."

McAllister knew he was lying but was not going to push him to reveal everything. If this were half as bad as he indicated, this administration would owe him a lot.

"Good luck in November, Aaron."

"Stay out of trouble, Alec."

Alec settled the tab with a decent tip and left the bar holding the folder with the second article. It was not the right time to give him that one. Asking for leadership change was one thing, asking for security from a threat within his administration was something different. If they won, they would come to him, and then he might offer it up.

Alec retrieved his car from the valet and headed home. He could not wait to see Adelle. Once out of the city, Alec would call her. He had not figured out the hands-free part of the new car, and the DC police watched closely for drivers talking directly on the phone. Especially when they tied up traffic in the numerous intersections that were the main arteries of DC. When he hit the parkway in Virginia, he made the call.

"How did it go?" Adelle asked.

"I think we are doing the right thing. McAllister was appreciative. It's up to them now. See you shortly."

"Hurry, Alec! I want to try a new spot for dinner tonight."

"You bet! The Mexican place?"

"That's the one."

"Excellent. See you soon."

He pulled up to his parking spot 30 minutes later. Rush hour was never a good time to drive the main roads, and it took him longer to arrive home than he anticipated. He jumped out of the car and walked up to the house. Adelle dressed for the occasion and was wearing a low-cut blouse and a pair of blue jeans. She finished off her look with cowgirl boots, which were starting to come into fashion as the weather changed. Adelle covered her top with a denim jacket. She looked terrific, and Alec couldn't help but look at her.

"Are you sure you want to go out?"

"Come on, Alec. We can come home early for dessert," she said in her playful way, closing the sentence with a twinkle in her eye.

"Okay – I need to make a quick stop, and I will join you outside."

"Great, give me your keys. I want to drive."

Alec fished into his pocket and gave her the keys.

"Be right with you."

Adelle walked out the door, sashaying her hips for him, and looked back over her shoulder to see if Alec had noticed. Nature called, and Alec was in too much of a hurry to return her gaze.

He washed his hands and was coming out of the bathroom when the windows of the house exploded, spraying glass into every corner of the room, cutting into his arms and face as small pieces of glass flew by. The house rumbled and felt as though it lifted off the foundation. Alec was blown backward into a chair and then on the floor. His mind reeled as he considered the various reasons for the explosion as he stood up and regained his balance. His vision was already cloudy from the cut across his head, leaking blood into his eyes, and Alec felt numerous small cuts on the rest of his exposed skin. He ran to the door. "Adelle, are you alright?"

He stopped before getting out of the door. His car lay in parts scattered across the street. Where his BMW was parked, a smoldering clump of metal consumed by fire was in its place. Numerous other homes had their windows blown out, and some of the small trees and shrubs were on fire. Car alarms from other vehicles beeped and buzzed loudly up and down the street. Neighbors poured from their homes armed with cell phones, all dialing 911 at the same time overwhelming operators trying to respond to the frantic reports.

Alec never moved from his front door, which hung loosely on one hinge. In shock and not able to comprehend all that was happening, he watched the arrival of the emergency response vehicles, each entering the scene in slow motion. An ambulance unloaded its paramedics, and one of his neighbor's arms rose slowly and pointed to him. The young man's sprint to him was surreal and in slow motion. Disoriented, Alec sat down on the stoop. It wasn't until he saw the paramedic yelling at him that he felt part of the scene around him. Alec still heard nothing but a constant ringing in his ears. Two other paramedics pulled a gurney from the ambulance and rolled it to them. Without understanding how he was on it, he was pushed to the ambulance. Placed in the back, he watched as the paramedics' mouths moved, but no words emerged. He saw one place a needle in his arm and provide fluids to assist his body that failed to understand the activity around him. Another placed a bandage on his head and cleared the blood from his face. His eyes blinked, then remained closed, bringing the blackness he craved to escape this moment.

CHAPTER 39

Adelle's family and friends began to reach out to him via text and email as he laid in bed at the INOVA hospital in Alexandria. Some caring person plugged his phone into a wall socket to keep it charged. The Good Samaritan also turned off the ringer. The hospital staff was most likely monitoring calls on his phone to see who they should contact to pass along information about him and his condition. He could hear the short vibrations of his phone announcing another inquiry into his health or Adelle's death each time a new text message arrived. He still felt as though he was in a daze and had difficulty making his thoughts coalesce. He envisioned one big puzzle scattered about that only when assembled would a picture emerge about his last 24 hours. He did not move when the orderly walked in, carrying his meal on a tray supported by a stand that allowed you to eat the meal in bed. The straw in the juice drink stuck up like the antenna on a radio. The orderly, a black woman of about 45, looked like she had seen suffering and overcome her own trials in life.

"Are you hungry yet?" she asked, upbeat and encouraging.

Alec was not sure if he answered or not.

"Ok, I am going to set this down here next to you on the nightstand."

The orderly positioned the tray and the meal on the

stand.

"Your cell phone is right here. I plugged it in for you this morning to keep it charged for when you want to start calling folks. The nurses know to let you keep it with you."

"Why did you do that?" Alec asked.

"Just because, honey. 'Nuff said on that. Would you like some sunlight?"

"Yes."

She pulled on a string next to the window, and the blinds opened, letting in the sun and removing the darkness from the room.

"The nurse will be in shortly to check on you and then the doctor in about an hour. I'm just a buzz away. You eat something now."

Her words were commanding but delivered like music. A nurse came in 15 minutes later and took his vitals, recording the result on her iPad. She also encouraged Alec to eat his breakfast and then left. Alec reached over and saw a familiar number on the list of missed calls. It belonged to a longtime friend of Adelle that lived outside DC in Reston, Virginia. She called numerous times and sent several text messages. Alec called her first.

"Alec, is that you? Is it true?"

"Donna, I'm sorry."

Alec could hear her choking back the tears as she continued the conversation.

"I saw the explosion on the news and recognized your address. The reporters say something exploded. There are very few details, but one station said they thought the car blew up!"

"Is that all they said?"

"They said there was one fatality. The news said it was Adelle?"

Donna clearly struggled with her sentence.

"She's gone, Donna."

He could barely say the words.

"Oh, my God. I am so sorry, Alec. Are you ok?"

Her voice began to strengthen as the need for assistance became clear to her.

"I don't know. Some cuts and bruises, I think," he said, unable to assess the damage to his body.

"What are you going to do?"

"I don't know."

"I will come to see you, Alec, and we can figure things out. We can get through this together. Let me handle this."

Most of what Donna was saying was foreign to him. He understood that Adelle's affairs needed to be handled, but none of it currently made sense to him. They were just words on the phone.

"Where are you?"

"Inova, Alexandria near Seminary Road."

"I can find it. I will see you in a couple of hours."

"Fine. Thank you."

Alec hung up the phone. The text messages were constant, and he regretted reactivating his old phone. The doctor made his rounds and wanted to keep Alec one more night. He needed sleep. The doctor scheduled the hospital psychologist for an appointment at 4:00 that afternoon. He told Alec that if the psychologist gave his approval, that he would be released tomorrow.

He had one more message to answer and focused his thoughts on the task. He picked up his phone and responded to a text that contained a question mark only. "Not yet," he typed back. "If something happens to me, publish."

True to her word, Donna arrived at the hospital. As he and Donna talked, he felt his energy and mental capabilities begin to return. They spoke briefly about a service for Adelle. Donna was right; having a purpose was a great motivator to healing, whatever the reason. Their discussion turned personal and opened the door to his and Adelle's relationship. While Alec felt uplifted sharing their best moments with Donna, he switched to another subject as the memories became too intense, and he felt depression begin to seep in.

Throughout the conversation, he discovered many things about Adelle that she never shared with him. Donna revealed that Adelle told her she wanted to be cremated, and her ashes spread from a mountain top into the wind. Alec smiled. That sounded just like her. That decision was made, and they agreed to meet and spread them together. They also concurred to hold a service in Reston and let the network know the details to share with its employees. Donna would host at her house since Alec's was in no condition for guests. Donna told him she would handle all the details. They would talk soon. When Donna left, she provided him a hug and whispered, "one day at a time" in his ear. He smiled and thanked her for her help. The day's planning helped sharpen his mind again and provide him focus. Alec thought one thing heading to his 4:00 appointment down the hall. He needed to convince the doctor that he was okay while holding back his real emotions. He was going to make those responsible pay.

◆ ◆ ◆

Adelle's service was one week later. Donna chose a non-denominational church off the Reston Parkway. The church was perfect and would be what Adelle would have wanted. A beautiful building, it was nestled in surrounding trees of rural Reston in a chapel filled with natural light pouring in from the outside. Over 350 of Alec and Adelle's friends attended the service to say goodbye.

As the service concluded, Alec stood at the back of the chapel to visit with friends that traveled from New York. Donna approached the conversation Alec was having with two executives of the network and sharing memories of Adelle. She waited for the discussion to end and stepped in before another started.

"Alec, could I see you a moment?"

Alec excused himself from a line that formed to wish

him their condolences and moved away from the crowd.

"Alec, a man, approached me and gave me this envelope. He said you would know what it was about."

"Is he still here?"

"I don't think so. It all happened very quickly. One minute I was talking with friends, and the next moment, a man handed the envelope to me and told me it was for you. He said it should be delivered immediately. Then he seemed to disappear."

Alec took the envelope.

"Thank you, Donna."

She offered a small smile and turned back into the crowd, beginning a new conversation with someone in line waiting to see Alec. The envelope was white with no markings and felt light. Alec opened it, and inside was folded piece of paper with a printed message, simple in its intent:

Are you ready to talk? 8:00 pm tomorrow,
86190 Mercure Circle Sterling, VA.

Alec calmly folded the message and placed it inside his suit coat pocket. He looked over at Donna and smiled, letting her know everything was fine and that he was ready to re-engage. He walked toward the waiting line filled with sober faces and embraced by a woman that worked with Adelle in DC.

"I am SO sorry," she said as she hugged him.

"Thank you," he said graciously. He knew it was the calm before the storm.

CHAPTER 40

The sun was setting below the horizon as Alec parked his rental van a quarter of a mile from his meeting place outside of Sterling, Virginia. He checked the watch on his phone. 7:10 PM. The address was about a seven-minute drive from Dulles Airport. He wondered if they moved the BWI operation from Maryland to Virginia. He wanted to review his plan one more time, all too aware of the technology that would be used by the program to monitor his arrival. It would be minimally staffed if the building were like the one at BWI. This would be his advantage.

To get inside, he needed additional items from his house in Alexandria. Three days ago, he returned home. He found it strange to see his windows now covered with plywood. Fortunately, the electric and gas companies turned the utilities back on, and one of his neighbors hired the local handyman to re-hang his front door. The yellow police tape was gone, and the neighborhood looked like it had returned to normal. There was no sign of where his car burned in the street, except for a black slanting scar in the road where the flaming vehicle melted the tar off the asphalt on top, exposing the old brick underneath.

Alec walked on the glass-covered floor, accompanied by the crunching of each step. It was though an unseen partner was walking with him. He climbed the main stairs and reached his destination in the upstairs hallway. Alec pulled down the string in his ceiling, extracting a ladder that gave him access to his attic. He turned on the attic light and found the box marked "Christmas" that he'd prepared. This carton held the items Alec would need to complete his business with the Supervisor. Opening the box, he removed the carry bag and it was just as he remembered packing it. Inside were the two gas grenades that UT had given him the last time they met at the National Harbor. He also had extra .45 ammo, two protective gas masks, and the .45 silencer.

Not long after Alec's discharge from the hospital, he purchased another .45 pistol from a sporting goods store near Quantico, Virginia, outside the Marine Corp base on the Potomac River. He had time to pass the three-day check and encountered no problems with the purchase, listing its use for home defense.

His plan was bold. He would pull up to the front door and get out without his pistol or mask. He would carry a foot-long round 1inch diameter wooden dowel from a hardware store along the inside of his jacket sleeve. Assuming an agent would answer the door, he planned to subdue the guard, pull the grenades from his jacket pockets, throw them inside, and prop open the door with the dowel to keep the door from clicking shut. Once the door was open, he would go back to his car and retrieve his pistol and one of the police protective masks that Grant procured. Alec would enter the building wearing the gas mask, take out the agents, and find the Supervisor. Their sensors would see him coming, but have no idea he had the small grenades to unleash the hell he carried inside of him. The first guard would be the biggest hurdle. He would need to act decisively to knock him out once he was inside the door.

He rechecked the time. 7:48. Well, he would be early. He started the van, put it in gear, and started the drive from his parking spot. Unknown to Alec, a traffic accident on the toll road connecting Interstate 66 out of DC to Sterling backed up the evening commuters on the Dulles Access Road, causing the

Supervisor to be twenty minutes behind his 7:30 arrival time. Alec pulled up to the front of the building, just as the Supervisor's SUV arrived. This presented an opportunity too extraordinary to ignore. Alec saw the vehicle and all previous plans changed.

Alec opened the door to his van and stepped out. He started walking to the driver's side of the SUV about 20 feet away. The agents immediately parked the SUV and exited, pistols still concealed. The Supervisor remained in the back seat.

"I am unarmed," Alec said.

The driver side agent walked around the SUV and pointed a handheld device at Alec.

"He's clean," the agent said.

The Supervisor lowered the driver's side window and leaned through the vehicle.

"Well, this is a surprise," he said. "Mr. Richardson, it seems we are both off our schedule thanks to the rush hour traffic. Ironic, don't you think, that something as simple as a fender bender in traffic could influence a significant event like our meeting this evening."

Alec ignored the comment.

"What do you want to talk about?" Alec asked.

"I am here to so we can work something out for your future."

Alec looked at the building beside him.

"Do we have to do it here? You can understand my reluctance to go into any of your buildings."

The Supervisor thought a moment and did not see a downside to having their conversation in their driving vehicle.

"Perhaps we can drive and talk. Come to the vehicle and get into the back seat with me."

Alec approached the SUV, and both agents pulled out their pistols and trained them on him. Alec raised his hands. As he approached the vehicle, he opened the rear passenger door and got in. Both agents lowered their weapons and got into the car as well.

"Mr. Richardson, this is a little closer than I expected, but I think it will do."

The Supervisor then looked at the driver.

"Let's go, Willis."

The passenger side agent raised his pistol, keeping Alec covered and on alert. The SUV started and Agent Willis put the car in reverse. As the vehicle moved, Alec reached into his jacket pocket and pulled out the grenade. The Supervisor saw it and yelled, "Stop!"

Willis hit the brakes. The passenger side agent fired his pistol at Alec, but the sudden stop caused him to miss. The back seat puffed from the round's impact. Alec pulled the pin and dropped the grenade on the floor of the van under the Supervisor's feet, rapidly opened his car door and rolled out. UT had told him that the confines of the car would accelerate the gas' effect just as the pressurized room had at BWI. The Supervisor slumped over unconscious before he could exit his door. The two agents were affected quickly and fell unconscious, as well. Willis' foot slipped off the brake and pressed the accelerator. The SUV surged in reverse, hit, and bounced over a small parking space barrier causing the passengers to shift inside. The bounce caused Willis' foot to drop from the accelerator bringing the SUV to a slow stop.

Alec ran to the car and shut the back door to contain the gas within. He immediately felt light-headed and nauseous but did not collapse as he breathed deeply, pulling the night air into his lungs. Alec sprinted back to his vehicle and grabbed his mask, his pistol with the silencer, and his small bag of .45 preloaded magazines. He slung the bag over his head and moved the strap to position his ammo on his left side. Heading back to the SUV, Alec placed the mask over his face. He opened the driver's door and took the car out of gear to prevent the vehicle from driving further back into the street. He grabbed Willis and pulled him out onto the ground. Alec ran around to the passenger side and did the same with the other agent. Looking down on him, he felt the rage build within him and permitted himself to exact revenge. Alec fired two rounds into the agent's head and one into his chest; the silencer making the familiar "Pop, pop, pop" as each bullet left the barrel. He removed the lanyard from around his neck and put it around his. Alec returned to where Willis laid and fired three more shots, removing his credentials as well. He reached into Willis' pocket and pulled out the SUV keys and placed them in his jeans pocket. Lastly, he grabbed the Supervisor's lanyard from around his neck.

He ran to the door and recognized the card swipe. Using the Supervisor's access card, the door buzzed open. The guards inside were monitoring the activity of the supervisor's vehicle, but without specific information for what Richardson had done to cause the incident, decided to take care of him when he entered the building. As Alec opened the door, he was met immediately by pistol fire. Alec stayed on the outside as bullets hit the wall and failed to penetrate the door's steel composition. Pulling out his second grenade, he threw it into the building. The grenade exploded with a small pop and began to expel its product throughout the offices. As the yells to take action quickly ended, Alec moved inside; pistol at the ready. Entering the entrance hallway, he saw three agents sprawled on the floor. He dispatched one, reloaded his magazine, and dispatched the remaining two with a calmness that only vengeance can create. The hallway had two adjoining rooms, and when he checked, he found one remaining agent. He fired three more shots. He ejected the spent magazine into his hand and inserted a new one from his small bag. Once again, pistol at the ready, he moved through the remaining large room and into a smaller room separate from the outdoor loading dock entrance. Inside the smaller room was a technician passed out by his computer. He fired three more rounds, and with each shot, he felt a small part of justice embrace his purpose.

Alec successfully cleared all the rooms but the loading

dock. Upon reaching it, he surveyed the large area leading to outside. There was no movement. He closed the door and accepted the risk that no one made it out and would come back for him. He had no choice.

Alec moved back through the entrance hall and back outside. He walked briskly to the SUV. Alec knew he had limited time remaining before the gas wore off. As he opened the back door to extract the Supervisor, he heard him moan, coming out of the eight minutes of temporary sleep the grenade provided. Alec pulled him from the car, and his body collapsed on the ground. As he heard him moan again, he pivoted his .45 and brought it down onto the Supervisor's head. The moaning stopped. He reached down to pick him up into a fireman's carry but quickly found the Supervisor's build was more substantial than his appearance showed. Thinking fast, he grabbed him by the arms and dragged him the 50 feet or so to the door across the gravel parking lot, stopping every 10 feet or so to catch his breath.

"I have some questions to ask you," Alec said aloud through the muffle of his mask.

He swiped the card reader again, and the door buzzed open. Pulling the Supervisor through the door, Alec let it close. Once again, he grabbed his arms and dragged him through the main entranceway into the bigger back room. Going into the tech's room, Alec moved the technician's body aside into the bigger room and retrieved the chair. Checking the security offices, he found two sets of cuffs and keys. He grabbed them and an extra chair and returned to the Supervisor. He took a moment to regain his breath. Each task required additional effort with the protective mask he wore. Hoisting the Supervisor onto the chair was not easy either. He locked the rolling balls on the feet. That worked and kept the chair from rolling away from him while he lifted the Supervisor into the seat. He took another break, struggling to breathe through the mask filters. Using the cuffs, Alec secured the Supervisor's hands and feet behind the chair's frame. Sitting in the second chair, Alec positioned himself to see over the Supervisor's shoulder and observe the door to the loading dock. He was ready.

Alec stood and paced, still keeping his mask on and would do so until the Supervisor woke up, indicating the gas was gone. Reaching inside the Supervisor's suit coat, he removed his pistol from the holster. As Alec waited, the bile started to rise in his throat as he recalled the agents he just shot without a second thought. He could feel himself begin to shake as the calmness of his surroundings now enveloped him. Alec leaned over and put his head down.

Pull it together, Alec, he told himself. His thoughts drifted toward Adelle just momentarily, and stopped when the Supervisor begin to stir. The gas had dissipated. He removed the mask and threw it on the floor, inhaling deeply to fill his lungs with air. Breathing without the mask's filters calmed him, and his shaking stopped. Alec knew he needed to keep his emotions in check. He would need every part of his intellect to question the Supervisor. He stood up and pointed his adversary's own pistol at him.

CHAPTER 41

The Supervisor slowly focused on his surroundings and the turn of events that resulted in him handcuffed and sitting in a chair looking down the barrel of his own Sig P226 and the crazed man that was holding it.

"Does this remind you of BWI, with just a slight twist?" Alec asked pulling the chair close and taking a seat.

"An exceptional effort to get the better of me. What did you use to knock me out?"

"Someone taught me how to use a .45 as a club once."

The Supervisor nodded.

"Gives you a real headache."

The Supervisor eyed his captor, wondering what his next move would be.

"So, Mr. Supervisor, I hope you don't mind if we talk for a while, do you?"

It was clear now. Alec would not kill him immediately. Alec wanted answers and was seeking closure before his real purpose was known. He wanted a reason why for all that transpired. This was not what The Supervisor wished to discuss, but he was not in a position to determine the conversation yet.

"What happened to my two agents?"

"Dead. I killed them both. The ones in here too. There will be no help coming for you anytime soon. It's just you and me."

The Supervisor did a mental headcount. Six agents and one technician. Alec had the advantage and obvious motivation. He added revenge to Alec's agenda.

"Where did you get the grenade, or should I ask?"

"From someone else that planned ahead. You are not the only one with that gift."

Alec would not be forthcoming with answers. The Supervisor resigned himself to his temporary situation.

"Ok. It looks like we are going to be here for a while. What do you want to discuss?"

"Really, asshole?"

Alec raised the pistol and pointed it at the Supervisor, who was unaffected by the gesture.

"You have to ASK that question?"

The Supervisor thought for a moment; he needed to buy himself time. He knew that if the agents reported the incident before they were killed, the duress system would activate. Otherwise, the Supervisor was required to push a key sequence on his phone when he arrived, or the VLS facility would text him. If he did not answer or have the guards confirm, they would use the GPS signal on the phone and have a reaction force here in another thirty minutes. He had to stall for 45 minutes, and the best way he knew would be to walk through the events that Richardson wanted to discuss; chronologically.

"I guess I should have asked, where do you want to start?"

Alec lowered the pistol.

"I want to know..."

He choked on his emotion, unable to finish his question. Tears formed in Alec's eyes and then he pushed the words out through a twisted set of quivering lips.

"Why Adelle?"

The Supervisor knew the answer but watched as Alec, wrestled with his loss, his face moving through the ranges of emotion and grief. He was in no hurry to answer the question and needed Alec to diffuse so that their conversation would be meaningful, and by meaningful, he wanted an exchange of information that generated more questions, which in turn took more time. Each second mattered as The Supervisor began his next game of chess, pitting his mind against the emotional man across from him. He opened with his first move, silence.

Alec stood up and walked into the main entrance hall. The Supervisor tested his handcuffs and those attached to his ankles. He was not going anywhere. Richardson was obviously upset by his recent events. *I need to keep him off balance until help can arrive.* He watched as Alec started pacing outside of the room. He looked to the Supervisor as though he was carrying on an internal conversation that caused him pain with each step, and then he stopped.

Alec returned, appearing much calmer after his short break.

"So Mr. Richardson, are you ready to continue?" He intentionally asked the question with contempt, challenging Alec's manhood and insinuating that the emotional burden was too great for him to handle.

Alec walked over to the Supervisor and stared intently into his face. "You are a hard son of a bitch."

The Supervisor showed no emotion. Alec clenched his right fist and with all his might, landed a punch to the side of his captive's face, splitting his lip and causing blood to drip onto his suit. The Supervisor felt the pain move through his jaw as his head absorbed the blow and turned to the right.

"Answer my question! Or I swear to God, I will beat you until you can't talk."

The Supervisor moved his jaw around. Nothing was broken as far as he could tell, no teeth rattled. That was a well-landed punch. The game had changed. He looked up into the steely-eyed man that now hovered above him.

"Empty threats, Mr. Richardson. How will you get your answers if I can't talk?"

The second blow avoided his jaw and landed higher,

almost knocking him out. The Supervisor struggled to keep his consciousness. His lip poured blood down onto his white shirt, and his nose started to bleed. The Supervisor felt Alec pull his head back and saw the rage in Alec's eyes. *You can take a few more hits,* the Supervisor thought. He was making progress in this battle of wills and intellect. The Supervisor felt Alec let go of his hair, and his chin fell limply into his chest. Alec walked back to his chair and sat down again.

The Supervisor did a mental check of his injuries. He could still think and would need his mind to achieve this meeting's intent. Alec was in the game now; he responded to silence with aggression. Time for his second move. He looked up at Alec.

"Sacrifice, Mr. Richardson. The answer to your question about 'why Adelle' is sacrifice."

He had Alec's attention. "What kind of bullshit answer is that?"

"Without sacrifice, there is no passion for fueling your soul. There is nothing to drive a man to achieve greatness. There is no doubling down on commitment in the depths of despair."

The Supervisor stopped and spat blood onto the floor.

"There is no pain to push you to survive."

"Sacrifice. You murdered Adelle for sacrifice?"

Alec stood and walked toward the Supervisor. He flinched ever so slightly in anticipation of his next blow. Instead of striking again, Alec leaned over the Supervisor.

"What do you know of sacrifice?"

"More than you would care to know. I will tell you that without the loss of loved ones in my life, there would've been no passion for building VLS."

Alec backed away, listening with curiosity. He did not know the Supervisor's story.

"I would have lived my life as a civil servant, engineering solutions that might have made a difference to someone, somewhere. There would not have been the greatness of an achievement like VLS to change all of humanity for the better. You marveled at VLS when you saw it. You saw the potential it could bring and knew the magnitude of my desire for the program to survive. My commitment to the program's survival is what has kept you alive. You knew I would agree to terms before you printed the second story for just that reason."

"What I underestimated was the depth of evil you would order to keep your program, your greatness. You murdered seven people that I cared about!" Alec shouted.

The Supervisor spit more blood on the floor.

"Always the Pulitzer Prize author," he laughed and quoted Alec, "'the depth of evil.' You make it sound so ominous. You have no idea what evil is, Mr. Richardson, and by my calculations, our body counts are even after tonight. You've killed as many as I have."

The Supervisor made his second move; guilt, and ambiguity.

Alec was not going to take the bait to discuss numbers.

"So tell me. What causes the man that builds a marvel like VLS to contain evil, to become the very evil that he seeks to contain?"

"A good question, assuming I agree with what your definition of evil is; but I don't."

Alec retook his seat.

"Are you familiar with the concept of polarity, Mr. Richardson?" Time to press the attack. This chess game was on.

Alec remained silent. He knew his answer would not be correct, nor could it be in this discussion. Seeing that Alec decided not to answer, the Supervisor continued.

"Polarity is the concept where only the extremes are defined. It means that there is no way to measure the difference between those extremes. However, in reality, *they are both the same thing*. Let me ask you, just for the sake of our discussion, do you know what hot is?"

"Yes."

"Do you know what cold is?"

Alec remained silent and stood up, frustrated by the conversation that yielded no answers.

"Before you move to punch me again, to convince me to answer your questions." The Supervisor spit more blood on the floor. "How do you know where hot ends and cold begins? Indulge me. You have the gun."

Alec decided to play along.

"You don't know, it's a matter of measuring degrees between, but the temperature is different for each person," Alec responded.

"So now you have your answer. The people in society determine the standard for 'good.' Evil is also determined by those same people who use 'good' as a standard of measure. Said, another way, evil is the absence of good. But what happens to good and evil when an action falls between the two extremes?"

"I'm starting to lose my patience," Alec calmly said.

"Who decides what is good and what is evil for the actions in between the two? The person with the pistol; and if so, what is the basis for their decision? Remember, Good and Evil are both the same thing separated by interpretation or circumstances.

Who decides that the value of a program like VLS is worth the loss of a few lives? You've heard phrases like the greater good. Where does that come from, Mr. Richardson? What happens when things turn gray and are no longer black or white?"

"Are you saying to me that the continuance of the program justifies killing innocent people? What kind of crazy-ass thinking is that?"

"The people in the SOUP are not dead, Mr. Richardson. But let me answer your question with another question which does include death. Does the loss of a driver's life, justify the reporting to win a Pulitzer Prize? Especially when the writer caused that loss of life?"

"What are you saying? Where did you hear that?"

"I've checked you out, made a couple of inquiries. A driver that was found in the desert, mutilated almost beyond recognition by his wife. That man was there because you paid someone to make him go away. Your driver was never abducted by government officials, oh no. You made him disappear. He was reporting your every move to the government while also working for you. You found out about it, and your story was in jeopardy unless you used your other resources to make him go away. Who is evil now, Mr. Richardson?"

"They were only supposed to take him to the desert and keep him there until I completed my story. His removal would close the backchannel to the government. They were not supposed to murder him!"

"But they did because he was also reporting to the government on their illegal activity as well. They wanted that to stop and killed him to close *their* backchannel. You set the actions in motion and paid the men that killed your driver. And when you found out they killed him, you retrieved his body and buried it with his wife, and then you grieved with her. Did you feel guilty or mourn out of compassion for the family."

"Both."

"See Mr. Richardson, you do understand the concept of polarity. It won you the Pulitzer Prize, and you felt compassion and guilt simultaneously while you justified what you'd done. This puts your actions in the middle. Good intentions ended with a bad, unintended outcome because of you. Yet here you are a free man today. And until tonight, no one would call you evil, just the opposite. You have achieved! You are a Pulitzer Prize winner. You have become a great writer despite your driver's murder. Now, even with these laurels, are your actions tonight justified, Mr. Richardson? You killed in Afghanistan, and now my team is gone because of your desire for revenge. It sounds like evil to me."

"Shut up. That was not the way it was supposed to happen."

"Things happen because we cause them to happen. We

want to control the outcome, but we can't. The only control we have is deciding to act and the way we put our actions into motion. Once we put things into motion, we roll the dice and hold on until we observe what we produce. You wanted your driver abducted. He ended up dead. Tonight, you acted. Tonight, you murdered my team. What about the men and women you killed tonight? Did you know them? Did you know their families? Cause and Effect, Mr. Richardson. What will be your next action? After all, it's what you do next that determines what kind of man you are."

Alec paused for a moment and then responded.

"You have caused these deaths tonight, not me!"

"You pulled the trigger. You could have walked away."

"And you could have walked away from Grant and his family! From Adelle!"

"I did not set out to kill your friends. It was a roll of the dice based upon your previous actions. Let's not forget you talked with the *Guardian* about BWI and a new article. YOU forced my decision to take Grant's family. You tried to break them out and killed some of my people. YOU forced my decision to respond with my reaction force."

"Bull shit! You have control over your people and THEIR actions! You put them into motion."

"Do I? I have little control over my actions anymore. This program started in the beginning, to achieve something for this country. It was intended to be good for Americans and still can revolutionize our method of criminal punishment. But instead of an effective program, it's been politicized by people looking to expand their personal power. Your editor hopes to influence an election with your words about my program. My friend is caught between doing what is right for America and following our White House's orders. My program is being crippled by people in Congress that do not even realize that they are bringing about their destruction because they do not possess the vision to see it happening. It is a curse to think three steps in front of your opponent. It's a curse because you can see the destruction coming and can do nothing about it."

"Enough for tonight, professor. I'm getting tired of listening to philosophy. Are you ready to start answering my questions?"

Alec was countering with his attack, the Supervisor observed, but time was passing. Two minds, battling for the win. The Supervisor knew he would prevail. He made his points. Did Alec understand them? What would be his next action? What could he control? Time was his answer. He decided to provide Alec with his answers.

"Ask them," the Supervisor said.

"I drove my car all day. Why didn't the bomb detonate with me?"

"The explosives were placed in your car while you were at the Willard talking with McAllister by one of our men posing as a valet."

"That does not explain how it exploded with her in the car and not me."

"The ignition did not detonate the bomb. We used a cell phone as a trigger. Your house was under observation since returning from Utah. The command was issued when Adelle came out on her own."

"Who gave that command?"

"I did."

Alec processed the information he sought. The Supervisor ordered Adelle's death.

"How did you know I was going to the Willard?"

"Methods and techniques," the Supervisor said, making a standard reference told to Alec during his interview when the answers to his questions included classified information.

"Why did you start abducting innocent people and putting them in the SOUP?"

"To protect the White House."

"Why did you abduct Maggie?"

"To protect the program."

"Why did you kill Grant's family?"

"This is going to get tedious, Mr. Richardson. I've already explained the sequence and events behind my actions. See the big picture despite the cause and effects. VLS can solve many of society's problems. Sometimes trade-offs need to be made."

Alec was not buying it or being baited into a morality discussion. He wanted answers.

"Adelle and I were in DC. We were the lead car that day. Why weren't we killed? Your agents trained all their fire on Grant and his family."

"To my agents, Grant and his family were the escaped inmates. UT was, unfortunately, in the vehicle. You were an accessory to their escape. Our policies are clear; escaped inmates are our priority. Others will be apprehended if possible. The agents left quickly to avoid their role in what happened there. As you know, an incident like that could shut VLS down."

"And afterward, did you try to find us?"

"No."

The finality of the Supervisor's answer shocked Alec. He leaned forward in his chair.

"Why not?"

"Because I knew you would eventually come back to us."

"How could you know that?"

"You worked through the logic the same as me. You did as I would have done. You sent one story to be published that could serve your editor and your needs and held the other story for security. That story would have destroyed the program for both parties. You sent both stories to me to make sure I understood your intent and desire to reach an agreement. We found you, and you negotiated your lives based upon the second story. Pretty simple to reach my conclusion, do you agree?"

"Then why didn't you honor your agreement to let us

live peacefully? Why did you murder her!"

Alec stood as his suppressed anger manifested on his face.

"I've answered that question, Mr. Richardson. Sacrifice. Without sacrifice, we never achieve what we aspire to!"

"What the hell are you talking about?"

"You are a writer, you tell me."

Alec thought for a moment. *Greatness, sacrifice?*

"Mr. Richardson, didn't you ever take a class in at the University that involved a discussion of sacrifice and higher ideals?"

"Yes."

"Are you familiar with the quote, 'Power tends to corrupt, and absolute power corrupts absolutely. Great men are almost always bad men'?"

Alec answered, "Yes. The quote was used to explain values and morals of the real world and how personal opinions would affect the newspaper's storyline. The instructor used examples of famous leaders that advanced their nations, but also discussed the dark things required to achieve those advancements that most history books omit. He emphasized stories needed to be truthful, but not all the details needed to be written about if the overall result was beneficial to the people. Is that the price we pay? To use evil to achieve for society?"

The Supervisor smiled. "I see you are beginning to put your Afghanistan experience into perspective. As you said, Mr. Richardson: it's all questions of degrees. Who will judge us for our actions in the gray, and will they show mercy when they do? How great will you become when your second article, published with the deceased Ms. Hall's name, is next to yours? Imagine the greatness you will achieve from her loss. It will force my resignation and greater oversight of the program by the very people that caused the decisions leading to this discussion. To America, changes will be made. To the program, nothing will change because people don't; but each action will serve a purpose. Even your being here tonight, Mr. Richardson, serves a purpose. Hence, the invitation to meet."

"Purpose! What purpose? To be lectured by you, the man responsible for killing Adelle!" *He is stalling for time.* Then Alec realized the reason. *The duress system.*

"Did you always believe that you figured out answers far in advance of others? When did you become such a pompous ass?"

"When I discovered that sacrifice drives us to do the things that we must do for the good of all. We are always a pompous ass to those that do not understand what we do and why we do it."

Alec thought for a moment and nodded his head.

"And you. Why do you do it?"

"I am a patriot, Mr. Richardson. I lost my ability to love my family and replaced it with love for this country. I would do anything to keep its people safe."

Alec believed the Supervisor to be telling the truth, even if his moral compass was far from true north.

"Honesty, a trait that I can admire," he said.

Now it was Alec's time, to be honest.

"I know you have a duress system worked out with your team. I also believe you have kept us here talking long enough for someone to realize they need to send help. Am I right?"

The Supervisor smiled again.

"One thing about talking with you tonight, Mr. Richardson. Your conversation is impeccable though sometimes disrupted by flowery metaphors. A credit to your trade."

Alec stood up.

"I thought so. I don't care how great I become or about any of this crap you've said tonight. Stalling for time has taught me one thing. I saw fear in your eyes when I landed that second punch. You are afraid that *you* will not be remembered. That you will die here and no one will shed a tear for your life. You have suffered greatly, you said. No one cares. You built VLS as a result of that suffering. No one cares about your greatness. That's what you are afraid of most — dying in obscurity. No contribution to history, regardless of the sacrifices you've made. You are afraid that your life will not even be a footnote in the history of humanity."

The Supervisor sat still, staring at Alec.

"Unlike you, Mr. Richardson, I did not set out to achieve great things. My life events changed my direction. I did all that I could, not to achieve greatness, but to fix a great wrong in my life. I couldn't care less about how I'm remembered. *You* are the last part of the life I wanted."

Alec heard the Supervisor, but his words all sounded the same. Alec continued, "So I want to say this before I go. You set out to change a great wrong, but your actions led to killing an innocent family. You destroyed their future."

"Unintended consequences for the greater good. It was not my ambition to do so."

"Shut up! Enough already. You killed the woman I love. I don't need degrees or shades of gray or any of that other crap to see the wrong, and don't give a flowery metaphor about your philosophy of sacrifice. As you said, people determine what is good and what is evil. I've determined what you have done is pure evil. Talk time is over."

The Supervisor smiled. He had won. Checkmate!

Alec raised the Supervisor's pistol and fired one round into his head. It jolted it backward, removing most of the back of his skull and leaving the Supervisor's intellect on the floor and the wall behind him. He dropped the pistol where he stood and surveyed the room's surroundings. The Supervisor, cuffed in the chair, fell off to the side, tilting the chair sideways until its inevitable crash, landed the dead man onto the floor. Alec turned and calmly walked out, content in knowing that he no longer cared around his future.

Adelle enabled this to happen tonight. Her comment about a "Doomsday Strategy" gave him the strength he needed. Standing in that room, trying to control his emotions was impossible as long Alec thought about saving his own life.

Once he realized the simplicity in no longer trying to escape, seeking revenge for the people he lost brought incredible clarity. When he no longer cared about his own life, it made his next actions with the Supervisor academic and easy to perform. Both of them would die: the Supervisor by his hand, and Alec by the agents that would find him. Total destruction. One thing he concluded: the Supervisor miscalculated. He should have left him something to live for; because in mercy, he too would have offered the same. Not everyone seeks greatness.

He reached into his pocket and pulled out the keys for the Supervisor's SUV. He walked outside, unlocked the vehicle with a beep, opened the door, and stepped up into the driver's seat. Having no place to go, he started the car and would leave his destination to the fates, a roll of the dice. He pulled out onto the main road and started heading west. The moon was full and shining into the SUV through the trees, making a slight white glow through the windshield. And then he noticed it. At first, it looked like a small portion of the windshield cracked, and then Alec saw that the crack was getting bigger.

Slowly, several inches at a time, the view in front of him began to come apart as the very make of the windshield was pulling apart bit by bit. The phenomenon moved across his windshield and down onto the console. He still could not understand until his car disappeared and suddenly he was in a room with Adelle and Grant. *He was in CT at the facility outside BWI.*

They were in the room with the six boxes on their way to the facility. They were trapped and could feel the pressure increase in their ears.

He moved to be with Adelle, who was standing rock solid as her mind searched for what was happening around her. Some outer material instantly covered the windows. He looked into her eyes, and she looked back and smiled.

"I love you. I will never let anyone hurt you. Trust me," he told her.

She nodded her head quickly up and down and stared into his eyes. He pulled her close, running one of his hands through her hair in an attempt to comfort her, and she hugged him back.

His mind clutched for some physical reality around him, but there was just darkness. In a moment, he knew.

All of what happened: Grant, his family, Adelle; nothing was real. Somewhere they were all alive! Were they in the SOUP like him? He felt hope that brought him to weeping. He felt grateful that somehow they were still living. Adelle was alive. He felt love that surrounded and overwhelmed him with a joy because of her. *Adelle, Adelle. I will gladly give my life for you. I would willingly sacrifice my life for yours.* And then he understood sacrifice. *If I have to die to keep you alive, then so be it.* Adelle was the last name he remembered and spoke it aloud before seeing a bright light that faded quickly into a dark abyss filled with peace.

Outside, the staff was unable to access the locked door to the VLS environment room. The Supervisor ignored UT and the Warden as they pounded on the door, trying to reason with him to stop what he was doing. Each watched with finality as the large display screen in the room showed a digital counter approaching zero. At zero, the crown disengaged, the rear door of the containment box opened, and the coffin moved into the crematorium. In a flash of fire, Alec Richardson was no more.

CHAPTER 42

T he *Washington Guardian* broke the news in a digital update to its website, which would follow in print in the
next morning's edition. It reported that the Pulitzer
Prize winning author, Alec Richardson and his finance, network executive Ms. Adelle Hall, were missing in Jordon. The
article took half a page. Several eyewitnesses stated that the
two were investigating conditions in Syrian refugee camps in
the region and were last seen near Zaatari. No bodies were
found, and local authorities were continuing to investigate.
The remainder of the article talked about their careers and
achievements in the field of journalism.

Earlier that week, found on a rear page of the back of the
Washington Tribute was a small article about a Metropolitan
Police officer, Jefferson Grant that was reported missing while
investigating a major drug ring in South East Washington, DC.
An anonymous source stated that foul play was suspected.
The Chief of Police was quoted as saying, "we are committed
to finding Officer Grant and will not rest until we do so."

The Warden looked around the room at her assembled
staff. The press releases were produced after the BWI incident.
Each version relied on realism to cover Richardson, Hall and
Grant's entry into the SOUP, and followed every procedure
to include providing the supporting documents like plane
tickets, emails that documented personal decisions and new
plans, and valid eyewitness accounts to keep the most likely

questions answered. It had taken time to assemble the back-stories with prepared documents, but the program was now able to release them with the confidence they would work. Placing the three into the SOUP at Baltimore was not her call, but now she had to deal with the consequences of that decision. The next item for her to address was more significant, which is why she called the staff together. *The press had just printed the information on the three and now this!*

She had taken over operations of VLS after Alec Richardson's death barely three hours ago. Richardson's death surprised everyone. The Supervisor was one of the steadiest, most honorable men she worked with. Yet for some reason, he revoked the staff's security access to the doors of the environment room and put Alec Richardson into cardiac arrest. Afterward, he returned access, walked out of the room, and calmly said to Dr. O'Neil,

"The system logs and audits will show that I introduced significant current to Alec Richardson and his container to cause his death. Effective immediately, I am resigning my position as the Program Executive. I will confine myself to my quarters and await action by the appropriate authorities. I will cause no problems nor make any attempt to leave the facility."

He then walked to his office and closed the door.

It was now her responsibility to ensure continuity in the program leadership. She needed to explain what happened, but more importantly, the Supervisor had created a significant security incident. The system needed to be examined to ensure no surprises were waiting for them, either placed in VLS by the Supervisor or malfunctions due to his actions. The staff assembled, and she began her meeting.

"All of you are aware of what happened here a short time ago. I am sure I can speak for everyone when I say we are all stunned by what has occurred. Despite our feelings about what the Supervisor has done, we are all professionals and our job now is to make sure that the integrity of the system is not compromised. As we speak, Dr. O'Neil is meeting with the head of the Committee to determine courses of action. Any questions before we get started?"

She looked around the conference room, and there were none. The Warden looked at the assembled group, then to a man standing nearby.

"Agent Willis?"

"The facility is secure. All systems check out and are green. We have posted an additional agent at the secondary elevator to control access and-"

He paused, then continued in the same steady voice.

"Prevent unauthorized use. We have the reaction force spun up and on standby if needed."

She nodded her head. The Warden did not think the Supervisor would try and escape that way but ordered the extra security.

"Williams?"

"We have done a complete diagnostic on the system. All environments are green and functioning normally."

"Intrusion protocol?"

"Finishing up the diagnostics in the next 20 minutes, but we expect it also to be clear."

"How did he introduce the charge?"

"He was right. What he did is all documented in the system logs. He deactivated Richardson's container safety and power routines and pulled enough power directly from our source to provide the charge. Only Richardson's container routines were off. All other inmates and their containers are providing green status."

"UT."

"I have monitored Mr. Grant and Ms. Hall's activity."

He stopped. He worked very closely with Richardson. His loss impacted him more than the rest of the staff and felt it more significantly than he anticipated.

"Both have created realities that we expected. Officer Grant is retired, living well with his wife, his daughter and son and law. She married a man that Grant was working with named Darnell Washington. His daughter is expecting a baby girl in three months. Officer Grant will be a grandfather. Ms. Hall ... and Mr. Richardson are married. Both are continuing their professional and personal lives together. In my assessment, the community database of the FFP is not significantly impacted by introducing the Supervisor's scenarios. Each scenario is tailored with the quantum tags specifically for Richardson."

The Warden pondered this a moment. Sometimes she found herself impressed with how each inmate lived in their own world, even though they used the memories of everyone in the community. The Warden still found it hard to comprehend that while Richardson was in the worlds with Grant and Hall, they were not aware they were involved in Richardson's reality as well. Each were busy creating their own simultaneously. Much like Richardson never knew he married in Hall's world, she never knew Alec was dead in hers.

"Your assessment of the scenario introduction capability?"

"It appears to have worked flawlessly. The Supervisor was able to introduce memories into the FPP community that were specifically tagged and used by Richardson. By introducing the scenarios, he was able to create a 'cause and effect' set of events specific for Richardson rather than the random reality creation we find in the inmate community. This is a significant breakthrough. It opens the door for directly influencing activity in the SOUP that could lead to inmate reform."

"Overall assessment?"

"I see no additional database entries or tampering with the VLS system that would cause a loss of integrity. My assessment remains: the Supervisor had a specific purpose with Richardson that did not affect the other inmates. I am confident that the community is green."

The Warden agreed.

"Gomez?"

"Major surveillance activities are confined to monitoring the Grant family. We provided notification to his wife before the press release and provided contact information. We observed the standard reaction of grief and worry from the family. The wife is a strong woman, and Grant's reality may not be far from the truth. It appears Darnell Washington is a part of the daughter's life. We have the standard procedures in place to handle family inquiry with the DC police. We will continue to monitor and make personal visits if the family decides to have the court declare Officer Grant dead. In the meantime, we will provide funding to the wife from the non-profit 'National Organization of Harmed Police Officers.' These funds should take care of any financial needs they have in addition to standard DC police benefits they receive if any. The website for the Organization is up and we are making routine changes as required. All communications from the site route to us."

The Warden contemplated this report. The introduction of the Family Protection Program required an expansion of her resources to support the various cover stories, provide unanticipated financial support, and higher levels of creative thought not tied directly to the program. *How many more loose ends would there be?*

"Mr. Washington's mother is also in the SOUP. UT?"

"Living a positive, happy life also. She is a grandmother and community hero though, in her reality, she does not know Michaela Grant. All appears to be normal."

"Gomez, your assessment of Darnell Washington."

"He was working with Officer Grant and provided some of the research that led them to BWI. The disappearance of Officer Grant and Darnell's personal life with Michaela appears to have taken away his immediate desire to investigate his mother's disappearance. I believe he has put together the pieces for his mother and Officer Grant but at this time, is not willing to act. This could be a cause for concern in the future. We will continue to surveil."

"I would like to add an incentive. I want Washington to get a promotion at his museum. A new job, additional money, and the potential for a new family could stabilize future exposure. Let's see if we can get the family as close to normal soon under the circumstances," the Warden said.

"I'm on it."

"Anything else?"

The room was quiet.

"Ok, we're done here."

As chairs rolled back and people stood up, the Warden began thinking about how the Committee would deal with the Supervisor. That decision was above her paygrade for now. Dr. O'Neil would know what to do.

CHAPTER 43

D r. O'Neal was scheduled to meet Senator Carter Hurst outside the US Botanic Garden on Independence Ave., which was a short five-minute walk from the US Capitol building. The Gardens were a personal favorite location of Dr. O'Neal; who, despite her Ph.D. degrees in Engineering and Artificial Intelligence, enjoyed a walk through the different rooms of plants where she admired the unique species that grew in environments around the United States. Her personal favorite was during the Christmas season when they put together a display of trains and a theme in one of the display rooms. It always appealed to her engineering mind how they built homes and structures out of the natural material. Her favorites were the White House and Capitol buildings, constructed entirely from plants and shrubs but capturing the detailed features of each building.

The sun was down, and the evening brought a cool breeze that was typical for October. She had not waited long when an official car with Carter Hurst pulled up midway on First Street SW, and Carter stepped out. He recognized Dr. O'Neil immediately and started walking to her. When he reached her, he extended his hand.

"Sandra, always good to see you."

"Thank you, Senator. I wish the circumstances were a bit different."

"Which program?"

"VLS."

He felt a pit grow in his stomach. Hurst knew something was wrong if she was here instead of his friend. Dr. O'Neil supported several programs and reported directly to him, but she never did so for VLS.

"Let's walk, sir," she said, looking towards Garfield Circle a short distance away.

While the distance was not far from the circle, it would keep their conversation from being overheard by some of the people walking by the entrance to the gardens.

"I don't know how to say this so I will just be direct."

Plenty of people were direct with Carter. Most of the time, he appreciated their directness. One more conversation without the tactful slant or Washington nuance of indirect conversations would allow him to process the information quicker and avoided the double meanings.

"Okay. Go ahead."

"Approximately four hours ago, the Supervisor locked the staff out of the VLS Environment room and directed electrical power into an inmate container, putting the individual into cardiac arrest, causing their death."

"Damn! Who was it?"

"Alec Richardson."

The name set off a dozen bells and sirens in his head. He knew the role Richardson was playing with the VLS articles and the hand selection by POTUS to write them. Hurst looked at her.

"Sandra, what is going on? What was Richardson even doing in the SOUP?"

"Approximately six months ago, you were at the facility. We briefed you on four options to identify the next step in our research to generate Cause and Effect Memory scenarios and Last Memory Jumpstart. Both of these are required, in our opinion, to incarcerate inmates with non-life sentences and teach subconscious meaningful reform."

"I remember the brief. The catalyst was a TV interview

staged by one of the news channels to discredit VLS."

"Yes, sir. On your authority, we created the Family Protection Plan community and began…"

"Wait, what do you mean on my authority? I told the Supervisor under NO condition was he to exercise that option. I told him I wanted him to find another way. The TV interviews stopped, and I thought he had."

"The Supervisor gave us the authority to proceed with FPP. We identified approximately 250 people that were candidates. Sir, we have almost 230 in the SOUP."

Carter's face paled even in the evening darkness around them.

"I can't believe this!"

"There's more, sir."

"There always is!"

Dr. O'Neil expected this reaction. Her experience taught her that it was not uncommon for programs like this one to spin out of control because of the political pressure put on the executives. She was there when Carter asked for a solution to provide to the Speaker and to ensure VLS played well in the press, translated into DC language, remained stable in the polls. Her boss made a decision, and she still wasn't sure if it was right or wrong.

"Two months ago, Alec Richardson, Adelle Hall, and a member of the DC Metropolitan Police Department named Jefferson Grant discovered our operations at BWI."

"How did they do that?"

"We are compiling a full report for the Committee, sir. I admit, I don't know all the details myself."

"What can you tell me now?"

Dr. O'Neil continued.

"They used the internet to identify family members living close to incarcerated inmates. They identified news articles that we gave to various digital newspapers that mentioned the names of the family members we put into FPP and cross-referenced them. Lastly, they used police computers and other sources to track an increase in the number of human remains transported to BWI."

"How could the Supervisor be so-"

Dr. O'Neil could tell Hurst was ready to explode, then he quickly changed his demeanor.

"Sandra, I think I know where this is going. Was Richardson the only one in the SOUP?"

"No, sir, all three were placed in the FPP community. We could not risk any compromise to the operation."

"So how do we cover this? If he is dead, people are going to start missing him. I have to tell POTUS."

Dr. O'Neil reached into her purse and pulled out her cell phone. She turned it on, and the *Washington Guardian* article was already cued.

"This will print tomorrow morning. Richardson's real death will never be known. We prepared these press releases to cover their disappearance after BWI. The timing is perfect."

She handed him her cell phone. Hurst read midway through the article.

"This is good. You are out in front of it. The President will buy this."

"There is a similar one in the Tribune for Officer Grant. He is reported missing in DC, investigating a drug ring. His family is being taken care of."

He nodded agreement with the damage control in place and decided not to ask about Grant's family. The less he knew about this, the better.

"If Richardson was in the SOUP, how were his updates being provided to the *Washington Guardian*? I read them."

"The Supervisor wrote them. We hacked Richardson's account, and sent them to the *Guardian* from his email."

Carter nodded. Maybe this part of the news was not so bad. Now what to do about his friend.

"So sir, I know you and the Supervisor were close. What do you want to do?"

"Where is he now?"

"He has confined himself to the facility. We have added additional security in case he runs."

"No, not him. He won't run. He's waiting for me to make a move."

"Will you notify the FBI or special security, Senator?"

"No. If this got out, heads would roll around the beltway for weeks. He has us. I can't arrest him, but if he has murdered Richardson..."

"Sir, I don't think this is IF. The staff saw him do it. The logs in the system capture his ID turning off the safety protocols and running the power to the container. And lastly, Senator, he admitted it."

"Old friend," he spoke aloud, ignoring the evidence just presented by Dr. O'Neil. "What are you trying to tell me?"

"Senator, do you think he acted on purpose?"

Hurst smiled. He knew his friend well; and yet this was vastly out of character for him. The Supervisor was the most brilliant man Carter knew. He appalled killing and dedicated a large part of his life to building VLS to prevent this behavior. Why would he do this?

"He never does anything without thinking it three and four steps ahead. He probably knows that we are talking about his problem right now. He wants me to do something."

O'Neil thought a moment.

"Sir, if you believe he did this to cause us to take action, I think I might have a solution to our problem; but I need you to keep this between you and me until we try."

Hurst agreed.

CHAPTER 44

Carter Hurst entered the Facility using the secondary elevator and began walking to the conference room. Dr. O'Neal and UT were with him, UT carrying a medical bag. The three had met above ground at the entrance and discussed the details of the upcoming meeting. Their conclusions were the same when their discussion ended. Now it was time. Hurst opened the glass doors, and the three entered and took their seats across from the Supervisor. He was sitting at the table, waiting for the three of them to arrive. He did not bother to stand when they entered.

"Do you know why I am here?" Hurst asked.

"You need to know what happened. You will have to assign responsibility. The Committee will want answers," he said.

The Supervisor looked at Hurst and then Dr. O'Neal.

"I accept full responsibility."

He paused for a brief moment.

"Who else on the Committee knows?"

"No one," Hurst said.

It was the truth. He kept Dr. O'Neal's confidence. This was his problem to clean up, and he did not need the VP over his shoulder playing quarterback. This was his friend, and he owed him that much.

"Are you ready to answer my questions?" Hurst asked.

"I am. As much as I can."

"Let's start with the Family Protection Program."

Hurst wanted to establish a chronology of events. He would take things in order.

"Alright, let's start there."

"Who gave the authorization to collect family members of convicted felons and put them in the SOUP?" Hurst began.

"I did."

"Why?"

"A primary research objective of this program is to develop methods to introduce and then remove inmates from the SOUP."

"Why?"

"So that society is protected from crime by putting *all* convicted felons into VLS. Once they serve their sentence, they are removed and free to re-enter society."

"But by releasing a felon into society, aren't you putting society back at risk?"

"Under our current system, yes. There is no reform in the SOUP. FPP is a separate community where we can evaluate our different reform protocols."

"What are these protocols?"

"We successfully discovered the procedures for introducing Cause and Effect memory scenarios into the environment. These are memories that act as a catalyst for the inmate to take action and learn from their activity. UT and Dr. O'Neil discovered how to attach the quantum tags we use to record inmate memories onto video, to each scenario so that it would target a specific inmate. We introduced scenarios into the community and monitored the reaction. Based upon how the inmate responded, we introduced a follow-up scenario to reinforce the behavior or, if not the right behavior, to correct it. Each time, a small part of the subconscious of the inmate changed."

"What would this achieve?"

"When we briefed the FPP to you, we told you that

science could not isolate the gene responsible for criminal behavior. The experts still believe criminal activity is a combination of genetics and environment."

He paused and looked at Hurst.

"We focused our test on the environment, Carter."

Hurst waited, knowing an explanation was coming.

"Let me ask you, Carter. What is the difference between a highly decorated Navy Seal and a mass murderer if both are genetically similar?"

"I would say the way they were raised. Their moral compass. Their parent's encouragement."

"Yes! And much more," the Supervisor said, nodding his head in agreement. "Our results showed that not only were our inmates in a positive VLS environment, but that our new approach was changing their subconscious and replacing their existing negative memories of their youth with positive ones. We discovered the method to bring about true reform!"

Hurst looked at Dr. O'Neil. She affirmed that the Supervisor was accurately reporting their results.

"But you are erasing their old memories!"

"Yes we are, and VLS provided the methods to create new, positive ones. All memories are created by experience. VLS creates experience! We provided the conditions for that experience and the context for the subconscious to learn."

This could be worse than Hurst expected. The program's achievements were stunning, but he was not sure the Committee was ready for someone to begin altering memories. He would address this with Dr. O'Neil later.

"I think I understand what you've achieved. But why take innocent people?"

"We needed a trial group — a new community with family members not influenced by the criminal activity of a parent. The inmates we have in the original inmate community would require much more effort. I am not sure they can ever be reformed, but our confidence is higher with lesser criminals. This also solved the problem you had with the Speaker and the media."

"So you have positive results on reform," Hurst said, ignoring the comment referencing prisoner visitation. "But you have yet to develop the inmate removal methods from the SOUP."

"That's my failure and the reason for the FPP." The Supervisor admitted. "While never removing or threating the life of an FPP inmate, we were able to run various trials to simulate removal."

"But they would come out only with their last memory. Like a coma, you told me."

"Yes, they would have no VLS memories; but with our new protocols using scenario introduction, their subconscious memories would be changed for the positive and remain that way after removing them from the SOUP. Carter, recidivism will drop significantly!"

"But without removal, your efforts remain only potential if you cannot bring inmates out of the SOUP."

"Yes. But it's only a matter of time before we figure that out too, Carter. We are so close!"

"But you have 230 innocent people in your facility!"

The Supervisor changed his voice from excitement to monotone.

"Our achievements require sacrifice, Carter. There are always the unfortunate few that sacrifice for the greater good. Is a crime-free world worth 230 people?"

Hurst would not answer that question. He was being led by his friend, but led to what? It was time to focus on BWI. Perhaps the answer was there. Between O'Neil and UT, they could put the facts together on this portion. Hurst began again.

"What happened at BWI?"

"A journalist discovered our operations. You know him, Alec Richardson, another media network person, Adelle Hall, and a DC police Officer name Jefferson Grant."

"Did you introduce these three into the SOUP?"

Yes, along with another woman named Jada Washington?"

"Why?"

"Their knowledge of our operations threatened the program. Richardson and Hall were going to write a story about our BWI operations for the *Washington Guardian*! That would have caused problems for your friends in the White House."

"But why put them in the SOUP? Couldn't you figure out another way to keep them quiet without killing them?"

"I made the decision, Carter. And I assure you, Ms. Hall and Officer Grant are not dead."

"But Mr. Richardson is," Hurst said.

"Yes."

"So let's get to that. How did he die?"

"I introduced an electrical current above the safety parameters into his Box. This caused him to enter cardiac arrest."

"Why did you murder Mr. Richardson?"

"Murder is such a harsh word, Carter," he replied, eying his friend with indignation. "My actions were based strictly on scientific method and Mr. Richardson's activity in the SOUP."

"Explain that to me."

"Mr. Richardson was my trial subject for using our memory scenario solution. We were testing positive memories within the FPP community. I wanted to see if I could alter a man's environment by replacing positive memories with negative experiences."

Hurst bit back his anger at the thought of his friend experimenting with humans and their minds. He took a deep breath.

"What purpose would that serve?"

"It would validate our hypothesis that subconscious memories could change with negative memories as well as positive. Mr. Richardson had a very positive childhood and adult environment. If I were able to change his behavior with negative memories, then there would be a chance that reformed inmates could also revert to criminal activity. He was a Pulitzer Prize winner, which qualified him for my testing. Could he be great, and still be good?"

Hurst immediately recognized the reference to the quote. He felt sickened by his friend's use of the words to justify his actions.

"So, you experimented on him!"

His anger surfaced.

"Science requires results to be analyzed to make progress! He was the only one in FPP that met my criteria for the experiment. If I could turn him, then reformed inmates could also be turned. Our protocols would need to be changed to prevent this from happening. We need positive reform and correction to make VLS work for all inmates. This will solve our biggest problem of reintroducing criminals back into society. Incarcerating criminals only works if they are reformed; otherwise, they place an incredible burden on the system. We've discussed this."

Dr. O'Neil, sensing Hurst's anger, provided the next question while Hurst calmed down. She could tell they were close to the Supervisor's rationale for killing Richardson but needed to ask more questions.

"Mr. Supervisor, how did you run your trials with Mr. Richardson?"

"I began by injecting the memory scenario where we took Officer Grant's family. This caused Mr. Richardson to conspire with Mr. UT to rescue them. Mr. UT's involvement was part of the injected scenario. Our next scenario was the unfortunate demise of Officer Grant and his family. This caused greater hate and deception in Mr. Richardson. Lastly, our final memory scenario was the death of Ms. Hall, which drove Mr. Richardson himself to murder several of my staff and my avatar in the scenario introduced into his reality. I realized that if a man like Mr. Richardson could be driven to commit murder, our approach to reform was incorrect."

"What does this mean, Mr. Supervisor?" O'Neil pressed.

"It means," he said with resignation, "My life's work will not be enough to save us. Richardson was an honest man, and he ultimately chose murder because of the scenarios I introduced. This means all people, if raised in the wrong environment, or driven to action by circumstance, will choose evil, and justify it."

He looked at Hurst.

"We are not going to be able to solve this problem, Carter."

Hurst intervened with the next question, as he listened to his friend talk calmly about his failure. He never talked this way. *What happened to him?*

"All of this makes a great science discussion, but why the hell did you murder Mr. Richardson in real space?"

"Mr. Richardson was a brilliant man in his field. I liked him. He even understood in his final moments the value of sacrificing yourself for a larger good for the people you love, much like my love for this country."

"God damn it! Why did you kill him?" Hurst exploded.

"Because Carter, it brought you here!"

No one spoke. It was though the air was sucked out the room, leaving everyone speechless. Hurst was right, Dr. O'Neil surmised. They were being led and had reached the point where the Supervisor wanted them. Carter Hurst was being forced into a decision. The Supervisor looked over at this friend.

"You once told me, Carter, that you would do 'whatever it takes' to keep criminals from doing what they did to my family to anyone else. My life was destroyed because of that man in Austin. He took everything from me; and now, we have the solution to prevent that from happening again! We need to perfect it. It's what I am trying to achieve."

"But you can't trade off innocents to justify your program objectives. We agreed every life was important."

"Whatever it takes! How do we advance without this, Carter? How will history judge us if we succeed? By the small number of lives we have affected or the large number that we will save?"

"When are the losses too much, Matthew? When do you have to find another way to save people instead of sacrificing them?"

Using his first name was a significant security breach. O'Neal looked at Hurst and understood. Using his real name was the keyword to initiate action with the Supervisor. Hurst had made his decision. UT stood up and left the conference room.

The Supervisor looked up from the desk. He had not missed the slip either and stared Carter in the eyes. This was the way the Supervisor had chosen. Richardson sacrificed his life to bring the program to this point. Now, he, too, would do the same.

"Dr. O'Neil, would you get me a glass of water?" the Supervisor asked.

She did as the Supervisor asked. She poured the Supervisor a glass of water from a pitcher next to the coffee maker. She reached into UT's bag, extracted a gelatinous pill, and dropped it into the water where it dissolved instantly. She made no effort to conceal what she did and remained standing next to him. The Supervisor accepted the drink and emptied the glass.

"Thank you, Dr. O'Neil."

The whole scene seemed very surreal to her. The Supervisor was willingly placing his life at risk with this new method, and accepting Hurst's judgment for his crime, solving two problems at one time!

"I know what you are thinking, Dr. O'Neil. We all make sacrifices to achieve our dreams. It is time for me to make my last one for this program. Carter..." the Supervisor's speech slowed as he completed his sentence, "Dr. O'Neil knows what to do. Trust her."

Dr. O'Neil knelt next to him as his head slumped forward. She lifted his head and sat him upright to inspect his eyelids and the pill's effect, looking for a deep red color in his eyes if he was reacting negatively to the drug. It was not there.

"Matthew, Matthew, can you hear me?"

"Yes."

His response was dreamlike.

"Senator, talk with him. He will respond to your voice. Take him back before the loss of his family. Have him focus on the positive aspects of these memories."

Hurst acknowledged his instructions with a nod. Leaning forward toward the Supervisor, he began. Even if it took repressing his own anger, he would try to save his friend's life.

"Matthew, tell me about your early days in Austin. Tell me about Elizabeth and the kids and your time with us, our friendship. I want to hear about your family and mine together. I love them almost as much as you do," Carter said.

The Supervisor closed his eyes and remained sitting straight in his chair. He took a deep breath and let it out, trying to relax while focusing on what Carter was asking him to do.

"There were the picnics on the Colorado River that we loved to do together," Matthew started. "And I remember us teaching the boys how to fish while Elizabeth and Ashley opened the wine and started talking about us. We were lucky men, Carter."

"Yes, we were Matthew. Keep talking about Austin," Hurst said.

"There was Lenny's Pizza. I don't think it's there anymore. The boys in little league and the river walk."

"Ask him specifically about his wife now, Senator. We have him in the right place," Dr. O'Neil directed softly, almost a whisper, transfixed by the event unfolding in front of her.

A man she highly respected, the genius behind VLS, was being walked backward in time to moments where he felt most alive. She was fascinated by observing science unfold and also conflicted with knowing the inevitable outcome. UT returned to the conference room and positioned himself on the near side of the Supervisor, Dr. O'Neil, on the other. Two agents were standing outside, waiting to assist.

"And what about Elizabeth, Matthew? Talk to me about how much you loved her."

"I loved her and still do with all my heart and soul. She was the love of my life. She could make me laugh when everything was wrong. She was a part of me, and I was a part of her. I will always love her," he said slowly.

Without warning, he collapsed toward the table. UT grabbed him to prevent his boss from falling onto the floor. Two other agents rushed into the conference room to assist. Dr. O'Neal was standing behind him with the empty syringe. Hurst looked at her and stood up to get out of the way while UT and the men lifted the Supervisor and carried him into the office across the hall. Already on the floor was the white jumpsuit, jacket, and container. Hurst followed them across the hallway and watched as the process began to insert the Supervisor, his friend, into the SOUP.

"UT, tell me that he will go into the SOUP with his wife as his last memory. He has got to start there!" O'Neil shouted.

As UT and the agents began undressing the Supervisor in a flurry of activity, UT responded, "This is the first time we have tried to control the last memory, but in theory, it should work. He knew this was going to happen and accepted it – almost welcomed it. That may be the element that makes this successful."

"Make his new life begin there," Hurst ordered, beginning to understand what was happening with his friend. "I want to know as soon as he makes his first contribution to the community, and we can record a confirmation."

"Yes, sir," he heard as he headed back to the conference room with Dr. O'Neil. This was going to be a long 40 minutes.

Dr. O'Neal and Hurst sat in the conference room. Neither speaking a word. UT knocked on the glass door and entered.

"Well?" Hurst barked.

"I've patched the video feed into the main loop," and pointed to the monitor. He turned on the TV with the remote, and the screen showed a black background with wavy white lines throughout. It was a paused video. In the top right was a date time stamp, the counter at 00:00 with the nomenclature I-231.

"Is he creating his own new memories?" Hurst asked UT.

"Yes, sir."

"How long will he live?"

"His medical condition is pretty good. We can only estimate, sir, but about 30 or 40 more years."

Hurst nodded.

"I thought you would want to see this video, Senator. It's all his. We were able to jumpstart him into VLS without any problems. He started creating his reality almost immediately."

"Play it," Hurst said quietly.

UT pressed the remote, and the video started. It was a much better image than the one during the first Committee meeting so long ago. The audio was still not perfect, but also greatly improved.

His best friend, Matthew Boyd, sat on the living room sofa in their house in Austin. He recognized it immediately. Next to him was Elizabeth sitting in her favorite chair. Both were reading in their pajamas: Matthew, a book on Physics, and Elizabeth the fashion section of the Austin newspaper. Their eldest son, Matt Jr., walked in and said something about going down to the river and asked if he could borrow the car. Matthew put some rules in place, not wholly audible, and pointed to the basket where they kept the keys. Erick, their youngest, came in shortly afterward and did a "walk by" past his parents, waving as he went out the door with Randy, Hurst's youngest son.

Hurst could not help but smile to see his son in the image knowing how strong the friendship was between the two boys. Elizabeth put down her paper, got up, and walked over, and sat in Matthew's lap on the sofa. Her eyes looked up at her husband, and she mouthed the words, "I love you." He responded with, "I love you, too." The screen went blank, leaving only the counter at the top, showing the full length played as 47 seconds.

Hurst was speechless.

Dr. O'Neil broke the silence and commented, "Nice job UT," and Hurst nodded his head.

"What is the probability that the Supervisor will access Richardson's memories in the community?" O'Neil asked.

"Less than one-millionth of a percent. Our quantum tags attached to the scenarios are very unique. If he does, for some reason, stumble across them, his actions will not be attached to causing Richardson's death because the death occurred-"

Hurst finished his sentence.

"He died in real space and therefore not recorded in the community. What about his death at the hands of Richardson in the SOUP?"

"Again, very low probability of him using that memory to create his reality."

Hurst looked down at the table.

"I think I need to think this through. Dr. O'Neil, will you stay?"

UT took his cue and left the conference room.

CHAPTER 45

Carter Hurst sat still, not making a sound. The barrier that held back the memories of his earlier life had broken when he walked Matthew backward towards his family. As each of the places and things were said, Hurst had relived them. Now, it was time to place each powerful recollection back into its place, buried with the other moments in his life that were too painful to confront. While he reflected on his decision, he knew deep down it was the right one. Matthew was robbed of his family and the life it offered. How ironic that he would be the one to create the tool that would reunite him with them. Anticipating the discussion ahead, Dr. O'Neil coughed lightly and broke the silence.

Hurst looked at her. She had his attention.

"You know, Senator, you were right. He planned all this."

"What do you mean, Dr. O'Neil?"

"I think there was no doubt with anyone that worked with him, that his vision for the future was true reform of the individual. He wanted each of them, regardless of their crime, to be able to start their life over. His ambitions were genuine, his intentions honest."

"I agree with you about his character and intentions, but something caused him to change, to murder an innocent man."

Dr. O'Neil nodded her head in agreement. "Perhaps it

will help you to understand now that you've seen the procedure. Two weeks ago, the Supervisor and I were reviewing preliminary findings on our mental retention and Last Memory Jumpstart, the process we just implemented. We were doing this to determine if and how our treatment would work for non-maximum criminals."

"What do you mean?"

"We were evaluating the possibility of all convicts being placed in the SOUP, as he told you when you questioned him. We were running into trouble determining the right memory to Jumpstart from, and then pulling them out of the SOUP. We had obvious questions such as, how will the inmate react to a loss of time in their life, and where do they begin their life when they return to real space? We knew if we could somehow find the right memory to use as our jumpstart point, we might have a better chance at reforming their behavior when released."

"Ok, what did you find?"

"To put it simply, we thought that if we could find their right memory and not their last memory as the system works now, they would have a reason for remembering when they woke up why their life had value. Why they were important to those around them.

Our results were preliminary, but we identified the right procedures for testing our new drug protocols. We found that if we *focused* the last memory before giving the SOUP injection, that memory would replace the last memory most have just before the injection. Much like if we could get our inmates to remember their life before their first crime, then when they came out of the SOUP, they would not remember anything about their criminal activity. It would be like rolling back time and giving them a fresh start. We saw this as the ultimate redemption for inmates."

"I remember this from the FPP brief you provided. I had no idea you were so close to a solution. Is this what you meant when we talked, and you said there might be a way to fix our problem?"

"Yes, we believed that by the inmate entering a relaxed or hypnotic state, they would be subject to different mental suggestions that would activate their last real space memory. To get them there, we would have to administer a pre-treatment sedative that would allow the mind to prepare for our suggestions. You saw me give him the pill in the glass of water. Then you took him back to his time before his family's murder with your line of questioning. His memory of his family replaced the memory of the conference room."

Dr. O'Neil paused, then said, "He needed to know if it could be done, if it would work."

"So did he target Richardson for some reason, to make all this happen?"

"No sir. I was not his intent to put Richardson or anyone in the SOUP. But when Richardson, his girlfriend, and the police officer showed up at our facility at BWI, he decided to use them in the new FPP community. Each one of them had the qualities he was looking for, most importantly committed to righting injustices and willing to sacrifice their lives to do it.

Shortly after he issued the order to begin FPP, we stumbled onto the answer for introducing the 'cause and effect' scenarios into the SOUP. Even I was impressed with the technology and what we were able to do in a short time."

"What next?" Hurst asked.

"Richardson experienced an event in Afghanistan when writing the series of stories that would eventually win him his Pulitzer. He was indirectly responsible for a good friend's murder, and afterward accepted responsibility and took care of the man's family. Richardson tried to right his wrong if you will. This impressed the Supervisor, so he introduced him to a variety of scenarios to determine if the good found in humanity, was real. In his first scenario, he kidnapped the police officer's family and fed Richardson the scenario that they were in the SOUP."

"Were they?"

"No sir. They are all alive today in real space. But the first test for Richardson was coming. As they attempted an escape, the scenario ended with the death of Officer Grant and his family."

"Why would he do that?" Hurst asked.

Dr. O'Neil could tell that Hurst was distributed by her revelation.

"The family's death was the first attempt to influence the "environment" around Richardson. As we briefed, we believe the environment is the primary cause of crime, and not the genetics. The Supervisor began to affect Richardson's environment to test our hypothesis; that if an inmate's subconscious could be changed by a positive environment in the SOUP using these scenarios, they could be reformed when they were eventually taken out of the SOUP. He also wanted to know if the opposite were true."

Hurst nodded his head, "Okay, I am following this but why murder him?"

She avoided the question, intent on providing the background before taking on the subject. "When we saw the results from using the scenarios, the Supervisor directed me to start working the Last Memory Reset solution with UT. We were getting close on a solution, and he wanted to try some of our experimental protocols to lock the solution down. He did not want anyone to know that he was performing these types of scenarios on Alec except me.
After the scenario with the attempted escape we lost Richardson in the SOUP."

"What do you mean, lost him?"

"This was the first time we had used the scenarios. We had not considered the implications to the Community database as well as we thought, and 'we lost him'. Once I figured out the problem we were able to resume our efforts," she said, avoiding the word 'testing'.

"Can you explain what you mean?"

"The community uses Quantum tags as we have briefed

before," she began. "And the community is a database of sorts."

Hurst nodded.

"Our scenario results were not entering the memories into the community. Once we identified this, it was a simple process to 're-index' the community including the new quantum tags. We are also learning as we go Senator."

Hurst dismissed the excuse. "Ok, I got it. Let's move on."

"The Supervisor prioritized the Last Memory Jumpstart work and asked if we could make Alec "disappear" in the SOUP from observation by the rest of the staff until we had a solution. I was able to do that and the scenario of "living out west" for a while was introduced to follow on with the first memories of their escape plan."

"This is all fantastic! We can really do this?"

"We created this environment Senator and we are just beginning to understand the additional capabilities VLS offers. Its potential is fantastic for solving some of our social problems. The Supervisor knew this, and those of us that worked with him closely saw his vision."

"How long did it take you to complete your work on the Last Memory Jumpstart?"

"Close to six months Senator, and when we had a solution, we introduced a scenario that brought Richardson back to DC. The Supervisor was now ready to continue running his test on Richardson. He introduced the scenario that involved the death of his girlfriend, Adelle."

"Why?"

"It would be the final test of Richardson's reaction to his environment. How would he handle each of these tragedies? Would he seek revenge or remain true to who he was? Would he show mercy? The Supervisor, because of his own personal experiences, wanted to prove that evil is chosen and not part of humanity's natural condition. If Richardson chose mercy, then we would know that true reform was possible."

"How was he going to prove this?"

"In the scenarios, he sacrificed Officer Grant and Adelle to lead Richardson to a final conversation with him, just the two of them. The Supervisor believed that Good and Evil are different degrees of the same thing, something he told us he called 'polarity'. He also believed that we all do things for private reasons that we can justify to ourselves, but ultimately it is a society that determines if we treat the action as heroic, criminal, or somewhere in between. This was key to his belief in reform. He believed that when evil is done to someone, their response will always be evil in return. He was hoping it would be different with Richardson."

"And so he killed Richardson because of something that happened in the SOUP?"

"Senator, you have to understand. This was not about Richardson. This was about humanity. The Supervisor felt when Richardson murdered his persona in the SOUP, as well as his staff, that humanity was destined to always respond in this way. He could not reconcile this with the loss of his own family, murdered by a man that was wronged by someone else and for a reason that the Supervisor would never know. He confided in me before his event in the SOUP with Richardson that he did not believe reform was possible and hoped his confrontation with Richardson would change his mind. It didn't."

"So he believed that he should just give up? That's not who he was!"

Dr. O'Neil paused to formulate her answer correctly, bringing silence back into the room, filling her with a heavy burden to relate the facts as she knew them.

"He told me that if Richardson ended the confrontation in the SOUP with his murder, he was done with the program, done with humanity. He directed me to focus on improvements and ways to remove the FPP inmates from the SOUP and find ways to return their lives to them. If you recall Senator, we discussed the idea that people would want to use the SOUP as their escape over suicide. While I would not call the Supervisor suicidal, I would say that the loss of his family, the use of the program by the White House and Richardson's response convinced him of what he needed to do next. He knew he had a possibility to reunite with his family."

"The Last Memory Jumpstart."

"Yes, and while I do not dispute his desire to reunite with his family, I do not condone the way he did it."

"Richardson's death."

Dr. O'Neil nodded. "When we discussed the Last Memory Jumpstart, we knew there where risks as there always is in science. We knew what UT had developed might not work and most importantly, once the drug was taken to open the mind to suggestion, it would require a second person to introduce the memories to create the Jumpstart point. If it did not work, he would be in the SOUP after his family was murdered and could never be with them. We had evaluated pre-recording his memories and pursued numerous other methods for him to do this on his own, but in the end, we knew we needed someone that had shared these experiences with him."

"Me!"

"Yes, Senator, you. But had we known *how* he would bring you here to the facility, we never would have allowed it."

"Why didn't one of you assist him?"

"The method was experimental. We had no idea that it would even work. We just knew that it had the best chance of success with you."

"Why didn't you ask me?" Hurst's voice was condemning Dr. O'Neil. "You are as much a part of Richardson's murder as he is!"

"As I said Senator, if we had known what he was going to do, we would not have allowed it!"

Hurst calmed, and Dr. O'Neil did as well. Hurst shook his head. It was evident to Dr. O'Neil that Hurst could not accept the explanation he was hearing.

"Senator, he did not want us to ask you. He knew you well enough to know you would never support his decision."

"He was right, I would not have."

"Try and view it this way Senator. Richardson died so that the Supervisor could live. In doing so, the Supervisor took a big risk with his own life in the hopes that this technique could restore hope and faith into this country's future and offer the SOUP for more than society's protection. He never gave up, he took a risk to further the program and if it worked, it would open many new ways to use the SOUP. If it failed, then Matthew knew he would sacrifice himself. He felt justified to do what he did with Richardson. As he used to ask us all the time, 'is one life worth the nation?'"

"He wanted this to happen," Dr. O'Neil stated again, perceiving the emotion and conflict that Hurst must be dealing with.

"Then, he knew what was going to happen?" Hurst spoke slowly.

"Yes, Senator, it's what he wanted. That's why when you asked him why he murdered Richardson, he replied..."

"To bring me here. How did he know I would make this decision?" Hurst asked.

"He believed in your friendship. He knew that you would not have him arrested for Richardson's murder. He knew this because he created something amazing for this nation. He did not think you would discount this. He also knew that you could not allow him to murder a man and go unpunished. I believe Matthew decided to be put into a reality with the family he loved. This drove him to conceive of this solution. His drive to reunite with his family influenced everything here."

"I still can't believe that he would take an innocent life."

"Senator, Richardson's life brought you to your decision with your friend. Maybe he believed enough in your friendship to sacrifice himself for you. I know he believed in this country. Last Memory Jumpstart works! It will be through your commitment to his memory and friendship, Senator, we can right the wrongs that were done to protect this program and utilize what he has given us. We have to make sure this politicizing stops and does not happen again."

"What do you mean?" Hurst wanted to know.

"I have watched each of you, both men of integrity, and focused on doing the right thing, throw it all away to keep this program viable for an election. Will the White House ever know the role they played in the Supervisor's decision or Richardson's death? How did it come to this? How did a program that could offer so much, be turned into something that caused the death of an innocent man, and disrupted the lives of 230 other people?"

Carter reflected on Dr. O'Neil's comments. *How did it come to this? Was it the politics, or the obsession to create the perfect solution? How could he justify his own decision to handle this problem?*

"Is this what it comes down to? Lost lives for the benefit of others."

"Only he knows the real answer to that question, Senator. I am good with the reasons we have discussed and he gave you today. He was always way in front of us with his thinking. I don't believe we can second guess him."

Always way in front of me, Hurst thought and then smiled. He could never beat his intellect as the mental chess game the two friends just played proved.

"Thank you, Dr. O'Neil, that information was beneficial."

"You're welcome, Senator. For what it's worth, sir, you made the right decision."

She stood up as did Hurst, and they shook hands, then she left him alone in the conference room. Running through his mind was the quote his friend told him and referenced again today. It must have driven his friend's behavior more than he believed. He reflected on his own life. The quote was accurate. "Great Men are almost always bad men." He thought it funny that most refer to the earlier quote as an abuse of power and corruption. His friend made him question not the power, not the corruption, but the motivation for using that power. We all had choices. Mathew broke down decisions to their necessary actions. Do you respond with good, evil, or chose something in between that our egos and society can accept?

Was it all for power? He sentenced his friend without a second thought. He placed him in the SOUP like the criminals convicted by judges around the country. He judged his friend because the politics would have killed the program if any of this information made it into the public. Carter felt his actions all seemed so clear, but were they correct? His friend was a great man. Was this the price of greatness that one day, his friend murdered to remain so? Was it called murder when your cause was for the greater good, and you sacrificed yourself?

Technology and VLS enabled him to bypass the legal system. To Carter, VLS was a just and fair punishment for his friend's crime. Matthew made this the center of his agenda for creating VLS. Protect society without compromising the lives of the guilty. While deserving punishment under the law, they too were human, and their punishment should fit their crime. He took his friend's life in real space and balanced humanity and compassion with the sentence. There was no law precedent or loophole to prevent him from acting in truth. Content with his decision, Hurst spoke aloud.

"Live well, my friend live well."

The tears rolled down his cheeks, finally able to release his soul of this burden.

CHAPTER 46

The Warden, now the new Supervisor, stood in front of the Committee and finished the details of her presentation concerning the Matthew Boyd event.

"Ladies and Gentleman that concludes my report. I recommend classifying the report at codeword level clearance."

Carter Hurst looked at the Committee members. None objected.

"Approved."

"Lastly, I would like a decision about our 'guests' currently in the Family Protection Plan community."

"Do you have a recommendation Ms. Supervisor?" the Vice President asked.

"I do, Mr. Vice President. My Program recommends retention. We now have 231 souls in the FPP and no scientifically proven method for restoring them to Real Space. We believe that until we find a way to recover them correctly, they currently receive the best care in the SOUP."

"And when you do have a way, Ms. Supervisor, will your recommendation be the same?"

"As I have heard you say many times in the media, Mr. Vice President, 'I don't comment on hypotheticals.'"

The Committee broke into laughter. The Vice President gave her a knowing smile and wink, evident to all that he liked this woman. She was not as solemn as the previous Supervisor.

"Any objections to the recommendation?"

There were none.

"Recommendation approved at codeword level clearance."

No question about clearance on this decision. *None of the Committee want their conclusion anywhere near a Freedom of Information Act request*, the Supervisor thought.

"That brings us to our next topic of discussion. The Potential for VLS," Carter said. "Ms. Supervisor, we await your presentation."

The Supervisor picked up the remote and pressed the play button. The next presentation was loaded.

"We have evaluated several options for VLS that members of this Committee and others have provided to us. Some will require further advances in technology or methods to facilitate the environments that you suggested. To keep our discussion realistic, we have narrowed the list to two. These two were selected because we have the technology now to make these options feasible."

She pushed the remote button and progressed to the next slide. It was titled "Access to Foreign Partners."

The slide listed foreign nations considered as potential candidates. The list included England, most of the continental European countries, Israel, and Saudi Arabia. Next to each represented the potential sales costs. The total sales amount listed at the bottom of the list was over $2.7 trillion.

There was a collective gasp as the Committee viewed the slide. The Vice President looked at the chart with reservation.

"That's REAL money! What's behind your numbers?"

"Mr. Vice President, the numbers consist of the cost of sale of the VLS alone to each of the countries. They build their own facilities. We provide them with the plans and intellectual property only. We believe that 80% of the sale is structured as a one-time buy to achieve Initial Operational Capability or IOC. The remaining projected costs are technology improvements, engineering design enhancements, and medical advances that support the environment for five years."

"Who owns this technology?" Congresswoman Sheldon wanted to know.

"We would recommend Congresswoman that the United States Government maintain ownership. Sales abroad would transfer ownership of the solution for operations only, but not the underlying technology to the government that purchased. We would not sell our secrets to foreign businesses."

"There are many risks if we provided this technology abroad. While we have the technological edge now, we could lose it in the next decade. These governments will figure out how it works."

Congresswoman Katz moved restlessly in her chair, feeling uncomfortable with the thoughts that any of the listed countries may eventually develop a better product or, worse yet, build a capability that made the United States second.

"These are only our recommendations, Congresswoman. We want to present all the options considered. We will send a complete analysis of each option to the basements for your review. This should provide the information necessary to assist with your decision."

"Why would we even consider selling our technologies to these countries?" the Vice President asked as leaned over the table.

"We believe, Mr. Vice President, that selling to these countries would assist them with their incarceration problem. Our biggest concern is our borders are still porous. We believe that since VLS is unclassified and our capabilities are known, these countries will begin to send us their problems.

At the end of the 20th century, we became the world's policemen. I don't believe that by the middle of this century, we want to become the world's prison. By selling to them, we keep the world balanced with this capability and encourage them to hold onto their problems. It is a two-edged sword –

sell the technology or open the door to their criminals, much like the 18th century."

"Do you believe countries today would do this if we did not sell them VLS?" Katz asked.

"Yes, Congresswoman, I do. As a quick fact, 22% of inmates in the SOUP are foreign terrorists or not US Citizens. I think it is a genuine possibility not only that they send them, but that our citizens are the victims, and then we pay for arresting and convicting them. This does not cover the time and cost to try and return them to their own country. It's clearly a decision that requires some thought."

The Congresswoman nodded.

"Thank you for your answer, Ms. Supervisor."

The Supervisor returned the nod.

"If there are no further questions, I would like to present option 2."

The Supervisor pressed her remote, and the second slide appeared. Its title was "Rent to US Businesses."

"Our second option is to rent the technology to US Businesses. Part of the agreement would stipulate that it would be illegal for the US Business to give any part of the VLS to a foreign business or government. This option keeps VLS a US capability."

"Why would we not sell the technology to them?" Sheldon asked.

"Our assessment, Senator, is that we would not want to give our businesses the freedom to innovate. Capitalism is a fantastic system if the laws can keep up with the technology. I think we would all agree that it is easier said than done. We believe our businesses would find new applications that we have not anticipated, and we may find that we create laws to fix one kind of problem and create several others."

Heads nodded in agreement around the table.

"So how would you make these leases work?" Sheldon continued.

"We would use a model much like Defense uses when building ammunition. It's called, GOCO or Government Owned, Contractor Operated. We maintain control of the Intellectual Property and the facilities. Businesses are awarded contracts to run the facility and make the ammunition using our formulae and procedures. We would envision the same business model for our use."

"Thank you."

The chart showed the names of US businesses that might be interested in leasing the technology as well as the business sector. The summary of projected income figures by industry area totaled to $535 billion at the bottom.

"I would like to highlight that the majority of contracts anticipated occur in the medical and elder care sectors."

It was Congressman Sweet that asked the next question.

"I like what I see here. Could you give me a health care example using the GOCO model?"

"Our analysis shows an immediate application in nursing homes and eldercare."

This captured everyone's attention as now all eyes trained on the Supervisor.

"Our nation continues to be an aging society and will continue until the baby boomer generation expires in roughly 20-30 years. We could see a national health care alternative, owned by the government where VLS exists for nursing home patients. All voluntary, of course."

The questions began and were too numerous to answer. Carter Hurst brought the Committee under control, raising his voice above the fray as he did many times before.

"Too many questions. Let her finish first."

This comment silenced the room.

"Ms. Supervisor, please continue," Hurst said.

"Our model would involve building new facilities for this purpose. Patients in elder care would be allowed to volunteer for the SOUP for a fee, comparable to their cost for existing care. The business running the facility would be entitled to a portion of the revenue to cover their costs and profit. The remainder would come to us to reinvest in the equipment, infrastructure, and research. They would have to sign up for the existing methods, which include cremation. We would offer visitation but only for the family to see the *quality* of care for their loved ones. There is also the possibility of providing videos of the memories and experiences in the SOUP. In time, I am sure we could also find options for cremation as well.

"There should be no doubt. This is available for nursing patients only and could be expanded to all aging citizens at a later date. Since we have not developed the technology or methods for removing people from the SOUP, it's an irreversible decision. As an upside, it offers the best health care for the resident, and because of the Last Memory Jumpstart used with Matthew Boyd, we can offer them a reality at any age they chose until their physical body dies."

"This is amazing!" the Vice President exclaimed. "The family could see their loved ones living full lives via the VLS videos, but not have to watch as they slowly die in a nursing home bed. The quality of the last years would be..."

"Exceptional," Carter Hurst finished.

The Vice President nodded. To prohibit additional speculation and unanswerable questions, Hurst followed up with, "Can you work the details of the program Ms. Supervisor and provide them in 90 days at our next update?"

"I would like assistance from the Departments of Health and Human Services, Social Security, and Medicare. These persons require Top Secret clearances."

"We can do that, Ms. Supervisor."

"Thank you, Senator."

Hurst needed to clear the room, or they could be there indefinitely discussing the ideas presented.

"If there is no further business, this concludes this meeting. All option discussions are classified as Top Secret. Ms. Supervisor, could I speak with you?"

The Supervisor looked over at Hurst. The remaining members headed to the exit, and their conversation moved away from classified topics as the doors to the chamber opened. The Supervisor's two-person team was securing the briefing and shutting things down. As they collected their items, she turned to them and said, "Nice job today. I will meet you outside."

It was her and Hurst now, while Dr. O'Neil talked with Congressman Sweet on the other side of the room.

"What can I help you with, Senator?"

"Sorry to keep you, but it's a personal question."

She anticipated this. It had been months since Carter visited the facility.

"How is he doing?"

"He is doing very well, Senator. They all are," referring the others placed in the SOUP as part of the FPP. "Their realities show a happy and prosperous life."

"Do you believe in fate, Ms. Supervisor?"

"I am afraid I don't. I am more of a free-will person myself, Senator. Why do you ask?"

"I find it ironic that he would build VLS because he lost his family, and the very system he built would reunite him with them."

"I have heard you say that before, sir."

It was apparent to her that Carter Hurst frequently contemplated his friend's life and his ultimate decision to place him in the SOUP.

"Senator, is everything OK?"

"Couldn't be better. From a program view, our leadership is stable. We can expect the VP and his continuity to remain now that the election is over, and his administration has four more years."

"Yes, sir."

Does he have a point, or do I need to start worrying about him as well? She wondered.

"Ms. Supervisor, in your assessment, was it the politicization of the program that caused him to make his decisions and ultimately give up?"

He wants honesty, she thought.

"Yes sir, that was a big part of it, in my opinion. As I have reviewed his research priorities, he truly wanted to provide a complete solution: not just for the high-security criminals but a chance for all convicts to be reformed. I also discovered that for each breakthrough we achieved, the capabilities were directly applicable to his personal objective to rejoin his family. I believe the political pressure he felt caused him to accelerate his development schedule. This caused him to make decisions like the FPP and Richardson. But sir, who is to say those decisions were wrong."

"History written by others will answer that question for us," he commented.

"When they find out about it in 20 or so years," the Supervisor added.

Hurst smiled.

"Thank you for your honesty Ms. Supervisor."

He looked at her and knew she would be very successful in her new role. She was trained under his best friend but unconstrained by a motivation to achieve a personal objective at all costs. 'At all costs,' he remembered the time he said those words.

"Ms. Supervisor. From this point forward, I will do everything in my power to prevent this program from being used politically by this administration or any administration ever again. You have my word."

Carter Hurst extended his hand, and the Supervisor shook it.

"Thank you, Senator."

She smiled and walked back to her desk to pick up her remaining items.

He had lost a friend. In exchange, the United States possessed a capability that he built that could change the world. He reflected on his friend's often used quote again, "That almost all great men are bad."

"'Almost all' my friend, 'not all of them." Carter Hurst said aloud and walked out the Chamber door, determined for the world and history to remember his friend as a good man.

CHAPTER 47

D r. O'Neil had sat quietly in the rear of the room during the committee meeting and watched the new Supervisor explain the unique capabilities that VLS could bring to the world. She smiled when she saw the response to the eldercare option and knew that it would have the support to be done. As the meeting ended, she observed the discussion between Senator Hurst and the new Supervisor and concluded, something personal was occurring that she would not intrude upon. As she was waiting for the Supervisor's conversation to conclude, Congressman Sweet approached her. He started the conversation immediately.

"What has happened to Carter Hurst?" the Congressman wanted to know. "He has changed not just personally but also politically."

"I not sure what you mean, Congressman."

"Come now, Dr. O'Neil. The media is filled with reports of Hurst, and his willingness to work with the other party to find common ground. 'A changed man,' the press is saying. Do you have any idea what is going on?"

"Truly Congressman, you received the Boyd report today. You know what I know."

Unconvinced, Sweet asked, "You would tell me if there was something else?"

"Yes, of course, Congressman." Dr. O'Neil had watched the conversation between the Supervisor and Hurst conclude.

She needed to talk with the Supervisor a moment. "If you'll excuse me," Dr. O'Neil said extending her hand. "I need to talk with the Supervisor."

"Of course." Congressman Sweet shook her offered hand and headed to the door. Dr. O'Neil walked toward the Supervisor as she was gathering her items from the table.

"Ms. Supervisor, do you have a moment?" she said.

The woman looked up to acknowledge Dr. O'Neil.

"Dr. O'Neil, good to see you as always," she said extending her hand. "You were very quiet in the meeting today."

"Good to see you again too," she said, accepting the professional gesture. "Well, you are the one in charge now. It's your show."

"What can I help you with?"

"Do you have a few moments, we need to discuss something. It should not take any longer than about five minutes."

"Sure, I can always take a few minutes for you," she said.

Getting straight to the point, Dr. O'Neil started, "I don't want this to sound like I am starting to second guess anything that you are doing but, your report on Matthew Boyd to the committee is incorrect."

"Oh?" the Supervisor responded. "How so?"

"You reported that you and UT witnessed Boyd introducing electric current into Richardson's container and saw on the video, the container enter the crematorium."

"We did, it is all confirmed in the system logs and..." the Supervisor stopped, realizing she was talking to the one person that knew every circuit, element, and quantum component of the system. "What did we miss?"

"Yesterday, I removed several restrictions on your visibility of the system."

"What does this mean, removed restrictions?"

"Trust me when I tell you, if you look at the system now, your inmate count is wrong. You have one more inmate than you previously thought. Only *you* can see the change."

The Supervisor looked at Dr. O'Neil, and a smile slowly

formed on her face.

"I knew it!" she exclaimed. "How, when?"

"Ms. Supervisor, please lower your voice."

The Supervisor blushed, knowing her excitement had earned her the admonishment. "Not very professional," the Supervisor said. "It's just that I admired Boyd very much. I could not believe that he murdered anyone."

"I know, we all admired him."

"So, he did not murder Richardson?" the Supervisor asked, still unable to believe, but overjoyed at what Dr. O'Neil was telling her.

"No, Richardson is very much alive. You will be able to see him as I300. This also means that now you, UT, and I are the only ones that know the truth. This will be our secret."

"So again, how and when?"

"As you said, Boyd could never murder anyone. It ran counter to everything we *all* believed in. We knew that would never happen, but we needed *the perfect reason* to get Hurst to be part of the trials for Last Memory Jumpstart. Boyd insisted that Hurst be the one to 'walk him back.'"

"So you told him that Richardson was murdered, knowing that he would decide to put him in the SOUP rather than bring in the authorities."

"Yes, Boyd was insistent that he be the one to try the new procedure. He told me he had the most to gain if the new protocol was successful."

"What if Hurst had decided to prosecute?"

"Unlikely, but the Supervisor was willing to tell him the truth if needed."

"Did he say anything else?"

"What do you mean?"

"Last instructions? What happens if we find a way to bring inmates out successfully? Does he want to re-enter real space?"

"Not if we were successful and he was able to re-join his family." Dr. O'Neil paused, "He said to me that you were ready. You could take the program to new applica-tion areas like eldercare, for the 'good' of the nation. He believed that you needed to make the system a benefit to society again, to fix the direction of the program."

The Supervisor nodded her head that she under-stood, "He really wants to stay?"

"He wants to live the rest of his life with his family. Had we not made LMR work, he said to bring him back when we figured out how, but under no conditions was anyone other than us three to know the truth about Rich-ardson."

"So, you lied to Senator Hurst?"

"Yes, but he was also not truthful with me. He told me he had not authorized FPP. Boyd told me he had. I be-lieve Boyd."

"I believe him too," the Supervisor said soulfully and then continued. "I can see real benefits to what you and Matthew have made possible. Last Memory Reset is going to change the world."

"He knew you would see the potential of what could be accomplished."

The Supervisor nodded while sensing the opti-mism of the moment. "Where was Richardson when his container entered the crematorium?"

"We had already moved him."

"How did you...," and the Supervisor stopped again, knowing that Dr. O'Neil was the genius that built the 'mirror' called VLS. The Supervisor witnessed first hand the reflection of each inmate's true nature and the lives of crime they created for themselves in the SOUP. Unfortunately, VLS also reflected the potential for evil by those around her as well.

"It was not easy, but fortunately we did not have

to disconnect the Crown, just transfer the containers. We saw that Richardson entered into a short CT as we did so, but he re-entered the community quickly. This is a procedure that we want to evaluate more. CT should not have happened but it appears that transferring the Box does have some interesting, unexpected outcomes."

The Supervisor nodded agreement.

"I know this is a lot for you to absorb right now, but UT and I would like to meet with you next week. There is so much we need to share with you. The Cause and Effect scenario results are fantastic! Some of those involving Richardson were hidden from you as well, but show huge potential for our mission here."

"I look forward to our meeting Dr. O'Neil," she said. "I do have one last question."

"Yes?"

"Don't you believe Senator Hurst should know that his friend did not murder Richardson?"

"You've seen the press on the Senator?"

"Yes, very positive," the Supervisor responded.

"He is serving this country better with the knowledge that Richardson is dead than if he knew the truth. Perhaps Richardson's death will inspire each of the committee members to rise above themselves and focus on trying to be great leaders, without the ugliness that goes with it. Hurst seems to be trying to put aside his political views in favor of achieving national objectives. Who knows, he could bring about real change in our system by his actions." Dr. O'Neil looked at the Supervisor, and envisioned a Congress that focused on the needs of the Nation first without thought of personal political victory. "Seeing the change in him makes me believe that this is one of those times when the truth is best left untold."

The Warden understood. "I am looking forward to working closely with you Dr. O'Neil," she said, offering her hand.

Dr. O'Neil shook it and smiled warmly. "Me too. We are going to do some great things with VLS."

As Dr. O'Neil turned and started walking toward the door to the meeting room, she thought, *Thank you Matthew, for so much.* It was going to be a much better world.

EPILOGUE

The Mirror's Other Side

The sun hung brightly in the sky over Central Park in New York City. The park was experiencing spring in the last days of May, always a wonderful time in the city. Adam Spear started his morning run and was going for a personal record. He was trying to build his stamina to qualify for the New York City Marathon coming in November. Each weekday Adam ran his 8 miles in a particularly circuitous route that he mapped out within the park. His weekend runs were longer to help attune his body to the longer distances he would have to master to complete the 26 miles required.

He was fortunate to have the time to train in between his classes at Columbia, where he was majoring in Biology in hopes of going to medical school. He liked to put his mind into something he called the "bio-zone," and think about his school work when he ran. When Adam discovered that he could work through his Organic Chemistry lab and the complexity of carbon bonding during his runs, all topics became fair play to be reviewed while his legs carried him wherever he guided them.

He glanced at his wristwatch and his run time. He was a good thirty seconds ahead of his pace when he made the turn at Waffles and Dinges and headed for the pond. Today felt fantastic. Each stride filled his lungs with air, feeling as if it turned him into a machine with unlimited capacity. He reached the pond, and once he was across Gapstow Bridge and hit the "four walks" intersection just beyond, he was done. He kicked in his reserves and crossed the bridge at top speed. Midway across the bridge, a young woman stepped back from leaning against the bridge wall without warning. Adam unavoidably collided with her, sending both sprawling in different directions.

Adam rose to his feet and determined the only thing he injured was his personal record. He was only 150 feet from the finish. The young woman also stood and was shaking off her blue jeans and jacket, appearing to have a small abrasion on the palm of her hand. Adam immediately walked over to her.

"I am so sorry! Are you okay?"

The young woman turned to face him.

"I think so, what happened?"

Ever the gentleman, Adam said, "It was my fault. I was running too close to you over the bridge. Is there anything I can do to help, your hand looks scrapped."

"It will be fine, I think. I've had worse. I have three brothers, all older."

"You come from a large family?" Adam asked.

The woman looked at him suspiciously, and Adam saw her facial expression.

"I'm sorry, my name is Adam," he said, extending his hand. "I should have at least told you my name before asking about your family?"

The woman smiled and shook his hand.

"Maryland, like the state."

"Well, nice to meet you, Maryland, like the state."

Adam's eyes observed the woman's body language warm and become more open.

"So Adam, what brings you out sprinting on a day like this?"

"I'm trying to work up for the Marathon in November.

It's a personal goal of mine."

"That's great. I've never been much of an athletic person."

"Ah, a woman with a mind, no doubt."

"No doubt," she said coyly.

"Are you in school?"

"Yes, how about you?" She deflected his question back to him perfectly.

"I go to Columbia. I'm a Biology major."

"Hoping to go to med school, no doubt."

"No doubt," he said, smiling while mimicking her earlier response.

Maryland laughed out loud, watching Adam imitate her coyness. It filled the bridge with the last missing piece of spring as Adam felt the attraction begin.

"And you, Maryland? Tell me about your mind."

He was anticipating a pleasant talk over coffee that would fill his afternoon.

"I'm a second year in Law School at Columbia."

"I hear Columbia is a great school."

They laughed at his attempt at humor.

"You are very cute," she said, recovering from the laugh.

"Why, yes, I am."

Here was the moment.

"Would you like to get a cup of coffee and get to know each other a little better?"

Her expression changed, and he knew rejection was coming.

"I would love to, but I am meeting someone. Here he comes now," and she looked in the direction of the four walks intersection and the street beyond.

Adam turned to look behind him and saw a tall, well-dressed man wave in her direction. He began walking towards them. He arrived before Adam could make his exit, and Maryland introduced them.

"Adam, this is Jeff."

Jeff extended his hand.

"Hey, how's it going?"

Adam shook it.

"Pretty good."

He turned to Maryland.

"Well, nice bumping into you – no pun intended."

"Same here," she said. "Good luck with the marathon."

Adam waved over his head to her as he started his jog in the direction of the Met to begin his cool down from the run. *She was pretty nice*, he thought, *but a second year in law school and me going to med school, nothing serious could come of that anytime soon. We would both be buried in books, and that's not where he wanted to spend all of his time.*

"Not to worry," he said out loud to the park, "I've got plenty of time to find the right woman."

◆ ◆ ◆

Freda Spear held her daughter Mariam's hand as she walked down the brightly lit hall on the way to number 754. It was a marvel of engineering with bright lights reflecting off the white-colored walls. There was not a shadow to be found in the corridor. Placed approximately every 5 feet was a gray plate that indicated the presence of a person behind the name and number. When they reached number 754, Freda stopped and looked at the dull gray plate. It was finished using a method that made the plate look like a slate rock, professionally done with gold finish. In the middle of the slate was the name Adam Spear and the date of birth, 1938, brightly displayed in digital numbers.

Looking up at the name, Mariam asked, "Is that Granddad, Mommy?"

"Yes, it is, baby."

"Did Granddad die?"

"No, Mariam," she smiled, "not at all. He is VERY much alive."

Acknowledgments

To Cherie Farrington for her endless hours listening to me talk about this story. Her love, patience, and contributions to my creativity are immeasurable.

To Doris James for her encouragement and positive words that provided the incentive to keep the story alive.

To Vern James for his assistance with navigating the world of publishing.

To Dr. Claire Cuccio, Beth Miller-Herholtz, Blanche and Gene Powell, Andrew Hurst, and Bryan DeWitt for their editing, story validation, and the proper comma placement advice.

Made in the USA
Middletown, DE
23 November 2020